To Rose

All the best to you ..... your family

From the Author

George Robert Peabody

MAN WITH THE BANJO

Man with the Banjo

Published by Wheatmark®
1760 E River Rd Ste 145 Tucson, AZ 85718 USA
www.wheatmark.com

ISBN: 978-1-60494-667-3 (paperback)
ISBN: 978-1-60494-707-6 (hardcover)
ISBN: 978-1-60494-706-9 (Kindle)
LCCN: 2011937908

This is dedicated to Captain Eddie and his Four-String Harp, and the happiness he brought to the many lives he touched throughout his career, and to my wife, Carol, for her love, patience, and encouragement throughout.

murus aeneus conscientia sana

This story is fiction but is based on actual events.

AUTHOR'S NOTE

Eddie Peabody, labeled "The King of the Banjo" by enthusiastic fans and the press, lived the show-business and naval experiences outlined in this novel. Much of what is known about this unique personality was derived from interviews with family members, personal letters, various published entertainment news articles, and other popular publications of the day. I want to personally recognize and thank Lowell H. Schreyer for his tireless research on Eddie's musical career, outlined in his 2000 publication, *The Eddie Peabody Story*.

I also want to thank Jim Woods, Stephen Mertz, Jeff Rake, and Malcolm Levin, PhD, for their time, inspiration, and professional critique of this manuscript. And thanks to the folks at Wheatmark Publishing for a job well done: editor Lisa Boucher, proofreader Susan Wenger, interior and cover designer Jack Martin, account manager Lori Leavitt, and publishing information manager Atilla Vekony.

FOREWORD

For nearly five decades, in the world of show business and contemporary music, the name Eddie Peabody brought a smile to millions of fans. Eddie Peabody is forever remembered by many as "The Man with the Banjo." Tireless energy, a bubbly personality, and the sheer magic in his presentation of the banjo inspired thousands of listeners to take up the instrument.

A sandy-haired, wiry man who was five feet, five inches in height, Eddie joined the navy during World War I when he was fourteen and a half years of age. Eddie's mother and father had divorced just prior to his joining the navy. Times were hard in those days, and Eddie's mother, Ella, had to send his younger brother, Wilbur, to live in an orphanage—an event that troubled Eddie for many years.

A self-taught musician who loved stringed instruments, Eddie took up the banjo to entertain his shipmates. After Eddie's discharge from the navy, the popularity of the instrument in dance bands at the time and his virtuosity propelled him into a successful musical career.

His career was so successful that by the age of twenty-three, Eddie was making the front page of *Variety* magazine, selling fifteen to twenty thousand copies of his recordings per week, and signing million-dollar contracts with some of the largest theater chains on the East Coast. What most people did not know, however, was that one of his biggest fans was the president of the United States, Franklin D. Roosevelt.

Throughout his show business career, Eddie developed many friendships with other performers with whom he came in contact. George Gershwin, for example, was a guest with Eddie on a popular radio show in the 1930s when George insisted that Eddie perform George's famous composition *Rhapsody in Blue* on the banjo. But no performer had more of an impact on Eddie's career than Rudy Vallee, the most popular singer in America of that era. Eddie's close relationship with Rudy lasted more than a decade and was the spark that led him to his first successful European tour. Though Eddie's musical career took a significant detour during World War II, he is credited with doing more than any other performer to kindle the interest in America's "four-string harp," particularly when tastes in popular music nearly rendered the banjo obsolete.

Eddie married Maude Kelly, a Texas girl, in 1924. Maude took an active role in Eddie's early career. She served as his booking agent, valet, publicity agent, and business manager. Events in this story commence during Eddie's successful return to the New York theater scene during the Depression.

MAN
WITH THE
BANJO

A novel by

GEORGE ROBERT

Hamburg, Germany
Winter 1938–39

Through the dirty windowpane he could see the starless sky begin to change from cloudy to clear. The change was sudden, like the opening of a shutter. A few dingy lights under a half-moon were casting eerie shadows along the dark, ice-encrusted banks of the river Elbe. He mused, *Looks like another butt-freezing front sweeping in from the north.* He scanned the quay: no visible activity.

It wasn't long before the tension and fatigue began to take their toll on Eddie. The bone-chilling wind dancing along the surface was mesmerizing as he tried to slowly trace the water's edge. His eyelids drooped. *Nothing, no movement at all—just that damned wind.* He turned away from the window.

A loud *crack-crack!* echoed across the river. He flinched and felt the nerves in his neck tingle. *Damn, shots fired.* He quickly crouched below the windowsill. Across the quay, emerging from the shadows, he caught a glimpse of two men dressed as dockworkers. One was holding his leg and limping as if wounded.

Both men ducked between two adjacent buildings and again disappeared.

All seemed quiet again, eerily quiet. *What the hell is going on over there? Where's security? The police? Troops? Somebody?* As he traced the building shadows along the river's edge, he thought he saw something moving near some crated material lined up along one of the buildings. He watched the area for several minutes, but no one appeared. *My eyes must be playing tricks on me.* Nothing seemed to be moving.

His hands and feet felt icy cold. Turning away from the window, he took some deep breaths and cupped his hands while breathing warm air into them. He marched in place, remembering to wiggle his toes to ease some of the frostbite pain he'd contracted in the last war—"the War to End All Wars." *I need to get the hell outta here and stretch out.*

To ease some tension, he rotated and exercised his neck, but that didn't seem to help. With his head throbbing and eyes bleary, he couldn't keep his mind from wandering. *Germany is gearing up for something. I can feel it. Uniforms are everywhere, except where you'd expect them. And where the hell is the damn submarine launch Greg was sure would take place?*

His scattered, anxious thoughts only added to the frustrations of the evening. The sound of boots marching across bricks and concrete suddenly interrupted all his thoughts. He shook himself awake and peered over the sill. Twelve uniformed, armed men appeared at the side of the nearest building. He crouched to one side for a clearer view. The men divided into three groups and dispersed on the run, away from the quay, between the buildings. Eddie continued to watch the unfolding drama. But now, a sudden lower back pain forced him to stand and stretch. *Damn!*

He pulled a straight-backed chair away from the wall, flipped up the collar on his topcoat to warm his neck, and eased his tired body onto the hard wooden seat. He leaned back and felt a popping in his spine. *This cold, damp air will be the death of me.* He glanced at his watch: almost 4:00 AM. He tucked his hands into the warm softness of his coat pockets. *God bless cashmere coats.*

The thirty-seven-year-old sandy-haired man always dressed smartly. Everyone seemed to notice, but few, except Dix, would comment. And tonight was no exception. He'd brought three tailored suits on this tour, but the one he'd donned after this evening's performance now felt like a limp rag. *Life seems to just happen—especially when you're making plans.* He grinned to himself as he reminisced about one of Maude's favorite expressions. *That woman was always spouting something.*

He leaned back on two legs of the hard wooden chair and continued his thoughtful drift with an imaginary conversation. *So, now you think you're a successful entertainer—well, some folks thought so. The press has even pinned a label on you: Eddie Peabody, the King of the Banjo. And unbeknown to your lovely German hosts, now it's Lieutenant Commander—holed up here in a cold, damp apartment, freezing your butt off, hoping for a glimpse, and one good photo, of the newest member of the German submarine fleet. And who gives a damn? Our thirty-second president, that's who. If the Germans are breaking treaties and are adding to their submarine fleet, then the bastards have to be assembling them right here at one of these shipping docks.*

His eyes adjusted to the darkened room and caught the outline of Dix. *At least she looks comfortable.* In a threadbare armchair directly behind Eddie, Dixie slouched in slumber. She sat upright and shook herself awake: her sudden, albeit delayed, reaction to the sharp sounds emanating from across the river. "Did I hear something? Sounded like gunshots." The twenty-four-year-old multilingual, leggy chorus girl stood an inch taller than Eddie but fit like a glove when in line with the other girls in the stage show. She ran her fingers through her short, bleached-blonde hair as she curled up in her floor-length wool coat. Exhaustion had enveloped her as well. Marian Graham, aka Dixie, also unbeknown to the German authorities, was a highly recruited naval officer working undercover with Eddie in the same musical stage production of *American Jazz.* At this moment in her life, however, all she could visualize was getting back to Boston and her mother and refocusing on her music—well, maybe immersing in a lavender-scented steamy bath would do in the meantime.

"Yeah, Dix, you did. Two guys ran out of one of the buildings and then disappeared. I think one of them was hit. Some troops are scouring the area, but all looks and seems quiet now." His wiry, five-foot, five-inch frame ached as he stood to move the chair closer to the window. Leaning against the windowsill, he peered out: still nothing.

Dixie and her chair occupied the middle of a ten-by-ten-foot creaky wood-floored room that smelled of dust, mold, and damp, cold air. Located just off a street called Brooktorkai that paralleled the river for a short distance, the two-room apartment was modest by German standards. The unit was small, sparse, and lacking in adequate heat, but two windows faced north and west, commanding a good view of the Elbe and its curiously busy docks along the north bank.

Unable to stand it any longer, Eddie leaned over the armchair. "Dix, I'm heading back to the main room. I'm freezing." The adjacent room contained a kitchenette and a table with two wooden chairs crowded into one corner. Another threadbare lounge chair occupied most of the wall nearest the door. He crouched over the floor's heating vent, warming his hands. *And here I thought I was done with living in dumps like this.*

Dixie nearly stumbled as she shuffled over to the lounge chair near the door. "Well, whatever. I'm ready to head out whenever you are. I'm too thrashed to do much of anything, so wake me if anything happens."

He walked over to her and pulled the collar up on her coat, softly rubbing her shoulders. She was asleep in a minute. He left one hand on her shoulder as he listened to her breathe. An audible sigh escaped his lips as he stared up at the ceiling. *My God, but you're beautiful, Dix!* He turned away and stuffed his hands in his pockets. *What the hell is the matter with you, sailor? You're a married man! Yeah, but . . . but what? What the hell, Maude? Maude, Maude . . . all you've done for the last year is bitch and complain. The president himself asked for me—can I help that, or deny the man? Damn it, woman, I love the navy. Why can't you see that?*

He shook himself to clear his thoughts and then pulled a kitchenette chair over the heating vent. He was feeling restless and achy when, quite suddenly, something alerted his senses. Then he began to discern a distant rumbling sound that he couldn't quite identify. He wasn't sure what the noise resembled, but it was too distant to worry about. *My ears must be playing tricks. This country is an icebox! Gestapo goons everywhere and watching everyone—just waiting to send you and your family . . . These bastards are planning for another war! Now the damned SS has been put on high alert—arrested a Brit for spying last week, right here in Hamburg. Swell! And here I am with my four-string harp, trying to plunk out a few tunes, entertain the folks, and maybe put a smile on their faces. I wish someone would just tell me to get the hell out of this nest of vipers, and pronto!* The rumbling of heavy equipment was now louder, and Eddie quickly realized that the noise he'd been hearing was real and getting closer. "Dix, wake up!"

Bleary-eyed, she lifted her head. "What is it?"

"We've got to get the hell outta here, and fast. I think heavy trucks are moving into the area, maybe our neighborhood. And that, to me, means troops. They could be searching all the buildings in the area for anyone or anything they think is suspicious. Remember that Brit they caught nearby snooping around the docks last week? Charged the poor bastard with spying! Now let's get moving, girl!"

Dix was on her feet now. She grabbed the camera, and neither spoke as they quietly left the apartment.

ONE

The White House
Late Spring, 1934

The temperature had dropped ten degrees since sunrise, and rain began to fall steadily. A cold air mass from the north was meeting with warmer, moist air from the south, right over Washington DC. At an informal morning staff meeting before the rest of the cabinet arrived, President Franklin Roosevelt, George Dern, and Claude Swanson were having coffee. FDR was sitting comfortably in his wheelchair, preparing to light up his first cigarette of the day. He loved a good smoke, especially while watching the rain.

As he was adjusting the cigarette holder, FDR asked his two coffee companions, "Say, did either of you gentlemen catch Eddie Peabody's musical performance on Rudy Vallee's radio program last night? That man's virtuosity on the banjo is nothing short of phenomenal."

George took a sip of coffee and offered, "Well, that Peabody fellow is sure popular out west." George was a politician's politician, though, as Eleanor had discreetly shared with her husband in private—a little too tightly wrapped, in her view. "My wife and her sister never miss any program he's on. He was in Salt Lake for only one evening, but my wife made me drop everything and make sure I had tickets."

"My wife seems to be taken with him as well," added Swanson as he stirred cream and a teaspoon of sugar into his cup. Here was a soft-spoken man with an eye for detail. FDR always admired that trait. "And she tells me that he just returned from a successful European tour."

Dern moved to the edge of his seat, clearly preparing to make a point. "Apparently, while most of our European brethren are embracing American jazz music, their governments appear to be preparing for war. You know, Mr. President, very soon we're going to have to beef up our embassy in Berlin. We have just *got* to find out more about this Hitler character. Did you read that last dispatch about the 'voluntary' dissolution of all political parties except the Nazi Party?"

"Yes, I did. And I find recent political events in Germany—the whole political climate, for that matter—very disturbing." The president turned to Swanson and spoke in a pleasant but firm tone. "Claude, I want someone in your group to do a background check on this fellow Eddie Peabody. But please do so quietly. I don't want anyone outside these walls to get wind of this. Submit your report directly to me."

"Yes, Mr. President. But may I ask, sir . . . ?"

"One of my secretaries informed me that he's coming to Washington next week to perform at the Shoreham Hotel. Eleanor asked me to contact him for a private Sunday afternoon garden concert she has planned."

There was a long pause as the president inserted a fresh cigarette into his holder. "I'm not sure why, gentlemen, but this banjo-playing ex-sailor fascinates me. I guess once a frustrated banjo player . . . " There was polite laughter from both cabinet members.

★　★　★

Staff Meeting
The Following Week

Claude Swanson coughed and nearly dropped his coffee cup. He cleared his throat. "Excuse me, sir. The coffee was a bit warmer than I anticipated." The president looked up from the document he was scanning. There was an awkward pause while all eyes turned toward the interruption. Swanson picked up the document in front of him and handed it to his boss. "Sir, I ran the background checks you asked for. And you were right—about Peabody being a sailor, I mean." He fumbled about in his case and retrieved a manila folder. "Looks like he did some time in battleships and submarines and was discharged from the S-14 in San Pedro in 1921. Oh, this was interesting, sir. Three of the vessels on which he served were sunk. A freighter rammed one, and the other two were shot to pieces by merchant ships. He was one of the eight survivors on *Subchaser 209*. Apparently, he floated sixteen hours on a chunk of ice, clutching his violin case. He and only a few others made it to shore."

Roosevelt nodded. "I remember that one, a damned sugar steamer from Havana. No radio, no signal, no warning shots . . . just one unlucky lob down the ammo storage. I wanted that convoy commander fired, but I was overruled."

"You have a remarkable memory for detail, Mr. President."

FDR ignored the comment. "What else have you got, Claude?"

"Well, I asked an acquaintance who works in the Bureau to give us a brief summary of Peabody's show-business career."

"And?"

"Well, after his discharge, it looks like our banjo man had some clear sailing. Several *Variety* articles indicated the boy hit the big time around 1925. And he's remained popular, even with the demise of vaudeville. He may have performed in a mob-syndicate theater or two during his career, but he doesn't appear to be linked to any organized crime. He just recently finished a European tour, and from the news accounts, it appears he was well liked in England. Oh, one last point, Mr. President. He earned the rank of Eagle Scout and has been very active in the Boy Scouting movement, both here and abroad. He's married, but currently there are no children. In short, he appears to be a solid citizen who's served his country well as a first-class quartermaster. And he has been damn successful as an entertainer and citizen ambassador since his discharge."

Roosevelt flashed his famous campaign smile. "Eagle Scout, you say? I knew there was more to this guy." The president wheeled his chair to the nearest window. He stared at the budding trees as they shimmered in a short gust of wind. He began to speak in a quiet but firm tone of voice. "Gentlemen, I'm going to share some private thoughts with you. And I don't want a word of what I'm about to say to leave this room." He wheeled around now to face his morning guests and to take note of each man's reaction.

"It's no secret that our intelligence gathering in Europe is nonexistent." He waited for some rebuttal, but no one flinched. "And what I've been thinking is, this . . . this Peabody character, or someone like him, may be just what we need for some firsthand, on-site European intelligence gathering." Again he waited for comment. *Not even a raised eyebrow? Perhaps they're in shock.* He continued, "Current gossip from our embassy in Berlin is that Hitler is planning to construct an armada of submarines. If he is, well, I for one want to damn sure know about it." Roosevelt silently finished his thought: *And Eddie Peabody knows ships.*

Roosevelt wheeled back to his desk. "I'd like to know how serious this gossip is. If Hitler is building submarines—where, exactly? Likely near Hamburg. And is he basing them there? And just what the hell is the mood over there?" Roosevelt lit another cigarette. "I'm aware that our embassy staff and naval attaché in Berlin are being constantly watched, by the Gestapo. Perhaps someone undercover, like this banjo-playing sailor, could find out a lot . . . and right under their damn noses."

Roosevelt looked up from his desk for any comments or questions. The room was quiet. Roosevelt pushed himself upright in his chair. "That settles it, then. I want this man recruited."

George Dern cleared his throat to get the president's attention. "Sir. I believe that what you are proposing will, and rightly should, be classified as top secret. Accordingly, I recommend that an operational plan, a letter of intent, or some official directive— signed by you, of course—is in order."

The president didn't reply to his secretary's demand. He merely glanced at Dern with a nod: not necessarily a nod of approval, but one that communicated clearly that he understood the man's concerns. The president then wheeled his chair back to his desk and began signing documents. "Thank you, gentlemen. I look forward to your draft report on Friday."

The cabinet members exited to the nearest hallway. In the hallway Dern grabbed Swanson's elbow. "I believe the boss is thinking of instigating the reinstitution of naval intelligence. I recall that this was the very active top-secret branch within the Navy Department under Roosevelt's term as undersecretary during World War I."

Swanson motioned with his head for the two of them to continue walking. When he felt they were past listening-in distance, he spoke quietly out of the corner of his mouth. "Without an official declaration of war, this is going to be no small task, my friend." Claude was silent. They continued walking toward the stairway.

When Swanson again spoke, Dern could feel the tension in his words. "I see no way around naval regulations. The boss didn't say it, but I got the picture—Congress be damned! I am sorry, but I'm going to insist that every agent assigned to this group be a commissioned naval officer."

At the stairwell Dern turned to look at Swanson. "Okay, I see your concern. But now what the hell do *we* do about Eddie Peabody?"

Swanson raised his eyebrows but didn't answer. At the bottom of the spiral staircase, after gathering his thoughts, he spoke softly. "If the boss wants civilians in this group, either a new regulation is needed, or all civilians are going to have to submit to the requirements for reserve officer status." A devilish grin suddenly appeared on his face. "So, George, how do you envisage the process unfolding—taking this world-renowned entertainer and secretly running him through officer's training without one word leaking to the press?"

Dern could almost taste the sarcasm. "Well, that will definitely be a challenge, but I see a bigger hurdle before we even start. I didn't mention it to the president, but his favorite sailor only has a grammar-school education. Oh, his fitness reports indicate that he's smart enough to pass his exams for promotion, but to pass the exam for officer's candidate school—and without any college preparatory? I just don't see how that's possible. If we were at war, perhaps a field commission might fly. But truthfully, I simply don't know how the hell to go about this."

Dern's mind was racing through a myriad of what-ifs on this subject. He felt frustrated that the president hadn't directed someone to be the lead on this issue. *And where did Roosevelt get the idea that a naval threat from Germany is something we need to worry about? Germany needs us—they need our goods and services, our raw materials. And they certainly aren't going to send a bloody armada just to take whatever they need. What the Germans do in Europe is their business. Congress and the American public are not going to tolerate our participation in another foreign war.* He tried to force an unconcerned smile. "I was just thinking—I agree that inasmuch as the president likely wants a naval intelligence group, and not an army/ navy intelligence group, I think you should take the point on this one. Of course I'll back you at every turn, and add my two cents worth, when asked."

Claude Swanson could feel the tree limb he was clinging to start to bend. They cordially shook hands before parting ways. He was still uncomfortable with what FDR wanted, but he especially didn't like Dern's last comment. *Pass-the-buck politics . . . damn it!*

Swanson returned to the Oval Office after lunch. The president's appointment secretary, a plain but pleasant woman of middle age, told him in her normal, no-nonsense and don't-even-think-about-interrupting, steadfastly firm manner that the president had but five minutes before his next scheduled appointment.

Without waiting for a reply, she stood away from her desk and abruptly opened the door to the Oval Office, and then she quickly closed it after Claude had entered.

"Mr. President, I apologize for not elaborating at our earlier meeting, but I feel strongly, and I'm sure you'll agree, that those individuals within the naval intelligence-gathering business should, at a minimum, be naval reserve officers."

FDR, leaning on his desk with his jaw cradled in his right hand, stared at Claude with probing eyes. "Go on."

"Well, sir, the problem I'm grappling with is how we can bring this civilian entertainer, Eddie Peabody, into the ranks of naval reserve officer when his formal education only extends to grammar school. I mean, his service record indicates—"

The president chuckled. "Looks like you've got your work cut out for you. Look, I know in my heart this man is navy from his nose to his toes. I can feel it without even glancing at his service record. The highlights mentioned earlier only served up more convincing evidence. You're a good man, Swanson. I picked you myself for the job of secretary. I know you'll do whatever is necessary to accomplish what I truly believe is in the highest interest of our national security."

The secretary swallowed hard. He knew he was being dismissed. "Yes, sir, and you know I'll do my best, sir."

Sensing the secretary's discomfort, the president held up his hand and motioned him to a nearby chair. "Please sit down a minute, Claude. I've just finished reading a classified report from the Brits. It seems that this guy Hitler has a national press or propaganda secretary named Goebbels who now has a post in the government as minister of enlightenment. He has personally put a radio in nearly every German household so he can broadcast lies to the populace round the clock." FDR suddenly slammed his fist on his desk. "This new Bavarian corporal the German people have chosen as their leader scares the hell out of me. I don't give a damn what Lindbergh thinks, or anyone else, for that matter. I believe that Hitler is planning for war, and his man Goebbels is broadcasting peace, prosperity, and any other damnable lie that will mollify the masses. We need to know firsthand what's going on over there, and we need to know it now."

Claude had never witnessed a response from the boss this strong or emotional, on any issue. Without commenting, he looked at his watch and stood up. "Thank you, Mr. President, for sharing your thoughts. A draft outline will be on your desk first thing Friday morning."

FDR never looked up from his desk.

TWO

Schutzstaffel (SS) Headquarters, Berlin
Midsummer 1934

Reichsführer Heinrich Himmler and most of his staff were gathered for a meeting. At Himmler's side, as had been the case since he joined the SS in 1931, was his deputy Gruppenführer Reinhard Heydrich. Several *Schutzstaffel* and *Sturmabteilung* (SA) officers that had participated in the recent *Reichsmordwoche*, "Operation Hummingbird" or "the Blood Purge" drafted by Heydrich, were also in attendance. This operation was nothing more than a lethal purge of Adolf Hitler's potential political enemies in the SA. Heydrich had personally decorated three officers, Colonel Friedrich Ault, Captain Wilhelm Meyer, and Captain Carl Beck. And all were promoted for their bravery and loyalty to the Reich.

Due to a very pale complexion and a slight build with rounded shoulders, Himmler was not a physically intimidating man. But behind that slightly bloated smoothness of his face, the closely trimmed moustache, and the steel blue-gray eyes was a conscience-less efficiency and intelligence that commanded the focused attention of everyone in the room. When he finally addressed the group, his voice was soft and deliberate, requiring everyone to strain their hearing to catch each word.

Himmler stood at parade rest as he surveyed the room. Without introduction or fanfare, he began. "Gentlemen. There is no question that the enemy will attempt—today, tomorrow, or the next day—to break into our fortress here in Europe. The British, the French, and quite likely the Americans are at the top of the list. At one point or another, this will undoubtedly be the case." He paused and again glanced around the room. "Gentlemen, I believe that the best political weapon we have is the weapon of terror. Cruelty commands respect. Men may hate us when this weapon is brought to bear, but we don't ask for their love—only their fear. It is our duty to penetrate our enemies. We must learn of their treachery before they set foot on our soil. To accomplish this, I have ordered Gruppenführer Heydrich and the *Sicherheitsdienst* to set up organizations—right in the homelands of our enemies— to inform us immediately of all suspected enemy agents. We, of course, will then arrest and detain these spies the minute they cross our borders. Now, Herr Gruppenführer, if you will continue with the details."

Heydrich stood at attention with a loud click of his boots. He too came to a parade rest as he looked over the assembled group. Heydrich stood over six feet tall and was the living embodiment of the Aryan ideal: blond; fair complexion; cold, penetrating blue eyes; educated in the classics; walked with a confident swagger. He was articulate when he spoke, clear and distinct, but he struggled, as he had throughout most of his early life, with a high, almost falsetto voice. "Gentlemen, your orders are in the folders given to each of you as you entered. I will work with each two-man team in your respective area assignments. And I will personally review the background checks on every new recruit. For the next three months, Colonel Ault will be traveling with Captain Meyer and Captain Beck to and within the United States. They will report to me directly. Our objective in the United States will be the same as our objective in Britain, France, Belgium, Holland, or Denmark. You are SS officers and you will be working within existing

German-American expatriate groups. In the United States there are large groups of loyal German expatriates, especially in New York and Chicago. A network of trusted informants and direct radio communication with *Schutzstaffel* headquarters will be the first priority. Upon his successful return, Colonel Ault will be assigned to Berlin headquarters. He will be in charge of coordinating all forwarded field information and, in my absence, will review all background checks." Heydrich paused as he looked over the assembly. "Are there any questions, gentlemen?"

The silence in the room was deafening. Himmler pushed away from the table, and Heydrich called the room to attention. After the *Reichsführer* had departed, the assembly began to break up.

Colonel Ault approached Heydrich. "Excuse me, sir. Do we have any additional background information on this Herr Schwindenhammer in New York? I know a family in Munich by that name."

Heydrich continued to collect his meeting folders as Ault spoke. He then turned to face the man and spoke almost in a whisper. "We will discuss this subject in more detail once we are at sea, Colonel. Now, if you will excuse me." Colonel Ault watched the man adjust his cap, arch his back, and march out of the room. Those men still in the room waiting to depart parted like the Red Sea as they heard Heydrich approach.

THREE

New York City
"The Talk of the Town," Rudy Vallee

HIS BANJO GETS HOT AND SMOKES, reported the *New York Times*.

Rudy Vallee folded the paper and turned to his producer. "Jack, get us a couple of tickets to the Brooklyn Fox Theater tonight. I want to get a look at this banjo man Eddie Peabody. The press seems to think that this guy is a hot act, and we could sure use a fill-in for next Thursday's radio show. I'll be at the club most of the day, but I'll call you about noon, all right?"

Rudy Vallee was the image of Ivy League sophistication: A six-foot, wavy-haired, dashing crooner with a megaphone, he was the idol of many vaudevillian performers and hopefuls. His New York syndicated radio show was known nationally and boasted a listening audience of more than one hundred million. He held court, and often gave press interviews, at his spacious and elegantly furnished apartment near Central Park.

Jack Turner, Rudy's Heigh Ho Club producer, secretary, schedule keeper, and overall personal assistant, was a short, overweight, nervous man that never stood still. But he loved the view of the park from Rudy's balcony, and though he was listening as Rudy barked orders from an overstuffed lounge chair, he caught himself starting to drift as he took in all the activity around the pond. He jerked abruptly as he turned to answer his boss.

"Will do, Rudy, and you're right—they say this guy's like lightning. Maybe he could give that German guy in the band—what's his name? Heinz, I think his name is—a few tips. No, now that I think about it, if this banjo man sat in, who knows what Heinz would do? We've got to fire that guy, Rudy—send him back to Germany. He's an accident waiting to happen. Anyway, I've heard this banjo wizard Peabody can really dazzle 'em, Rudy. Maybe he could give you a few tips."

"All right, all right, now, knock it off. I bet he can't sing or play the sax, and I'm sure he can't excite the ladies with 'Your Time Is My Time.'" Rudy grinned as he crooned a few bars of his transnational hit. "I'll call you in a couple of hours. Do what you have to regarding the German fella. And make sure the Brooklyn Paramount has my stage settings for the guest appearance on Saturday."

"You got it, boss."

Jack connected with the Fox Theater manager and reserved four seats, two rows back from the orchestra. Rudy, Jack, Rudy's program manager, and one of the WEAF radio station secretaries whom Jack had been dating all arrived separately but within minutes of curtain call. As the orchestra was warming up, Jack leaned over the secretary and copped a quick feel while he whispered to Rudy, "Looks like the Fox tries to run things on time."

The lights dimmed. The orchestra opened with classic *1812 Overture* kettle drums and cymbals, and once again little Eddie came sliding down the neck of a large wooden banjo stage prop, landing with a bang, and immediately he warmed up his fingers to the *Poet and Peasant Overture*. The little guy in starched white sailor trousers and a short red jacket was one awe-inspiring bundle of energy. He bounced around on a tiny stool and delivered as many crisp musical notes as a concert pianist. His enthusiasm bubbled over when he smiled—everyone knew this guy loved performing for them. Some in the audience held their breath as they marveled at his fingers dancing up and down the instrument. The applause after each number was thunderous.

When Eddie finished his segment of the show, Rudy stood from his seat. "Did you watch that guy's hands? I've never seen anything that fast. Let's get backstage and see if we can get him for a guest spot."

"Eddie!" Jack was yelling over the cacophony of the performers and stagehands. Eddie headed toward his dressing room, carrying his banjo like a rifle with the neck resting on his shoulder. Rudy touched Jack's arm. "Jack, look at that bright, happy-faced smile, his touch, the enthusiasm, and the warm and friendly greetings from nearly everyone in the show—it's infectious!"

"Eddie, excuse us, please." Jack extended his hand. "Jack Turner here. Could we have just a minute of your time? You know Rudy here, I'm sure." Rudy had that well-known effervescent smile of his beaming at Eddie as he gingerly shook the man's hand while resting his other hand on Eddie's shoulder. No one in North America, let alone show business, could ever mistake Rudy Vallee.

"Eddie, Jack and I just caught your show, and you were sensational!" There was deep sincerity in Rudy's voice.

"Well, thank you, my good man. Coming from you, that is a compliment indeed. Let's move to my dressing room, away from the crowd here, shall we? At least we should be able to hear ourselves think in there." Though the man was not long legged, both Rudy and Jack had to hustle to keep up with the little sandy-haired ex-sailor. Once the door closed, Rudy began to slowly pace in circles. The room was small: too small for Rudy's nervous pacing.

"Eddie, I'll come right to the point. I want you on my radio show. You'll have my listeners dancing in the streets. Now, I've got Kate Smith booked for guest spot this week, but how about you and I doing a duet or something, with a short interview, the week after?"

Rudy's antics were so distracting and comical that all Eddie could manage was a burp and a grunt. Rudy now stood in the middle of the room with his hands folded behind his back. He looked at Eddie with a facial expression that clearly communicated, *What the hell are you doing? Have you heard anything I've said for the past five minutes?*

Eddie broke the short silence and motioned for Rudy and Jack to take a seat on the small couch crammed against one wall under a large framed mirror. "Rudy, you're a very persuasive man. I'll do your guest spot."

FOUR

Rudy's Villa Vallee

The Villa Vallee Club was the swankiest nightclub in all New York City. With its marble floors, crystal-encased lighting, and mirrored wall panels, the place looked like it came directly from the palace in Versailles. And the nightly clientele represented the city's upper crust: senators, congressmen, state legislators, judges, police chiefs, and anyone else in the political spotlight not wanting to be seen frequenting a nightclub.

Rudy warmly greeted his new friend. He placed his hand behind Eddie's elbow, as if to guide him. "Come on back to the office for a minute, would you? I've got something I need to talk to you about. And maybe you can show me some more of your—" Rudy was suddenly distracted.

"Good evening, Your Honor." Rudy beamed. "Glad to see you could join us this evening. Mayor, may I introduce you to Eddie Peabody? Eddie's going to help us celebrate tonight. And this is . . . ?" Rudy turned to greet the absolutely stunning young lady accompanying the mayor. She blushed and was absolutely shell-shocked when the nationally famous heartthrob Rudy Vallee leaned over and kissed her hand. "Your name, sweetheart?"

She blinked, shook her head, and breathed heavily, "Emma." After a brief moment of silence, she erupted into a woodpecker-like laugh that had everyone within earshot turning to see what the commotion was.

The mayor and two rather husky gentlemen quickly hustled the young lady into the adjoining dining room.

With a Cheshire cat grin, Rudy turned back to Eddie and rolled his eyes. "Ah, yes, the essence of beauty, with a voice like a bird. Let's head through the kitchen and up to my private office . . . hi-de-ho."

Rudy's office was more extravagant than anything Eddie had ever seen. A large, polished wood desk was the centerpiece, with luxurious leather chairs angled at the front for visiting guests. A leather couch with a coffee table sat against one wall, facing a floor-to-ceiling bookcase along the opposite wall. A draperied window covered the wall behind Rudy's desk. Rudy manipulated two handles attached to the bookcase, revealing a hidden private bar. The glassware behind the case was crystal, glittering like polished diamonds. The labeled decanters contained nothing but the best: blended Canadian whiskeys, Cuban rum, and Russian vodka. "Pretty swanky, Magee," Eddie quipped, as his eyes tried to take it all in.

"What'll you have, my good friend?" Rudy took out two tumblers and threw in some chipped ice from a small container nearby. "All I've got is Canadian whiskey, rum, and vodka, but if I may recommend the Canadian—it is simply superb. Now, what's your pleasure?"

"The Canadian would be fine, Rudy. Damn it, man, you have quite a setup here. I don't think I've ever seen anything quite like it. If Maude saw this she'd—"

Rudy was quick with, "Where did you say your wife was off to?" He handed Eddie a drink and directed him over to the leather couch.

"She's in Texas, thank God, visiting her folks. Her father is not well. She's a fine business manager, my friend. But I'd be lying if didn't say I was happy havin' her outta my hair for a coupla weeks."

"Eddie, I need your help, good friend."

"Just name it. Damn, this is the smoothest I believe I've ever tasted. Boy oh boy, I bet you don't share this with the poor people."

Rudy laughed, loosened his collar, and began to relax.

"Well, my friend, I've been trying to find a rhythm banjo player for the club band for more than a week now. Jack hired some German fellow, and he has been nothing short of a disaster. Not only was the SOB a lush, he couldn't carry a tune in a bucket. On top of that, he has tried to pick a fight with damn near everyone in the band."

"Really? I'm sorry to hear that. Well, I usually bump into several banjo players after the Sunday matinee. I'll put the word out and see if anyone is interested."

"Thank you, my friend. Anything you can come up with would be a blessing. Would you believe he nearly started a fight on stage with that hot jazz violinist I'd hired last week, just because the guy was French? This guy was German, of course, but I can't remember his name. I think it was Blintz, Mintz, or maybe Heinz. I am glad we fired that hothead, anyway."

"I truly am sorry. Your club band has a great reputation. I will ask around and see what I can turn up for you, pal."

"Thanks. Oh, and there's one other thing I'd like to twist your arm on." Rudy's eyes lit up, and he moved to the edge of his seat. "I'm hosting a private party tonight in one of the adjoining ballrooms—actually, entertaining a few special patrons. I'd like you and your banjo to help me out, if you're game. It should be a barrel of laughs. What do you say?"

Eddie understood the part about Rudy wanting him to help entertain some influential folks, but he was silently waiting for the other shoe to drop. The man was acting like he just stole a pig.

"This affair is going to be wide open, my fine, feathered friend. Sort of no-holds-barred, if you know what I mean. And any raids tonight, and the state of New York will have to elect a whole new state legislature, and maybe a few from the Supreme Court as well."

Eddie stood up and touched his glass to Rudy's with an audible clink. "Terrific! So let's get down there and see how this bacchanalia is progressing, shall we?" They both refreshed their drinks.

"And wait till you see the chorus girls Jack has lined up for tonight. And wouldn't you know the floor plan of this marvelous building requires that we travel through their dressing room to get to the ballroom." Rudy was smiling broadly and swirled his index finger in the air, as if ready for the foxhunt to begin.

Eddie gave out with a chuckle, feeling giddy and lightheaded. He wasn't sure, but it felt like he and his friend were about to do something quite naughty. "Well, hi-de-ho, I say, and let's go."

Rudy led him through a maze of hallways and stairwells, winked, and then opened a door. The noise level jumped ten decibels.

"Rudy, if my life depended on it, I don't think I could find my way outta here."

The room they'd entered was narrow, with a dense screen of tobacco smoke. Eddie could see showgirls on both sides of the room in various stages of costume change. He tried not to stare. *My God, they'd be more covered up with just . . . !* He was trying his best to smile at everyone.

By now, Rudy had snaked his way into what looked to be the kitchen. Trying to keep an eye on Rudy, and not paying attention where he was walking, Eddie proceeded to step on one of the showgirl's feet, and bang into her nose-to-nose, sloshing some of his drink down the front of her costume. The cold liquid caused the young lady to throw her arms up with an ear-shattering screech. Realizing what he'd done, he reached in his pocket for a handkerchief. "Oh my, I am sorry, my dear." He dabbed at the spill as much as he thought appropriate, while she glared at him with an angry, annoyed look.

Rudy, noticing that he'd lost his friend, returned to find the man sheepishly dabbing away. "What on earth?" The expression on the showgirl's face when she saw Rudy gradually evolved into a toothy grin. She extended her hand. "I'm pleased to make your acquaintance, Mr. Vallee."

Rudy smiled and cordially grasped the lady's hand. "I hate to interrupt this lovely rendezvous, my friend, but we're on a bit of a tight schedule."

"Right you are, skipper." Eddie bowed slightly to the showgirl and again apologized.

The ballroom wasn't large, but it was luxuriously furnished and decorated for the festive occasion. Rudy glided over to one of the tables. Three men and one woman all smiled and waved in a toast to what they knew would be a grand evening.

Rudy graciously greeted everyone in his patented self-assured yet humble tone of voice. "Senators, and ladies . . . so good to see you this evening. I do hope everyone is comfortable? And may your evening be most memorable."

The band had already started to tune up. Eddie recognized many of the musicians. The piano and bass were from Rudy's band, but the drummer and most of the brass were theater musicians. There was no spot for a rhythm banjo. *No wonder Rudy invited me down here tonight.* Rudy's instrument was sitting on a stand behind the piano. *And it looks like my friend is hoping for another duet.*

Rudy was chatting with the acting master of ceremonies for the evening. "Eddie, this is Paul Scofield." Paul Scofield was a short, wiry man with thick black hair, stylishly slicked back. His angular face and deep-set eyes gave him a serious and focused look. "Paul arranged the music for this evening and will direct all the dance sequencing."

Paul described to Eddie the choreographed all-girl show. "This is Rudy's appreciation dinner-show for some of his influential political friends, Eddie. You bring your wife at your own peril, if you know what I mean. Nothing but the best tonight—imported champagne, USDA prime, and the best show in town."

"Paul has some hot numbers for the chorus line, Eddie. And you and I will just be adding some backup on two of the numbers toward the end of the show. I'll sing sixteen bars of 'Sweet Georgia

Brown' about forty minutes in, with you on rhythm banjo—and Eddie, I mean rhythm on this one. You can pull out the stops on the last stanza, and on 'Bye Bye Blues' when Paul gives you the high sign. Got it?"

"Sure, Rudy. I'm just a visiting fireman, remember? Oh, by the way, I noticed that there wasn't a spot in the band for a rhythm banjo. What were you going to do if you couldn't get hold of me? Perhaps that German banjo man from upstairs . . . " Eddie started to snigger.

"Damn it, man! Don't even joke about that guy. That guy scares the hell outta me, and I wouldn't put it past him to do something dastardly." Rudy clenched his fists and took a deep breath as he closed his eyes. "Okay. No more talk . . . " He put his arm on Eddie's shoulder and directed him back to where the band was starting to tune up. "My friend, the last time I sponsored one of these outings, one of the state representatives got so carried away that he took off all his clothes. Then he commenced to carry one of the showgirls out to Forty-Second Street." Rudy motioned for Eddie to slide over to an empty table near the kitchen. With a snap of Rudy's finger, a waiter came through and deposited two beautifully displayed plates with generous portions of sizzling filet mignon. "Sit down, pal, and let's sample some of New York's finest."

After they'd been served, Rudy began to nervously look at his watch. It was almost 10:00 PM. "The stage show should commence in about fifteen minutes. Enjoy yourself tonight, my friend. We're all amongst friends, but don't get in the way of any wandering politicians."

The show commenced without introduction or fanfare. There were five different skits in quick succession, with lots of singing and dancing. All the girls were in tuxedos with top hats and walking sticks. When Eddie looked back toward the stage, the girls had stripped off the tuxedos to reveal sequined underwear and were grinding away to some very bawdy music. The crowd roared its approval.

The pace of the show and the noise in the ballroom had

elevated considerably. Eddie could feel the tempo, the mood, and the excitement, and his pulse start to accelerate.

"Ten more minutes and we're on, Eddie." Eddie rose from the table and quietly moved to the back of the bandstand. He shouldered his banjo and grabbed a short stool that was near the piano.

When Rudy sang his portion of "Sweet Georgia Brown," a lone spotlight caught just him, with Eddie silhouetted in the background. As the number rolled to a close, Rudy jumped back onstage and motioned for the audience to sing along. "How are we doing out there, ladies and gentlemen? Is everyone enjoying themselves?"

Some of the guests began banging on tables. An inebriated gentleman at a front table slurred out, "We love you, Rudy, but you aren't what we came to see." The room filled with raucous laughter.

"Hang on there, sport. Ladies and gentlemen, it is my sincere pleasure to introduce to you my good friend and King of the Banjo, Eddie Peabody." For the finale, the band transitioned very softly into "Bye Bye Blues."

As Eddie banged out the melody, the chorus line entered with a Radio City Rockettes precision-style dance routine. They snaked around all the tables for the finale. The noise was now deafening. The band kept on playing some popular dance tunes.

A whistle noise suddenly blared out from one of the room's corners, and the band stopped playing immediately. One of the waiters yelled, "It's a raid!" Several women started to scream.

The show's producer grabbed a megaphone and tried to calm everyone. "Please remain calm, folks. All is well. One of our security men has jumped the gun, and there is no cause for alarm." He wasn't having much luck. People were in a panic. The showgirls began to exit quickly through the dressing area. "Ladies and gentlemen, for everyone's safety, the waiters will usher you out in groups of four."

Rudy grabbed Eddie by the arm and shoved him toward one of the exits. "This way, my friend. It'll lead to a passageway around the kitchen and back to the stairwell."

Eddie was hanging on to his banjo with a death grip.

Rudy noticed. "You'd probably save that thing if the building was on fire."

"From where I stood, pal, either there was a fire, or somebody just sent in the troops. I thought I'd better save something."

FIVE

Ernie Heinz sat in his apartment at a wobbly wooden dining table, thinking about lunch, sorting through the mail. A short, stocky man, balding with long, curly, unkempt locks on the back of his neck, he resembled a troll. His eyebrows were bushy, and he sported a short, untrimmed mustache from his nose to his upper lip. He was staring at a letter that had been forwarded from the German restaurant where he was employed.

With dirty gray walls, his one-room flat seemed as cheery as the recent weather, dismal at best. It was clear that dirt on the floor or spilled food were Heinz's last priorities. The floor had so many warped boards that sweeping was nearly impossible. He glanced at the metal-frame bed, pushed to one corner, with wooden slats to support the thin cotton mattress. There he had laid out his prize possessions: his banjo and his sheet music. He heaved a deep sigh. *That swine Rudy Vallee! I hope his fancy club burns to the ground. Well, I've still got work at the Hofbrau Haus.*

He tried to focus on a letter he'd dropped on the table last

31

evening. It was addressed to Herr Gruppenleiter Earnst Heinz, Hofbrau Haus, 302 W. 35th, New York, New York, USA. It was from Munich, but he didn't recognize the address. It had to be from Alfred and Aunt Frieda. They'd said that things were so bad all over Germany that they felt like moving but didn't know where to go. Maybe they were thinking of coming to New York and staying with him. He stared at the envelope. *Herr Gruppenleiter.* He smiled. *A waiter, yes . . . a banjo player, yes . . . but a group leader? Not unless the Hofbrau is a secret Boy Scout troop.* He laughed out loud.

My God, I don't earn enough to support my family. I work two jobs. I'm always broke. And I'm treated like a second-class immigrant. The Wassersteins, with their sophisticated upper-class Jewish attitude—"I'm a better German than you." He tore open the envelope.

Dear Earnst,

How are you doing in America? I hope this letter finds you well and that you are still playing your music that you so love.

We really miss seeing you. I know Mom or Dad would never say, but we all appreciate the money you sent. It helped all of us, and it gave us hope.

Things are much better in Germany now, for all of us. There is new construction everywhere—even the factory has reopened. People are going to the theater and to cabarets. It seems that new sidewalk cafes are opening on every street. You would have no problem finding work here in Munich, especially with your experience in America.

You can see from the address that we now live on Hochbrucken. It's a big apartment, Earnst. There's plenty of room if you decide to come home, which we all are hoping for.

I do have some bad news. Uncle Alfred died this spring. They said his heart gave out, but I still think it was because he drank too much. He wasn't the same after he lost his business to those heartless Jewish bankers. Aunt

Frieda now lives with her son, our cousin in Augsburg. We see them often on the weekends when the weather is nice.

Dad has a guard job back at the factory and I'm working for the *Nationalsozialistische Deutsche Arbeiterpartei*. Oh, Earnst, there is so much political excitement these days. And the party I work for has the most brilliant and dynamic new leader in all of Germany. You would love him, Earnst. Soon you will read about him in America, I'm sure, after we win in the upcoming elections. His name is Adolf Hitler, and he comes from Bavaria. He's not an aristocrat like those stuffed pigs from Prussia, or one of those boring intellectual politician puppets of Hindenburg. And you should hear him speak. It's like he knows what we are all feeling. We believe and pray that he will be the one who leads our homeland to greatness.

Oh, dear brother, I'm sorry, but I do ramble on. Please write me all the news from America, and please, please, please do think about coming home, if only for a visit. We do miss you so.

> *Alles Liebe,*
> *Deine Schwester,* Della

Heinz was completely surprised. *Things have really turned around in Germany. And Della, she must be a grown woman by now. How long has it been? I can't believe it. She's now working, and interested in politics as well. I do miss seeing her. Maybe with my experience, I could land a good job with a band at a restaurant or theater. I should write her.* He made his way to the icebox and opened a bottle of beer.

My God, this stuff is awful. What this country couldn't do with a really good glass of beer. I must answer Della's letter this afternoon, before I get busy and forget. Yes, I want to return home, but I'm so broke, I might have to stow away on a freighter. When Heinz came to America six years ago, he worked his way over as a cabin helper on a converted passenger ship. The captain had been fond of him, and at the time, Heinz really hadn't minded bathing and massaging the old goat.

He hustled through a lunch of sausage and kraut and began

to write his sister a quick letter. He wrote of how pleased he was to hear from her and said that yes, after reading her letter, he was thinking about returning to Germany. He asked her if she would write to him about the restaurants and theaters in Munich, and whether or not the jazz craze had infected Germany the way it had America. He told her that he had learned to play the banjo. And he had a job at a German restaurant, playing polkas.

Heinz picked up a theater ticket from the table where he'd had his lunch and brushed off some breadcrumbs. *Tonight I'm going to see a real banjo player.* The entertainer he was going to see was featured at one the city's great theaters. He had been reading about him for weeks. He'd even purchased one of his records, though he couldn't bring himself to part with the kind of money needed to buy a record player. There was a recent news article and advertisement on his nightstand. *I think I will send the article to my sister and ask her if she's ever heard of this fellow.*

The advertisement read as follows:

Jack Loeb and the Fox Theater Proudly Present
New York's Newest Recording Star
"The King of the Banjo"
EDDIE PEABODY
And his Versatile and Talented Band

He reread the article before stuffing it into the envelope. *I thought his recording of the* Poet and Peasant Overture *on the Edison Diamond Disc was a one-and-only, but it says here that he had recordings with five other companies. This guy must be making more money than those Jews down at the Hofbrau Haus. I have got to find a record player.*

The Fox Theater's architecture was ornate, and with the huge window over the entrance, it looked more like a cathedral than a stage theater. Everything about the Fox was built on a grand scale, and it was magnificent. The auditorium was accessed through four great arches of beautifully carved hardwoods. The theater contained more than three hundred deeply padded red velvet seats. The chandelier that hung from the ceiling in the center of the auditorium was more than twelve feet in diameter. The carved, dark veneer extended all around the theater walls to a grand sculptured crest that covered a series of pipes mounted between the top of the stage and the ceiling. The pipes belonged to a huge pipe organ. Elaborately appointed elevators carried patrons to every balcony level. On either side of the thick-carpeted walkway, large wells opened views to the theater's grand promenade below.

Tonight, the Fox Theater was packed. Excitement and tension filled the air as patrons bustled about, and young ushers helped the lost find their seats. With a loud, ear-splitting shrill from the brass section of the orchestra, the lights dimmed, and an announcement came from behind the closed curtains. "And now, ladies and gentlemen, the sensation you've all been waiting for—New York's newest recording sensation, the one and only King of the Banjo, Eddie Peabody!"

After initial applause, a hush blanketed the audience. The curtains opened quickly. Nine band members, dressed in red blazers and white pants, were centered round a giant wooden banjo that glowed with one hundred light bulbs outlining the instrument. At the top of the giant banjo neck, on a sliding platform, sat little, sandy-haired Eddie with his banjo tucked in his lap. Eddie was also dressed in a red blazer and white baggy pants. The stage was dark except for the lit-up stage banjo. A spotlight flashed on Eddie and his effervescent smile. Some of the women at the front of the auditorium were captivated by the scene and started to swoon. The platform atop the brightly lit giant banjo began to descend. The kettledrums in the orchestra began a chest-pounding, thunderous roll. When the little platform reached the stage floor, Eddie began to wallop out an arrangement of the *Poet and Peasant Overture*, to thunderous applause. He then played a medley of several favorite tunes of the day, many of which he had formally introduced over the radio. Chorus girls were used to spice up the last refrain as the medley built up to a foot-stomping finale. Eddie varied the pace of the performance by soloing on other stringed instruments—the awesome harp-guitar, the soothing, soft-sounding Banjoline, and the violin. One song on the violin used the upper reaches of the neck to produce a sound mimicking the melodic call of the mockingbird. But it was his bejeweled plectrum banjo that seemed to stir the most excitement. The public had dubbed him "The Man with the Banjo," and that was what they'd come to see and hear. After he'd performed George Gershwin's *Rhapsody in Blue* on the banjo, there was a standing ovation and applause lasting for more than three minutes. For ninety minutes it was just little Eddie—no intermission.

This was the most spectacular show Heinz had ever witnessed. Overwhelmed by Eddie's virtuosity, Heinz was exhausted from concentrating on Eddie's technique. *I must meet this man.* He noticed some reporters moving against the crowd and heading for one of the backstage entrances. He slipped in with them and followed the group to the dressing room area. He noticed Eddie sitting in a corner, toweling off and cleaning the strings on his banjo. A young reporter for the *Times* entertainment section was sitting next to him, jotting down interview notes. Suddenly he was jostled and knocked backward by four teenage kids who were seeking an autograph. "Excuse me, sir—Herr Peabody?"

Eddie looked up from signing programs. He glanced at the disheveled, sweaty man with the thick accent. The youngsters showed their irritation verbally as the guy elbowed his way to the front of the line.

"My name is Earnst Heinz."

Eddie smiled and nodded, but continued to autograph programs. When he'd finished he turned to Heinz and said, "Please, have a seat, sir . . . Mr. Heinz, is it? It'll only take me a minute to finish packing up."

Heinz was now feeling dumbstruck, and began to stutter as he tried to continue the conversation. He craved a cold beer. "Herr Peabody, you have the fastest hands that I have ever seen." He felt stupid the minute he'd finished.

"Thank you, sir, for your kind words. I'm afraid all I have to offer you is water."

"No, no, thank you. I am a banjo player too . . . perhaps you've heard of me. I'm currently working at the Hofbrau Haus. I came by to invite you to have some good German food and listen to our band. We play polkas, and sometimes a little jazzy stuff."

Eddie stood and reached out with his hand. It was time to usher this guy out the door. "Thank you very much, Mr. Heinz. Perhaps my wife and I will be able to stop by, oh, say sometime after the matinee on Sunday."

SIX

Even though it had been almost ten years since the end of the war, strong anti-German sentiment ran high with many in America. Recently, a group of German merchant ships, accompanied by a German warship, docked at the New York harbor. The *Times* carried a picture of the German warship as it entered the harbor. There was also a picture of veteran doughboys marching in protest. A sizable German neighborhood not far from the piers catered to the locals. There were several good ethnic restaurants, including the Hofbrau Haus.

Sunday afternoons were always chaotic at most of the local restaurants near the docks, and today was no exception. Many of the merchant crew and a few German navy sailors from the warship were ashore. All, of course, were looking for a good meal and a good time.

The band at the Hofbrau House had just finished a sing-along, including several German patriotic songs, and was preparing to take a break. Heinz had been helping himself, since before noon, to some exceptional *bockbier* that had been smuggled in by one of the merchant ships. Looking up toward the restaurant entrance, to his surprise, he noticed Eddie Peabody enter with a woman, perhaps his wife.

He noticed that the woman was tall, taller than Eddie by an inch or two. She was large but striking—not because of her physical beauty, though she was not unattractive. It was her razor-straight posture and self-assured manner that caught Heinz's eye. *She has to be of sound German stock, if I'm any judge.* He suddenly felt a hush falling over the din of the restaurant clatter. He noticed that all eyes were turned toward the entering couple.

The proprietor's wife, Mrs. Wasserstein, approached the couple. She was a short, round, wiry-haired lady, but she always wore a pleasant smile as she greeted her customers. Over her dress she wore a short apron with edelweiss embroidered around the edge.

To Heinz, however, Mrs. Wasserstein was the living embodiment of everything he detested. First and foremost, she was a woman, and she made it clear to everyone in her employ that *she*, and no one else in this restaurant, was in charge. He approached the incoming couple, but his negative attitude and the copious amount of beer he'd consumed made it difficult for him to walk and think straight. "Eddie, it's very good of you to come." He couldn't keep from slurring his words. He looked towards the tall woman and could tell she was very uncomfortable.

In awkward silence, Eddie grabbed Maude's elbow just as Mrs. Wasserstein pushed Heinz to the side and barked, *"Du bist ja besoffen."* ("You are drunk.")

Heinz was now seething with anger. *Bitch! A few beers just might make you tolerable. Besides, it isn't every day that a good glass of beer can be had in this godforsaken country.*

Mrs. Wasserstein ushered Eddie and Maude to a front table just off the bandstand, where the air was a little clearer. Eddie leaned across the table and whispered, "Did I smell a brewery, or do you suppose the man has had too much sauerkraut?"

"How could anyone mistake that horrible smell? You say he

performs here? In his condition, I don't see how that's possible. Where do you find these characters?"

A young man approached their table with a chalkboard that explained the sparse menu. The man's accent was thick and difficult to understand, but they were able to recognize a few items. They each ordered sauerbraten and potato dumplings with kraut, one of the house specialties. Mrs. Wasserstein personally brought them each a glass of contraband German Rhine wine that, she was proud to announce, had just been brought in that day by one of her old boyfriends.

Eddie leaned over again. "You know what they say, hon. When in Rome . . . "

Maude smiled courteously but gave him a sarcastic look, with her arms folded. "Alcohol merely detracts from performance and lowers alertness." He reached across the table and touched her hand—the lecture was finished.

Without fanfare and with Heinz on the banjo, looking less than alert, the band began playing some nice German and Austrian waltzes. A few couples danced, but most of the diners were just humming along with the music. After three nostalgic songs, Heinz stood at attention and slurred an announcement. "The Hofbrau Haus has a very special guest this evening—direct from the Fox Theater—Eddie Peabody, the King of the Banjo."

There was light applause. Most of their patrons had never heard of the Fox Theater, let alone Eddie Peabody. All eyes began to look over at their table. The audience shouted words of encouragement as Heinz gestured for him to get up and come over and sit in with the band.

Eddie reluctantly got up and walked over to politely decline, but Heinz quickly jumped down from the small bandstand and handed Eddie his banjo, then stumbled to the back of the restaurant. Eddie glanced at his wife, and her face said it all: *Let's get outta here.*

The accordion player started to play a polka while the bassoon and sax players joined in. Eddie jumped up and sat in Ernie's chair, reached in his coat pocket for one of his own banjo picks, and after briefly retuning the tenor instrument, he began to strum out chords of accompaniment to the polka. After the medley, he asked the other band members if they knew any Southern tunes. They all nodded encouragement for Eddie to lead away. He began with "Old Folks at Home" and even got some of the patrons to sing along. He then went into "Swanee" and concluded with "Waiting for the Robert E. Lee." By the time he'd finished, everyone in the restaurant was clapping and stamping their feet to the music. Eddie stood and looked for Heinz, so he could hand him back his banjo. The audience was shouting for more. He bowed, thanked the other band members, and laid the instrument on Heinz's chair.

The band played one more waltz without Heinz and then took a break. Mrs. Wasserstein brought their coats while Eddie paid the bill. As he turned toward Maude, the men's room door burst open with a bang.

It came open so quickly, and with such force that Eddie tripped and bumped his nose on the edge of the door. He stumbled backward but was abruptly grabbed by the lapels of his coat. When he refocused, he saw that he was about to be punched out.

"*Schwein*," growled Heinz. "Did you enjoy making me look like a fool?"

Like a whirlwind, Mrs. Wasserstein stepped in pushed them apart. She was glaring at Heinz. She spoke sharply in German, almost spitting her words. Then she turned to Eddie and Maude. "Please, *mein Herr*, I am very sorry. I apologize for this drunken employee Heinz. We very much enjoyed your playing this evening."

Eddie nodded politely, grabbed his coat from Maude, and then hustled her outside. In silence, they walked hurriedly up the street. Maude was first to open up.

"What just happened in there? What did that man say to you?"

"I honestly don't know, hon, but I think you were right. That was one drunk sailor back there. And he sure as hell didn't want me playin' in his band."

"So why did he ask you, and in front of everyone?"

"How the hell should I know?" Eddie paused to burp. "Damn kraut always gives me gas anyway."

Mrs. Wasserstein had given Heinz a tongue-lashing that had most of the men who were within earshot holding their sides with laughter. He felt angry and humiliated. All he wanted to do was slap the Jewess across the face and burn her precious restaurant to the ground. He grabbed his banjo and, in a fit of anger screeched, "Get stuffed, all of you!" He stormed out.

I'll be fine once I'm home—no, home in Germany. Tomorrow I'm going to book the first steamer passage back to Germany. The cold New York air was bone-chilling. He leaned against a light post. He began to spit out words, to no one in particular, but to all those he loathed at this moment. "Shit! This country, these people, these Jews . . . all of you, you're not even food for pigs . . . shit! *Mein Gott,* I'd like to strangle that bitch!"

He slept in fits and starts that night and awoke drenched in sweat. His head felt like an anvil. He stumbled to the sink and threw up the vile, acidic remains in his stomach. He tried to swallow water, but it came up before hitting bottom. He stumbled back to bed and tried to will away the pounding in his brain. He couldn't remember what all happened last night, but he felt sure his employment was finished. His brain had turned to oatmeal. Even though he wasn't sure why, he knew he had to find his way to the German-American Club.

The walk in the cool, crisp air the following day cleared his head and gave him time to reflect on what took place the evening before. He was sure he had made a fool of himself, and he remembered Frau Wasserstein yelling at him. A cold chill ran up his spine at the thought of returning and confronting the wicked witch. If there were any final wages to collect, he knew he'd need every cent he could scrape up.

The entrance to the German-American Club was off an alley with only a small sign over the doorway. Just the initials GAC were stenciled in old European script under a carved griffin. In the upper center of the door was a small circular window that was covered from the inside by a sliding metal plate. Only card-carrying members were allowed in when elections were being held, but those were few and far between.

Heinz had only been to the club a couple of times, and then only when he'd heard they'd received a shipment of *bockbier*. Upon entering, he heard, "Herr Heinz, come join us." He recognized the two merchant seamen that had been at the Hofbrau last night. They seemed genuinely glad to see him.

"Good evening to you, my friends . . . Karl and Fritz, is it, yes? May I sit with you?"

"Of course. Say, Heinz, where is your banjo?" The two sailors immediately started to chuckle, but they ceased when they noticed their acquaintance wasn't amused.

"We are sorry, my friend, but last night—we can't remember so much fun."

After a long swallow of beer, Heinz belched so loud that it resonated throughout the room. "Well, I'm sorry too. I can't seem to remember shit." That aroused instant laughter from his two friends. Heinz was not in a jovial mood. He wanted to change the subject quickly and get their undivided attention. Without warning he slammed his open palm on the bar. "Please, my friends, I came here not because I wanted to entertain you with what happened last evening. Seriously, I would like to book passage back to Germany. Who do I need to talk to, and what do you think it will cost me?"

One of the men, Fritz, was annoyed at Heinz's theatrics and wanted to needle the man a bit more. "So, you want to go home, eh? Maybe you think that American banjo player wants your job, *ja*?"

"No, I'm quite sure that isn't the case. And I don't think he would put up with that bitch at the Hofbrau for one minute."

"Stop your worrying, friend, and don't let Frau Wasserstein's bark get to you. She barks at everyone." The two merchantmen continued chuckling and poking each other.

"I just received a letter from my sister, begging me to return home. I've been thinking about it now for a while. She said that things were much better in Germany. What do you two think?"

Karl spoke now but never lifted his eyes from his beer mug. He directed his words to no one and spoke quietly. "If you're asking if people have forgotten about the war, they haven't. Oh, people may be partying more today than five years ago, but the government still doesn't know what it's doing. And people just keep voting in those idiots. Every time you turn around, there's another election. And the French! Those swine are just pushing for another war. I don't know what's going to happen, but *ja*, some people say things are better. There seems to be a lot of new construction, and that's good for my brother and the company he works for. Now he thinks he makes enough money and wants to get married."

Fritz cleared his throat and coughed. "I need a smoke." He grinned at Heinz and slapped his back. "I think you will do better in Germany, Heinz. There are too many Jews and niggers in this country. There is no discipline . . . too much freedom. It will collapse."

A tall, blond, well-dressed, middle-aged gentleman strolled over and introduced himself. "Good evening, gents. I am Herr Schwindenhammer. *Wie gehts?*" He was a strong, jovial man with a robust handshake. He pulled up a chair from an adjacent table and joined them. "The beer is good here at the club, *ja?*" Schwindenhammer quickly became serious and leaned into Heinz and his two friends. He pointed his finger at Fritz. "Be careful in what you say, my friend. There are many in here that think you are correct . . . this country is crazy. But others might take offense at what you say." He put a finger to his lips. "Me, I look at who makes all the money. Here . . . gangsters, Jews . . . baah! In Germany the Social Democrats are the same. If real Germans are not careful, Communists will take over everything."

Heinz tried to look interested but was too impatient to listen anymore. "Excuse me, sir. I would like to talk to you more about this, but I would very much like to know if you could help me. I need to book passage back to Germany. Perhaps one of you knows of a ship that could take me on?"

"Ah, had enough, *ja?* And now you want to go home? I am the club president and do have some connections. When do you want to go?"

After an uncomfortable pause, Heinz finally answered, "Actually, I'd like to leave as soon as possible—that is, if the passage is not so expensive. Oh, and my German passport expired."

Schwindenhammer replied quickly, "The passport is no problem. I can start the paperwork here. A relative must meet you when you arrive in Hamburg, and you should encounter no problems." The large man smiled broadly, showing off two gleaming gold crowns. "The passage will cost you one thousand marks."

"I don't know the exchange rate anymore, but I'm sure I can scrape up five hundred dollars US, maybe a little more." Heinz knew that he had about that much in the bank, but he wasn't sure about any severance from the Hofbrau Haus.

"That should be plenty, *mein freund*. I will talk with the dockmaster tomorrow and find us a suitable ship. You get your money and come back in two days, *ja*?"

They touched glasses to a mutual *Prosit*. The beer had given Heinz a surge of confidence. He felt ready to face Mrs. Wasserstein. He bid them *Auf Wiedersehen* and walked out into a chilly, noisy New York afternoon. Upon arrival at the Hofbrau Haus, he found that Mrs. Wasserstein had already prepared his severance check. *I'd better hurry and cash it before the bitch changes her mind.*

SEVEN

Rudy Books Eddie on a Musical Tour of England

Their steamship sailed for Southampton, England, at 10:00 AM, and Eddie's sea legs returned to him quickly. He loved the ocean air and was either on the bow or with the captain on the bridge, looking over charts and instruments. His wife, Maude, however, needed help from the ship's doctor as soon as they left the harbor. She had grown up with horses, but any sideways motion of the ship made her dizzy and ill. And it didn't help having a sailor for a husband, who seemed to enjoy every damn pitch or roll!

On the third day of the voyage, the captain, being a fan, talked Eddie into playing a few songs for the passengers. He was happy to accommodate. The dining room had a six-piece band that played dance music for the passengers from 6:00 to 10:00 PM. After the lunch crowd had departed, Eddie sat in with the band for a quick rehearsal. A few late-lunch diners lingered and were enjoying the event of an unscheduled rehearsal with one of *Variety's* top headliners. They were reviewing "Walking My Baby Back Home" when Eddie heard the distinct bang made by a five-inch gun from a US destroyer. Several lingering diners abandoned their drinks and ran out to the railing to see what was happening. Everyone else stood frozen in place. Eddie dove under a nearby table, clutching a violin his father had made for him at the turn of the century.

The shelling continued for another four minutes and was accompanied by .50-caliber machine-gun fire. The captain approached the side of the ship where most of the passengers had gathered and held up his hands in a calming fashion. "Ladies and gentlemen, please don't be alarmed. The gun noise you've all heard is indeed from US Navy ships on maneuvers—they are not pursuing any enemy vessels. The exercise should be over any minute now, at which time the ship should be able to resume its original course and speed."

One of the passengers asked, "Will this delay our arrival in England?"

"Our arrival at Southampton, England, will only be delayed an hour. Thank you for your patience and understanding, folks. Oh, and complimentary champagne will be served on all decks."

Eddie was up and about now, as were the other members of the band. He caught the eye of the piano man and started to play "Walking My Baby Back Home" in a hot, up-tempo rhythm. Soon everyone within earshot of the toe-tapping rhythm headed for the dining room. The champagne began to flow, and in no time, everyone's concern about gunfire had floated away.

Eddie and Maude were whisked away to their hotel as soon as the ship arrived in port. The banjo man's English tour would launch from the Astoria Theatre in London. Rudy had originally arranged for Eddie to showcase the Paramount chain of theaters in Britain and was guaranteed seven weeks with two daily performances. The show proved to be so popular that Eddie was held over for another twenty-five weeks. During this period he made several Columbia 78-rpm recordings, including popular British songs of the time like "Just a Crazy Song" and "This Is the Day of Days." Rudy had also booked him in revues at clubs in Amsterdam, Brussels, Paris, and Monte Carlo.

EIGHT

After the evening meal, President Roosevelt enjoyed listening to music on the radio, along with a good glass of brandy and a smoke. Eleanor partook of neither but did sit quietly with her husband. The distraction that he derived from this simple pleasure was a much-needed tonic after a grueling day of political maneuvering. "Eleanor, this Peabody fellow actually performs Gershwin's *Rhapsody in Blue* on a banjo! I remember listening to him on Rudy Vallee's show when I was governor. The virtuosity of the man—on a banjo, mind you—is simply incredible."

She, of course, preferred the classics, but she did admit that this banjo player was quite talented, and if it pleased her husband, well, then she would sit politely and listen.

New York City
Spring of 1934

The window curtain opened and closed to the rotations of the small fan that was oscillating atop the dresser. It had been a long night. Morning sunlight was dancing over Eddie's face and the wall. When the phone rang, Eddie leaped from the bed to the floor like a spring-loaded trap. He snatched the receiver. "Yes . . . hello?"

"Eddie, you were sensational last night."

"Thanks, Rudy. What the hell time is it, anyway?"

"It's eight o'clock, and a lovely morning it is, my friend. I wanted to catch you before you got away this morning. I've booked the two of us for a private party at the Shoreham Hotel in Washington DC next Saturday night."

"Kinda far to travel for a private party, wouldn't you say? And you booked the both of us? Who's payin' the tab?"

"Look, you know I've been working on a radio show for you. Well, the Pure Oil people are hosting some congressmen at a private party at the Shoreham, and one of the execs called to book the entertainment. And who knows, maybe the Harvard boy himself will attend this one."

"Sounds good, Rudy . . . I'll leave the politics to you, though."

"According to my contact, these oil people want permission to drill and look for oil off the coasts of California and Louisiana. All I know is if we wow those congressmen and Pure Oil, maybe we'll find us a sponsor for a new radio show. What d'you think?"

Eddie was pacing the floor. His wife sat up and tried to hear what was being said. He stopped pacing and grinned into the telephone. "What do I think? I think that you have been busy, to say the least. And yes, we will knock the socks off those stodgy old congressmen."

"Say, listen, Eddie, before I forget. Jack got a call yesterday afternoon from the White House. They wanted to get hold of you and asked if you could get with . . . let me see . . . a Dianne Petit as soon as possible. I think the first lady is having a garden party or something and—damn, where did I put that number? Jack did tell whoever was calling that you and I were booked for a party at the Shoreham next Saturday. Well, sorry, but I'll just have to get back with you when I find that number, all right?"

"Sure, Rudy, and don't worry about it. Are we still on for tonight?"

"Right you are. So tallyho till tonight, my friend."

"Tallyho yourself, and thanks, pal."

Maude was wide awake now. "Was that Rudy?"

"Mm-hmm. He's booked the two of us for a private party at the Shoreham Hotel in Washington next Saturday night."

"You mean you and Rudy?"

"Yes. It's a private party for some oil executives. I hope he's bringing a few of the band boys." Eddie sat back on the bed. "Rudy's trying to squeeze these guys into sponsoring a radio show for me over at NBC."

"That's wonderful, hon. Does he think there's a chance?"

"Well, you know Rudy," Eddie said. "What I do know is that the man has been a godsend since we came back from England. With vaudeville gone and theaters closing left and right, I wasn't sure of anything. Oh, and I almost forgot. Someone telephoned Jack from the White House, wanting to know how to get in touch with us."

Eddie gathered a change of clothes and headed for the bathroom. Maude lay still for about two seconds as the door closed and she heard him start the bathwater. She sat bolt upright. *The White House? Oh my God! What will I wear?* She put on her dressing gown and went to make some tea. On pins and needles with excitement, she busied herself setting the table and tidying up. *The White House—just think! If Eddie doesn't come out of that bathroom soon, I might just have to knock the door down!*

The door opened, and Eddie went about getting dressed, unaware that his wife was about to burst at the seams.

"Well?"

"Well, what?"

"I assume they were calling about you—the White House, to ask you to perform at some function. So, who called, and how do we confirm?"

Eddie waved his hand. "I was so absorbed with Rudy's scheme—some gal named Dianne Petit had called. Rudy couldn't find her number. He thought the first lady was having a garden party or something of that sort."

Maude jumped off the bed and grabbed the telephone. She immediately dialed the local operator and asked her to connect with a Dianne Petit at the White House in Washington DC.

He dropped his shoe and looked up in surprise. "Maude . . . what the hell? It's just a private party."

She ignored him. "Hello, is this Miss Petit? This is Maude Peabody calling . . . Mrs. Eddie Peabody. We received word this morning from Mr. Vallee . . . Who? Rudy Vallee, the singer . . . you know . . . Yes, that Rudy Vallee. Well, he indicated that you were trying to reach us for a booking. A garden reception, you say—a week from Sunday—at two in the afternoon?" She looked over at her husband with a Cheshire cat grin. "Yes, my husband will be in Washington that Saturday for a private party at the Shoreham Hotel. You knew? I see . . . The fee? Well, will this be a public affair, Miss Petit, or will the guest list be small? Yes, formal or informal? Semiformal, all right. Well, the fee will be one hundred fifty dollars, Miss Petit. Oh, wonderful! No, no. The pleasure is mine, Miss Petit. If you would forward a letter of confirmation to me here at the hotel in New York . . . ? Very well, then, and thank you very much, Miss Petit." She hung up the phone and hugged herself, then jumped up and ran over to Eddie. She squeezed him so hard, he had to cough.

When he broke free, he held her by the shoulders. "What in God's name?"

"You, my good husband, are going to perform for the president and the first lady, and a few of their selected guests—which, I was told, is confidential. I do know one guest who'll be there, and with a beautiful new dress, I might add. You were through in the bathroom, weren't you? I've got to get to Macy's before the crowds."

"This is just going to be another private party, Maude. We're going to be in and out of there in short order."

"I think the young lady said it's a charitable event, for groups who support polio victims. Why, the publicity alone—every newspaper in the country will likely carry it. Think what that will do for your career, dear." When she finally emerged, she had a towel covering her and another wrapped around her hair. She sat on the bed and sighed; her eyes started to tear up. "I'm sorry, but to be invited to the White House and to meet the president and first lady . . . I've never been a society girl, and now look at me. I just want everything to be perfect for you, dear."

The White House Garden Party

The Shoreham party was a resounding success. Rudy secured the Pure Oil sponsorship, and the company execs were pleased to be able to lobby a few congressmen.

On Sunday, Maude spent most of the morning fussing with her hair, while Eddie read the morning papers and relaxed in the lobby with a pot of coffee. The White House had arranged for a limousine to transport them at the appointed hour. It was a short ride from the hotel to the White House.

As they approached the front gate, Eddie noticed a marine guard; there was a crisp salute as the car passed. As the car rolled to a stop, Eddie patted his wife's hand, flashed his effervescent smile, and, in a tone of voice that bubbled with confidence, casually commented, "We'll no doubt meet some very nice people at this party, Maude, two of whom just happen to be Mr. and Mrs. Roosevelt. You are going to be just fine. So now let's go meet the first lady."

As a uniformed doorman opened the rear car door, all she could manage, after taking a deep breath, was a thin wisp of a smile. She gave her husband a close inspection as he exited the limo. Her smile widened as she absorbed the sight and smell of the handsome figure standing next to her. And he did look sharp in his crisp, white summer tux. Feeling self-conscious, she straightened the collar on her long-sleeved satin blouse, which was neatly tucked into a beautifully tailored apricot skirt with a matching double-breasted jacket. Her shoes were dyed to match, and her only accessory was a small needlepoint cocktail purse that her mother had made. She reached over and brushed back an errant strand of his hair.

Another marine appeared and directed them to a yard side entrance that led to a lovely lawn garden. A large canopy had been erected that shaded a small stage and a podium. Chairs had been set up for more than fifty guests. Maude noticed a lovely young lady in a smart, dark blue suit coming toward them with her hand outstretched. She was not as tall as Maude, but she was very trim and athletic looking with her short blonde hair.

"Good afternoon, and welcome. I'm Dianne Petit, and you must be Mr. and Mrs. Peabody. I think I talked with you, Mrs. Peabody—last Wednesday, was it?"

"Yes, and please call me Maude."

"And you, sir, must be the famous banjoist who has the president tapping his foot as he listens to the radio every Friday night. I know they are both very excited that you were able to attend the first lady's Warm Springs Foundation tea on such short notice. Please come over, and Ralph will show you where they would like you both to sit. You can set your instruments next to the stage area. Ralph will want to take a quick look . . . security, you know. But I assure you everything will be quite safe out here."

Eddie carried his instruments the short distance to the canopied stage area, just as Ralph appeared, seemingly out of nowhere. His tone of voice was all business when he asked Eddie to open the instrument cases, and then meticulously he inspected every inch.

Dianne sensed Maude's tension and tried to distract her with the magnificent garden area where they were standing. "Did you see the roses, Mrs. Peabody? My office faces a portion of this garden. I never tire of the view, even in winter."

When Ralph had finished, he signaled his "okay sign" to Dianne. She glanced at her watch and walked quickly over to Eddie. "The president would love to meet you, sir, before the charitable event begins and he is swarmed by the press." She turned quickly to Maude. She was smooth, quick, and to the point. "If you would like, I would be pleased to give you a mini tour of the house while the president and your husband are chatting."

Maude tried to maintain what she thought was her end of the conversation. "That would be lovely, and very gracious of you."

"It's my pleasure. I do love this place, and giving tours is really part of my job here." Without missing a beat, she turned to Eddie. "If you'll follow Ralph, sir, he'll direct you to where you'll be meeting with the president."

Ralph was standing beside him, motioning with his hand. "This way, sir." A quick glance at the man's neck and shoulders, and Eddie could tell that this was no ordinary soldier. *If this guy wanted to, he'd have me on my keister in nothing flat.* Eddie smiled and nodded to his wife. He turned and followed Ralph down a hallway to a small but well-furnished conference room.

Upon entering the conference room, Eddie noticed that the room felt different, as though he were standing in some sort of chamber. It was the air pressure, or the sound—he couldn't quite describe the feeling. Ralph noticed Eddie's puzzled look as he closed the door. "The room is soundproof, sir."

Eddie remembered the same feeling when he had recorded for the Columbia Company in London.

"May I bring you a glass of water, some wine, or a cocktail, sir?"

"Actually, Ralph, I could do with a nice cold glass of milk. Is that possible?"

"Yes, sir. I'll have it brought right up." Ralph picked up a phone just as the door opened. Claude Swanson, the secretary of the navy, came in and introduced himself.

"May I order up some refreshment for you, sir?"

"No, thank you. Ralph here has sent out for a cold glass of milk."

"Why, that sounds marvelous, Eddie. Oh, Ralph, would you order me up one as well?" He turned toward Eddie. "I wanted to thank you for accepting our invitation. It is nice that we could get together with you on such short notice. The president and the secretary of war will be along shortly. I also wanted to extend my sincere thanks to you for your exemplary service to your country and the navy during the war years. You may know that the president was undersecretary of the navy during that conflict—before, of course, he became governor of New York."

Okay, now what? This guy must have been looking at my service record. Now, why would he be interested in that?

The door opened suddenly again. Secretary Dern walked in, followed closely by the president in a wheelchair. Both Eddie and Claude Swanson stood as soon as they noticed the president. FDR wheeled directly over to Eddie and extended his hand. "Eddie Peabody. This *is* a pleasure. I tune you in every chance I get. My son even found two of your records for me. Let me introduce George Dern, my secretary of war—and I take it you've already met Claude. Gentlemen, gentlemen, please be seated!"

This was one of the most powerful men in the world. Anyone could see the strength in his facial expression: the self-assured grin that had inspired millions. He was clear, confident, and in charge. Eddie felt humbled as he took notice of the wheelchair. *A great man confined by some damnable, crippling disease.*

The milk that Eddie and Claude Swanson had ordered arrived. "Milk!" bellowed the president. "What a splendid and refreshing idea. Say, Ralph, would you please bring me a glass as well?" The president glanced at George, but the secretary just shook his head. "Well, I guess it's just the three of us, then. Thank you, Ralph."

Swanson interjected, "I was just telling Eddie how grateful we are for his naval service during the war with the Kaiser, Mr. President."

"Yes indeed, Eddie. And as one navy man to another, we may need your service again, sailor." The president smiled at his guest. He turned his chair so that it faced him directly. "Eddie, the gentleman who's replaced the Kaiser is one scary guy. And our friends, the Brits, are sure he's building up his armed forces—against the terms of the Treaty of Versailles—faster than everyone thought possible. He has assumed so many executive powers that virtually all his political opposition has been crushed. You were in England recently, weren't you? What, in your opinion, was the mood of the people over there? Were they worried about Germany, Hitler coming to power? Or was everyone just getting on with things?"

After a long swallow, Eddie wiped the white mustache from his lip. His choice of beverage didn't have the calming effect he'd hoped for. "Well, first of all, Mr. President, let me thank you for your warm hospitality—and the kind words on my humble service record."

The president chuckled and stuffed a cigarette into his ever-present silver-tipped holder. The security agent was quickly at the president's side with a match.

"Yes, sir," Eddie continued. "I returned about six months ago from a very successful tour throughout England. And we had a couple of stopovers on the continent as well. The audiences, all the people we met over there, were just wonderful to Maude and me. I was booked into the Paramount theater chain, mostly around London, for seven weeks and wound up staying for the rest of the year. My main interest was to just entertain the folks, but I did visit several banjo clubs and Boy Scout troops along the way. I even had the pleasure of meeting with Lord Baden-Powell."

"Did you, now? Well, I haven't seen the general in years— great movement he started, the Boy Scouts. I had the pleasure of working with several of the Eastern Councils when I was governor. He sent me a personal cable, with his congratulations, when I was awarded the Silver Beaver. Tell me, how's his health?"

"He looked fit as a fiddle, sir. And he presented me with a badge that he'd created as a token of his appreciation for my work with the Boy Scouts."

"That's wonderful, Eddie."

"Regarding events taking place in Germany—well, sir, folks we talked with that had worked in France were naturally concerned. Some gave the impression that they simply mistrusted the Germans, but they also didn't care much for anyone else, including the English and Americans. My wife and I looked through the local papers daily, but I'm afraid, Mr. President, our primary interests were entertainment reviews. General Baden-Powell did express some concern about the events unfolding in Europe."

"Did he? And what exactly were the ol' boy's concerns?"

"Well, sir, he felt sure England would one day wind up in another war with Germany. He only hoped that this time 'our American brothers,' as he called us, would be bloody prompt with their support."

Roosevelt let out a loud "Ha!" at this comment.

"Well, I told Lord Baden-Powell that we kicked the slats out of the Hun once. And if it turns out they're up to their old tricks, we'll just have to kick them again, only harder this time."

Roosevelt leaned back in his chair with a wide grin. "I do hope, my boy, most Americans feel as you do."

"Lord Baden-Powell also said that if the Hun ever quit eating sauerkraut, he was sure their ornery reputation would clear up." This brought raucous laughter from everyone.

The president was now leaning forward in his wheelchair. The man's eyebrows narrowed as he began to speak. "I'm going to level with you, sailor. We need to know more about what's going on over there. We need to know firsthand, by men like you." FDR now turned and gazed around the room at those assembled. "But to get Congress on board, without a declaration of war—I have to find a way to get top men, like you, back in the navy."

Eddie heard the words, but little registered. The puzzled look on his face said it all.

"I know that this is sudden, Eddie. But I want you to think about what we've said here today. We'll talk some more in the near future." He glanced at his watch. "Say, we'd better get out to the Rose Garden pronto." Sporting that world-famous grin, FDR wheeled back from the table and announced, "Gentlemen." The meeting was adjourned. Everyone in the room stood as he wheeled toward the door. Before exiting, he turned to his guest. "Eleanor and I are looking forward to your concert this afternoon, Eddie."

Eddie simply bowed his head as the great man exited the room. A sense of pride was enveloping him, one that he hadn't felt since his submarine days.

The secretary of war tapped his pen on a glass. "Excuse me, gentlemen. Mr. Peabody, in case Ralph or Dianne hasn't briefed you, this conversation, as is every conversation with the president, is confidential. You're not to discuss what was said here with anyone, including your wife. Do you have any questions for us before we depart?"

"No, sir, no questions—I understand, completely."

"There is one more thing. After the charity presentation this afternoon, the president and Mrs. Roosevelt wanted to invite you and your wife for tea. On a personal note, I am certain you'd be doing your country a great service if you do decide to join our team. Now, gentlemen, shall we . . . ?"

Eddie followed the Cabinet men into the hallway. His mind was racing. *I do enjoy the fast pace on the path my life has taken, but this . . . I'm here to play a few tunes for the first lady's afternoon garden party . . . now the president wants me to reenlist?*

The president spoke without turning in his chair. "You gentlemen go on ahead to the Rose Garden. I will make a quiet entrance in a minute or so."

The men all exited the White House together and approached the canopy. The president waited by the large doorway until the others were out of earshot. The security agent that had escorted Eddie from the Rose Garden to the conference room now stood behind the president, holding onto the wheelchair handles. "What'd you think of our banjo player, Ralph?"

"Well, sir, he did seem a bit awed by it all. But he's also all that I've read about him in his file. Uncomfortable at first, but seemed to relax a little some when Secretary Swanson arrived."

"No hidden agendas?"

"I don't believe so, sir."

"Yes, I too was impressed." The event coordinator turned and caught the president's eye. "Well, it looks like it's showtime."

NINE

The Presidential Squeeze

Eddie was still replaying in his mind what had just taken place. *How the hell am I going to keep from telling Maude?* He walked over to where he had left his instruments. Maude was already seated, beaming from ear to ear.

The noise level diminished. Dianne, in clear audible tones, announced, "Ladies and gentlemen, the president of the United States."

Everyone was standing now as FDR wheeled himself out and under the canopy. He was smiling broadly. He wheeled to the front of the gathering and gave a warm, welcoming wave, and gestured for everyone to be seated. "Ladies and gentlemen, I do thank you for attending today, but in all honesty, this is Eleanor's party. So, without further ado, I give you your first lady. And, I'm given to understand, my dear wife has arranged for Eddie Peabody to provide you with some splendid entertainment after the formalities. So please enjoy yourselves. And thank you again for all your generous contributions and tireless effort in helping to develop the Warm Springs Foundation."

The weather stayed cooperative, and the Warm Springs Foundation charity agenda proceeded like clockwork. The first lady gave presidential citations to several members of Congress, and to a doctor and his wife for their generous contributions of time, talent, and treasure for all polio victims. Uniformed staff wheeled out a staggering buffet of caviar and assorted stuffed biscuits, salads, meats and cheeses—enough food to feed an army. After guests had sampled the delicious display, the first lady asked everyone to please return their seats. "Friends of Warm Springs Foundation, thank you for coming this afternoon, and please continue to enjoy this lovely buffet. Now, as an additional treat, it is my pleasure to introduce to you a very popular entertainer that some of you may have had the opportunity of seeing recently at the lovely Shoreham Hotel. Ladies and gentlemen, please welcome a man who once was described as a wizard on stringed instruments, but who is better known today as the man with the banjo, Mr. Eddie Peabody."

Eddie was now in his element. He sat on top of one the lawn chairs, placed the harp guitar to the side, and started to tune up his banjo. "Thank you, Mrs. Roosevelt, for that wonderful introduction. And thank you, ladies and gentlemen, for your support of this wonderful foundation that will benefit so many—I'm honored to be here today. And while you're enjoying these fabulous groceries, I'll sit here on my perch and play a few of your favorite tunes. Most of you know me—give me an instrument, a perch, and look out—I'm all ham. Seriously, folks, if you have a favorite tune, and it's in my repertoire, I'd love to play it for you."

A lovely lady in the back, without hesitation, stood up and shouted, "Indian Love Call!" Eddie looked up, smiled at the request, reached in his pocket, and installed a violin mute on the bridge of his banjo. There were couples sitting in a semicircle around him now. He had been playing for about thirty minutes when he took a short break. His security escort approached. "Excuse me, sir. The president would like you and your wife to join him for coffee before his afternoon exercises."

Eddie made eye contact with Maude and motioned for her to approach. "The president would like us to have coffee with him before his afternoon exercises." His wife's eyes widened, but she said nothing as she returned to her seat.

After playing requests for about an hour, Eddie turned to the group and said, "Thank you, ladies and gentlemen. I have had a wonderful time with you all this afternoon. I hope you enjoyed as well." While taking a bow, he noticed two marines start to carry his musical instruments to a waiting car. Maude approached, and they graciously retreated toward an open door where two other marines stood at parade rest. As they reentered the awe-inspiring grand symbol of American strength, Eddie quipped, "I don't think we'll have to worry about anyone walking off with our lunch around here." Maude pushed him on the shoulder. Ralph, the security agent, rushed in from one of the adjoining hallways to greet them. He now, however, addressed his comments to Maude. "The first lady will join you and your husband shortly after she's met with staff on tomorrow's appointments, Mrs. Peabody. She did want me to convey her sincere thanks to you and your husband for coming this afternoon, and on such short notice. And she wanted you to know that she will have a check delivered to you prior to your departure, if that is satisfactory."

"Oh, thank you, sir. How thoughtful of the first lady. My goodness, she is one busy lady, isn't she?"

"Yes, ma'am, she is. On many days, her schedule rivals that of the president's." As Ralph was speaking, he slowly moved his left hand behind Maude's right elbow and began leading her toward a narrow hallway. "Now, if I may direct you—we're going to go down two short hallways to a small reception room. The president and Secretary Swanson will be arriving shortly, but I believe coffee and some refreshment await us." Ralph extended his right arm, illustrating the way. "Shall we?"

Eddie was listening, and he followed along, but he was curious as to what exactly was going to be discussed after refreshments were served. *After that confidential warning, what the hell can I say?* Ralph opened the right door of a two-door entry to a large room.

To everyone's surprise, the president was already there. He was in his wheelchair, next to an exquisite old table. On the table, which was inlaid with leather, sat a beautiful silver tray with a silver coffee pot, a silver creamer, and four cups and saucers. To Maude, the room was something out of a European magazine. Every stick of furniture was antique, exquisite, with leather-bound books on the shelves, oil paintings on the wall, beautiful brocade drapes—she could feel the arms of the room's history envelop her. Then she noticed the real oddity. The president was holding onto an old tenor banjo. She and Eddie quietly sat in nearby straight chairs adjacent to and facing FDR. Eddie could now see the banjo and could tell it was a bit worse for wear and had seen better days.

FDR didn't look up when they entered. He was looking at the neck of the instrument as though trying to remember finger positions for chords to a favorite song. Eddie could hear the man softly singing the words to "Ain't She Sweet."

Suddenly, FDR looked up. "Ah, there you are, my boy. Thanks for coming by for a cup. And this must be your lovely wife. Maude, is it?"

Maude strode over when she heard her name, curtseyed, and held out her hand. "Mr. President. This is indeed an honor." The president looked up from his banjo and waved her to a nearby chair.

"Mrs. Peabody, you're being way too formal here, especially when you embarrassingly caught me with a banjo on my knee, trying to remember songs from my adolescent days." FDR set his banjo on the floor and wheeled around to the coffee table. "Please, make yourselves comfortable, Eleanor should be by shortly. May I pour some coffee while we wait?"

Maude, somewhat startled, sat gently on the edge of the antique chair. *I would die to possess just one item in this gorgeous room.* She tried to calm herself, smile, and breathe normally. "Why, yes, thank you, Mr. President."

"Eddie, I haven't touched this old tub since my undergraduate days at Yale. But on occasion, and with tolerance from Eleanor,

I do enjoy getting the old thing out and reminiscing. Can I con you into tuning it up for me? I'm afraid I've neglected to keep up on what little I once knew." FDR turned his chair to face Maude. "Now, tell me, Mrs. Peabody, how were the hors d'oeuvres out on the lawn today? Eleanor always fusses about the food, you know."

"The food was simply scrumptious, Mr. President. I don't believe that we've ever been to a more lovely or meaningful presentation." The president began wheeling back toward Eddie, now that he noticed his banjo being tuned by the master.

"Oh, you're far too generous, my dear. And, oh—did Dianne give you a little tour of the people's house?"

"Yes, sir, she did. Dianne was very gracious to me, and the tour was delightful."

As he always did with his own instrument, to stretch the wire strings, Eddie pulled on and vigorously snapped each string at the head of the president's banjo. And, as so often happens during this exercise, a string breaks—which is exactly what happened as he was tuning FDR's prize possession. "Well, that's a fine how-do-you-do." Eddie reached into his coat pocket and pulled out several packets of banjo strings. "Not to worry, sir. I always carry a pocketful of these things."

The president grinned and started to chuckle as he watched in amazement. With the speed of a hummingbird, the man seemed to work effortlessly, restringing his prize banjo.

"This usually happens to me on stage, Mr. President, right when I'm in the middle of a song. And while the band boys are stumbling over themselves, wondering what to do next, I usually turn to the audience and say, 'Well, folks, it'll only take me about a half an hour to get things back together here—so if you haven't already got one, now is the time to buy that program, and don't forget that the washrooms are in the back.'" In the time it took to tell that story, Eddie had installed the new string.

"Eddie, you are simply marvelous. Why, if I tried to change a string on that thing, it would likely take me to the next election before I completed the task."

While Eddie was changing the string, Eleanor quietly entered the room. She nodded to her husband, and he began pouring her some tea. She strode over to Maude. "Mrs. Peabody—excuse me, Maude—I'm so glad you could join us."

Maude stood as Mrs. Roosevelt extended her hand. Mrs. Roosevelt could feel Maude's unease and discomfort. She gently motioned with her hand for Maude to be seated. "May I pour you a fresh cup?"

"Yes, thank you." Maude nervously handed Mrs. Roosevelt her cup.

"Well, this certainly has been an eventful day, and I don't mind saying that it feels wonderful to be able to sit down. I feel as though I've been on my feet for days on end."

"I certainly don't know how you do it. Just to organize that presentation for the foundation would exhaust me for a week."

"Well, that was a labor of love, my dear . . . and please call me Eleanor."

The president cleared his throat. "You ladies may not know this, but Eddie here was a first-class quartermaster, serving aboard the submarine S-14, when I was undersecretary of the navy." Mrs. Roosevelt knew, from the tone of his voice, that her husband was about to reveal the real purpose of their unscheduled meeting with Mr. and Mrs. Peabody. She smiled, took a sip of her coffee, and nodded to her husband.

The president turned his chair to speak directly to Maude. "This afternoon I, along with Secretaries Swanson and Dern, briefly discussed with your husband some current events taking place on the Continent. And although I admit it was a bit sudden, we offered your husband an opportunity that I'm sure he has been pondering most of the afternoon. Well, Eleanor has made it clear that it would be pure folly to think that any man could make a decision, especially a critical one, without the guidance and support of his life partner. I can truthfully say that I am living proof of the wisdom in that axiom."

Eleanor smiled and set her cup on the nearby table. Franklin sat back in his wheelchair and placed a cigarette in a holder. In silent communication with her eyes, she indicated that he'd better not light that thing in here.

The president smiled at his wife as he laid the cigarette in a nearby ashtray. "'I'll come right to the point. Maude, we've asked your husband to consider becoming an officer in the United States Naval Reserve. With Eddie's background, he—and perhaps others like him—could be invaluable to our country. We need all the intelligence we can muster to counter any threats that may arise, before they come ashore." He paused and fingered his cigarette and holder. He glanced at Eleanor and then continued, "We were unprepared for what the Kaiser unleashed during the Great War—to say nothing of what the English or the French suffered through. Well, world problems do occur, and most of the time we can diplomatically head them off—before we have to send our best and brightest out to sea."

Maude sat rigidly on the edge of her seat, listening intently. She tried to look relaxed, but this *was* the president of the United States, and he *was* talking about her husband.

FDR turned his chair. "Eddie, you mentioned Lord Baden-Powell this afternoon. Well, I'm of the opinion that the good general and I are on the same sheet of music on this. And if he were present, I'm sure he'd say, 'Sailor, your country needs you.'" He set his cigarette in his lap and looked at his watch. "Egad, where has the time gone? Folks, I do apologize, but the doctor is adamant that I keep to my exercise schedule. So, if you'll forgive me." Eddie, Maude, and Eleanor stood as the president moved toward the door. He stopped and turned to face Eddie. He extended his hand. "I know you'll make the right decision on this."

"Yes, sir, I have. The decision seems clear to me now. I will be of service to you in whatever way that I'm able. I only hope that I'll be able to live up to everyone's expectations."

The president grinned and continued to shake Eddie's hand. "God bless you, sailor. And quit worrying about expectations that have yet to surface. Now, Claude's people will be in touch with you shortly. I'm not sure what all has to be done to get you commissioned, but he's been instructed accordingly. So relax, my friend. Everything will fall into place in due time."

Maude was completely unaware. She felt a deep sense of pride in the president's words, but so much had happened this one day. *Why didn't he consult me? What will this do to his career?* It made her dizzy.

FDR had turned toward Maude, but she was staring at the ceiling, unaware. She was startled and nearly stumbled when he extended his hand. "Mrs. Peabody—Maude—it's been our sincere pleasure to meet with you today. I do hope that you and Eddie will have time to dine with us sometime in the future." He leaned in and whispered, "Take care, now, and give him all the encouragement you can." A White House security agent had quietly moved in behind the president's wheelchair and began pushing him slowly down the hallway.

"If you'll please excuse me now, I must see to Franklin's diet. The doctors at Warm Springs are very strict with him on this. Dianne will see you out. Well, goodbye, and please do excuse my abrupt departure. I do hope we'll have an opportunity in the future to meet more casually over a quiet dinner."

"Thank you so much, Mrs. Roosevelt—Eleanor—for all your gracious hospitality. And yes, we'd pleased to dine with you and the president, anytime."

Dianne ushered them out to a side entrance and to their waiting vehicle.

Once in the limousine, Eddie whispered, "Babe, this whole afternoon was like a well-scripted show. And I'll be damned if the only players in the dark here weren't you and me."

Maude sighed audibly. "I don't know. I'm trying to replay and absorb all that's happened to us today. It seems like a week has passed. All I could think about after the president's speech was, why didn't you consult me?"

Eddie stared out the window but offered nothing. All that could be heard were the limousine's tires hissing along.

"While you were meeting with the president this afternoon, I must have looked at my watch a dozen times. Dianne was like an encyclopedia. She recounted each room's two-hundred-year history! I, of course, gawked like a schoolgirl. And you . . . drop whatever you're doing and rejoin the navy!" She looked up. She felt the driver staring directly at her. She searched his eyes in the rearview mirror.

TEN

Eddie dozed in the overstuffed armchair in the corner of their room, his head resting on the back. He tried to replay as much as he could recall: the meetings, the people, all that had happened at a whirlwind pace. The president had said the country needed him. How could any American refuse a request like that? *Why doesn't Maude understand? What the hell am I going to tell Rudy?* Someone would be in touch, they'd said. "Well, great, but who and when?"

Maude looked up. "What? What are you doing? And who are you talking to?" She tried to make eye contact, but he seemed to be staring at the picture the hotel had hung over the bed, a print of Pieter Brueghel's *Winter Landscape.*

"Damn it! What in the hell am I going to tell Rudy?"

"Please don't swear, sweetheart." She turned to face him. "I do hope you're not thinking of giving up your chance at a nationwide radio show, are you?" She paused. "Because if you are, you know you can kiss your career goodbye."

Her words stung him. "Thanks for your encouragement." He was tired, and her words pushed his button. He felt the grip of

71

anger welling up. *Of all people . . . we've been together . . . how long?* *Surely you would understand.* Angrily he reached for the phone to call for a porter.

★ ★ ★

The first-class train compartment was comfortable and quiet. They hadn't said a word to each other since leaving the hotel. She knew that anything said could spark a confrontation. She needed a snack. "I'm hungry. Can I bring you back anything?"

"No, I think I'll shut my eyes and take a snooze."

She smiled. *Sleep is probably the best thing. He'll see the light when he's rested. He'll see that his career has to come first . . . after all, I've got a stake in this too. Why do boys always want to play soldier? And I had to marry one who wants to play sailor—and give up his successful career, a career that I shaped and managed. Give up the spotlight, the money . . . our whole lifestyle . . . over my dead body!*

The ride back to New York seemed shorter. Their New York hotel room, however, seemed less inviting. They both were tired and tense. They'd no more than opened the door when the phone rang.

Eddie dropped what he was carrying on the bed and answered. "Hello . . . Rudy! How the hell did you know we'd just got in? Spies, you say? Well, a guy begins to wonder . . . No, I don't think the john is safe either. What's up? Lunch, tomorrow? Sure, pal. I'll be there with bells on."

He's smiling—a good sign. "What did Rudy want?"

"He wants to have lunch at his club tomorrow. Some people from Pure Oil will be there, to finalize a contract."

She lit up, clasping her hands to her chest. "So you've decided to do the radio show."

Is that a question? He was tired, and frustrated with her. *Either I do the radio show, or I can kiss fame and fortune goodbye.* He sat down on his side of the bed, facing away from her.

"Look, I'm going to do the damn radio show." He was deliberate and firm. "But I also want you to know that I'm going to do

72

whatever I can to be of service to our thirty-second president. And if that means rejoining the navy, then so be it. And if you cannot support my decision, then . . . " His voice trailed off to a whisper.

The shock of his words stunned her. She had to remind herself to breathe. *That was a calmly delivered ultimatum.* She waited a moment to see if he had anything more to say. Defensive and angry, she felt her face flush. She waited a moment more to calm her desire to lash out. She forced a smile, to give the illusion that she was in control and not bothered by his fantasy. "I do love you, Eddie. But listening to you makes me wonder whether or not you have your feet on the ground. I have worked hard at managing your career, and it upsets me to think you'd throw it all away to join the navy. I knew you were going places since the first time I set eyes on you. But you know that no amount of fame lasts forever. Please give this some more thought, for my sake. I'll always be yours, whatever you decide." She waited for a response; nothing but aggravating silence. She sat back in her chair with an audible sigh. She wanted to cry but willed herself not to. This was almost more than she could stand. "Please forgive me. I'm simply too exhausted and overwhelmed to continue."

Eddie no longer felt the need to sit quietly and contemplate justification for his decision. *You either understand what duty, honor, responsibility, and trustworthiness really mean, or you don't!* He walked around the bed and touched her shoulder. "I'm not sure what to do, babe. All I know is that for me, of all people, to be asked by the president—I feel honored beyond anything I could imagine. And I was counting on your support. Right now, I need a drink. I'm going downstairs. I'll be back when I think . . . whenever."

As he reached the door, she felt the need to say something. "Tomorrow will be a new day . . . for us both."

The door slammed shut.

Did he even hear what I'd said? Maude was frustrated. She felt that she was somehow being manipulated. *And there isn't one damn thing I can do about it.*

The following morning, he was still tired and a bit hung over. He readied himself while Maude pretended to be still asleep. It was past mid-morning when he slowly headed out for his meeting with Rudy. He didn't much care for Irish food, but it was Rudy's favorite.

"Eddie, over here, pal!" Rudy and Jack were sitting in a corner window seat. The wood-paneled walls gave the place a dark, clubby atmosphere. The pub was full and noisy as hell. *Noisy bastards. Why doesn't everybody shut up and eat . . . and give my head a break?*

Eddie did his best to muster a smile and an enthusiastic wave. "Top of the mornin' to you, lads."

"We're having corned beef on rye, Eddie. Waitress, please bring us another, would you please? Oh, and tell the barman that we need another Guinness for our friend here." Rudy caressed the waitress's arm as she wrote down the order. "So tell us about the White House, my boy. What was the president like, or did you get to meet him? Do tell us, man. We've been dying with curiosity."

Eddie smiled as he looked up. Rudy was busy wiping stray mustard and sauerkraut off his mouth. Jack, with a who-me expression on his face, was just finishing his beer. *Okay, now what the hell do I say?* He took a long swallow from the water glass. "Well, fellas, I'm sorry to disappoint you, but it was just a garden party. The first lady was hosting a Warm Springs Foundation celebration. You know, a kind of spa for polio victims. But the food, boy oh boy, was it something."

"But did you get to meet the man himself? I didn't vote for the Democrat, even though he hails from New York. But for a Harvard boy, I must say . . . " Rudy's voice became garbled as he sipped his beer.

"Yes, I did meet the president, as a matter of fact. And a nice man he is. Say, I'll bet you guys didn't know he likes to thump on a banjo."

Eddie felt uncomfortable from the look Rudy gave him. Fortunately, the waitress appeared with his sandwich and a beer. The awkward moment passed. He picked up his glass and examined the dark, almost black beer. "Damn, Rudy, this looks more like molasses. I think I'll leave this stuff for the Irish."

Rudy held up his glass "And look, it even leaves a ring around the glass." When the laughter subsided, Rudy leaned forward to redirect the conversation. "Well, whatever took place on Sunday, my friend, couldn't possibly compare with the first-rate job you and your lovely wife accomplished at the Shoreham. The Pure Oil people have had their attorneys in high gear all morning, driving us simply mad. We should have a signed contract by this afternoon."

"That's wonderful. You and Jack have worked hard on this one, and with some good acts, I know it'll pay off big time for you." Eddie suddenly let loose with a rather loud involuntary belch that embarrassed him.

With a mouth full of sandwich, Rudy mumbled, "Don't you just love this place?"

"Well, gentlemen, on board ship, if Cookie didn't hear at least one belch, his feelings would be hurt for a week."

"I knew there was a story there. But listen, thanks again for your good work Saturday night. We should all be going to the bank with a new show at Radio WJZ. In the meantime, Jack here needs some fill-in at the Hollywood restaurant. If you would be so kind, we'd like you to work with him and mix up the programs with some new blood. You know what I'm looking for—young talent who could maybe use a professional helping hand." Jack handed Eddie a schedule worksheet.

What do I say if suddenly I have to report to the Navy Department? Rudy's last comment brought him back to the present. He looked at the dates Jack had given him. Rudy did love young, new, exciting talent, and he was good for them, good for their careers. "Sure thing, boss. I've been out of circulation for a while, but I'm sure Jack and I can come up with whatever it takes to keep the Hollywood Club the talk of the town."

Rudy leaned back and smiled broadly. He loved the thought and was savoring the moment, now that his favorite protégé was back in the fold.

★　★　★

In Washington, Claude Swanson had summoned to his office an instructor from the Naval Academy, Commander Patrick Scharf. "Pat, we're going to have to accelerate our schedule on a training course for Eddie Peabody. The boss wants to be kept informed of his progress, and that means he wants to see results. I want you to contact Peabody tomorrow and set up an appointment."

The commander looked up from his notepad. "Mr. Secretary, may I ask how much time we have? We need give the man a sample exam to know where to begin. I would like to develop a syllabus for each of the test sections."

"Not a problem, Commander. When the president sets his mind on something like this, though, I know he won't sleep until he has what he wants. I'll drive up to the academy tomorrow and have a chat with your boss, the commandant. He may have some suggestions. Keep in close contact with me on this, will you?"

"Will do, sir."

Scharf met Eddie at the Washington station the next morning and then drove the two of them out to the Naval Academy. Eddie spent the next three hours answering written multiple-choice questions. He was exhausted. "Commander, I appreciate what the secretary is trying to do for me. I do have some signed contracts that I'm obligated to perform, but I'll do everything in my power to meet your expectations."

"Thank you for your commitment, sir. We'll review your exam and be in touch. And sir, mum's still the operative word on this."

When Eddie returned to the hotel, he called Rudy to confirm an afternoon rehearsal. Maude was sitting near the window, reading *Variety*. "Well, tell me how it went."

Eddie slumped on the bed, rolling his shoulders, trying to relieve the tension in his neck. He was more anxious than she'd seen him in some time. "That was one tough exam. I will definitely need your help on this one."

"I told you I'll work with you, and we'll get through this."

"I do thank you, and I may need your help with Rudy and Jack as well."

"What do you mean?"

"We can't say a word about what I'm doing, hon, and how to keep my comings and goings with the navy from Rudy, I don't have a clue."

Within two days Eddie had received a telegram from Scharf. Washington, the Department of the Navy, had arranged for a private conference room in the New York offices of the FBI. He was going back to school, and the commander would be his instructor. *I've got to pull this off without affecting any of my scheduled bookings, and I can't tell a soul. What the hell am I going to do?*

Maude could see the anxiety building on his face. "This navy business is really important to you, isn't it?"

"Yes, it is. But I'd be a liar if I said I thought that getting through this schooling was going to be a cakewalk. It scares the hell out of me."

"Please don't swear, sweetheart. We will get through this, and Rudy and all the others will just have to be patient. We'll think of something to say to those who get curious, when the time comes."

Rudy, in the meantime, had been offered a starring role in a movie. He immediately thought of Eddie and wanted to put the squeeze on him to stay on in New York permanently. But the classwork and the study time were endless and grueling, and the man was starting to wear down. Rudy took notice. He desperately wanted some time with Eddie to talk over his proposition, but the man never seemed be available. So he invited Eddie and Maude to his club for dinner.

Eddie was well known at Rudy's club. Several patrons immediately pestered him for an autograph, while Rudy sashayed around to greet and glad-hand as many of the patrons as he could. "Eddie, look at how popular you are. They simply love you here. If I'm not careful, I may have to find a permanent spot for you."

"Rudy, you fox. You know damn well it's Rudy Vallee that folks around these parts come to see, and for good reason."

"Flatterer! That's why I'm so fond of you, my King of Instrumentalists. Actually, I did want to talk to you about a business proposition. I'll be heading for Hollywood in two weeks. The Paramount moguls are going to make me a star in a new motion picture. I haven't actually seen the script, but I'm told that it will be a love story with a lot of singing. But enough already, before I get carried away. Let's enjoy a nice dinner and some good champagne to celebrate."

As the wine was served, Rudy continued. "Eddie, I'll come right out and say it. I want you to help me here at the club while I'm cavorting around Hollywood. I need someone like you to crack the whip and keep the mix new and exciting. I'd feel a hell of a lot more comfortable if I knew I had you at the helm, holding down the fort here in New York. What do you say?"

Rudy's proposal caught both dinner guests completely by surprise. *The man has been kind and generous, and he's helped bridge a lot of career gaps. But how can I possibly take on another job, especially now? And I sure as hell don't want to sound ungrateful.* There were several moments of uncomfortable silence.

Rudy saw immediately that he'd misjudged the reaction. He quickly added, "I'm offering to pay you handsomely for taking on this job."

"Rudy, Rudy, Rudy. You continue to flatter me beyond anything resembling the truth. But the truth is, my good friend, as you no doubt know, I've got more than enough on my plate right now. I'm completely buried for the next three months. You need someone full-time for this job."

"What do you think I've been offering you, my friend?"

Maude tried to add some calm to the conversation. "Rudy, you know we have a little Spanish hacienda and orange ranch in Riverside. So why don't you stay there while you're in Southern California? It's very quiet and quite comfortable. Eddie and I would love to have you as our guest."

Rudy was momentarily distracted but still befuddled. He could get by without Eddie's help, but he always liked to have insurance. He sat back, smiled, and placed his hands behind his head. "I thank you for your generous offer, Maude. Let me think on it. I'm at the beck and call of Paramount on this one." Without warning he sat up suddenly and laid his napkin across his plate. Without saying a word, he stood, kissed Maude on the cheek, and pointed his finger at Eddie. "Ciao, my friend. We'll talk later, okay?" Before Eddie could answer, Rudy had wandered off to greet another table of guests.

Maude said it for the both of them. "Sur-prise!"

Eddie leaned on the table with a deep sigh. "So now what?"

"He's getting on with his career." She paused. "Maybe now is the time to think about getting on with yours?"

He just looked at her. *Damn it, woman!* "Let's go."

ELEVEN

Rudy was nervously fidgeting with the silverware, and he stood up when he saw Eddie approaching. "Welcome, my friend." Eddie looked genuinely happy to be there, and that put Rudy at ease.

Eddie extended his hand before taking a seat. The meeting was awkward and uncomfortable. "This is nice, my friend, as is always the case anytime I share a meal with you." He took a sip of his water as Rudy glad-handed a patron.

As Rudy turned from the passing fan, Eddie touched the man's arm. "My friend, you and I have been pals a long time. And I can't tell you how grateful I am for all you've done for me over the years. I couldn't begin to name all the wonderful bookings and appearances you've arranged for me. I owe you a lot."

Rudy always enjoyed accolades but somehow felt self-conscious and a little embarrassed, and he couldn't say why. The discomfort turned his cheeks rosy and made it difficult to sit still. He lowered his head. "You know, I truly like you as a friend, and I do believe you are the Prince of Entertainers." He now sat up straight and started on the speech he'd been rehearsing. "Now, I've got an agent already in California . . . " His voice trailed off. He could see that Eddie's mind was elsewhere.

Eddie had been rehearsing a speech of his own. With his head tilted, now wearing his too-familiar stage smile, he commenced. "My friend, I think you know that Maude and I have been very happy here in New York. The Big Apple has been good to us." He lifted his eyes to check on his friend's reaction.

Rudy was caught off guard. "Get to the point, will you?"

"Right. Well, you may have noticed that I've been preoccupied for the past couple of weeks. Actually I've been getting up at 6:00 AM every Monday through Friday and working my ass off."

"Doing what?" Rudy was puzzled, and he twitched nervously as he interrupted. "Just where are you going with this?"

"I'll get there. Be patient, will you?"

"Look, I have been rehearsing a speech ever since our last meeting. Now why do I feel like I'm being upstaged?"

Eddie glanced around where they were sitting. Rudy, of course, felt he was just being rude and disinterested, not knowing his friend's desire to see who might be listening in on their conversation. Eddie once again surprised Rudy as he leaned over as close as he could to his friend and started to whisper. "Pal, just listen to me for a minute, please. I've been working on something that may be the most important thing I've ever done in my life. And the gods' honest truth is, I can't tell you one damn thing about it. As a matter of fact, I could probably get my butt kicked severely if the people I'm working with knew I was even talking to you, about any of this."

Rudy said nothing but was perplexed and fascinated at the same time. He started to rub his chin nervously.

Eddie continued, "So what the hell does any of this have to do with you or your generous offer? Well, unfortunately I expect to be tied up with this project for the next three to four weeks. So, you see, I simply couldn't take on anything more." He sat back with an exasperated sigh. "I am truly sorry, my friend. I do hope you understand. And please, please don't ask me any questions."

Rudy couldn't imagine what the hell the man was talking about. He had never encountered anyone so evasive. *It must have something to do with that ridiculous instruction book he published last year.* Nervously he looked at his watch. All he wanted to do now was leave. *What more can I say?* He stood and touched his friend's shoulder. "I'll see you at rehearsal tomorrow?"

"Yes, sir." Without thinking, Eddie nodded and then gave a crisp salute.

Rudy departed without comment.

Well, that's that.

When Eddie arrived in Washington to open the Earl Theater, he had two more weeks to study for his exam. He thought he was ready and wanted it over with. When the day finally arrived, it took him more than eight hours to complete, and he was thoroughly wrung out from the ordeal. When he arrived back at the hotel, Maude was in the process of ending a phone call. She smiled when he entered and handed him a celebratory glass of bourbon.

Eddie was not in a celebratory mood. "Well, who the hell was that?"

I just hate it when he swears. "That was Dianne Petit. You'll need to get your suit and a shirt cleaned . . . for we, my dear, have a dinner invitation for Saturday night." *And I need to find a dress!* She was suddenly overcome with the excitement. *We're having dinner with the president.*

TWELVE

The presidential residence was decorated for Christmas, and it was more splendid than anything they had ever seen. After dinner the president invited guests for coffee in an adjacent card room that he favored. The room contained, in addition to three walls of recently published books and magazines, an upright piano. There were also two beautiful inlaid-wood card tables and some scattered but very comfortable furniture.

FDR sat in one of the straight-backed card-table chairs, his wheelchair to one side. He picked up his banjo from the floor, placed there by a staffer who'd served the president for many years. The president's son and son's girlfriend sat nearby on the piano bench and started a duet of old college tunes. The president, after attempting to tune his old and somewhat abused instrument, tried to accompany them by thumping out some rhythm on his banjo.

Eddie had brought along his Banjoline, hoping to play a few favorite tunes for his hosts. Watching the president and the singing couple, he realized he was developing a genuine fondness for this family. The tunes were simple, and Eddie had no problem making the trio sound like a polished group.

FDR was truly enjoying this. He ordered port wine for every-one. Eleanor gave a disapproving look and said, "Do you think you should, dear?"

"Balderdash! One glass couldn't possibly hurt him, mom."

The president chuckled at his son's ready support. "That comment will definitely win you another term at Harvard, good son that you are."

Eddie and Maude stayed and enjoyed themselves till after midnight.

Upon his return to New York, Eddie was notified by telegram that he'd passed the Reserve Officer's Qualification exam. The following week, in Washington, the secretary of the navy com-missioned him as a lieutenant. With the completion of his engage-ments in New York, he returned to the land of sunshine and his beautiful Riverside ranch. On weekends he drove down to a training facility near San Diego, but he spent most of his time in Long Beach at the Naval Training Center.

One weekend, while in flight school, he crash-landed a paper-winged biplane trainer into a tree. He'd walked away unharmed. The Department of the Navy was panic-stricken when it heard of the incident, and it informed the president of its concerns during a staff meeting. FDR's reaction to this news stunned everyone.

"I knew this guy was tough, and I'm damn proud of him." He turned to Claude Swanson. "Claude, as this man's training progresses, I want you and George to develop a strategy for his deployment. And if you can, try to keep the State Department folks' involvement in this to a minimum."

"Yes, sir, but that may be difficult just now, sir. Some congress-men see things heating up, with boatloads of immigrants flooding our shores. There is real concern, and they want support from the Navy and the Coast Guard to help divert any German immigrants to Cuba, or some other island in the Caribbean. I'm sorry to say it, sir, but it appears that anti-Semitism flows right under the surface with a lot of folks. The elaboration of German police-state power under Hitler is continuing. Any opposition or dissent is simply not tolerated. And under one pretext or another, virtually all property owned by Jews is confiscated."

"Yes, I've read those reports from our embassy. It seems that after Hitler decreed that all Jews were to be dismissed from government service and none were being allowed to remain at universities, many left the country. Hell, I'd leave too. Those that remain risk everything."

"Yes, sir. The man is also busy doubling the rate of rearming the Fatherland. He's reintroduced conscription. He wants to create a peacetime army of thirty-five divisions or more. This is a direct violation of the Versailles treaty."

There was little doubt in the president's mind that this Hitler was an uncompromising nationalist, with intentions to overthrow the peace settlement of 1919, rearm, and establish German hegemony in Europe. "Claude, do continue to keep me informed on Eddie's progress, will you?"

"Yes, sir. I'll start on the strategy draft immediately, Mr. President."

The president tossed the daily edition of the *Cleveland Press* on to his desk so Swanson could read the circled article: EDDIE PEABODY BEAMS WHEN HE TELLS FRIENDS THAT HE HAS QUALIFIED AS A LIEUTENANT IN THE NAVAL RESERVE, AND AS A PILOT.

"Mr. President, we must put the squeeze on the man to keep a lid on this! He is due back here at the Shoreham in a couple of weeks, and I'm told that with the able help of NBC Artists, we should be able to arrange a European tour for him on short notice."

"Thank you, Claude. We'll discuss this after the staff meeting."

Swanson handed the president a folder. "My staff continues to peruse a number of publications, and they're assembling a file of articles on the man."

Variety: FDR is reported especially fond of Peabody's banjo instrumentalizing . . .

BMG (Banjo Mandolin Guitar): Since receiving my commission we have, on several occasions, been guests of President and Mrs. Roosevelt . . .

The Cleveland Press: Eddie Peabody and wife Maude have been guests repeatedly at the White House. Since they stopped off here last, they were guests of Franklin Roosevelt on the official yacht from which the President watched one of the younger Roosevelts row for Harvard.

The Washington Post: After his last stop here in May he went to Dallas, where he was guest of President and Mrs. Roosevelt and the Texas Exposition. Then to California where he played before half a million at the state Democratic Convention. (Thereby showing he was with the popular majority.)

BMG (Interview with Mrs. Peabody): Incidentally, I might mention that we recently had, once again, the great privilege of being the guests of President and Mrs. Roosevelt (both of whom have been most graciously kind to us in many ways). While there the President invited us to be his guests at the National Convention in Philadelphia, where Eddie had the honor of appearing before an audience of 200,000 assembled in Franklin Field to hear our President accept the nomination for re-election.

After glancing at some of the content, FDR dropped the file on his desk with a thud. "It's clear to me that it's going to be near impossible to keep a lid on this very much longer."

"I quite agree, sir. But I also believe that it's quite unlikely that the Nazis are reading *Variety* or the *Cleveland Press*. We may even have an advantage here, sir."

"How's that?"

"Most entertainers, including Eddie Peabody, are very public figures, we all agree. People are around this guy almost day and night. Fans come up in restaurants, on the street, just for an autograph."

"I'm not sure I follow you."

"Well, sir, field information could be transferred to public figures, like Eddie, more easily than someone in, say, the diplomatic corps. We believe that with some extra effort on local promotion, within two weeks of a performance, we could have our banjo man as recognizable on the streets of Hamburg as he is in Cleveland."

"It seems to me that there's a lot of information out there for the casual observer to ask some very poignant questions. With as much publicity on his commission, the visits we've had here at the White House—I don't know. I would hate like hell to send our man over there, only to be browbeaten by Himmler himself, or one henchman." The president placed a cigarette in his custom holder and began to light up. "Now, tell me about our German contacts. The wrong local could make or break our operation."

"I agree, sir. Our main contact over there currently is a director at the American School for International Studies. He's an American citizen but was considering German citizenship before the Nazis took power. His name is Greg Ziemer."

"Excellent! And how were we able to recruit such a distinguished gentleman?"

"Actually, he came to us, sir. The State Department has been working with him for some time now. He's been instrumental in getting some influential German Jews out of the country. I believe the State Department indicated he's been responsible for relocating over one thousand families. Turns out his mother was Jewish, but fortunately there is no record of that in Germany. Even more interesting, we're told he's also friendly with Hitler's man in charge of all German security. He secured some student placements at American University for children of some prominent Nazi Party officials. He has a reputation among the German hierarchy of providing great service to the Fatherland."

The president snuffed out the remainder of his cigarette. "Thank you for that update. I'm sorry, Claude, but I still have an uneasy feeling. I know there are henchmen out there that would profit handsomely from incriminating information on one of our agents, especially a public figure like Eddie Peabody."

"I believe you're right, sir. We do have the FBI closely monitoring all German radio traffic. We're told that coded traffic at this point is minimal. We may be able to get in ahead of any potential leaks if we accelerate our schedule. But there will always be some risk once an agent is in-country."

"I'm aware of the risks, Claude. But we must find out just

how many submarines and how big a fleet that paperhanger of a chancellor intends to muster." The president turned his wheelchair, indicating that he intended to leave the room. "And I want to know what else that little Austrian corporal is up to."

THIRTEEN

Seattle, Washington

The hotel room was cold and damp. The audiences had been very receptive to Eddie after an eight-year absence. Sunday matinees, however, were exhausting. This afternoon, the crowd seemed restless. It was as though they were daring him to entertain them. But, as intended, he won them over by the third or fourth tune. In his dressing room, he was changing the head on his banjo when the man he'd hired to arrange tunes and manage the show burst in and handed him the latest *Variety* review.

Eddie Peabody returned to Seattle as headliner on this week's vaudeville billing to take right up where he left off eight years ago in "wowing 'em." In the days when MCs flourished like dandelions but were treated like orchids, Peabody set this town on its ear with a length-of-stay record that still remains untouched. Seattle has changed in the years in between, and many of its theatergoers had forgotten the magic of the diminutive banjoist's personality.

His reappearance this week recalls it and re-demonstrates his ability to bring forth encores.

"A good article, don't you think, boss? The local newsboys will be quoting from it till we move on to Minneapolis."

Eddie read the complimentary article but never looked up or offered any comment. He returned to tightening up the banjo head.

His lack of comment surprised his manager. Lloyd's tone reflected his frustration. "I'm sorry for the interruption. Is there a problem? You seem to be elsewhere."

Eddie dropped the nut wrench and laid his banjo in its case. "Sorry. Just a million things on my mind, that's all. The article was great, and no, you're doing a terrific job, Lloyd."

The man left the room without responding.

The suspense was starting to drive Eddie nuts. *Why haven't they contacted me? Report somewhere, say, to Bremerton?* He remembered Scharf's warning. *Not knowing is part of it. Patience, Eddie, patience.* He silently repeated this to himself. He was feeling out on a limb, lonely, and a little scared. He decided to call Maude. *Maybe I can convince her to join the tour.*

She answered abruptly when he called. She said she was glad to hear his voice, but she too had a lot on her mind. "Sweetheart, I'd love to join you, but I'm exhausted—not feeling well, to boot. Your new manager—isn't he up to snuff? I thought he was Mr. Wizard and that's why you hired him."

Eddie thought he heard her start to cry. "Maude, are you all right? What's the matter with you? Look, I'm sorry about this tour. If I could—"

She interrupted, saying, "No, no, it has nothing to do with you, the tour, or your new man." There was an awkward silence.

"Then what is it? What's bothering you, hon?"

She took a deep, audible breath. "We both know I'm overweight, even though I'd never admit it. Well, lately I've been feeling weak, and awfully thirsty. My girlfriend suggested I see a doctor, and after a battery of tests he called and said I was diabetic. He felt certain from the tests, and he was emphatic that if I didn't stick to the diet he gave me, I could start having serious complications—problems with my vision, my skin, digestion, even tuberculosis." Maude's voice rose and quivered uncontrollably as she elaborated on the prognosis. "And if that wasn't enough, he added that two of his patients that didn't follow instructions fell into comas and died within a month!"

Eddie held the phone away from his ear. "Sweetheart, listen. I'll cancel the tour and be on the next—"

She quickly interrupted before he could finish. "No, no! You stay right where you are!" She paused to catch her breath and calm down. Her voice was now soft and contained, but he could tell she was working at it. "I'm sorry to be burdening you with this. But right now I simply don't know what to do with myself. I want to see another doctor, for another opinion." She paused again. He could hear her breathing heavily. "I'm going to hang up before I start to blubber again. Please tell me you still love me."

"Maude, you know that—"

Again she interrupted, her voice squeaking. "I've seen the internist that Marge says is so great. Please don't worry about me! I do love you, Eddie." She disconnected abruptly.

He was stunned, and he felt numb as he sat on the bed, staring at the phone. He tried to organize his thoughts. Everything seemed so confused, so uncertain. He was feeling out of control. He stretched out on the bed. Just as he began to doze off, the phone rang.

"Lieutenant Peabody?"

"Yes?"

"This is Chief Rice calling. Sir, you've been ordered to report to our Twin Cities Lake Minnetonka facility at 0900 tomorrow." The chief relayed the address but offered no more.

"Okay! Yes, Chief, I'll be there. In uniform?"

"Yes, sir, winter uniform. You'll be directed to base head-quarters for sign-in. And sir, please bring your identification card with you."

"Yes, Chief. Anything else?"

"No, sir, that's all."

After settling into the hotel and checking out the theater, Eddie drove to the small facility and signed in. He was directed to proceed to the building just behind the flagpole, where Commander Scharf was waiting for him in a small assembly room. He greeted Eddie with a smile and a vigorous handshake. "It's been a privilege working with you, Lieutenant. And you have impressed all of us in Washington. Now, as directed by the president, it is my privilege to present you these." He handed Eddie a pair of gold oak leaves signifying his promotion to the rank of lieutenant commander. "Congratulations! Oh, and those oak leaves were mine, Eddie. I like to think they brought me some luck. I sincerely hope they do the same for you. Now, we do have some serious training to accomplish here, so let's get started, shall we?"

"Thank you, Commander. I didn't think I was due for promotional consideration for another year."

"No, you've progressed right on schedule, albeit an accelerated one. And the boss thought it was time. You'll be dealing with embassy people soon, so you'll need all the rank we can muster." He glanced at his watch. "Oh my. We'd better get over to the training yard before the chief has a coronary. I know he looks meaner than a shipyard dog, but he's the best we have when it comes to covert operations."

The training was rigorous, and Eddie's endurance was pushed to the limit. When he finally returned to the hotel sometime after dark, he was exhausted. He had two phone messages, one from Maude and another from Lloyd.

Eddie called his wife. She answered in an angry tone. "I want you to know, my gentleman-rancher husband, that the income from the sale of the oranges on this property is insufficient to pay expenses. And we had a small earthquake right in the middle of crating—one whole truckload was ruined. To think of all the effort I've put into this harvest! I'm exhausted. I simply can't do this anymore, hon. You're just going to have to hire a full-time manager if you want to keep this place."

Thanks, Maude, I needed something else to worry about. He was out of breath just listening. He didn't know what to say.

The silence now was deafening. A minute passed before she spoke, in a calmer voice. "I saw another doctor yesterday. He concurred with the earlier diagnosis."

Eddie sighed into the phone. *So that's what's been in her craw.* "Maude, I've been talking with a doctor at the local naval base here, and he felt strongly that if you stuck to your doctor's diet, you'd be on your way to controlling this thing."

"Oh, for crying out loud. You know how hard that would be. These quacks told me that there's a new treatment—insulin injections. The thought of having a needle stuck in me every morning makes me want to faint." She paused. Then, as though nothing at all had happened, she turned the page. "So, how's the tour going? You're playing in a review up in Minneapolis, aren't you?"

"Yes, hon, I am." *Should I tell her what else happened today?* "I was promoted to lieutenant commander at the training center today, hon."

"Congratulations. By the way, is the government paying you for all this work you're putting in?"

Ah, yes, another one of her sore subjects. He didn't respond. "Look, I'm sorry about all the hassle with the harvest. Why don't you catch a train and meet me in Cleveland? We could have a small celebration, maybe go to dinner at the same place we had our reception dinner. What do you say?"

"That does sound nice." Eddie could feel her demeanor change. She breathed heavily before she spoke. "I just got off the phone with my brother, and he wants me to come to Texas—to see what he and his wife are working on near Fort Worth. I could go from there—meet you in Baltimore?"

"Maude, I—"

She interrupted. "You know, I planned to be with you in Washington anyway. I just know the Roosevelts will invite us for Christmas again—and what to bring them? Oh well. I'm sure I'll find something in Dallas." She fell silent again. "I'd ask you what's going on with the navy, but you'd probably just tell me that it's secret and you can't tell a soul. They're not sending you out somewhere, are they? Or can you even tell me that?"

His patience was wearing thin. "Maude, I'm not being sent anywhere. Tell your brother hello for me, will you? Please give our neighbors a copy of the tour itinerary, will you?"

"Yes, I will, sweetheart, tomorrow morning. And don't worry about me here at the ranch. I'll take care of everything, as usual, before I leave."

"That's fine, dear. Thank you for all your help. I'll send you some of the review clippings, okay?"

That was certainly depressing. He threw on his topcoat and headed out the door. Once outside, he tried to absorb the beauty of the fall evening. *I need to clear my mind.* The moon crested over the horizon and shimmered through the clouds. *Life has been good to me.* He couldn't stop thinking about the one-way conversation with Maude. *She didn't hear a word I said!* He stopped to exchange greetings with a young family. They had tickets for the Sunday matinee. *Maybe she'll calm down once she visits her brother. She wouldn't miss seeing the Roosevelts for love nor money. Damn it all— now she has diabetes!*

The show moved on to the Loew's State Theater in New York. He telephoned his friend Rudy Vallee.

"Eddie! Are you in town?"

"Yeah, pal. I'm back in the Big Apple, at Loew's for two weeks."

"Is Maude with you?"

"No, she's in Texas, visiting with her brother. She'll be up when the tour moves on to Baltimore."

"That's terrific. We'll have to get together and paint the town before she arrives. By the way, who booked you at Loew's? NBC?"

"Yeah, I'm still with NBC. And so, how are things with you?"

"Great! Have you seen my newest movie?"

"No, I'm sorry I haven't, pal. It isn't playing here, by chance?"

"If you've got any dead time, I'll be happy to get sloshed and sit through it with you. I'll point out who's sleeping with whom."

"Actually, I do have a few things I'd like to talk over with you, if you've got some time—maybe your favorite joint for a corned beef. What do you say?"

"You know I'll always find time for you. Say, I've been reading about how our president has taken you under his wing, made a Democrat of you, got you to publish a song of his as well."

Eddie went cold listening to Rudy's words. *Damn it!* "Rudy, Rudy, you know those newspaper bastards. What they don't know, well, they make up. Right?"

Rudy sensed his comment had made his friend uncomfortable. *But why? A relationship with FDR—one hell of a feather, I'd say.* "Say, you're going to be my radio guest this week, aren't you?"

Eddie was silent. It was a pause that was too long for Rudy.

"Your reaction says that someone has threatened you with Chinese torture if we chat on the radio. Did I guess right?"

What can I say? "We'll talk all about this at lunch, okay? Now let me get going here and get settled over at the theater, will ya?"

Rudy mused at the maneuvering. "You got it, my friend. But it'll be just you and me, sailor. Jack is busy as hell these days—busy with the job I'd hoped you'd take."

"Talk to you tomorrow, pal." Eddie rang off quickly.

FOURTEEN

Eddie arrived early. He wanted a table away from the noon crowd. After they'd been served their standard fare (corned beef on rye with a half-pint of stout), Rudy resumed his interrogation. "So tell me what you've been up to, my friend. And what is all this I'm reading about you and the Democratic National Committee?"

"Democratic national what? What the hell are you talking about?"

"Well, I just assumed that after all your stumping for FDR at the convention during the last election, and all the hoopla about your visits to the White House, at some point you'd be a prominent member of the DNC or at least running for office somewhere. So, which is it?" Rudy had always wanted to be up to his eyeballs in politics.

"Rudy, Rudy, you incredibly talented man. I'm not running for or from anything." He paused to gather his thoughts. "The Roosevelts are very nice people. You'd like them." He paused again and took a deep breath before continuing. He tried to make eye contact, wanting his undivided attention. "Look, you know I love kidding with you, whether we're on your radio show or at your club. But what I'm telling you now is very important, and I hope you understand."

"Understand what? So far, you haven't told me anything."

"I simply can't talk publicly about my relationship with the president, period. Look, he sometimes likes to jam after dinner, and I've shown him a few new chords to help him along. But on air, live on your radio show, I simply couldn't talk about anything more than what I've just told you. Can you understand and accept that?"

Rudy had shut out all the other table talk and was listening intently. "You really are good friends with the man, aren't you?"

"Well, I'd like to think that I'm a good friend of yours as well."

"Oh, you know you are. I'm just jealous, that's all. But listen, I remember when you were working your butt off, studying for some admission exam."

"What are you getting at?"

"Nothing. Just trying to put the pieces together. I do know this—folks would tune in by the droves to not only hear your banjo wizardry, but also hear how you've become personal friends with our president."

Eddie leaned back with a sigh of exasperation. He ordered another Guinness for Rudy and a glass of milk for himself.

Rudy took notice. "Don't you know that if you mix Guinness and milk, you could die from terminal flatulence?" The comic relief was a much-needed icebreaker. Eddie felt more comfortable now and motioned for Rudy to lean in closer so he could whisper.

Rudy smiled and placed his hand on his friend's shoulder. "I haven't offended you, have I?"

"No, no, no, no! Listen, you know I'd love doing a spot on your radio show, play some duets like we used to, jam with the band, whatever." Eddie looked around to see if anyone might be listening in. He continued, "Look, pal, there is no way I can make any public statements about the navy or my relationship with the Roosevelts." Eddie sat back and nervously shuffled his feet under the table. He leaned forward again. "And I can't tell you any more than what I've just said. As a matter of fact, I know someone who might say that I've already said too much. So please, pal, don't ask me any more questions. And please, please, please don't you or Jack contemplate pulling a fast one to try to catch me off guard . . . or I'll just have to beg off from doing your radio show."

Rudy was stunned by his friend's words, and he sat back. "Eddie, please don't ever think that I would ever deliberately embarrass you publicly." He waited for a reaction. "Okay, my friend. No more about the navy or the Roosevelts." They smiled and shook hands across the table as though a business deal had been consummated.

"So, when do you want me on your show?"

Rudy suddenly felt noncommittal. He nervously looked at his watch. "I am sorry, pal, but if I don't retreat to the club, Jack will surely have apoplexy. I've been late for rehearsal this whole month." Rudy pushed back his chair and prepared to leave. "But thank you so much for the delightful lunch and the stimulating conversation. I do hope you'll share some more with me at a later date. Ta-ta."

Upon returning to his hotel, Eddie called Maude at her brother's ranch in Texas. The call surprised her.

"Oh, hello, dear. Why on earth are you calling? Is something wrong?"

"No, no, no. I just wanted to know how you're feeling and if you're still coming up to Baltimore. I'd like to know when you're arriving so I can arrange to meet you, that's all. How's everyone in Katy?"

"Everyone is fine here, dear, but to be truthful, I haven't booked passage as yet. My brother wants me to fly, but I'm still afraid of flying. Besides, the seats on those little planes are so small. So I'll likely take a train. Anyway, I'd be arriving from Dallas sometime next week, so I'll call your hotel once I've confirmed a reservation. How are the shows going? I read *Variety* every day, and it seems that they like what they see."

He placed his hand over the phone fearing he'd say something in anger. *Well, if it's too much trouble, why don't you just stay put?* He tried to change the subject. "I finally caught Rudy for lunch. We

talked about doing his radio show sometime this week or next."
There was a hissing on the phone, and he thought they'd been disconnected. *Now what the hell do I say?* "Maude, I'm worried about
your diabetes, and I've missed you."

"I'm fine, sweetheart. I really am, and I'm looking forward to
a dinner with the Roosevelts. I do hope you're not going to be too
busy. I want to send my brother and his wife something special
for Christmas, from Washington. They've been so nice to me."

Well, at least I know what your priorities are. "I understand. You'll
have plenty of time to shop, dear. Oh, I almost forgot—I've got to
get ready for another European tour, sometime this spring."

"So soon? This isn't for the navy, is it?"

No one spoke. *Damn it, woman, you are not in charge of my life!
When are you going to get on board?* All Eddie could hear was the
long-distance phone hiss. A roller coaster of emotions passed
through him, but he knew he didn't want a fight over the phone.
"We'll talk some more about it when you get here, hon. Please give
my love to your brother and his wife. Love you. Bye now." *Every
time the navy comes up, I can feel her fingers poking at my chest. Damn
it, doesn't she see I need support from her, not confrontation?*

No sooner had he set the receiver down when the phone again
began ringing. "Yes?"

"Eddie. Commander Scharf here. Just called to bring you up
to date."

He sat back down. "Yes, skipper."

"First, several things have been scheduled during the week
you're at the Shoreham in Washington. So please leave your
calendar clear for daytime meetings during that week."

Eddie had grabbed a sheet of hotel stationery and begun
jotting down some notes. "I don't see a problem, skipper."

"Great. We're all new at the intelligence-gathering business,
Eddie. So everyone up the line, including the boss, wants to make
sure that every precaution, every contact, every contingency—
simply said, the boss wants everything covered prior to your
departure. And that date is fast approaching."

"Really? Can you be more specific, Commander?"

"I'm sorry, I can't. You'll be contacted shortly, though. Scheduling is tight, and things will be happening on short notice. We're accelerating the schedule of another agent, who will cross paths with you in France. I know this is pretty thin, Eddie, but we will be close by from now until you leave the country."

"I see. Okay. Well, you know my schedule. Oh, and my wife should be joining me next week."

Eddie listened for a follow-up from Scharf, but none came. Again all he could hear over the phone was a loud hissing, and then the line went dead. He returned the instrument to its cradle and pondered the abrupt conversation. *Another agent? I wonder what his thoughts were concerning Maude . . . likely she should stay home and be a good, supportive navy wife.*

Shoreham Hotel
December 1938

Maude had arrived by train and was lounging on the bed in Eddie's room when the phone rang, startling her. "Yes, this is Mrs. Peabody. Who's calling, please? Oh. Why, yes, the lieutenant commander is right here." When Eddie looked up, she silently mouthed the words, "It's for you dear. The White House."

Eddie turned his back to her and began speaking softly. He quietly replaced the receiver.

What is wrong with him? He knows I'm on pins and needles. "Well?"

"Well, what?" He bristled, not at the question but at her demanding tone. Realizing he was getting on edge, he tried to soften his reply. "Look, I'm sorry. But I've been called to attend a short-notice meeting." He looked at his watch. "I should be back in about two hours." He could feel the tension in the air begin to rise, and he'd just ushered it in. He walked over and stood close to her. "Maude, sweetheart. I am really sorry. But this meeting is with the secretary of the navy. You understand, don't you?"

He looked at her face. She seemed elsewhere, staring at

nothing, and then she looked up at him with tears in her eyes. "I haven't seen you for months, and now you're deserting me."

He put his hand on her shoulder and gave a comforting stroke. "You'll be more comfortable here, I'm sure. I promise I won't be long." Then, at the blink of an eye, he was out of the room and headed for the lobby. *Jesus, what am I going to do about her?*

The bell captain, Bert, always seemed pleased to accommodate his favorite hotel guest, Mista Banjo. Eddie always took time to exchange small talk and encourage him whenever he could. "Bettah bundle up, Mista Eddie, if you goin' out in dis. We in fo' a major stoam today, an' maybe tomorrow too. The radio said it would be worse than the one in nineteen thirty-three. So you take care now, *heah?*"

"I will, Bert, and thanks." Eddie tipped him generously.

Bert smiled when handed the gratuity. Life was good. He loved helping Mista Banjo.

FIFTEEN

Seated in the conference room was Secretary Swanson, a young man introduced to Eddie as David, Swanson's undersecretary, Commander Scharf, and a young navy WAVE lieutenant.

Claude Swanson formally opened the meeting. "Good evening, ladies and gentlemen, and thank you for attending on short notice. I would like this to be short and to the point. We'll be discussing the schedule for insertion of Lieutenant Commander Eddie Peabody. Commander, I'll get right to it. It is our intention, if all goes according to plan, to send you into Germany. We haven't worked out all the details yet, but we do have an excellent contact currently in place. And we want to make the best use of him while we still can. Hitler is getting more aggressive every day, and many of us, here and in Europe, are very concerned. Our embassy contacts indicate that Germany's war-machine factories are working nearly twenty-four hours a day. We don't have many photographs, but what we do have, along with eyewitness accounts, indicates that the military manpower he is assembling will be larger than France's by the end of the year."

He poured some ice water and then went on. "Right now, by all accounts, Germany is fully employed. Times are good over there—unless, according to nearly every dispatch from our Berlin embassy, you are Jewish. And the German press is working overtime to suppress the atrocities that have already occurred." He paused to gather his thoughts. "Though it is regrettable, this German global business boom has caused many otherwise honest and forthright governments, after years of recession, to turn a blind eye to Germany's military buildup and its expropriation of Jewish businesses and property. They are chalking it all up as merely a German nationalistic need, after their humiliation at Versailles."

A White House server entered with some coffee and a glass of milk for Eddie.

"One of our closest in-place contacts has had remarkable success in getting many prominent Jewish-German business-people and scientists out of the country. His name is Greg Ziemer. And he, Commander, will be your direct contact once you're in-country." Swanson glanced at his watch. "One of our concerns, and the president's in particular, is the current size and buildup of the German submarine fleet. As you may remember, they were pretty effective during the last conflagration with the Kaiser. Well, we believe that with your background knowledge and with Ziemer well established in-country, we should be able to learn exactly what kind and specifically where the Austrian corporal is constructing these submarines."

Commander Scharf cleared his throat. "Excuse me, sir. Perhaps this is the appropriate time to let the commander in on some background information we have on Mr. Ziemer?"

"Of course, Commander."

A large personnel folder was handed across the desk to Scharf. He glanced briefly at the file before commencing. "Mr. Ziemer is a director at the American School of International Studies in Berlin. The school enjoys a prestigious reputation. Many of Germany's international business leaders, and some political leaders, are recent graduates. Heinrich Himmler, Rudolf Hess, and Admiral Erich Raeder have all taken world business courses from Ziemer. Himmler is head of Security Services, Hess is a Reich minister, and Raeder is Secretary Swanson's counterpart. Mr. Ziemer currently enjoys a great deal of latitude in his current position. And we all pray that this continues to be the case."

The conference room door suddenly opened with a bang. Nearly everyone in the room jumped, and then they stood as they recognized the familiar hand grasping the doorway for leverage. The president smiled at everyone as he rolled effortlessly into the conference room. The white shirt he wore, with open collar and rolled-up sleeves, was crisp and bright. Sunshine had wheeled into the conference room, and everyone could feel the commanding presence.

Eddie thought the president looked tired, as though he'd been dealing day and night with a heavy burden. But there was no doubt in his mind that he'd follow this man to hell and back if he had to.

FDR gave a quick salute to all present. "As you were, people. I do apologize for being late. I just caught the end of your briefing through the door. Do continue, gentlemen."

Swanson stood and began to summarize. "Well, Mr. President, I'm not sure what more the assembled staff or I could add—unless, of course, there are questions." He looked around the room. No one moved, let alone spoke. You could hear a pin drop.

The president turned to face Swanson. "Did you mention any timing for Eddie's insertion?"

Eddie looked up and came to attention in his seat when he heard his name. Was the president himself directing this operation? *One thing is for sure—me and my four-stringed harp are about to embark on one tough performance.*

Swanson looked directly at Eddie. "Yes, sir, I believe the commander understands that the countdown has begun. And he will be contacted on a weekly basis by Commander Scharf until departure."

A staff assistant entered the room, carrying a glass of milk FDR had requested. "Splendid, splendid." The president leaned on the conference table as he spoke directly to Eddie. "I want you to know that I've taken up your habit, especially when the days get long, like today. And Eleanor is convinced that you've stumbled onto something of miraculous medicinal value." He paused and took a long swallow. "Commander, I know we've discussed the misgivings many of us have regarding Hitler, and what he and his Nazi thugs are doing in Germany these days. And from what I read in the papers, things are starting to heat up. Our mustached friend is reintroducing military conscription—a clear violation of the Treaty of Versailles. This is troubling to me, but apparently not to my esteemed colleague, Prime Minister Chamberlain. For reasons known only to the prime minister, a naval pact was negotiated between England and Germany, without consulting France. Germany will be allowed to construct ships totaling 35 percent of Britain's fleet. Here's where you come in, Commander. The agreement allows Germany to maintain a submarine fleet equal in size to Britain's. The bottom line is this—I believe that trust is the correct operative here, but by damn, verify!" He leaned back and finished his milk. He leaned forward again before continuing. "Since the Franco-Soviet mutual assistance treaty, Hitler has denounced the Locarno Pact and remilitarized the Rhineland. And with civil war in Spain, the German chancellor is now rubbing elbows with Mussolini, plotting who knows what. I know I'm in a minority opinion right now, but it seems to me that if France and Britain don't quit their petty bickering and keep an eagle eye on this man, before we know it we'll all be caught up in another damned war. And that thought makes my blood run cold." He took a deep breath and then glanced at everyone at the table. "Now we're going to find out what the little SOB is up to."

Eddie's feet began to twitch.

FDR turned to Claude Swanson. "Have I said anything out of school?"

"No, sir. I think you've just summarized, in short order, the sum and substance of this meeting. The commander's European tour is still a work in progress, Mr. President, but he'll be shipping out for England no later than mid-April."

Swanson turned to Eddie. "Commander, we do want you within a day's drive of Washington until you ship out, so we've arranged your schedule accordingly. We have secured spots for you in Pittsburgh and at the Metropolitan Theater in Boston. So, for the next two months, please don't leave the immediate area unless you clear it with us." Swanson looked up and noticed Eddie indicating that he wanted to speak. He nodded his approval.

"Thank you, Mr. Secretary. I wanted to say that I'm at your disposal and I will be wherever, whenever you want me. Everyone here has worked very hard, and I want each of you to know how much I appreciate all the time you've spent trying to get me up to speed. I will not let you down."

The president grinned broadly as he leaned forward in his chair. "Commander, that is exactly why you were chosen for this assignment."

The secretary handed Eddie a small slip of paper. All it contained was a Washington DC telephone number. "Please memorize that number, Commander, and then destroy that slip of paper. At our next meeting, before you move on to Pittsburgh, we will go over your tentative booking in England, and we'll brief you on your contact while in that country. This mission will be labeled top secret, Commander, and the Brits won't have a clue as to what you're up to. So you'll be on your own."

FDR signaled that he was ready to leave. Everyone stood as the president rolled toward the doorway. He stopped and grabbed Eddie's arm. "My son will be home from college this weekend. Why don't you and the missus come over for dinner Friday night, after your show?"

"It will be our pleasure, sir."

Everyone was still standing as the secretary followed the president. "We'll continue to be in touch," he reassured Eddie as he motioned for him to follow.

In the hallway, near an antique chair with a small coffee table, he stopped abruptly and grabbed Eddie's arm. "Commander, you'll likely be jerked around quite a bit in Europe, at least until schedules are firmly in place. On this assignment, once you're in place, you will be on official business, and perhaps even in harm's way."

Eddie nodded but said nothing.

"And, I'm sorry to say, on this assignment we can't allow your wife to accompany you. We know that will be difficult to explain, but I think you know that it would be in everyone's best interest if you and your wife said your goodbyes around the first of April. I do hope you understand that we need to do everything we can to ensure your successful return."

"That won't be a problem, sir." His thoughts drifted. *Maude isn't feeling well, and she should be glad to stay home and rest. But then again, she'll likely throw a fit and bitch till we're both mad as hatters.*

A staff security officer entered the hallway to escort Eddie back to a sitting room. Two staff attachés were walking rapidly down the hallway, talking to each other but not taking notice as they passed by. "I hope he can pick his way outta there as well as he picks that ol' banjo of his. I wonder if our banjo man will be as enthusiastic . . . "

The security officer touched Eddie's elbow. "This way, Commander, and pay no attention to the young motor-mouths." When Eddie was finally seated in the backseat of a staff car, he stared out the window at the wintry scene, trying to gather his thoughts. He tried to imagine a conversation with Maude.

I've just come from one of the most important and intense meetings in my life.

Why don't you tell me about the meeting, sweetheart? I know, I know—it's all secret stuff. You can't tell anybody anything. But you've got to share something with somebody.

He tried to rest his eyes as he tapped his fingers on the window. *What the hell do I tell her?* He awoke with a start when he felt the wheels start to brake. They'd reached the hotel and rode the slow elevator up to his third-floor room. Maude was dozing in a chair, but she stirred as he entered. He threw his coat on the bed and strode over to her. He began to speak rapidly—so rapidly that it sounded like familiar music, but played in staccato. "Well, from Washington, I'm booked into Pittsburgh, and from there we head to Boston, then back to Baltimore. Then from there, I'm not sure. What I am sure of is that through March and into April, NBC will be booking me into clubs and theaters not more than a day's drive from Washington."

He could see that Maude had a concerned look on her face. "And what happens in April?"

"Well, you'll head back to your brother's place in Texas or back to the ranch in Riverside. Rest up. And get this diabetes business under control."

"And you? What are you going to do?" Maude grabbed her husband's waist and held tightly.

He dropped his hands. Their eyes met. He softened his tone to a whisper. "I'll be going overseas." Eddie bit his lower lip as he struggled for words. "Look, sweetheart, even if you were feeling tip-top . . . "

Tears started to well up in Maude's eyes. "So where are you going, or should I say, where are you being sent?"

He was at a loss for words. "Look, I'm sorry, hon. You can't come with me on this one."

Maude sat down hard. She felt light-headed, out in the cold. "Do you know how long you'll be away?"

He turned from her, reaching for his coat, and shrugged his shoulders.

Maude slammed her hands on the arms of the chair and stood up. "Damn it, I'm your wife. And I have a right to know where you're going and for how long! I'll bet that Eleanor Roosevelt knows exactly where FDR is every minute!" She slammed her fist into her palm. "I'm going to tell Eleanor exactly how I feel about all this nonsense. She'll agree with me and make FDR tell me whatever I want to know."

Now Eddie was mortified. "Look, I know you're upset. Okay, okay, I'll tell you what I know, which isn't much. But you must promise me that you'll not mention a word of this to anyone, especially the Roosevelts."

He could still feel her anger. He caught himself and took a deep breath before he too said something he'd regret. "Do we have a deal?"

She winced, feeling awful. *What is wrong here?* Her eyes started to tear up. "Oh dear. Please forgive me, I don't know what came over me."

He took her hands in his. "I'm sorry to have upset you. So much has happened in the last few months. Sometimes I feel caught up in something that I have no control over." He started to pace around the room. "For more than a year now, the Navy Department has been training me for a mission. They even arranged this tour to be sure I was where specialists could train me. It's no coincidence that we wound up here, or that all our *Variety* reviews are glowing."

It was hard for her to believe what she was hearing. She was filled with questions. "But . . . "

"Shhh. No questions now. I know this is hard to understand. And you've probably figured out that the president is behind all that has been happening to us. So bringing any of this up to Mrs. Roosevelt will do absolutely nothing. But it will surely get me the boot, maybe scrapped from the program. Look, I've said this many times before, and I'm going to say it once more. I love my country, and I love the Navy. And yes, everything that has happened, and all that is about to happen, is scary as hell. But I've never felt more alive, never felt more a part of something larger than life itself, than I am feeling right at this moment. And when this is over, I'm sure no one will ever know exactly what took place." He paused, searching for words and hoping for some sign that she'd understood. "But if I'm to succeed, sweetheart, I'll need all the help and support you can muster."

Maude sat with her hands folded in her lap. "It's no wonder you chastised me for giving out too much information to *BMG* magazine, telling our friends about our relationship with the Roosevelts. But there is still so much I don't understand. What about the two shysters in Chicago trying to push you into manufacturing banjos? Is the government in the musical instrument business too? Why did you invest all that money? You seem to have forgotten what I've been doing for you ever since we were first married. Now you're telling me to stay home and mind the ranch."

At a loss for words, he just smiled at her.

"Stop it! This isn't funny. It's like you're living a separate life, one without me. Is that what you want?"

"Sweetheart, please. I've said that I need you—now, more than ever. I'm sorry for all the misunderstanding. But I have to do this assignment for the Navy—for the president. God knows I owe that man more than I could ever repay. And no, the government has nothing to do with our investment in the instrument company. People ask me every day where they can buy an Eddie Peabody instrument."

She could see the futility in discussing this further. "Let's go downstairs and get something to eat. I need more time to absorb all this, and suddenly I feel starved."

SIXTEEN

In Pittsburgh, Eddie shared the billing with a couple of jazz head-liners: Red Norvo and Mildred Bailey. There was also a dance group with two dozen leggy girls who worked in a banjo-strum-ming number as an intro to Eddie's Southern medley. On a cold and blustery Saturday after the evening performance, Eddie's ever-vigilant favorite commander entered his dressing room. But tonight Commander Scharf was dressed in civvies: white shirt with a wide gray-and-red-striped tie, dark gray slacks, and a sport coat. His shoes had the look of a military high-gloss spit-shine. Eddie was walking about in his boxers, brushing up his shoes, when the door opened. "Hey, hey, hey. Shut the door, please . . . the damn heat . . . Commander?"

The commander extended his hand. "I'm a civilian tonight, Eddie."

"Wonderful. Now come on in and sit down while I finish putting away my monkey suit. What brings you down here? I thought you'd be calling me at the hotel."

"Well, we thought it would be better if I introduced the two of you here at the theater."

Eddie turned abruptly. "Introduce? Who?"

"She's right down the hall. Shall I fetch her?"

"Sure, sure. Just let me get some trousers on." He grabbed his suit pants, slid them on, and threw the suspenders over his T-shirt. "You know what they say in the navy . . . " He looked up just as the commander reentered his room with a woman closely in tow. She looked college-aged as she strolled in wearing a knee-length wool skirt and sweater outfit. Her hair was cut short: bleached and bobbed like the other girls in the show. This young lady, however, was unlike other showgirls that Eddie had been introduced to. She was poised and self-confident, and she radiated maturity beyond her age.

Scharf could sense her effect. He broke the awkward silence and introduced the young lady as Marian Graham.

Eddie thought he recognized her, but when she spoke, he sensed a slight accent. "Very pleased to meet you. Marian, is it?" He extended his hand. She greeted Eddie and then sat on the small couch that faced his dressing table.

The commander pulled open a folding chair that was resting against the wall. "Marian will be in Europe touring with this dance group. I wanted you two to meet before you went in your separate directions. We, of course, are trying to align schedules such that you both are booked at the same theater in Paris, or at least theaters within the same district."

The commander paused to see if Eddie was following. "Marian is fluent in German and French, Eddie, as well as English. And she will be your best—perhaps your only—ticket out, should you ever be compromised."

Scharf paused while Eddie moved his ironing board and sat atop his dressing table. He continued. "Marian is a graduate of the Sorbonne school in Paris. Greg Ziemer, whom we talked about in Washington, was able to evacuate Marian and her mother in 1936. Her mother is Jewish, Eddie. And after the Nuremberg laws, her father, even though he was non-Jewish, was pressured to resign his university post and sever all ties to the government. Unfortunately, a month before they were all to leave Germany, he became gravely ill. His heart. Sadly, he died before he could be evacuated. But Marian and her mother continued on and settled in the Boston area. And now I'm pleased to say that, after some mild persuasion, she is a lieutenant, junior grade, in the Naval Reserve."

Eddie leaned over to congratulate her. As he extended his hand, she glanced at his wall clock. Abruptly she stood up. Both men stood as well.

"Guys, I'm sorry, but if I don't meet my roommate downstairs in two minutes, she'll leave without me. It's been a pleasure meeting you, Commander." She shook Eddie's hand and gave him a mock salute. "And, I look forward to reconnecting with you on the Continent." In a flash, she was through the door and down the hall.

Eddie turned and looked Scharf squarely in the eye. "Just what the hell do you guys need me for when you've got someone like her? She speaks the language, is drop-dead gorgeous, and could likely get into places I sure as hell couldn't."

"She knows nothing about submarines, Commander. You do. And if our intelligence gathering is working at all, by the time you arrive in Germany, you should be a person of particular interest to the German hierarchy." He glanced at this watch. "Oops, got to go, Commander."

They both stood and shook hands. Eddie gave the commander a puzzled look. As Scharf approached the door he turned and gave Eddie a reassuring smile. "Not to worry, Commander. You're in good hands." A cold chill ran up Eddie's spine. *I sure as hell hope so!*

NBC sent down a choreographer and stage manager to redesign the show so it could be moved on to the Hippodrome in Baltimore. During that two-week period, Eddie and Maude took some time off and booked a quiet country inn on Martha's Vineyard. While they were dining at a small seafood restaurant in Edgartown, a messenger interrupted and handed Eddie a note: *The president would be pleased if you and Mrs. Peabody could join the*

family for cocktails and an early dinner on the presidential yacht when it docks at Woods Hole on Saturday. Please indicate your response to the messenger.

Eddie verbally accepted the invitation.

Maude was visibly disturbed by the interruption. "I don't understand it. How in the world could anyone find us? We didn't know ourselves where we'd be until we got here." She cautiously looked around the room. She whispered, "Someone must be following us!"

"So?"

"So? So what kind of a life . . . ? But no, you have to go and rejoin the navy."

Eddie could see that she was getting worked up and had more to say. He took a sip of wine, smiled, and then put his finger to his lips to signal to her to calm down.

She leaned forward and whispered loudly, "We escape for a weekend, and then someone—"

He raised his hand for her to stop. "But I thought you liked having dinner with the Roosevelts. Besides, we've never been on the president's yacht. It should be fun."

The ferry from Martha's Vineyard docked at Woods Hole. A sailor met them as they disembarked and drove them some three hundred yards to where the president's yacht was docked. Two marines stood guard at the entryway. Eddie and Maude could see no one on board. A hostess quickly appeared from one of the salons and greeted them. She told them that the president and first lady were attending a Democratic Party planning luncheon in Hyannis Port, and she suggested that they relax, have a cocktail, and catch some sun. "The president should return within an hour, so please make yourselves comfortable."

Within minutes of the president's arrival, the ship was filled with people. The ship cast off and sailed out past the Vineyard toward Nantucket. The weather was cooperative, the winds were light, and the temperature was cool but comfortable. The sun was beginning to set, and the white clapboard mansions along the coast of Martha's Vineyard seemed to glow as they motored by. Eddie was in the salon, where the president had a small upright piano. Soon music and liquor began to flow, and Eddie entertained the guests for more than an hour.

As the gathering began to settle down, FDR wheeled up to the ship's bow, where he saw Eddie leaning over the railing, watching the ship cut effortlessly through the dark, calm water. The president filled his cigarette holder and lit up. "You love the sea, don't you, son?"

Eddie turned, somewhat startled, as he hadn't heard the man approach. "Yes, sir, I do."

"You know you're about to ship out, in a couple of weeks, I believe."

"Yes, sir, I figured we were close." The moist salt air was invigorating and seemed to clear his head of all worries. He breathed deeply and leaned back against the railing. He stared up at the star-studded sky. "I believe everyone has done their best preparing me for this job, sir. Maude heads back to Riverside in two weeks. And now I'm anxious to get on with it."

"I know you are, sailor, and I, for one, am damned proud of you. I only wish . . . " FDR's words trailed off as he pointed westward toward the last vestiges of the setting sun. "Red sky in the morning, sailor's warning—red sky at night, sailor's delight. Magnificent. Isn't it?"

Eddie glanced at the sunset but felt drawn to FDR's face. He didn't understand much about politics or the War Powers Act; he didn't understand Washington, for that matter; but he did love this man. "I'll do my duty, sir. And we will find out just what that little bastard is up to."

FDR broke into that famous broad smile but continued to watch the fading sunset. "I know you will, my friend." He took a drag on his cigarette. "Be careful over there. We don't have the kind of allies we really need right now. Stay close to your contacts. And if anything goes awry, don't hesitate for one minute to get the hell out of there." He reached out to touch Eddie's arm. "I had a great time today. I want you back here and in one piece."

Eddie saluted. "That makes two of us, sir."

Eleanor approached. "Franklin, it's getting cold, and I want you to come inside and wrap up."

Commander Scharf met with Eddie nearly every other day, while Eddie spent much of his downtime reviewing dossiers on many of the higher-ranking members of the German government.

Maude could see her husband becoming more and more absorbed. One morning, after he had showered and shaved, Eddie caught her sitting on the bed, thumbing through a report on General Wilhelm Keitel, Hitler's chief of staff. He quickly grabbed the report off her lap and mildly admonished her for looking through a folder that, he pointed out, was clearly marked CLASSIFIED SECRET.

She folded her arms somewhat defiantly. "If it's meant to be secret, why don't they just put it in a locked box?"

"Would that have stopped you?"

"Well, a wife's got a right." She turned away.

"Look, hon, the Navy wants me to be on my toes, be the gracious ambassador. Should the Germans let me in, I must be able to recognize cabinet ministers and other high-ranking military officers." He glanced at his wife and could see the pensive, frightened look on her face.

She squeezed his hand. "We've always been together, whatever crossed our path. And now? I'm sorry, but this Navy business scares me to death."

SEVENTEEN

Finishing his coffee, Eddie opened the envelope containing his tentative itinerary. *The Shakespeare Theater in Liverpool on April 14, then traveling north to the Tivoli Theater in Aberdeen, Scotland. A roadshow, British Decca Recording Studios . . . This is a fine tour of England, but I don't see any dates for the continent, or Hamburg, for that matter.*

A handwritten note from Commander Scharf was attached.

Eddie,

We're still firming things up, but it looks now like the earliest we'll be able to get you in-country will be December or January. Remember your accompanist from your first tour, Jonathon Pitts? Mr. Pitts has dual citizenship. He's a Brit and has a German passport as well. He's fluent in the language, and he knows Mr. Ziemer.

The picture was now complete. He liked the idea of Johnny being his accompanist and booking manager. Things were looking a little brighter.

★ ★ ★

Maude was packed and ready to go, but her mood was dark. The phone rang.

Eddie picked up and was pleased to recognize Scharf's voice. "Have you had a chance to review the itinerary and my note?"

"Yes, sir. It's in my pocket, but I looked it over earlier this morning."

"We've been scurrying like mice, keeping an eye on the German embassy. We wanted to see if anyone's been following you."

"And?"

"So far, nothing. But we've had a couple of sleepless nights. Is Maude still with you?"

"She will be starting back to Riverside tomorrow."

"Right. We'll have someone keep an eye on Maude till you're on your way. We shouldn't be discussing this over the phone, so I'll be brief. German intelligence is strong over here. But to date, we haven't uncovered anything more than normal written correspondence. The State Department believes that the German hierarchy is pleased with our War Policy Act and figures we'll remain neutral like Switzerland, should they start stirring the pot."

He could see that Maude didn't want her mood disturbed by any idle chitchat. "It'll all work out, babe—you'll see. And before you know it, I'll be back and needing your advice on how to market banjos from our new factory. This European tour will just be another feather in our cap."

"Look, you and I both know that right now you're so tied up in this navy business, a team of wild horses couldn't pull you away." She waited for her him to deny her accusation. He didn't bite. She continued, "And while you're over there, traipsing all over and doing who knows what, I'll be stuck in California. And if those two charlatans from Chicago ever set foot on our property, asking for more money, I'll send them packing with buckshot in their britches."

"Feel better now?"

A man sitting in a lobby lounge chair rustled a newspaper. Eddie and Maude both stared at the bold-faced headline:

GERMAN TROOPS OCCUPY AUSTRIA

THE UNITED STATES ALONG WITH
GREAT BRITAIN AND FRANCE LODGE PROTEST
AUSTRIAN CHANCELLOR, KURT VON SCHUSCHNIGG, STEPS DOWN

Maude stopped suddenly as a chill ran down her spine. "Now I'm really frightened." She turned to face him, touching his shoulder. "I want to go with you. No! Actually, I don't want you to go!" She covered her face with her hands. "Oh, dear God, I don't know." Her breathing became shallow, and her eyes teared.

Eddie grabbed her hand and squeezed it hard. "Calm down, sweetheart, and try to relax."

Maude's luggage had been loaded, and the limousine was ready to depart. Eddie opened the rear door for her.

"Aren't you coming to the station?"

"I can't, love. I've got rehearsal in forty minutes. Phone me when you get back to Riverside." He clutched her face and kissed her, hard. "Now, remember, Johnny Pitts will be with me over there. You remember him. He knows the ropes." He patted her on the butt as he helped her into the backseat. "I'll write you weekly, and call when I'm able. I love you, babe. Don't worry, everything will be peaches and cream."

Maude returned to the ranch safely, and her brother consented to spend the summer with her in Riverside to help her with the orange harvest.

Eddie boarded a passenger ship in Boston on April 7 and arrived in Southampton, England, on the twelfth. The voyage was uneventful. The ship sailed west from Southampton and up the coast to Liverpool, its final destination.

Jonathon Pitts greeted him at the dock in Liverpool. He was a tall, thin man with light reddish-blond hair not unlike his own. Eddie remembered him as Johnny, always well groomed, with an engaging smile—an excellent technician, but wound very tight. After a cordial greeting, Johnny helped him hustle through customs. He then made arrangements with one of the local transport companies to transport Eddie's gear to the Shakespeare Theater. *This talented accompanist and arranger is always nervous and uptight—must be his German blood.*

They took a cab to a nearby hotel. Eddie noticed that the lobby bar was small; there was only space for two stools and not much standing room. *What the hell? The bar in Rudy's office is larger than this.* They found an unoccupied corner in the adjacent room.

"Well, Johnny, my good friend, here's to you. You're a sight for sore eyes. And it was damn nice of you to meet me at the dock today. When the commander indicated that you—"

Johnny put his finger against his lip. "You know I always enjoy working with you. This is an opportunity of a lifetime." Eddie noticed that the man's eyes darted around the small room. "You must be very tired from your journey—probably want to call home and let your wife know you've made it. I'll take you over to the theater for introductions after you've had a bit of a rest."

He could see that his friend was nervous and in a hurry. He grimaced as he threw down his drink. "Damn it! When are you people going to discover ice cubes?"

"Why you Americans would ruin a perfectly good drink with ice is a mystery that the world has pondered for more than a hundred and fifty years."

Johnny escorted Eddie to his room on the pretext of reviewing some sheet music. He immediately surveyed every lamp and behind each wall print. He looked out the window and scoped out the immediate area. "Sorry about cutting you off in the lounge, old chap, but I'm afraid Europe—and England, for that matter—has hotted up since you last visited." He closed the curtains around the one window in the room after he finished his inspection. "Right now it seems that caution is the better part of valor." Feeling confident that Eddie's room was free of any listening devices, Johnny began to relax; he loosened his tie and sat in the upholstered chair between the window and a small desk. "I'm sure your Navy Department has told you all about me by now, so I'll cut right to the chase, as you Americans are so fond of saying. I've been setting up shows and traveling between here and the Continent for about six years now. In my opinion, Germany is a powder keg just waiting to explode. To make things worse, it seems that everyone in London, if you believe the papers, is either pro-communist or pacifist. Everyone is deathly afraid of another conflagration. The prime minister has been quoted saying that he would do most anything to avoid confrontation with the Germans. Fortunately, not everyone in Parliament agrees."

Eddie listened intently, but he was unaware of who England's prime minister was or what was happening politically in Europe. His brow furrowed in puzzlement.

His friend read the look. "The bottom line is that today there are enough German spies in England to fill that ship you just came in on. And the last thing I want to happen is for some eager young Nazi to look twice, at either you or me. So from here forward, we stick to music and theater scheduling whenever we talk outside these walls. Okay?"

The intensity in Johnny's voice clearly indicated that now was not the time to joke about. "You got it, skipper. And if I get out of hand, or whatever, don't hesitate to give me a quick kick in the slats."

The break in tension felt good, and Johnny chuckled. "By jolly, it's good to see you, and to be working with you again, my friend. And listen, once we get into our routine, we'll forget all about who's a Nazi and who's not. Quite likely it'll be several months before we get the go-ahead anyway."

"That long? Why's that?"

"Two reasons, really. First, I don't have solid confirmation for a theater in Hamburg. Second, the Germans are fond of American jazz in general, but you are relatively unheard of on the continent. What we've got to do, and in short order, is to get you so much exposure and press coverage here that the theaters in Germany come screaming at me to get you before you head back to the States."

Eddie pulled out the itinerary that Scharf had given him.

"What have you got here, mate? Bloody 'ell. Well, this looks pretty much up to date. I've taken an option with the Decca studio, and we'll have to take a train to London this coming week to take advantage. I've also managed to wangle an advanced spot on the production line. So if we're lucky, we should have recordings by Mr. Banjo in the shops—and on the radio, for that matter—by the first of June." Johnny crossed himself in the traditional Catholic manner.

"That's wonderful, pal. Say, if you don't mind, I'd like to walk over to the theater and check my instruments."

"You want to see what they broke, eh? Righto!"

Eddie found it difficult to know when Johnny was kidding and when he was serious. He could see that the man had been dead serious while inspecting his room, but when it came to casual conversation, he turned nervous and uncomfortable.

The Shakespeare Theater was in need of some repair, but it was not too different from many of the theaters in the United States. He checked over his instruments and concluded that the shipping trunks had done their job. The theater's show producer indicated that dress rehearsal would be the following day at 10:00 AM.

At the hotel, a telegram had arrived, confirming their studio time in London. The two men reviewed some tune selections and then headed down to a local pub Johnny liked for their fish and chips.

That evening, Eddie called Maude. It was nearly 7:30 AM California time the next day. "Hi, sweetheart, I'm in Liverpool. Sorry about the connection and the time difference. All is well here, and the trip over was uneventful."

"Good gracious, it's good to hear your voice. Oh my, I just looked at the clock. Did you connect with . . . oh, what's his name? And how's the show? The papers are full of stories about all the troubles over there. Some editorials are saying that war is imminent. I'm frightened to death, dear."

"Everything is fine, and yes, I did connect with—you remember—Johnny Pitts. He's been a godsend. So, how are things at the ranch? When is your brother coming over?"

"He'll be here next month, and all looks well right now. But I can't say the same for those hooligans in Chicago. Do you know they had the audacity to ask me for more money?"

Eddie could sense the conversation deteriorating, and he wasn't up to it. "I'll deal with those guys when I return, sweetheart. And if they call again, just tell them to put everything on hold till I return. Okay?" There was a swooshing on the line that sounded like an incoming wave. "Maude, are you there?" No answer. "I love you, sweetheart." No answer. Eddie sighed and returned the phone to its cradle.

Johnny had worked previously with the show's producer and was able to anticipate song selections where he knew the show needed a boost. He also wanted to increase Eddie's stage time. "Audiences will love the little banjo boy from America, I tell you. It will be a moneymaker you can count on."

Early Wednesday morning they boarded the train for London, and after a short cab ride from Victoria Station, they arrived at British Decca for their recording session. After four hours of recording, though exhausted, Eddie felt upbeat and had a sense of accomplishment. "We knocked out a couple of good ones this morning, eh, pal?"

"Aye, mate. By the end of summer, everyone from Inverness to Monte Carlo should be clamoring for you. All we need now is an interview on BBC, and we'll be on our way. Say, inasmuch as you've brought us good weather, why don't we have a walk down past the park for some fresh air? I know a nearby pub that serves a great ploughman's."

"Fine with me. I could use the walk."

They walked past the roundabout, toward Marble Arch. Eddie looked left instead of right and nearly stepped out in front of an oncoming taxi. With an audible gasp, Johnny quickly grabbed him by the collar. Eddie felt embarrassed, and a prickly feeling traversed the back of his neck. He looked around at the people scurrying about but saw nothing out of the ordinary. At Hyde Park large crowds had gathered around two young men standing on orange crates, yelling at each other. They approached, and Johnny stopped to comment on the two men in Speakers' Corner. "Here, my friend, anyone can turn up unannounced and talk on almost any subject."

Eddie, however, looked frozen in place. He was staring intently off to his right.

Johnny tried to ascertain what had caught Eddie's eye. There, leaning against a tree and looking directly at both of them, was a man; he was about Eddie's height, but he had a square jaw jutting defiantly outward. This man was definitely not English. "That man leaning against the tree, looking over at us—do you know him?"

"I don't know. But I can't explain it. I was looking over the crowd and caught sight of this guy. I was about to call out his name when you said something."

They both looked up toward the tree, but there was no one about.

Eddie broke the silence. "He looked an awful lot like someone I met some time ago in New York—someone I'd forgotten about and hoped I'd never see again."

"Well . . . ?"

"I think he was a banjo player at a German restaurant in New York. But that doesn't make any sense, does it?"

"Do you think this man, for whatever reason, followed you here to London?"

"It doesn't make any sense if he did."

"Well, the fellow seems to have disappeared—for now, anyway."

The two young men were still debating one another atop their respective orange crates. One of the bespectacled men, dressed in a tattered tweed coat and a bow tie, was speaking. "People! Listen to me! The proletariat's advance guard will lead all of us to a new political, economic, and intellectual life. The Nazis tell us of a new order! Yet they are unable to realize that our new order, and their own people, will swallow them up."

The other speaker, a tall, very young boy with close-cropped blond hair, was wearing a uniform. Eddie thought at first glance that he was a fellow Boy Scout. The Nazi armband on the boy's sleeve, however, clearly indicated otherwise. He noticed several more young boys, also in uniform, dispersed within the crowd. *What a shame!*

"You communists are always talking about your world revolution. Well, we'll see whose destiny it truly is to rule the world—the superior Aryan race, or your humble and ignorant proletariat. Look at Austria. Chancellor Seyss pleads for troops to restore order after you communists resort to street fighting. People, I ask you, who speaks the truth? Is it our beloved führer, or that inferior Slav in Russia who can do nothing but incite riots and murder his own people?" There was a spontaneous *"Sieg Heil! Sieg Heil!"* from the boys surrounding the young Nazis.

Eddie had never seen or heard anything like it in his life. He turned to his friend. "What the hell is going on here?"

"This is Speaker's Corner, mate. Just a bunch of communists down from Cambridge to have a holler at the Nazis. Nothing more. They've been getting after it maybe once a month this summer. Anybody can speak his mind here if they sign up, and nobody seems to bother. We can't see them, but I'm sure the bobbies are nearby."

Just then, someone standing near the two men began shouting out in an American accent, "And workers around the world will unite! They will bury the filthy-rich capitalists—warmongers, who do nothing but take bread out of the mouths and break the backs of working people at every factory—like Roosevelt. As far as I'm concerned, he may as well be a Nazi."

That did it. Eddie was incensed. He moved toward the scruffy young man twirling his fist in the air and spewing what Eddie thought was nothing short of treason.

Johnny looked up when he saw Eddie moving and tried to follow. The throngs of young people slowed him. He'd heard someone shout something, but he hadn't been paying attention.

Eddie had weaved his way close to the boisterous individual.

He could see that the unkempt man had a bottle of beer in his left hand and was unsteady on his feet. To his surprise, the inebriated man turned suddenly. "So what's your problem, buddy?"

Within a blink of an eye, Eddie reached out with his left hand and threw the man's beer in his face, and then he punched him square in the nose with a reaching right. "You, you traitorous son of a bitch."

The man was startled and fell backward, his head bouncing off a tree. Johnny was there by now, and he forcibly ushered Eddie away from some stunned onlookers. "Move it, mate! Quick time, now! And don't even think about looking back." He guided Eddie across the street and down an alleyway, into the back entrance of a small pub that faced Piccadilly.

They slid into a corner table next to a window overlooking the street entrance to the pub. Johnny quickly ordered two plough- man's and two half-pints from a barmaid. When she was out of earshot, he leaned across the table. "What the hell got into you, mate? One minute we're listening to some loud-mouthed kids, the next you're givin' a clip to some bloke!"

"Did you hear that son of a—"

"Look, I don't bloody care what the hell he said or didn't say. The last thing you or I need right now is a bunch of local Nazis, commies—or the bloody king, for that matter—taking any notice of us! If the bobbies had pinched us, the next day, people would be reading how Eddie Peabody punched out some bloke on Hyde Corner. And that, my friend, would surely finish this mission!" The barmaid interrupted the conversation with two plates of bread, cheese, and salad. "Blimey, I had no idea you were such a loose cannon—with one hell of a right cross to boot, I might add."

Eddie started to chuckle, and both men began to relax. "Sorry about that, my friend. I lost my head, and one punch. I hope my right hand cooperates this afternoon." Eddie wriggled the fingers of his right hand. "Oh well. It's nice to know I've still got it."

EIGHTEEN

Reporters were on hand when Eddie visited the local *BMG* club in Aberdeen, Scotland. After playing several tunes with the local players, the club president took several photos of Eddie clowning with members.

Johnny corralled all the reporters interested in a story. A young man in front shouted the first question: "Tell us, Mr. Pitts, how does Mr. Peabody balance his musical career with a military career?"

Johnny was suddenly at a loss for words, and he looked perplexed. The reporter noticed, so he continued, "I telephoned the archives secretary in London yesterday. It seems that Mrs. Peabody forwarded a yearly review of her husband's career to the *BMG* editor. The magazine printed excerpts from her letter."

Johnny's hesitation had the others scrambling for their notepads. The reporter maintained his attack. "Perhaps we should interview Mr. Peabody directly?"

Johnny raised his hands, palms up. He knew he needed to deflect this query. "Gentlemen!" He lowered his voice. "Please, I'm aware of Mrs. Peabody's letter of December of last year, I believe. You caught me off guard. I didn't expect to be grilled right out of the barrel by someone obviously having done some homework, especially way up here in Aberdeen." Laughter broke the tension, but he could see that pencils were at the ready. "Now, let me first of all answer the question by saying yes, Eddie was performing in the Washington DC area in December. And the Roosevelts did invite him, and Mrs. Peabody, to a White House Christmas party." He started to pace and couched his words with as much feeling as he could muster. "Now, please listen carefully, gentlemen. I'm going to let you in on something completely off the record. So please, no notes. Okay?"

They all nodded, folded their small notebooks, and inched closer to catch every word. The noise level had dropped to where one could hear the squeak of a new pair of leather shoes.

Johnny let out a deep sigh and then proceeded to fill them in with the story he'd concocted only seconds before. "President Roosevelt is fascinated by banjo music, especially the stuff this little guy performs on his four-string harp. The president befriended Eddie and coerced him into revealing some of the tricks he routinely performs on the banjo. As a token of his appreciation, the president granted Eddie an honorary commission, just like the honors the king regularly confers on this bloke or that. So you can clearly see, there's no other career for little Eddie, just his banjo and the magic only he can strum up. And gentlemen, please, Eddie guards his relationship with the president and his honorary commission very closely. Anyone would—wouldn't you agree? So again, please, if anything I've just told you winds up in print—well, Eddie will be hopping mad, and so will I." He stopped pacing, folded his hands behind his back, and faced them with a smile. " Now, if you would like to write about our tour, the theater production, or his new recording releases, please open up your books. Gentlemen, I guarantee you'll have your exclusive."

The gamble had worked. Pencils were flying over paper as he started with the new recordings and went on to their scheduled bookings. He hoped and prayed there would be no further mention of the president or Eddie's commission.

Soon radio stations were playing "Lambeth Walk" and "Love

Walked In," by the new jazz sensation from America, Mr. Banjo. By the time Eddie opened in Edinburgh, the BBC had run a twenty-minute special on "American jazz hits the Highlands, featuring the American jazz banjoist Eddie Peabody." Theater attendance swelled, and shows were held over.

The waiter came over to warm Eddie's cup of half hot milk and half very strong coffee. Eddie turned to Johnny and asked, "what'll you have, my friend?"

"Just coffee, please. Yes, white, please. Mate, this is just what the doctor ordered. The coastal stations on the continent will pick up on what the BBC is playing, and soon Mr. Banjo will be in demand everywhere. I've got to get in touch with London."

"What's up?"

The waiter poured Johnny's coffee from two containers. "The Palace Theater in Hamburg, mate. Surely there's been some communication from them by now."

Eddie had picked up a copy of the local paper, and he began to peruse the headlines.

Sudeten Minority in Czechoslovakia Rally for Greater Autonomy

Hitler Demands Cession of the Sudetenland to Germany

His grasp of European geography was poor, but he could see that with the annexation of Austria, and now a portion of Czechoslovakia, it was looking like Hitler had a premeditated plan. The question was, how far would he go? *It's just a matter of time. Will England and France continue to put up with this arrogant bastard?*

On the train to London, they sat quietly and tried to relax and catch up on some much-needed sleep. As the train approached King's Cross Station, Johnny saw that Eddie was starting to wake up. "Nothing beats first class when you need a little quiet, eh?"

"Right you are. Boy, I was out like a light. I guess I needed it. So, anything new on the agenda?"

"I received a call last night from my contact at the US embassy. They're targeting December for our insertion."

"December?"

"Right. That gives us about two more months to build up your presence and whet the appetite of our German friends. They're living pretty high over there right now, and the marks are flowing freely for everything from Swedish steel to lavish French cabaret shows. So if they'll soon be wanting to hear and see the great American jazz musician in person, that is precisely what we'll give them."

They returned to their favorite Argyle Street hotel; both were beat, so they took in a casual dinner at a nearby pub. On the way Eddie noticed that Harry Reser, the great British classic banjoist, was performing at one of the private clubs near Regent Street. "You know, I should probably stop by and perhaps meet the gentleman."

"That's a private gentlemen's club, mate. And without a membership, you might get a courtesy look-about. Then again, you might not get past the doorman."

"Well, maybe I'll just join this gentlemen's club!"

"Right. Do be careful, won't you, old boy? Perhaps I should go along? You know, bridge the cultural and language barrier."

They both started to laugh. Eddie put his arm around his friend. "Perhaps you should go along. I'm afraid I do need a keeper."

They took a cab to Trafalgar Square and walked past the National Gallery toward Regents Street. They found the club, but the doorman quickly informed them that this was a private club for "Special Service" government employees. No amount of money, nothing short of an invitation from the king himself would allow them past this formidable man. He politely informed them that he would let Mr. Reser know that a Mr. Peabody and friend send their regards.

They walked off to flag a cab. "Is this Reser well known in America?"

"No, no. I recently read a letter he sent to the editor of a trade magazine. He said he thought my showmanship was just a cover for my lack of technical ability."

Johnny stopped and looked at his friend. "Really?"

"So I thought I'd pop in and have a listen. Maybe he'd like to play a few tunes with me. You know, for the folks in his audience—they might like a little cross-cultural entertainment."

"Bloody 'ell, am I glad that bloke at the entrance stood his ground."

The following afternoon, after rehearsal, two groups of booking agents, scouting for the Scala theater in Berlin and the Moulin Rouge in Paris, sent a messenger with an invitation for Eddie and his manager to dine with them at the Carvery that evening.

"The blokes scouting for the Scala are Nazis, I'm sure of it. Germans love American jazz, but since the '36 Olympics and Jesse Owens, the bastards won't grant a black musician a visa for love nor money. Please, my friend, avoid talking to these blighters if you can. Remember, our mission is to gather information—not engage the enemy."

"Relax, pal. I promise not to provoke an international incident. Anyway, the show at the Moulin should be a lot more interesting—the girls are prettier."

That evening, as they were reviewing some arrangements they'd been working on, four arrogant-looking young men entered the large room. Three were wearing poorly tailored dark gray worsted wool suits. The third young man was wearing a brown uniform with a leather strap draped diagonally across his chest, and a Nazi armband. One of the young men looked like one of the speakers arguing with the communists in Hyde Park.

Suddenly, a fifth man entered in a rush. As he approached Eddie, recognition began to set in. He was certain that this was the same guy that had been following him in the park. All were now surrounding them at the bar. The fifth man stepped forward and, with a smile, extended his hand. "Herr Peabody, I do hope you remember me . . . the Hofbrau House in New York? Earnst Heinz."

He greeted the man with a handshake and a nod.

"I am with the band at the Scala Theater in Berlin now." The man was clearly pleased with himself. He had moved up in the world and was watching Eddie's reaction. "We are here to book some new acts, for the holidays. And of course when I heard you were in London, I persuaded my colleagues here to help me scout you." Heinz swept his arm to indicate the unkempt Nazi goons that had accompanied him. He cleared his throat. "It's strange that none of your records have made it to Germany. We did hear one song on the radio near Amsterdam." Heinz grinned like a schoolyard bully as he rocked back and forth from heel to toe. "I am doing much better now that I've returned to a country that rewards its loyal citizens. We have been sold out every night since I started at the Scala. And the press—they have been so good to me—I'm embarrassed to speak of it. But if you were headlining there, with me . . . *mein Gott!*"

The other two gentlemen were noticeably uncomfortable and annoyed with Herr Heinz's monologue. Their sharp, unblinking eyes spoke volumes. One gentleman, who seemed in charge, gave a brief, courteous bow to Eddie and then began reviewing available dates and standard fees that would be reviewed and adjusted after a set period.

I didn't think I'd ever see this sorry excuse for a musician, ever again. And why, why the hell have you been following me? "Ernie, tell me, how did you know I was in London?"

A frown crossed Heinz's brow, and he cleared his throat. "I was speaking at one of our newest Nazi youth . . . " He stretched his arm to introduce Eddie to the young man in the brown-shirt uniform.

One of the suits quickly stepped in front and interrupted the introduction. He smiled thinly at Eddie and, in a controlled, thickly accented whisper, informed him that he and his partner regularly visited Paris and London to scout out the traveling American jazz singers and musicians. "The world today seems fascinated with everything American—their clothes, their cars, and especially their music. And many in Germany, to the wonderment of every sensible Wagner enthusiast, seem especially fond of their barbaric, African-influenced jazz."

"Really?" The ignorant young man was goading him. *What the hell is going on here?*

Johnny was looking up toward the entrance. Two well-dressed gentlemen and a drop-dead gorgeous lady wearing a large brimmed hat were promenading toward a corner table. The lady caught everyone's eye.

The gray suit sensed he'd agitated the American. He politely told his comrades, in German, that they had concluded their business and it was time to politely leave.

Heinz, however, was clearly obsessed and wanted to continue to harass his nemesis. He'd been shadowing the man all day, hoping to find something revealing. He knew in his heart that this man with the banjo was a fraud, maybe a closet Jew.

Johnny was able to secure firm theater dates, and they exchanged telephone numbers. The Germans (except Heinz, of course) seemed pleased with the conclusion of their assignment. As if on cue, they bowed and began a fast-paced walk toward the exit.

The expression on Heinz's face masked the deep frustration he felt. He jerked suddenly when his comrades took their leave. "Well, have a nice tour, Herr Peabody. I expect the next time we meet, you'll be in my country." He tried to smile as he quickly turned and hurried to catch up with the others.

"Who the bloody 'ell was that odd fellow you were chatting with? He seemed to know you but was acting very strange."

Eddie relaxed his shoulders and felt a sudden release of tension. "I'm not sure I can explain that guy or his behavior. Right now, though, I feel exhausted."

"Order something special for yourself, my friend, and relax. I'll be off schmoozing with the Paris scouts that just came in. So enjoy your peace and quiet."

Johnny approached a corner table with his arms spread wide. There were the normal hugs and kisses and Johnny noticed that champagne was being served.

After the appropriate toast to everyone's good health and a prayer for continued peace with Germany, the Parisian agents indicated that they were in London to check out Fats Waller, Florence Desmond, Max Miller, and Eddie Peabody for some upcoming dates at the Moulin Rouge.

Johnny returned to his friend, and they retreated to a quiet corner of the lounge. "We'll have no troubles getting you booked into the Moulin—they loved you, mate. And if another of your tunes hits the charts, they'll be clamoring all over Europe for Mr. Banjo. It's probably the only time I ever heard the French agree on anything. Now, not to worry about the road show here in England, mate. Danny Farrell, the producer, will rewrite the show to accommodate either Ken Harvey or Freddie Morgan."

"Freddie Morgan? Hey, neither of those guys can do what I do."

"That's quite right—spot on, as we say over here, mate. But don't forget what you're over here for." He grabbed Eddie's arm. "We're at bloody war over here—it just hasn't been declared as yet." He loosened his grip and ran his other hand through his thinning hair. "Sorry, mate. We've both got important jobs to do now, and neither one of us wants to muck it up. Oh hell, jolly good show this evening, my friend."

At the Decca studios, Eddie and an eight-piece British group knocked out five songs that were included on two new 78-rpm records: "Strike Up the Band," "My Heaven in the Pines," "When the Organ Played 'O Promise Me,'" "Love's Old Sweet Song," and "Desert Song." They were immediate hits, getting radio time on Dutch, Belgian, French, and even German channels as well as the popular English stations.

The road show toured most of the borough theaters that surrounded London. At the Empire Theater in Hackney, Eddie was getting ready for a show in his dressing room when, without a knock or introduction, an attractive young woman abruptly walked in. At a quick glance he noticed that her hair was bobbed short and she wore a dark pleated wool kilt and a sweater that accentuated her showgirl figure. She walked casually over to one of the dusty dressing-room chairs. Her eyes caught his, and she smiled.

He returned the smile. "Good evening, Lieutenant."

"Good evening yourself, Commander. Sorry to barge in on you, but our troupe was just informed that after we close in Scotland, we've been booked into Paris, the Moulin Rouge. And rumor has it that you'll be performing there in early December. Any truth to that?"

He took a deep breath. "Yes, that's correct . . . Marian, isn't it?"

She nodded and then quickly put two fingers to her mouth to indicate that they should cease talking. She listened for a second as several sets of footsteps passed by, and then she shrugged her shoulders in a gesture of false alarm. She startled him again when she suddenly jumped up. "Well, gotta run. I'm glad we've finally connected. See you in Paris. Bye." And in a flash, she was gone.

Eddie saluted as she closed the door. He continued to adjust the bows on his tie, then turned and looked into the mirror. *Damn nice to see you too, babe! Never a dull moment!*

London Entertainment Review, August 22, 1938

The London Palladium Show, which opened this week, is again replete with outstanding showmen, particularly Eddie Peabody, no stranger to this country, but making his first appearance at the GTC "ace" house. Peabody gives dynamic performances on banjo, a 16-string harp guitar, and a violin, showing virtuosity upon each instrument . . . At the end they were yelling for more from the pint-sized Mr. Peabody.

Johnny was waiting on Eddie reading the review. They were on their way to a record signing in Chelsea. "Bloody 'ell, another fine review. And have look at this—record sales continue to climb! My boy, you're going to be the biggest thing to hit Germany since the Graf Zeppelin. And by the way, I just got a call from a radio station just outside Amsterdam. They want to do a two-week special on American jazz artists, and they want you to kick it off in early December. They're even bugging Decca for an exclusive in Belgium and Holland. It might be our first in on the Continent—that's if our bosses give us the thumbs-up. I'll swing by the embassy in the morning."

Eddie was happy with the review but felt apprehensive. The mission was about to begin.

"Everything seems to be fitting in nicely, mate. We should have a firm commitment from Amsterdam soon, then confirmation from Berlin, and Hamburg should follow. This is just what we've been waiting all these months for." They both left the hotel in silence.

At the American embassy, the message was short but to the point. *Lobster Pen is a go.* Johnny stuffed the message in his coat pocket and quickly exited. He stopped on the walkway at the iron fencing surrounding the building and looked up into the sky. *Only the London naval attaché and the Navy Department in Washington have knowledge of Lobster Pen—and me, of course. Well, mate, here we go!*

"We're on, my friend. We've been given the go-ahead. Tomorrow I'll get us our visas and some decent hotel accommodations, then we're set. Let's have a pint and celebrate, what say?"

"After waiting nearly six months, I'd love to tip one with you."

"Say, you know I'm feeling so confident of late that I might even ask for more money. Cheers, mate. And may you bloody colonists finally get it right one day." They both had a chuckle and enjoyed the moment.

NINETEEN

Eddie set aside the morning *Times* with its glaring headline:

ECONOMIC CRISIS IN FRANCE DEEPENS

GOLD STOCKS IN THE BANK OF FRANCE SHRINK—
FRANC TAKEN OFF THE GOLD STANDARD

He opened a letter sent to him from the editor of *BMG* magazine.

Dear Sir,

Regarding the controversy about America's or England's Greatest Banjoist, I am surprised at Harry Reser's letter in the June issue of *BMG*. That he is picking holes in Eddie Peabody's playing is very evident and it is beyond me that a player of Reser's ability should waste time decrying the efforts of an outstanding performance like Peabody's. Anyone interested in the Theater World (not the Concert World) knows that billing acts such as The World's Greatest Banjoist is the idea of the booking agents to boost the player concerned and, providing the player can entertain the public 100 percent, everybody is quite happy. For Reser to talk about educating the public to understand the difference between the player and the player-showman is futile. The public desires entertainment, not education. If Reser could imitate birds and wave his body about sufficiently he would find that the public would pay him handsomely for his efforts. Perhaps his inability to do so makes him envious. I have just had the pleasure of seeing Eddie Peabody imitate birds and slide up and down the neck of his banjo at the Pavilion Theater, Glasgow. And I can say that in Eddie's show we, undoubtedly, have the finest banjo act ever to hit these shores. His performance will do more to popularize the banjo than that of any other vaudeville artist I know. Good luck Eddie. Mr. Reser would profit better by getting on with his job than slinging mud.

Sincerely Yours,
Fred Beattie
Past President BMG, Glasgow

He smiled to himself as he folded up the letter. *Well, now, aren't we a wee bit glad we didn't get into that fracas a couple of months ago? And as dear old Dad used to say, if you really are good at something, you don't have to tell anybody about it.*

Johnny had pulled out an adjacent chair and quietly sat next to his friend.

Eddie glanced up. "Damn it, man! Where the hell have you been? I was about to call the embassy." He could see that his friend hadn't shaved, and his hair was more askew than usual. "You've been hiding in Soho, haven't you?"

His friend gently turned over his coffee cup as a waiter came over. "Her name is Hilda. She's just returned from the continent. She said that things are getting tougher and tighter in Germany, even as we speak. She said that except for military escorts on goods coming into the country, most civilian border crossings have come to a halt."

"Well, well. Hilda, you say her name was. I always knew you were a gentleman and a scholar, my friend. The *Times* here says that the French are running out of money. So how are our bookings holding up?"

"Don't believe any of that crap in print. No one really understands the French and their politics. French socialists and communists have been fighting each other since before the war. And now all they do is follow Neville Chamberlain around like a bloody puppy dog." He leaned back and took another swallow of coffee. "I'm happy to say that the Moulin Rouge has been around longer than any French republic. And as far as we're concerned, we're cleared to travel to Holland, Belgium, France, and Germany— first-class accommodations all the way."

"That's terrific, pal."

"Yeah, well, last night Hilda was saying she saw the bloody German SS in every major European city from Paris to Amsterdam. We'll have to be on our toes every minute once we cross the channel."

"So, when do we go?"

"Thursday, after the first dinner show. We've got the manager a fill-in act for the weekend, and they start a new show on Monday. We catch the nine o'clock up to Harwich, then board the ferry across to Holland."

Eddie sat back, albeit with an apprehensive smile. He arched his brows and whispered, "Well, okay!"

The trip across the North Sea was rough. And many, including Johnny, were seasick the minute they left Harwich. It was windy and cold when they docked, and it was a major effort just to get him off the boat. "Just get us to the hotel, if you would, please. Otherwise send my body back to Hilda."

A Mercedes limousine was waiting at the dock, as ordered, but the driver spoke little English. Eddie did his best with hand language and pointed on a map to the hotel near Kattenburgerstraat, his friend moaning and sprawled out on the backseat. The driver tried to make conversation, but he could tell that his passengers didn't understand a word, so they traveled the few kilometers into the Amsterdam city center in silence.

Eddie was tired and on edge, with survival training clouding his thoughts. He now wished he'd paid more attention during those tedious briefings. It was late, but he could see uniformed sailors strolling the deserted streets. He tried to recognize the insignia. Their driver turned down a street adjacent to one of the many canals. A German patrol unit was paralleling them across the canal. The unit was in rigid formation; officers wore black dress uniforms with the distinct swastika armbands. The patrol halted as their limousine crossed a bridge connecting the two streets. The officers turned and watched the passing vehicle.

They turned onto Beursstraat and approached a lighted square. There were several groups of people crossing the street, some with bicycles. They all appeared nervous and agitated. In the crowd were a dozen or more men with beards and long curls of hair hanging down past their ears, dressed in long black coats and wearing black felt hats.

Johnny was now sitting up and watching the commotion. In a whisper he explained, "They're Jews—Hasidic, orthodox—likely emigrated—more likely they've just escaped from Germany. They're more than likely trying to find friends or family. Or some, maybe, are trying to find their way to Palestine, or Britain, or even the United States."

Eddie remembered seeing some similarly dressed Jews in New York's diamond district. Rudy Vallee had taken him there. "I've only seen whiskers and curly hair like that in New York."

"Right, mate. We'll likely be seeing more of these chaps, on account of we are now in the diamond capital of the world."

"Really?"

"That's right. After the Spaniards ran all the Jews out of Belgium in the sixteenth century, many of the finest cutters in the world settled here."

Suddenly the German patrol turned a corner and started to march into the square. The group started to shout in a language he'd never heard and scattered immediately, several dashing in front of the car.

"Welcome to 1938 and the Continent, my friend."

"Why on earth would some Jews in Amsterdam be afraid of a German shore patrol?"

Before his friend could answer, the driver had stopped in front of their hotel.

The next morning Eddie awoke with a start, after catnapping most of the night. Johnny was sitting in the lobby, reading what looked like a local newspaper. "Ah, there you are. I'm famished. How about you?"

"I hope they've got good, strong coffee over here. I feel thrashed. What are you reading?"

"Well, either my German has turned to mush, or the Nazis simply don't give a rat's apple what is going on over in Britain. I couldn't even find a listing of the most popular songs. Last year every German edition of a Dutch, Belgian, or French paper had a whole section devoted to popular music. Some included all the jazz happenings around town. Now . . . ?"

"Let's get something to eat, pal. I've had a better night's rest in the boxing ring." He made a beeline for the restaurant.

"You know, for a guy with short legs, you walk faster than a thoroughbred coming out the bloody gate. I'm sure they won't run out of kippers. Anyway, I'm still sloshing from that rough crossing."

A hearty Dutch breakfast consisted of cold cuts of ham, beef, blood bologna, sausage, English kippers, several cheeses, and hard rolls with butter. Eddie ate what he recognized but left most of his plate untouched. After three cups of strong coffee with warm milk, he was ready to move on.

They hailed a cab and headed off to a Dutch radio station. The station was a small stone building located near Utrecht, about forty kilometers southeast of Amsterdam.

Throughout the journey Johnny tried to converse with the cabbie, using a few common German words and a lot of hand language. He learned from the cabbie that German military traffic along the Amstel and Rhine rivers had increased tenfold over the previous year. He also learned that commercial traffic on the river is often held up for days at a time. The cabbie's brother operated a barge for a fishing company, and twice he'd been stopped at gunpoint.

On the return trip to Amsterdam, they could see one or two barges moving in the narrow, open center channel. Most of the other craft along the riverbanks were frozen in the ice pack. A few pedestrians were heading to or from the small number of food stalls that were open. Something seemed out of place.

"I don't see any cars or trucks."

His friend didn't respond; he only nodded. *It's fear, mate. People stay home when they're afraid. I can feel it. It's as though everyone is looking over his shoulder. You can't always see them, but the Nazis are always there, like a cancer.*

They dined that evening at one of the high-end clubs on Rembrandtplein. "This is one of the more famous squares in all of Amsterdam, my friend. And if I remember right, there is a company record store nearby. Wouldn't you like to see what promotional stuff they have in their window?"

"By all means."

They could have taken a canal boat in the summer months, but not tonight. The canals were frozen solid, and the wind was now getting strong enough to cut through the heaviest wool. Rembrandtplein, just off Amstelstraat, was only a five-minute taxi ride from their hotel. Many of the nineteenth-century houses were heavily decorated for Christmas. The cabbie, wanting to demonstrate his knowledge of the area, stopped and pointed directly at the statue of Rembrandt. "This square was once a butter market. We have many fairs here. Would you like to have a look?"

"Yes, we'd like to walk around a bit."

"Okay. There are many good pubs and restaurants about, so enjoy." His English was near perfect.

"Don't be shocked, mate. I did mention that the Dutch are a bit more liberal than the English."

"I'll be on my best behavior, pal. I promise."

They could hear music, and there were lights everywhere. Alongside one of the buildings, they noticed what must have been fifty bicycles. The air was cold and crisp. They proceeded toward an old Georgian wood-and-plaster inn. A blast of warmth from a fireplace that took up nearly one whole wall of this tiny pub enveloped them as soon as the door swung open.

As they looked casually around the tiny pub they saw two German officers in uniform, with spit-polished boots, sitting with two young Dutch girls. They decided to move on.

Strolling around the square, they heard ragtime piano music coming from one of the noisier pubs. They passed a corner building with a glass display window on their way to the noisy pub. Eddie couldn't believe his eyes. Sitting in a red chair on a small red-carpeted stage facing the street was a beautiful young girl. She was bare-breasted, with only a feather boa covering her shoulders. She smiled and beckoned them with her finger to come on in.

"Come along, old chap. I told you they were a bit more liberal over here. Or perhaps you'd like to negotiate with the young lady?"

"I thought I'd seen just about everything. Rudy Vallee wouldn't believe this for one minute."

They entered the small but jam-packed pub. A black man in a tuxedo was banging out some serious ragtime in a corner of the room. Eddie recognized him as Fats Waller. He motioned to his friend with his head.

"Right. Some of these pubs pay handsomely to book popular black American jazz artists. The French love this music, but the Dutch, of recent, seem to be fascinated with American jazz. They come from miles around to catch a show like this."

Fats recognized Eddie and came over to their table after a short medley set. Eddie took advantage of the opportunity and invited Fats to jam with him on one of the upcoming radio shows. Eddie leaned back in his chair and smiled. "Fats, I have to say that in this land of good cheese, ice skates, picturesque windmills, and the not-so-subtle German cultural invasion, it feels good to come across a familiar face."

When he returned to the piano, Fats made a short announcement to the local patrons. "Ladies and gentlemen. I am pleased to announce that the undisputed 'king of the banjo,' Eddie Peabody, who happens to be with us tonight, and yours truly, the ever-irreverent Fats Waller, will soon be jammin' on Dutch radio! So do stay tuned." With that, he rolled into a European favorite, "Sweet Georgia Brown."

"This sure is one hell of a popular place, my friend. Good food, good drinks, good music, and hookers to boot. I'll be damned. Rudy Vallee would think he'd died and gone to heaven."

The radio show went well. Following the interview, the station manager provided a Mercedes and a driver to chauffeur them to their first record store. The Rotterdam store was jammed, and the local press was on hand to cover the event. It was dusk when they'd finished their tour and headed back to the hotel.

Eddie dropped Johnny at the hotel and told the cabbie to take a drive near the docks. The Amsterdam docks were right behind the central rail station and not far from the hotel. He wanted to see what ships were in port. As they slowly traversed several miles of port facilities, all ships appeared to be commercial and were flying the German flag. *With all the German sailors in port, I felt sure I'd see at least one sizable warship. If this Nazi chancellor isn't preparing for war, what exactly is he up to?*

Over a nightcap Eddie relayed to his friend what he'd observed. "What do you think? With the shore patrols we've seen, I'd expect to see at least a frigate or a battlewagon docked out there somewhere."

"Well, mate, right now Germany is importing more war material than its North Sea ports can handle. Hamburg is their largest port, and it's my guess they want to keep their shipbuilding away from as many prying eyes as they can. They'll make best use of as many close-in ports as they can."

Eddie shook his head in exasperation. "Right, and while the English and French are politicking, the Hun is preparing for battle."

Eddie's popularity was catching on, and he was often besieged by groups of teenage fans. Local musicians were starting to play

"The Lambeth Walk." Johnny continued to work closely with the local press.

Their train trip to Paris was uneventful, but Eddie was startled when the conductor passed by and collected both passports.

"Don't get your knickers in a twist, mate. It is standard procedure these days to collect all passports. We'll be getting them back as soon as we get off in Paris. They'll stamp our passports in Belgium, as well as France, which should be of help when we leave for Germany. Should be less hassle at the border, you know. Trust me, mate."

TWENTY

It was about a six-and-a-half-hour train ride from Amsterdam to Paris. Except for the lighted stations they passed through, there was little of the countryside to be seen. Not seeing any German uniforms in their midst, they treated themselves to a light dinner and an excellent bottle of French wine. The atmosphere was relaxing, so unlike the cattle-car experience traveling from New York to Washington. Another welcome change was the service people, especially in the dining car; they were always friendly and accommodating. The two men would often listen in on adjacent conversations and try to guess at what language the folks were speaking. When a waiter approached, everyone seemed to automatically switch language—as though they instinctively knew what native language was the common courtesy, either to communicate their needs or just engage in friendly conversation. But the private compartment, where everyone could decompress at his or her leisure—they could not understand why American train travel had not embraced this clearly superior idea.

Eddie was dozing comfortably when the train began to slow as it approached Antwerp. Glancing out the compartment window he noticed that several uniformed officials were about to come aboard. He poked his friend to alert him to what was happening.

Johnny was starting to nod off when he felt a jab. "Merely customs officials, mate. Another group will board and check passports and the passenger manifest when we cross into France. They check and stamp everything. They usually keep a copy of the passenger manifest for their records."

The train pulled into Gare du Nord, Paris, a little after midnight. Three men and a woman were holding a sign: "Eddie Peabody—Bienvenue à Paris."

The woman approached and waved recognizing Eddie as he disembarked. "Welcome, Monsieur Peabody. I hope your journey was pleasant. *Oui?*"

Eddie, dead tired, managed to smile and shake her tiny hand.

Johnny stepped forward. "Michele, is it? From the club?" He extended his hand as she greeted him graciously.

"*Oui*, and you must be Monsieur Pitts. No?"

"*Oui* . . . ah, yes. Are any of these gentlemen here to transport the instruments and other equipment?"

Michelle nodded and motioned to two burly young men. "Everything will be sorted out at rehearsal tomorrow afternoon, if that is satisfactory."

"Yes, that will be fine."

Michelle barked some curt commands at the two young men and then guided Eddie and Johnny to an awaiting Citroën.

Eddie bumped his friend and gave a quick twitch with his eyebrows. Who was this very pleasant and well-organized woman?

Johnny wasn't sure he comprehended the sign language, but he whispered a reply. "She's an assistant manager at the Moulin Rouge. Quite nice on the phone and, I must say, even nicer in person."

While unpacking, Eddie reflected on how different he felt being in Paris—a discernible change from what he'd felt in Amsterdam. *Here we are in Paris, and all seems right with the world—the openness, the gaiety, the total lack of concern for anything other than an evening out. Yeah, well, I know damned well all isn't right with the world.*

After a short night and a French breakfast of croissants, confiture, and strong coffee, they took a taxi to the Place Pigalle, just off the Boulevard de Clichy, at the foot of Montmartre. The temperature was cool, with a light breeze. Because rehearsal wasn't scheduled for another two hours, they decided to walk about the neighborhood and check out other Métro stations and restaurants within walking distance from the club. They could see the landmark Moulin red windmill off to their left on nearby Place Blanche, and the club's modest marquee:

La Revue Américaine—Le Spectacle de Cabaret—Jazz—avec
Eddie Peabody et soliste Florence Desmond aussi
Chester Fredericks et Gloria Lane

Johnny pointed to the line connecting the Place de la Concord, near their hotel, to the Place Blanche and the Moulin Rouge, on a small Métro map. "I'm reasonably comfortable with the Paris Métro, mate, but when we get to Hamburg or Berlin, we'll bloody need to either do some trial runs or stick with a cab."

Eddie had his hands in his pockets but listened politely. *He's anxious over the damn trains. That's the least of my worries.*

As if he'd read his friend's mind, Johnny added," Look, mate, if the Hun decides to bollix things up for us, we may need to exit in a hurry, wherever the hell we are—and we will get the hell out!"

"Easy, pal, we're not bollixed up yet. So tell me, what are we looking at over there?" Eddie put his arm on his friend's shoulder and turned him around to look northeast at an old church on a hill.

"That's the basilica of Sacré-Cœur. There's a lovely view of all of Paris from the top of the dome."

"Well, let's mosey over and take a look. Looks like . . . what, about half a mile from here? There's probably a nice spot nearby to have lunch."

"Right. Capital idea, Peabody. And it won't take a cabbie five minutes to get us back to the club."

They found a small bistro off Rue Gabrielle. A young couple sitting near the front of the restaurant commenced yelling at each other. It looked to be a lover's quarrel.

Eddie looked at his friend. "Did you understand any of what they're fussing about?"

Johnny started to chuckle. "I caught enough to conclude that the young lady was chastising her boyfriend for not paying attention to what the Nazis are up to. I think the young man is a socialist, but I'm afraid his lady friend is a communist."

"You got all that?"

"Well, I admit I'm filling in a lot of blanks, but I definitely heard her say that Hitler was planning to march into Paris. She also said a friend of hers living in Germany has been sent to a concentration camp, just for being a communist. Her boyfriend was admonishing her for being hysterical and paranoid."

Eddie shook his head. "Hell hath no fury . . . "

"Right you are, mate. But it looks as though some of the folks over here are concerned enough to wonder what that little Austrian rooster is up to."

"Well, it scares me, pal, to think that the only two powers over here able to put a stop to this guy's shenanigans have their bloody heads in the sand. I'm afraid something is going to pop over here, and sooner rather than later."

The chorus line rehearsal was finishing up, and the producer called a fifteen-minute break. Johnny handed out music to the orchestra, while Eddie checked his instruments in his dressing room. A soft knock on his door caused him to look up. It was Lieutenant Graham. He felt off balance and couldn't remember her first name. *She's beautiful. Her hair is shorter and lighter, but those eyes—dear God, but I love those eyes.*

In the awkward silence she whispered, "Commander?"

"Marian, Marian, please come in. I'm sorry—it was a short night. How are you? How long have you been here in Paris?"

She could tell that he was flustered and that she'd startled him. She gave him an affectionate smile as she touched his arm, and then she quietly closed the door. The room was sparse and small, and she sat in the only chair near his dressing table. Eddie sat gingerly on the edge of narrow dressing table, with one foot on the floor.

"It's good to see you too, Commander. Well, we've been here, as a group, for a little more than two weeks now. And I've been learning the ropes and basic routines. The regular Moulin girls have been very patient and quite friendly. And, I'm happy to say, my French is getting to be better than passable. Oh, by the way, I'm now known in the troupe as 'Dixie.' One of the English girls nick-named me that after a Southern medley at a theater in London. It stuck, and so I've gotten used to it. It also seemed prudent to change my name on the roster to my mother's maiden name. I thought about being in Germany, and with my family's past and all . . . I hope you understand."

Eddie felt mesmerized but tried not to stare. He tried to take in all she'd said, but he was tongue-tied. A minute passed while they just looked at each other.

Dixie was feeling uncomfortable in the awkward silence. "And we've been hearing your song "Lambeth Walk" on nearly every station since last week. The club manager plans to really promote this American show. I swear a dozen people after every show want to know when Eddie Peabody will be here."

He now realized he hadn't talked with a friendly female in months. He missed Maude, but her letters were stiff and cold. He'd tried calling once a month, but the connections were bad, and it took forever to connect.

Again Dixie broke the silence, this time with a cough. "Excuse me. Well, Commander, I'd better be getting back. I've got to sub for one of the regulars tonight. Anyway, it's good to see you, and I'm glad you're finally here."

Eddie stood and touched her elbow as she moved toward the

door. "Marian, please forgive me. It's just that . . . well, I haven't seen or talked with a friendly female face in months. And when you came in, well, I just fogged up. Please have lunch with me sometime. Will you?"

She smiled at him and put her hand behind his neck. She gave a quick squeeze. "Sure, Commander. I'd be happy to. But I do hope you think of me as more than just a friendly face."

After rehearsal the two men took the Métro back to their hotel. With Marian still on his mind, he tried to call Maude. The phone finally rang. "Hello, Maude?" There was swooshing static, and then a groggy voice answered.

"Hello. Eddie, is that you?"

"Yes, sweetheart. I'm in Paris, and everything is all decorated up for Christmas. It's beautiful. I wish you were here to enjoy it with me."

"Do you know what time it is? Why, it's not even 5:00 AM! What time is it there?"

"Dear, it's only 8:00 PM. I'm getting ready to go down for dinner with Johnny."

"Oh. So, how are the shows going? Oh, by the way, I'm leaving for Texas tomorrow, to spend Christmas with my brother. So if you call on Christmas, I'll either be at his place or Mother's."

He felt the wind drop out of his sails. She was half asleep and not really interested in conversation. "Johnny's been a real pal, Maude. I'd be lost without him. And the shows are going great. Remember when I wrote you about recording 'Lambeth Walk'? Well, it's a hit from London to Paris."

"That's wonderful, dear."

She said it with little enthusiasm. He wished he'd never mentioned it. "You go back to sleep, dear. I just wanted to hear your voice and tell you I'm still alive. Give your family my best, and tell them I'm sorry for missing out on Christmas. I'll try to call you Christmas Day. There won't be any shows on that day. Love you, babe."

"Love you too, dear. You will take care of yourself, won't you?"

"Bye-bye, Maude. I'll call on Christmas." Eddie hung up and

let out a long sigh. He felt a dull ache in the pit of his stomach. *I need to call Marian. What am I thinking? How do I get in touch with her? More importantly, what do I say to her?* He picked up the phone and started to dial up the Moulin. Before anyone could answer, he replaced the receiver.

The opening show at the Moulin Rouge was spectacular. The staging, the lighting, and the girls' costumes were all profession-ally done to perfection. He'd never seen anything in vaudeville to compare, even in New York. Every detail had been attended to. The two men were standing in the wing, waiting for the grand finale. The orchestra was playing a medley of tunes that had been performed throughout the show. The girls were on a back staircase platform, doing a dance routine in soft light. Eddie and Johnny couldn't see what the audience was seeing, but they could hear the cheers and clapping. They looked at each other with raised eyebrows and an expression that said wow.

After this dance routine came the closing sequence. The lighting level raised, the girls filed out on both sides of the center stage, and the other show performers ran out onstage as the girls returned for a final bow. They were watching the stage manager closely now as the girls began to exit to the wings.

Eddie had been around pretty, hardworking stage girls his entire career. But when he glanced over his shoulder as they began to line up, he felt his chin drop. He could feel their body heat as they got closer. Standing directly behind him, expression-less and looking straight ahead, was Dixie—Lieutenant Marian Graham. Her beautiful sequined swimsuit with fishnet stockings and polished, high-heeled tap-dance shoes were stunning. Her outfit also included white gloves and a top hat with silky plumes. There were colorful feathers, strategically wrapped toward the front, decorating the sides of her suit. There was only one thing missing: the top of her suit. *My, oh my, no wonder the audience cheered the finale.* He felt someone push him; he'd missed his cue for the final bow. On stage, Eddie was standing next to Florence Desmond.

She smiled as she whispered, "Leave it to the French. It's a wonder they didn't ask us to strip down as well."

The newspapers reported that mainstream Paris was now beginning to pay more attention to politics than to the latest American dance tune, though the show at the Moulin was a smash success.

When he could, Eddie traveled around the city, looking for jazz clubs on the left bank of the River Seine. He took time off to catch a set at the Caveau. He liked the cavelike atmosphere and enjoyed one evening sitting in with a hot French Dixieland band.

After Saturday's evening performance, Eddie was changing into his suit pants when once again his dressing room door flew open, and there was Dixie. Other than some missing feathers, it appeared that she hadn't changed from her grand finale costume. The lieutenant looked out of breath, as though she had been running. "Lieutenant, what's up?"

She put her fingers to her mouth to signal quiet. They could hear footsteps. Of course they could hear footsteps. This was the backstage of the theater.

Dixie had one ear nearly resting on the door. She was clearly listening intently. She turned and began to whisper. "Commander, please listen. From this point forward, you must only refer to me as Dixie. I'll only refer to you as Eddie, and I'll try to be formal about it when we're in a crowd. Okay?"

"Okay, but what's happening?"

"Look, I'm sorry for barging in, but some Germans came backstage this evening. They were trying to hustle some of the girls for a party back at their embassy. All I could think about was someone overhearing me refer to you as Commander. I panicked. I had to warn you."

"Marian—er, Dixie, I—" Just then the door started to creak open. Dixie threw her arms around Eddie and kissed him. He was startled but was thoroughly enjoying the kiss. The feel of her bare breasts on his chest was too much to ignore. A quick glance revealed the intruder was only Johnny.

"Oh, sorry, old chap. The producer cornered me, and I thought with the delay that you might . . . But I can see you're in good hands, so I'll say cheerio."

When the door shut, Dixie broke the kiss and stood back slightly. They looked at each other in startled silence. Eddie smiled, leaned over, and whispered, " You want to catch a jazz set at a cave with me tonight?"

After modestly covering her breasts and turning sideways, she agreed, though she couldn't hide the nervous quiver in her voice. "Okay . . . sure. Just give me ten minutes to change. We'll meet back here. Okay?"

The Caveau club band recognized Eddie as soon as he walked in. He and Dixie sat at a nearby table. A waiter brought over a bottle of champagne, courtesy of the piano player, Jock. After a regular band break, Jock came over and welcomed them. His English was deliberate and heavily accented.

Eddie mentioned to Jock that Dixie was with the show at the Moulin.

"Wonderful, mademoiselle. And what part do you play in that beautiful show?"

She answered him in perfect French. "I'm part of a rotating dance routine at the Moulin, but in Brussels, in addition to the chorus line, I sang two solos.

Jock's eyes lit up while she spoke. He stood and offered her his hand. "Please, come with me. Let's do a tune. What do you say?"

Why'd I have to say so matter-of-factly that I could sing? Now she was embarrassed. She inhaled her champagne. "Sure!"

Up they went, and in a deep and sexy voice she began one of her favorites, "Am I Blue?" The music seemed to resonate from her soul. Those who were near enough to catch her improvisation went wild with applause. She could tell they wanted more. But with an effervescent smile, she bowed and returned to Eddie.

He quickly refilled her glass, then leaned over and kissed her.

"What was that for?" Her hand unconsciously moved to cover her breast but retreated when she realized all was well.

"Because you were sensational, girl."

For the first time since she had returned to the Continent, she was truly enjoying herself. For the moment she'd purged her mind of all that was happening around her, and she felt terrific. She smiled and tilted her head backward and then turned toward Eddie. She was about to tell him how wonderful she felt when suddenly a door slammed shut with a bang! Nearly everyone in the club jumped. She turned to see what had happened. The euphoria disappeared instantly. With her senses now on full alert, she knew she needed to get out of there. With stooped shoulders, she leaned toward Eddie as she glanced at her watch. "I'm having an incredible time, but sorry to say, if I'm going to get any sleep tonight, I should head back across the river."

He slugged the remainder of his champagne. He touched her hand affectionately. "Well, I couldn't have asked for a better time. Okay, then, shall we?"

Dixie felt surprised; he hadn't fussed at her wanting to leave, and part of her was disappointed. *I know he likes me. So, why doesn't he . . . ?* Looking disappointed, she stood and sighed as she took one last look around the club. She wanted to remember every detail. She smiled at Eddie as she reached for his arm. "After all that champagne, I think I'm going to need all the help I can get." Outside she breathed in the cold air and walked arm in arm for roughly a block to a taxi stand. "This has been simply wonderful. I can't remember when I've had such a good time."

"You were the sensational one tonight."

She stopped and put her arm on his shoulder. Then she leaned over and gave him a kiss on the cheek.

"What's that for?"

"For just being you."

The next day at breakfast, Eddie was perusing the *International Tribune*. Without looking up, he began to converse with his friend. "Dixie mentioned to me some German embassy boys lately have been getting a little aggressive."

"I've heard that as well. And I also heard that a couple of them were getting rough with the girls. So, is that what you two were discussing in your dressing room when I popped in?"

Eddie smiled at his friend's deliberate understatement. "Yep, and wondering what I'd do if one of those goons came barging in. About then, you stuck your head in."

"Well, ol' chap, I certainly am glad you decided to think about it rather than try for another one-man international incident. Tell me, do you always get that . . . ah . . . close when you're thinking?"

Eddie dropped the paper just below his eyes and looked directly at his friend, but he chose not to reply.

A few nights later, Dixie dropped by his dressing room after the performance. "I don't think I mentioned this, but on the evening we stopped in at the Cave, two girlfriends went to a German embassy party. Little happened, other than everyone drank too much. Though there were some roaming hands, neither girl was forced into bed. They did have some difficulty rousting someone to drive them back to their hotel when their dates fell asleep. One of the girls learned, however, that a young officer she'd met that evening worked directly for Heinrich Himmler. Before he passed out, he alleged that he was on a top-secret assignment from Berlin. He also mentioned that he knew that the American troupe was scheduled to be in Berlin within the month. To impress her, he boasted that he would recommend the show to all the high-ranking SS men he worked with."

Eddie was feeling very uneasy and anxious listening to Dixie. "That sounded like you were reading from a tabloid scandal sheet, Dix. We're not at war, Dix, but I'll be damned if it doesn't feel like we are. I'm getting the uneasy feeling that every German official who comes in contact with the show acts as though we're all spies." *It's got to be my imagination, but damned if I don't always tighten up like an overwound clock when I hear those guys are around. And in two days I'll be in Hamburg.*

TWENTY-ONE

The train left Paris on time, heading back to Reims, then east to Verdun and finally north to Luxembourg. From the Luxembourg border the train traveled on to Trier along the Mosel River.

It was too dark to see a station name, but Johnny turned from the window and spoke in a whisper to his friend. "Bloody 'ell if we're not in the Hun's playground now."

Eddie was wide awake and could feel the tension in his hands, his feet, and the pit of his stomach. He took a deep breath and tried to relax, but his mind wouldn't allow it. *Okay, so now we're in Germany. What did he casually mention last night? And you know, ol' chap, that without the proper documents, our journey could be delayed by as much as a day. The damn bureaucrats would take whatever time they felt necessary to sift through every piece of baggage. And heaven help anyone offering a bribe to expedite the process.*

The train did stop at Trier, but only for a short time. Looking out the window, they noticed two German officials enter the train. A porter passed their open compartment and stopped. He communicated in French that their next stop was Koblenz. He added that if German customs wanted to inspect any cargo, or if they intended to check for any expired visas, it would happen there.

Johnny relayed the porter's message and suggested that they remain on board until the train had cleared customs. "And whatever happens, mate, please don't you take a swing at a bloody agent. Understood?"

"Aye, skipper." He could tell that his friend was as anxious as he was. He smiled and tried to look away. *Damn, Johnny, you look as if you're about to walk a gauntlet of queers buck-naked.* "How about a nightcap, pal? It would do us both a lot of good right now."

The man was glued to the window, however, trying to discern what was happening. *Blimey, but these bloody scary, black-booted high-steppers give me the creeps. Greg Ziemer said that every bureaucrat was simply unforgiving for the least little infraction . . . so be on your toes. Being with Eddie Peabody on this trip is certainly going to be an experience—a damned dangerous one.*

Eddie quietly slipped past and headed to the bar.

On his way he noticed a woman that he swore looked familiar. She was in a bathrobe, heading back toward standard class. When he returned, he touched his friend on the shoulder.

"Bloody good of you, mate. Is that a bock beer for me?"

"Sure thing, pal, just in case of fire or theft."

Johnny knocked down a few swallows and then turned back to see what was happening outside. It was pitch-black. He couldn't even see the river. He leaned his head back against the bench seat cushion, briefly raising and lowering his shoulders, trying to release some tension. He was very preoccupied now, but he knew there was little he could do.

Again Eddie quietly stepped out past his friend. This time, however, he thought he'd check out the standard-class carriage. Entering the first car past the bar and dining area, he realized that he'd stumbled into a sleeping car. Heavy curtains separated each small bunk bed. *Peabody, you're intruding here.* He did an about-face. Quite suddenly, and with force, he felt a hand grab his thigh. He almost lost his balance. Another hand emerged and pulled him onto the small bed. After thwacking his head on the metal rail of the upper bunk, he heard a throaty whisper. "Good evening, Commander."

"Dix, is that you?"

She kissed his ear but didn't answer.

He sighed and leaned back against her. "You know, you almost made me pee my pants."

She stifled a laugh and snuggled against his neck. "Shhh. We don't want to wake the whole line, now, do we?"

Eddie breathed heavily through his nose.

"I couldn't sleep, so I thought I'd snag some company."

"Well, I certainly am glad you snagged me and not one of the Kraut customs agents. You know we're in Germany now?"

She kissed his cheek.

Eddie tried to roll over to face her. He got about halfway. "Oh damn, Dix. I'd better get back anyway. Johnny is so nervous right about now, he's likely to come looking for me. And I couldn't do that to the poor guy." He kissed her on the nose. "But I will take a rain check." He tried to push himself quickly off he bunk and thwacked his head again on the overhead bunk. "Son of a . . . "

The person above groaned. "Knock it off!"

Dix gave him a push as she stifled a giggle.

It was 2:00 AM when the train left Central Station in Koblenz. They watched a cadre of officials enter and leave the train, assuming passports were being checked against passenger manifests. The French weren't as fastidious about their record keeping as the Germans. Delays were commonplace. As the train jerked, starting to pull out of the station, both men let out audible sighs of relief.

"Only two and a half hours to Hamburg now, mate."

"Where are we staying in Hamburg, pal?"

"At the Vier Jahreszeiten just off Jungfernstieg. It's quite nice, and there are a couple of fine restaurants nearby as well. If the freezing rain wouldn't turn us blue, we could walk to the Palace."

Looking out the window, trying to establish a sense of direction, Eddie asked, "Write that down on a little map for me will you, skipper? I may need to give directions to a cabbie, just in case we get separated."

After they unpacked and threw some cold water on their

faces to wake up, they met in the coffee shop for some breakfast. The coffee was great, but Eddie, though famished, found hard rolls and cold cuts of pork and lamb a little heavy for breakfast. In a small gift shop they had purchased three maps; a walking map of the city center, the Hamburg metro system map, and a roadmap covering a forty-kilometer area around the city. They used the walking map to locate a nearby bank to deposit checks and exchange their French francs.

The weather gods were good to them as they walked toward the theater. Sunshine was peering over some ominous clouds east over the Binnenalster waterway; the wind was light but penetrating. They walked east across a main intersection at Ballindamm and continued on to the Palace Theater.

It wasn't long before Eddie felt his fingers start to stiffen up. "Damn, this cold, damp air goes right through me. I don't see how people stand it. Where, oh where is that warm California sunshine?" He spied a wood-burning stove in a corner of a nearby pastry shop. It looked warm and inviting and was decorated with greens for Christmas. A large, happy-faced man was polishing some glasses on one of the tables. They entered and sat near a counter.

"My friend, you'd better count your blessings. Because if we ever decide to emigrate to California, your much-touted promised land, you'll be stacked up just like the rest of us sardines."

The rotund, happy-faced gentleman approached with a complimentary pastry and asked if they would like some coffee. His smile was infectious. "Velcome, English."

Johnny thanked him in German for his kind generosity and nodded at his suggestion of two coffees. A young waitress returned promptly with two very large cups of coffee. It looked as though she were carrying bowls of soup.

"Right, mate, as you can see, not every German is a ruddy member of the SS, eh? Some, like these folks, are right nice." He paused and gave a slight nod. "Well, are we ready to brave the cold and have another go at it?"

The proprietor walked over to hold the door for them. In a

surprise gesture, he grabbed Eddie's hand and shook it vigorously. "*Wo wohnen Sie? In Amerika, ja?* Velcome, velcome."

Johnny answered, "*Ja, ja,*" and smiled.

The theater was less than a five-minute walk from the shop. They entered from the front, as neither of them saw anyone about. Once inside, they couldn't help but notice the elaborate and festive decorations throughout the lobby. Past the large velvet entry curtains was the main seating arena, and onstage the Moulin dance troupe girls were rehearsing a complicated number.

In an astonished tone, Johnny quipped, "Good grief, the temperature in here is only marginally warmer than outside. I cannot imagine doing anything that strenuous after that ruddy awful train ride. I knew German producers were sticklers for perfection, but this seems ridiculous. I certainly hope they break soon, or one of them will be nursing a sprained ankle, or worse."

They checked all their equipment and were relieved that everything appeared to have arrived safe and secure. Eddie began his ritual of oiling up and cleaning the strings on his instruments. There was a knock at his dressing-room door.

"Dixie!"

She hugged him, but he could tell it was an effort. "I wanted to give you this as soon as we were settled." She handed him a slip of paper with three addresses on it.

He stared at the small paper scrap.

She leaned in close to his shoulder. "The first address is where the rest of the troupe and I will be staying, the Alte Wache, about two blocks south of your hotel. My room number is 114."

He looked up from the slip of paper, straight into those beautiful brown eyes.

She broke the moment by redirecting him. "The second address is a restaurant club two doors south of our hotel. If I'm not here or in my room, that's where I'll be. The last address is my mother's cousin's house in Harburg. It's a small town a few miles south of Hamburg. This will be my last-resort rendezvous point. If you can't locate me anywhere, look for me there. Her telephone number is next to the address. Her name is Ilsa, and she understands and speaks English. Remember, this will only be used as a last resort, because I want to draw as little attention to Ilsa as possible."

He was staring at the slip of paper as though he were trying to burn the letters into his brain.

She touched his hand to distract him. "Otherwise, Commander, we should be seen together as much as practical."

That comment brought a smile to his face.

Loud footsteps just outside broke the moment and caught their attention. She quickly put her arms around his neck as she was facing the door, but no one entered. She abruptly dropped her arms. "Any questions, sir?"

He gave her a quick kiss on the nose and turned back to his instruments. "I can't think of a thing. I know that with your skill and thoroughness, Dix, we can't fail. But please, no more sirs."

"Okay, but if this slave driver of a producer doesn't give us a break, whatever skill I once possessed will be reduced to nothing but muscle cramps and shin splints." She wriggled her fingers in a coquettish goodbye. She smiled to herself as she walked back to her dressing room. *I think the commander likes the togetherness part of this job.*

Johnny, in an excited rush, gave two knocks on the door and then entered. "I just met with the producer, mate. He said that he's booked the theater for a private preview on Thursday evening. A special convention of industrial engineers and military contractors will be in town, and he was persuaded by the mayor to provide them with some first-class entertainment. Our contract doesn't cover this, but he assured me that all would be amply compensated. Oh, and the girls' costumes should be here tomorrow. He said he wants a dress rehearsal by Wednesday. So there you have it. What do you think?"

"I think we need to convince His Nibs that if he drills those poor girls any more, all he'll have on Thursday is a chorus line of toothpick legs."

"That bad, eh? Well, his knickers did seem a bit in a twist, but he didn't touch on the rehearsals or how they were shaping up. I did hear some scuttlebutt from the stagehands. And from what I could discern, the boss couldn't decide on what routines to include. His own choreographer told him that it would take more than a week to write new stuff."

"Well, the matron and a couple of girls had suggested that if they used the Moulin routines, little would need to be modified."

"Right you are. Why, our girls could step off those routines in their sleep. Let's hope that even as we're speaking, they'll be successful in convincing the producer of their recommendation. God knows our girls could use a much-needed rest."

"I'm with you, pal. Now, I think I'd like to head back for a quick nap before dinner."

"Capital idea, my friend. Oh, I nearly forgot. Greg Ziemer will be stopping by this evening. He's a delightful chap—you'll like him."

"He's our contact, right?"

He could see the tension in Eddie's eyes. "Right—not to worry. Look, I know you and Greg will get on just smashing—you'll both likely forget all about poor old me, I'll tell ya. So, are we ready?"

So, now it begins.

The weather turned bad late in the afternoon, causing Johnny to uncharacteristically pace about in the hotel lobby, worried that their contact man, Greg Ziemer, was held up somewhere. He also kept a sharp eye out the front door, to catch any signs of the Gestapo.

Eddie was waiting in the restaurant, enjoying a brandy. Several of the restaurant diners that evening were German officers in dress uniform. He took special notice of one group of naval officers sitting at a large table. One wore captain's insignia; the other three were junior officers. There were two civilians that seemed to be part of the group as well. *Perhaps they're part of the military contracting group we're going to entertain at the Palace?* He took another sip of brandy. *Damn it! Why does just being here send a cold chill up my spine?* He looked up just as Johnny was entering with a slight, middle-aged man in tow, more than likely their on-site contact. As he took notice of the man, he remembered that the State Department had said that Ziemer blended in so well that he was almost transparent. He was wearing a dark brown, somewhat worn corduroy jacket and pants that obviously hadn't been pressed. *Typical professor.* His facial features were rounded, versus sharp, and the man's eyes were bright and alive. With his short-cropped hair and unkempt appearance, he did look like, as advertised, a college professor. Eddie sensed that the guy was friendly, warm, and genuine. The man smiled as though he meant it.

Eddie stood and offered Ziemer his hand. Now his gestalt feeling about the man was firmed up. Now he wanted nothing more than to get on with it, get the needed information, and then get the hell out of Germany.

"Greg, I'd like you to meet my boss and now good friend, Eddie Peabody."

Greg bowed slightly and extended his hand. He spoke perfect English with only a slight German accent. "I'm very pleased to meet you, Herr Peabody. I've heard so much about you. And recently, I am pleased to say, I have heard your music on the radio. I can truthfully say that I am now a fan of the American banjo."

Eddie returned a courteous bow. "Thank you, Mr. Ziemer. It is truly an honor to finally meet you."

"Please, it's Greg." There was a pause.

Eddie felt Greg's probing eyes.

"I'm sorry for staring, but for some reason, I feel we've met before."

"Perhaps, but not to my recollection. Johnny has been telling me your story on a daily basis. Now that we've met formally, I can say it is truly a pleasure."

The waiter appeared and broke the moment. To bridge the enthusiasm, Eddie ordered German champagne for the table.

Greg gently raised the palm of his hand. "My friends, I regret that I must limit myself to but one glass only. Though I would love to celebrate the evening away with you, I am teaching two classes tomorrow—the subject is political geography—regrettably not one of my favorites." With a wink and a nod, Greg toasted, "To good food, good drink, and especially to good friends. Merry Christmas. *Prosit!*"

No one noticed the German naval captain approaching their table.

"Herr Ziemer?"

Greg looked up, startled. Quickly he stood and with a plastic smile acknowledged the acquaintance, speaking now in German.

"Captain Schroeder, one of my best students! How nice to see you."

The captain didn't click his heels, but he did come to attention, and he offered a slight bow to the man he knew to be Herr Professor.

"Please, Herr Captain, sir. May I introduce my friends?" Greg never broke eye contact with the captain. He gestured with his left hand as Johnny stood and extended his hand. "This is my good friend Herr Jonathon Pitts, from England. An extraordinary musician who, on occasion, brings me a bottle of the most extraordinary scotch whisky."

Johnny extended his hand, acknowledging the captain in German.

The captain grasped Johnny's hand and pulled him close enough to whisper in English. "Upon your next visit to Hamburg, I too would appreciate a bottle of your excellent scotch."

He'd never been hit on so directly. All he could do was smile, nod his head, and try to disengage the captain's vise-grip on his hand.

Greg, feeling like the master of ceremonies, motioned toward Eddie with his right hand. "And this, Herr Captain, sir, is my world-famous American friend, currently performing at our fine Palace Theater here in Hamburg. May I present to you, direct from the United States of America, the wizard of strings and more widely known as the King of the Banjo, Herr Eddie Peabody."

Eddie was already standing at attention, offering his hand.

The captain and Eddie cordially evaluated one another. They both seemed to understand each other intuitively. Each man had earned his place in the world, and each man had earned his sea legs, as only an education on the high seas can bring.

The captain bowed as he shook his hand. "Several of us have tickets to the Palace for what we've been told is a special American jazz presentation, with lots of beautiful girls." His voice rose in emphasis. "I shall look forward to seeing your performance, Herr Peabody." He turned abruptly. "So, my favorite professor, it looks like you three are celebrating. So I think now I should take my leave."

"No, no, please. We're just toasting old and new friendships. And, I'm happy to say, my friends are buying."

The captain laughed robustly. *"Das ist gut . . . ja!"* He motioned for everyone to be seated. He acknowledged all of them once again with a bow. *"Guten Abend,* gentlemen."

After a moment of quiet, Greg began to explain his brief acquaintance with Captain Schroeder. "The captain is one of the senior dock commanders where many ships are being built or refurbished here, on the Elbe River. He, along with several other German officers, attended one of my British and American history classes at the university. Captain Schroeder, as I recall, was particularly interested in American naval tactics during the Civil and Spanish-American war periods. I spent several evenings discussing American political attitudes with him and two other officers."

Eddie was unconsciously twitching his foot as he tried to take in all that was being said. He breathed in deeply, leaned forward, and in a calm, quiet voice said, "Excuse me for interrupting you, Greg. But when can I impose upon you to take me for a little sight-seeing ride around the city?"

The conversation ceased as the waiter began delivering their first course. "How about Sunday morning? Traffic should be at light, and we should be able to stop more easily to take in the sights."

Eddie nodded. "That would be great. Say eight o'clock? Oh,

and could you bring a small camera so I could take some snap-shots? I didn't think to bring mine. All I've got is one of those bulky, oversized newspaper cameras anyway."

"Yes, I would be happy to find something suitable. We wouldn't want you to leave beautiful Hamburg without some shots of Germany's finest architecture."

Johnny, who had been feeling uncomfortable ever since they entered Germany, now felt relieved that he wasn't included in their sightseeing tour. "Well, then, gentlemen, it's settled. I'll leave you two to have at it, while I try desperately to catch up on some much-needed beauty rest."

Greg's mind accelerated as he looked over at Captain Schroeder's table; an idea was emerging. He quickly sorted out what he wanted to propose. "I'm not sure, gentlemen, but believe I may persuade the good captain to give us an off-duty private tour of his facilities. That is, if I'm clever enough to finesse an invite to one of his private parties."

Eddie added some encouragement. "Go for it, Greg! I'll bring my banjo, and we'll have everyone clinking their cocktail glasses and singing Christmas tunes in no time."

"And that, my friends, is exactly what I'm going to sell the captain on. With his ego, and his wife's need to be the social talk of the town, they won't be able to pass up an opportunity like this."

The Hamburg show's producer was very pleased with the dress rehearsal. He was a devout Nazi Party follower who wanted nothing more than to impress his superiors whenever possible. The mayor had mentioned to him at a luncheon that one or two Reich ministers might be present at the show's preview the fol-lowing evening. And the producer knew well enough that if the show flopped, he'd be out of work for the rest of the winter. It was only the finale he was fretting over now. Would Hamburg wives approve of topless girls in a musical performance? While on holiday in Amsterdam, he'd heard one of Eddie's songs that had been recorded in England. He'd persuaded the local radio station to play the song to promote the show, and advanced seating tickets were sold out.

After rehearsal, Eddie literally bumped into Dixie as she exited the communal bathroom. Suddenly feeling self-conscious, she smiled politely at him and tugged on her robe as she lowered her head.

He cleared his throat to redirect her attention. "Ah, excuse me, but may I ask you to join me for a drink before we head back to our hotels this evening?"

"Tonight?" She held her smile. "Sure. I'll meet you at the pub next to our hotel in, say, forty minutes?"

Eddie realized she was referring to the second address she'd given him to memorize. As he looked up, he noticed Johnny waving his arms in the hallway.

He exhaled with an exasperated sigh and walked over to see what his friend wanted.

"Want to share a cab, mate?"

Eddie said nothing, but his eyes said, *Not a chance, you klutz! You actually interrupted my moment with the most beautiful lady in the world, for a cab?*

★   ★   ★

The wind and rain had ceased, but it was still cold out, and the snow on the sidewalks had turned to ice. The cabbies seemed to know instinctively that there were fares to be had at the Palace. There always seemed to be at least two sitting idle whenever the two men looked out front.

Tonight Eddie asked to be dropped off at the pub address Dix had given him. He gave his friend a small slip of paper he'd scribbled it on.

Johnny sat back and stared at the address. "Do I really want to know what you're up to? If you'd wanted me along, you'd have said so, right?"

Eddie sat on the edge of his seat and gave him a mischievous wink. "I'll only be stopping for a short one. We're still on for dinner. So don't leave town without me, pal."

"Not to worry about me, mate. I'll look for you in the lobby, say half past the hour?"

Before Eddie could answer, the cabbie had pulled over to the pub. He made ready to exit and slipped some marks to the driver. "Half past it is, my friend."

Johnny noticed the small hotel next to the dumpy-looking bar. *A rendezvous, perhaps?* He sat back with an envious grin. *Looks like I may be dining alone tonight.*

The cabbie was watching Johnny's facial expressions. Before entering the main street, he turned around and looked straight at him. He wanted to remember his face.

Johnny was startled by the driver's reaction. *Damn! I hope this bloke isn't Gestapo! It's beginning to look like bloody goons are everywhere!*

Eddie walked into the dimly lit, somewhat seedy establishment and sat at the bar. The floor was sticky with spilled beer and smelled worse than a brewery. He ordered a brandy, and the barman looked at him as though he were joking. A quick scan of the room revealed a stage and a bandstand. He couldn't imagine a small place like this supporting live music. There were only three other patrons sitting at a corner table: two inebriated locals with numerous empty beer bottles scattered around the table, and a middle-aged woman who looked like she was trying to talk them out of whatever money they had between them. Dixie entered about five minutes later.

She walked over and casually sat on a barstool next to him. They never made eye contact or acknowledged one another.

"I'm told that in winter, a local band shows up on Saturdays. But they say the locals party pretty hard every chance they get."

Eddie listened as he continued to scan the small room.

"Shall we sit at a table?" Without comment, they both stood and picked a small table close to the front, out of earshot.

"I'm going to tour the city with Greg on Sunday, Dix. We met a naval captain, last night at dinner, who will likely be at the performance tomorrow night. Greg says that this guy has been a student of his, and he thinks he can get us a private tour of the shipbuilding facilities." He paused and looked around to see if anyone was trying to listen in. "I wanted you to know in case I need your assistance."

She pushed forward and leaned in to him. "I do appreciate that, sailor." She sipped some more beer. "I'll do the same if any of us get invited to a private party, or whatever." She wasn't sure what to say next, so she stared at her beer.

From the tone of her voice, he wasn't sure what she meant. He twitched nervously, wondering how to soothe the moment. When he looked up, she was wearing a devilish smile.

"I think it would be a good thing if you and I were perceived by the locals as an item, but discreetly—you know, as though we didn't want our spouses to find out." She leaned back in her chair.

He picked up and fumbled with his drink. "What should I say?"

"You don't have to say anything. Just look interested." She continued, before he could catch a breath, "That way, who knows? We might be invited to the same affairs. And we could have reason to bow out, if need be." She looked quite satisfied with herself. She rocked back and forth in her chair. "Don't you agree?"

Once again her quick thinking had caught him by surprise. *I think that this gorgeous lady knows exactly what she's doing. The question is, do I?* He took a slug of brandy, hoping it would help him muster some much-needed courage.

She could see that he was pondering her suggestion and was more than a little nervous. *I hope I didn't scare him. Surely he's a man of the world?*

He broke the silence with a slight stutter as he tried hard to look calm and in control. "I like your idea, Dix. I just wish to hell I could spend the rest of the evening talking with you."

She gave him an affectionate smile and put her hand over his.

He nervously glanced at his watch. "I am sorry, but I've got to get back and meet with Johnny."

She squeezed his hand. "Those two drunks and the hooker are watching us. Make sure you kiss me hard before you leave."

Eddie tried to look around casually as he stood. He grabbed her face abruptly, with both hands, and gently kissed her. He still held her face as he broke the kiss. *Dear God, but I love that smile.*

She startled him again by kissing him hard.

He turned toward the door.

Dixie walked with him the short distance and then patted him on the butt as she announced in a sexy, singsong voice, *"Auf Wiedersehen und danke, mein Herr."*

The two drunks, overhearing the exchange, raised their steins and yelled, *"Prosit!"*

Johnny watched from the hotel lobby as Eddie entered. He seemed pensive but quite happy, almost giddy, with a slight swagger as he dodged two couples as they hurried to catch a cab. *You lucky bastard!*

"What the hell are you staring at, pal? Is my zipper open?"

"No, no, it's nothing at all. You just look like you swallowed a canary, that's all. And I was marveling at how well you seem to be getting along in Hun country, that's all."

TWENTY-TWO

They arrived at the theater as people were being seated, and both men were trying to make mental notes of the number of German uniforms they saw. The reality of where they were began to set in. At the front entrance there were sentries posted and a red carpet down the steps to the canopy had been rolled out. They felt certain that one or more of the German hierarchy was going to be in attendance this evening. They both wished that Greg were near to help them decipher who was attending.

The band started its warm-up, and Eddie came bounding out of his dressing room, bumping shoulders with Dixie as she was running toward the chorus line. "Dix! You look, ah, stunning!" He touched her shoulder. "Absolutely stunning, in your all-but-nonexistent costume."

She blushed and tried to laugh off his comment. She leaned in closer. "Have you taken a look at the German brass in the audience?"

Habit took over, and he looked over his shoulder to see who might be listening in. "Yes! With all the security, I'd say we had a field marshal or admiral attending tonight. Now is when we need Ziemer. He could recognize who's who."

"Well, I've got a lovesick stagehand admirer. I'll quiz him and see what he knows." She saw a couple of her girlfriends hurriedly walking toward them. She grabbed him and kissed him full on the lips, then left to join her friends. "I'll try to catch up with you at intermission."

The first show proceeded smoothly; Eddie wowed them. He tried to relax in his dressing room between shows as he changed out a broken banjo string. *Well, it looks like we're going to be well received by the locals here. So here's hoping I'll get to see some things that I ordinarily wouldn't be privy to.*

Suddenly, his dressing room door opened with a thwack, and again Dixie bounced in. Her face was made up but shiny with perspiration from her performance. Her jaw was set, and her facial expression was serious. She kneeled next to him and motioned with her finger for him not to speak. "Just listen, please." Her voice was low and almost monotone. "In the audience tonight were three admirals, including Erich Raeder, the commander-in-chief of the whole German navy. The other two were Otto Schniewing, chief of naval general staff, and Kurt Fricke, chief of naval operations."

"Good Gawd! No wonder security is tight."

They heard footsteps approaching, and she jumped up and tiptoed back to the door. She listened for a minute. No one approached. She turned, gave him a quick smile and a short wave, and then quietly slipped out.

Eddie had finished changing the string and was tuning up when a stagehand poked his head around the door and held up five fingers, which meant five minutes till next curtain. He made a dash for the staging area, carrying his banjo on his shoulder, like a rifle. In jest he saluted some of the stagehands as he passed by. Near the staging curtain he saw his friend Johnny pacing in a small circle. The man's eyes were nearly bugging out. "What's up, pal?"

"Have you seen the brass in the audience tonight? One mishap, a fire or anything, and the whole German Kriegsmarine hierarchy could be kaput!"

"And quite likely all of us as well. So calm down, pal. What's come over you? We're not performing for Buckingham Palace, or even the Austrian paperhanger himself. So for cripe's sake, take it easy. These guys are just some sailors who want to see some pretty gals and be entertained by some American hotshots. That's all there is to it."

"Bloody 'ell, mate, if you aren't one for the books. You're cool as a cucumber, or I'll kiss the king's arse in Piccadilly, I will."

The show unfolded with flawless precision, and Eddie was cheered into performing an encore—"The Lambeth Walk," his newest hit. The theater manager was ecstatic. After the show, he poured champagne for the press, urging them to herald the show's success.

On Sunday morning Eddie and Ziemer met for breakfast at the hotel. During their quiet course of casual conversation, Greg expressed concern over their planned extracurricular activity.

"Maybe I'm tired from the pace, or the sleepless nights. I don't know. Lately, all I can think about is how this new Germany under Hitler continues to rattle its saber. First it was Austria, and now he wants part of Czechoslovakia. And now, more than ever, I'm beginning to get concerned about the Gestapo. They might be watching me more closely. If I do get dragged in for questioning, I sure as hell don't want you along . . . though I'm sure I'd appreciate the company."

"Look, we both know what the stakes are here. With what you've witnessed, we both know that somebody has got to tell Roosevelt and the rest of the world. Nobody in our country has the slightest idea about what's going on over here. Regardless of the risks, pal, I'm going to do my damnedest to do my job and learn what I can. Then we'll—and I do mean we—we'll get the hell outta here and let the boss know what exactly we think the German submarine force is capable of. We're in this together, you and me, and we will succeed!"

Johnny Pitts had not been sleeping well since they'd entered the continent, and last night was no exception. After his unsettling encounter with the taxi driver, all he wanted was to complete this tour as quickly as possible. But the truth was that right now he really didn't know what to do. He had nervous energy, so he decided to walk around the hotel before breakfast, to check out anyone suspiciously lingering nearby. Within a short while the cold air began to invigorate him. He'd seen no one standing in the entryway of the building across the street, or sitting in a parked motorcar. He started back to the hotel entrance and noticed Greg exiting and heading for his car. They waved to each other as they passed. Ziemer guessed that Johnny had been on one of his early-morning neighborhood walkabouts. They didn't stop to chat.

Greg waited for Eddie in his somewhat cramped but adequate little car. As he slipped on some warm gloves, he pondered his past association with Johnny Pitts. He'd run reconnaissance for Greg on several occasions while relocating some influential Jewish merchants.

Eddie opened the passenger door. He had to scrunch down into the passenger seat. "Well, it's a good thing we're both short. In the future, though, I may ask you to find me a sidecar."

Ziemer didn't miss the humor as he started the vehicle. He prayed that the inadequate heater would continue to function. "See anything suspicious on your way to the car?"

"No, I didn't. But then I really wasn't looking about, perhaps like I should have. Why? Did you see something?"

"No, no. While I was waiting, my mind started to wander, and you know how dangerous that can be. I sometimes get a little uncomfortable, and that usually brings on a need for extra caution." He released the handbrake, and they started off slowly down the narrow street. The car was warming up ever so slightly as he entered the Deichtorplatz roundabout. "I'm sure, by now, you've been briefed on my background. My primary mission, other than teaching at American University, has been to help some influential, and more willing, Jews consolidate their assets and flee the Nazis. It has been very difficult for many of them—they still feel that

Germany is their home, and they've endured anti-Semitism before."
As he navigated slowly through light traffic, he continued, "It may
also interest you that on several occasions, Johnny Pitts has helped
with the relocations. Most of our success stories settled in either
Britain or Canada, but some landed in the United States as well."

Eddie glanced out the window, trying to get a sense of
direction. The car turned abruptly, and a sign caught his eye:
ACHTUNG! DURCHFAHRT VERBOTEN. Greg translated, "Caution! No
thoroughfare."

Perhaps we're near the River Elbe. Eddie's intuition was confirmed when Ziemer pulled over into a narrow space near the
river's edge.

"Sit with me for a minute before you get out, would you? There
are a few things I want to share with you. Ever since the Munich
conference, the cession of the Sudetenland from Czechoslovakia
was inevitable, and the Nazis appear to be unstoppable. This time,
my friend, I believe anti-Semitism is going to get very ugly. I have
seen the increase in Gestapo surveillance—their eyes watching
every railway station, bus depot, port, and major hotel. And
through my scholastic grapevine, I've heard that Waffen-SS agents
are now in every country on the European continent, and my colleagues believe they're even in the United States."

Listening to his impassioned speech had a sobering effect. *I
should have been paying more attention.* Another cold chill traversed
his spine. He shook his head to refocus. *You have a job to do, Peabody.*

They exited the car and began a slow stroll along the quay.
Everything looked depressingly gray: the sky, the river, even the
buildings. There was no one, save one noisy seagull, within a
hundred meters.

Eddie, walking close to Greg, asked, "Can I pick your brain as
we walk along here?"

"Sure. What's on your mind?"

"Well, I'm sure you know more about the agreements between
England and Germany than I do. But I've been told that these
guys should have a submarine force of no more than twenty-four
thousand tons. Is that what you understand?"

"I'm sorry, but I have no idea what that means. I wouldn't hazard a guess at what a submarine weighs, so twenty-four thousand tons—it has no meaning for me."

"Well, take my word on it, but that's about twelve to fifteen subs. The Brits have been telling Washington that these guys have a lot more than fifteen submarines. And they think there's a hidden manufacturing facility right here in Hamburg. And with your help, my orders are to try and verify or deny any of this. So, my friend, if it were up to you, where the hell would you hide a submarine manufacturing plant around here?"

"Actually, I've no idea, but I've heard it said that the best place to hide a pebble is right in the middle of the rock pile. So if I did hazard a guess, I would say we should be looking somewhere near the left bank of the river—there are already ship manufacturing facilities there and a lot of quays that could hide a submarine plant. Now, for us to get anywhere near those facilities, well, I simply haven't a clue."

A loud whistle, near the roof of an old building across the river, let loose and startled both men. It was the noon hour, and workers wearing bibbed overalls spilled out by the hundreds all along the quay.

"You may remember Captain Schroeder, who came over to our table the other night. Well, he sent a messenger to where I was teaching a class to extend to us an invitation to tour his facility. I should think that a tour of his facility would be as good a place as any to start our search. What do you think?"

"Good grief, Greg! I think that would be wonderful. I had no idea where to begin, and here you come up with an insider tour. What a guy."

Though nothing as yet had been finalized, he couldn't restrain the telltale smile. "I'll phone Schroeder's office tomorrow and see if I can set something up for us later in the week. Oh, I nearly forgot—I suggest renting a room that overlooks the river. If they do have a hidden shipbuilding facility, then they'd have to float whatever they built up the river, right? And to avoid any nosy neighbors, launchings would have to be at night. And if we had a room overlooking the river, who knows? We might get lucky."

It was bitterly cold, and Eddie's fingers and toes were letting him know. He put his hands in his pockets and began to stamp his feet.

"One last item before you leave Hamburg. I would like you to get some pictures of some of the anti-aircraft fortifications the Nazis have built near Denmark. I simply couldn't believe what I saw when I drove to Esbjerg this fall. The Germans may not be talking war to world leaders, but from what I've seen, they damn sure look like they're preparing for one. Now, let's get you out of this cold air."

"On the way back, could we take a drive near those shipbuilding facilities across the river?"

"We'll give it a shot, my friend."

They were driving toward the St. Pauli Landungsbrücken, a narrow, man-made docking quay paralleling the north bank of the River Elbe. Ziemer was pointing out the Wallanlagen gardens and the Bismarck memorial. A uniformed soldier suddenly appeared and stopped them just before the Seewanstrasse intersection. They could see a military roadblock ahead. Ziemer rolled down his window, told the guard that he and his friend were sightseeing, and asked what the problem was. The guard approached and unceremoniously informed them that they were entering a restricted area. They were to leave immediately.

He smiled and quickly put the car in reverse. The guard would surely pass along the vehicle license plate number to his superiors.

After crossing the river, Ziemer turned into a narrow alleyway and rolled to a stop. "Before we head back to the hotel, what say we have a look for a flat near the river, one with a view?"

"Sure thing, skipper."

"I'd bet shillings to sausage that we were awfully close to something back there." He tried to maneuver the vehicle in reverse back toward the street. He stopped and slammed his fists on the steering wheel.

"What's the matter? Did you forget something?"

"No, no, it's nothing. But now I'm afraid they've likely reported my plate number. We'll have to find some alternate transportation for any future sightseeing, that's all."

"We could always borrow the theater manager's car. For that matter, oh hell, we could buy one.

Greg suddenly hit the brakes hard, causing Eddie to brace himself against the metal dashboard as the car slid to a stop. He was pointing to a building with a For Rent sign in one of the windows. "The river is only one block ahead, behind that building." He maneuvered the car into one of the adjacent driveways, hoping no one would object.

They both looked around for inquiring eyes as they walked in silence toward the apartment building. The building was not new, but it wasn't completely run down, either. They felt warmer as they stood in the entryway, away from the chilling wind off the river, but they soon realized that there was no warm air flowing from any type of central heating unit. Being next to the river, they were sure that every unit in the building would be drafty and damp, but those rooms facing the river would likely be perfect, at least for what they had in mind.

"Wait here, Eddie, while I try to locate the manager and get a look at what is for rent." The building manager's apartment was at the end of a narrow, poorly lit hallway. He very soon emerged with the manager in tow. The manager was a large, burly man with a two-day beard and scouring-pad hair. He was wearing gloves and a heavy coat and seemed somewhat disinterested. He took notice of Eddie rubbing his hands together and stamping his feet. He indicated to Greg that the building's central heating was under repair, and perhaps they should return in a week to view the apartment after repairs were complete.

Greg thanked the manager but said they both were anxious to have a look anyway. The manager shrugged indifference as he shuffled up wooden stairs to the second floor. The vacant apartment was the first unit on the second floor, facing the Elbe. Upon entering the main living area, they both realized that the unit was much larger than was needed. However, they continued to feign interest as the manager ushered them along on the creaky wooden floor to inspect the rest of the apartment. As they quickly walked through the two tiny bedrooms, they both noticed immediately that the second room had a window with a clear view of a large portion of the river, including most of the St. Pauli landing.

Returning to the main room, the manager began to spell out deposits required for utilities and damage insurance. Greg interrupted, indicating that they were only interested in renting by the month, but obviously a functioning heating system was essential.

The manager hemmed and hawed. "Sir, I assure you that the unit will be repaired by the end of the week." He suggested what he thought would be a fair monthly rent but continued to insist upon a deposit.

Given the scarce availability of rooms in the area, they both thought the price was reasonable. They shook hands and sealed the deal.

On the way back, Greg asked cautiously, "Eddie, do you think you'll be able to scrape up a couple thousand marks to cover what we'll need here?"

"That shouldn't be a problem. We've opened an account at the bank near our hotel, and I'm sure the embassy in London can wire as much as we need. I'll ask Johnny to arrange for five thousand, which should be enough for a month's rent on this dump and maybe another car."

Greg smiled. "Dump, is it? My friend, that apartment is much nicer than what most of my professional friends are able to afford. And yes, five thousand should be more than enough, for now."

"Look, forgive me if I offended you. I know you're doing incredibly important and dangerous work over here, and I appreciate everything you're doing for me. Without you, I know I wouldn't be able to get anything for the folks back home."

"No, I'm the one who should ask for forgiveness. Sometimes all the tension that continues to surround me, it just wears me down. And again, five thousand marks should be more than enough for what we want to do. I'll try to touch base with you in two or three days."

Eddie's hands were like ice. After warming them under the hot water tap back at the hotel, he called up Johnny. "Heya, pal, how's about you and me taking a short stroll before heading to the club tonight?"

"Bloody 'ell, I swear you Yanks butcher the King's English just to irritate civilization. I presume a warm coat and gloves are in order?"

"Right you are, mate. I'll meet you in the lobby in five." He rang off without waiting for a reply.

Before leaving the hotel, they both took a quick glance around to see who might be watching. All seemed normal: traffic was light, no one was sitting idle in a parked car near the hotel, and there were only a few pedestrians.

Once outside, Johnny was curious. "So, what's happening? Why the sudden need for a stroll, as you put it?"

"I need you to contact the embassy in London and get five thousand marks sent to our bank down here as soon as you can."

"Well, I guess you did have something important to discuss. You know, of course, that at your embassy, this mission has been a priority since you landed in England. Whether or not they'll advance me what you've requested, I simply don't know."

A cold wind had picked up while they walked along, and Eddie's hands started to chill up again. He tried to ignore it. "Greg hit a military roadblock near the St. Pauli shipyard. He's nervous about having his license plate reported to the Gestapo. So, at my suggestion, he's going to purchase another car. The man's neck is sticking out pretty far, and we couldn't possibly complete our mission without him. Oh, we also found an apartment with a bird's-eye view of the river, right across from the shipyard." He glanced around to see if anyone was within earshot. "I know you and Greg have worked together in the past, and you know there isn't anyone I trust more than you, but right now I think it would be better if you didn't know any more than you already do. Are you okay with that?"

"Certainly, I'm okay with that. The less I know, the better off I'll be if we get pinched. And tomorrow morning, first thing, I will call the American embassy from a secure phone. I'll encrypt what you've relayed to me and pass along an emotional plea. I can't imagine we'll be turned down." He put his arm around the shoulders of his friend. "I apologize if you thought I was being too nosy. But you know me."

The shows at the Palace were packed. Hamburg audiences were enthusiastic about the American performers, and the local press echoed that enthusiasm. With the number of uniforms at each performance, the port city appeared to be nothing more than an armed compound. The younger officers, of course, were smitten with the American chorus girls, and the girls' dressing room soon resembled a floral showcase. After a matinee performance, Eddie noticed Dixie carrying an armful of roses. He wanted to kid her, but Johnny caught him by the arm.

"We need to get back to the hotel straightaway, my friend. A visitor will be dropping by." He didn't elaborate.

Eddie nodded and suddenly forgot all about socializing with Dix.

Catching the last cab, they rode the short distance back to the hotel in relative silence. They'd agreed that when in a public conveyance, the less said, the better.

Eddie checked the incoming mail, while Johnny scanned a local paper. Greg, having arrived five minutes earlier, proceeded to Eddie's floor and entered his room with a key he'd obtained from a young, impressionable desk clerk. Quietly he scanned Eddie's room and began checking for anything that looked disturbed. He was especially concerned that small microphones might recently have been installed. After satisfying himself that the room was clean, he waited for Eddie in an unlit corner near the window.

Within a few minutes, Eddie opened the door and turned on

the overhead light. Greg's presence startled him. "Damn it, man! It's a good thing I haven't got a gun."

"Good evening, my friend. You do look surprised to see me."

"That I am. And just how the hell did you get in here?"

"Well, that was the easy part. I simply told the desk clerk that you had asked me to fetch one of your instruments. And as you can see, the young clerk didn't hesitate." Greg walked over to where Eddie was standing. "It was that easy. And you know that anyone wanting to look around, especially the Gestapo—well, they'd have no trouble at all. So I've carefully checked your room for any devices that may have been recently installed."

"Well?"

"Well, I'm pleased to say I didn't find any hidden cameras, microphones, or tiny, unexplained holes in the wall. And I found no evidence that any of the light fixtures had been tampered with. So I think it's safe to assume that—for now, anyway—your room is clean."

Eddie could feel his blood pressure start to rise. He was astonished to learn that access to his room was that easy, and that any Gestapo bastard that wanted to could spy on him just as easily.

"I can see that this is a new world for you. Try to look at it this way—the Gestapo wouldn't be doing anything that you or I wouldn't do in similar circumstances. So try to calm down. Take it easy."

While Eddie was mulling things over, Greg changed the subject. "I believe I've located another car."

"Really?"

"Right, it turns out an overly generous family that I'm relocating to the United States offered to give me their Mercedes. I politely declined. Also, Johnny mentioned that the money you've requested should be transferred to your account here in Hamburg by the end of the week."

There was a slight knock at the door. Johnny entered. "Well, good evening, gents."

"Greg, did you say these people wanted to give you their Mercedes? Good grief!"

"Yeah, how about that?"

"So now what?"

"Well, I told the people that vehicles were scarce in Germany these days, and that their beautiful car was worth far more than I could afford. However, I did tell them that I'd saved a little more than two thousand marks."

"Yes, and?"

"They told me that with the current anti-Semitic fever gripping their homeland, a Jew publicly selling anything today would raise nothing but suspicion. So, they said, they would consider it a blessing if I'd quietly take their car, at no charge."

"My God!"

"Right, but I still couldn't accept their offer, and I asked if two thousand marks would be an acceptable exchange. They accepted."

"That's terrific. What a story."

"Sorry, gents, but I've got to run and prepare for a class tomorrow."

"Right," Johnny interrupted. "As I said, we should have the cash by the end of the week."

Eddie shook hands with Greg as he strode past toward the door. After Greg departed, Eddie turned toward Johnny. "That'll work just fine. But I must say I have very mixed emotions. These people are so kind and generous—I can't believe they're so anxious to sell everything they own, for whatever they can get, just to be able to leave their homeland. Can you imagine? It breaks my heart."

Johnny was a little stunned by Eddie's more than empathetic reaction. He knew that many at the American embassy were unaware of what was happening in Germany today. When he'd related similar stories of people desperate to leave the country of their birth, most had reacted with emotional detachment. He looked at Eddie and knew he needed to stay upbeat with this guy—an American entertainer, with a short fuse, wanting to get involved in risky business.

Eddie had walked over to the window. He was staring at the pedestrians scurrying about below and wondering how many would jump from the current ship of state, if given the chance.

Johnny felt uncomfortable in the silence and tried to think of something upbeat to say. *Maybe I should just leave?* He cleared his throat and put on his everything's-okay happy face as Eddie turned away from the window. "I almost forgot. Greg mentioned to me that Captain Schroeder's having a holiday party at his home this coming Saturday. And he insisted that we attend. Of course I told Greg that you had a Saturday evening performance, but he was insistent. He went on to say that Schroeder's holiday parties were widely known to last into the wee hours. I told him that we would be pleased to attend if at all possible, but that I would have to ask you, knowing the show schedule at the Palace. I told him to please not count on you attending."

"Count me in, pal. This may our only opportunity. I'll do whatever I have to do to make this work. We need to call Greg and tell him I'll bring my banjo. We should have the ladies all a-giggle and singing 'Jingle Bells' in no time."

"Well, I'm sure the captain's wife will be too excited for words."

Greg had parked the Mercedes right in front of the hotel's entrance. The bell captain was pleased to watch over the big, shiny vehicle and handed him the keys as the three men approached.

"Good grief, man. Is that the car you just bought for two thousand marks?" It wasn't as large as some of the German staff cars he'd seen at the theater, but it was still one hell of a luxury item that he knew few locals could afford.

Eddie and Johnny sat in back, gawking at the ostentatious luxury of the spacious vehicle. Johnny leaned forward and asked jokingly, "Say, is anyone going to believe you'd give up a cushy teaching job just to usher around a couple of hotshot American musicians?"

Greg revved the motor and spun the tires, throwing the two men in the back against the seat.

"Whoa, slow down. We don't need to be explaining to some nosy constable why we're racing around in this fancy car."

Greg turned north toward the river and drove them to the apartment that he and Eddie had looked at a few days earlier. The building manager walked over from the alley to meet them at the front entrance. He smiled as he offered the three an enthusiastic and hearty handshake. He'd reviewed with the owner the rent amount he'd wanted to charge by the month, and all was okay with him.

Greg was immediately suspicious. Either this guy had gotten suspicious and gone to the Gestapo, or he was looking to slide by an outrageous price tag for the monthly rent. Either way, the guy looked like he'd just swallowed the canary.

As they walked up the stairs, the manager proudly told them that his son had worked on the heating unit for the last two days solid. They did notice that there was some heat emanating from a small cast-iron grill in the kitchen floor.

Greg motioned for Eddie to listen. "I think he's trying to roll one past us."

They strolled casually into the second bedroom to confirm that the river view was still intact. Greg and the apartment manager began the process of negotiation, parrying arguments.

"You'll find it impossible to find anything comparable," the manager insisted.

"Greg, tell the guy we'll need a bed, some linen, and a table with a couple of chairs." Eddie pulled out 750 marks and handed them to the manager, the two shook hands, and the deal was sealed.

Once outside, Greg spoke matter-of-factly to the other two. "That was an outrageous price we paid back there, but I think I fussed enough to not raise any suspicion. I'm hoping our manager will thump his chest and tell everyone what a tough negotiator he was."

"You did a good job on him, Greg. To me the room was perfect, and if he comes through with the other items we asked for, I really don't care what he charges us for the time we're going to be there."

"It is a good spot, and with a little luck, you may get a shot of what you came here for. Say, before we head back to the hotel, if there is time before you have to get ready, I'd like to take a short drive up toward Denmark for a little sightseeing."

"I've got two hours before I have to shave and clean up for tonight's performances."

As the three made their way to the car, the apartment manager standing next to his wife at a window was pointing out to her the guys he'd just scalped on the vacant upstairs unit. The wife inhaled with a gasp, putting her hand to her mouth as she focused on Eddie's profile. Her husband never took notice.

"I'm sorry, gents, but I need to beg off. I have an appointment to review some changes with the show's director. I do hope you don't mind?"

"Not in the least, Johnny. You take care of business. Besides, you've already seen much of what I want to show Eddie."

After depositing Johnny at the hotel, Greg drove Eddie another fifty kilometers north to Flensburg, a small town on the Danish border. The countryside, though it was the dead of winter, was beautiful, all covered in a blanket of white. Greg slowed the vehicle and pointed out several anti-aircraft fortifications that had recently been constructed. They were all manned by Germans. He slowed to a stop and fumbled under the driver's-side seat, retrieving a small Leica 35mm camera. The Leica was small, compact, and simple, unlike Eddie's Speed Graphic.

The air was freezing, but Eddie began discreetly to take as many pictures out the open window as he could. "There's a hell of a lot of activity out in this remote area, if you ask me. It looks like somebody is preparing for something, and it looks like they're expecting an invasion. There's more traffic out here than in Hamburg."

"Right you are, Eddie. That's why I wanted you to see all this for yourself. And none of this is Danish. There is no doubt in my mind the Germans are preparing for war."

As they slowed down while passing through a small village, Eddie noticed that many of the village buildings had been decorated beautifully for Christmas. He stared out at the frosted, frozen landscape. *What a contrast. Celebrating the Christmas season while preparing for war, right on top of Denmark.* Greg turned the large vehicle around at an intersection and returned quickly to the hotel.

The night of Captain Schroeder's party, Greg took the Mercedes to the theater and waited backstage for Eddie and Johnny. He helped load musical instruments and then drove slowly to Schroeder's home east of the city. They wound through a heavily wooded neighborhood where many of the trees were tall hardwoods. The noise of the big city had suddenly disappeared. The thick foliage would have blocked a street view, had it been summer. The homes were older and quite large: not mansions, but very elegant with their manicured landscaping. This was an old-world wealthy neighborhood.

"Scuttlebutt has it that all the local brass, and maybe one or two from Berlin, will be in attendance tonight. Apparently, the captain's wife's family is old navy, and all are very well off. One of my students commented that, short of placing an advertisement in the paper, the captain's wife and her mother have broadcast to nearly everyone that you'll be the guest of honor tonight. So we should expect people from the local newspaper milling about, looking for a story."

"Don't worry, Greg. I've done this sort of thing my whole life. I'll find a cozy corner somewhere and play my heart out, at least until the hostess is curled up on the couch. Give me a couple of drinks, and I'll have everyone singing *Yankee Doodle Dandy.*"

With an anxious tone, Johnny quipped, "Dear God, but I do love your reassurance."

"Just kibitzing with you guys."

At this point, Greg was also feeling quite anxious, but he put on a reassuring smile as he touched Eddie's shoulder. "There will be some serious politicking tonight. Stay close, if you can. Not knowing the language should be to your advantage. I'll do my best to keep you informed—who's saying what to whom."

"Right. My German is a bit rusty, mate, but I'll try to get the gist of what's being said."

"Eddie, my plan is to monopolize our host while you're entertaining guests with your musical wizardry. Who knows? Maybe I can talk him into a tour of his facility. I'll tell him I'm doing a research paper on the government's new emphasis on industrialization and the positive effect it's having on the German economy. That should flatter his ego sufficiently. I'm reasonably sure he'll want to show us just how impressive German industrial might truly is."

"Well, just point me in the right direction. I'll do my best to charm the ribbons right off his chest."

"Getting out of here in one piece is definitely in my plan, gentlemen."

They arrived fashionably late. The driveway, approximately a quarter mile off the main highway, was a frozen mixture of finely compacted snow and ice, with gravel as a base. The large Mercedes navigated the potentially slippery drive with ease. The Schroeders' nineteenth-century home was constructed of stone blocks that had weathered gracefully with age. Ivy covered much of the walls on either side of the entrance. The front lawn was covered with a thin crust of frozen snow that reflected the outside lighting with a frosty glare. A few pine trees were interspersed with the many hardwoods that seemed to surround the house. A stone walkway and steps led to the entry alcove from a circular drive. Two uniformed sentries guarded the foyer. Once they passed through security, the large, solid-wood door framed by tall beveled-glass windows slowly opened as if it could do so on its own. From inside, a white-gloved uniformed doorman appeared from behind the door with a welcoming bow. The captain and his wife stood to one side and formally welcomed their distinguished guests. The stately old house was large, with beautiful beamed ceilings, and decorated with delicate period furnishings. A perfectly shaped Christmas tree (a fourteen-footer, as the captain proudly pointed out) occupied one corner of the main room. Eddie was also pleased to see in the opposite corner a small grand piano, which he hoped was reasonably in tune. Greens were strung high, near the ceiling, throughout.

Almost everyone there was standing in a conversation group and sampling several selections from the sumptuous buffet. Standing near the lovely display in the dining room, the captain's wife announced that everyone should refrain from being shy, and sample as many of the rare delicacies as their uniforms would accommodate.

By the time they had traversed the sumptuous buffet, Eddie choosing only that which he vaguely recognized, the captain had appeared with a tray and offered them a glass of champagne. Greg and Johnny were standing in a deserted corner near the fireplace. They each took about four bites of the food they'd selected and set their plates on the hearth. The champagne seemed to go down much easier.

Many of the guests were now starting to separate into groups: men on one side of the room, women on the other. Eddie motioned to Johnny, with his eyes, toward the piano. He quietly carried his banjo over to the piano and sat nearby in a straight-backed chair. They began the process of tuning up.

As Captain Schroeder waltzed in with another tray of drinks, Greg captured his attention and began chatting him up. The captain was very forthcoming and candid with Greg. They were in close conversation long enough for the captain to realize he was neglecting his other guests.

"Greg, it is wonderful that you were able to arrange for Herr Peabody to attend this evening. He is well known by many of my wife's friends in Hamburg. How did the local press refer to him? I think it was the American Wizard of Strings, or was it the Man with the Banjo? Whatever—my wife has been on pins and needles all evening."

"Thank you for those kind words, Captain." He turned toward Eddie. "I was just telling the captain how you'd love to play some Christmas songs for the ladies."

The captain's eyes and face lit up visibly with excitement. "My house is yours, my friends."

"Wonderful, wonderful." Greg translated for Eddie.

"Greg, if you'll give me a poor man's introduction, we'll see if we can't find some tunes that everybody knows. I see a likely group of carolers right over here."

He translated Eddie's intent in the best humor he could muster, asking the ladies if they would be interested in some Christmas songs performed by the Man with the Banjo himself, Eddie Peabody. With a burst of handclapping and a giggle or two, the gathered group clamored its approval.

Eddie put the violin mute on the bridge of the banjo to soften the tone. He hoped the soft music would touch everyone with the spirit of the season. Soon verses of "Silent Night" and "Deck the Halls" could be heard throughout the house. By the time he'd removed the violin mute and started to strum out "Jingle Bells," the living room was jammed with people clinking on glasses with a knife or fork in time with the music. A raucous cheer and shouts of "Happy Christmas!" erupted when the song finally ended.

Greg came forward with a raised glass in a toast to the host and hostess. He thanked everyone for their gracious hospitality and wished them all a happy Christmas and a prosperous new year. The three men stood together for several minutes before cheers and whistles from the crowd began to subside. The captain and his wife rushed forward, continuing to applaud and gushing effusive thanks as the three meandered toward the front entrance.

Once in the car and away from the party's din, Greg revealed what he'd discussed with Captain Schroeder. "In summary, the captain said the brass leaves for Berlin on Wednesday. So he wondered if Thursday morning at 9:00 AM would be good for me to tour his facility. After I'd agreed, I graciously asked if I could bring along my American entertainer friend. He hesitated but then reluctantly agreed."

"Very good, Herr Ziemer."

Greg added, "We need to maximize our time with Schroeder. I've got to put together a plan."

"Well, you may not know it, skipper, but if you ever decide

to leave this cloak-and-dagger business, you've got one hell of a future in show business."

Greg chuckled at the implication. *What does he think teaching students is all about?*

Eddie was ecstatic about his pending visit to the shipyards. He too wanted to maximize their time with the good captain. Whether or not submarines were being built at this facility, he knew he'd be bringing back valuable information to Washington. He closed his eyes. *The Germans likely do have a secret shipbuilding site—and quite likely they've no intent of keeping the terms of any agreement they've signed with the Brits.*

The following evening, after the last show, he took a cab to the St. Pauli District where they had rented an apartment. The building still felt cold and damp. He quickly ran up the stairs, inserted his key, and was surprised to see that the manager had connected a small lamp on a table next to a well-worn armchair. He walked over and gently pulled the shade over the window. The apartment felt ice-cold as he moved slowly to the second bedroom's window. He stared out across the river, mesmerized by the lights from the shipyard and surrounding buildings. He could actually see some ship movements, and he wondered if Greg's camera would be able to pick up much detail. He remembered Greg's lecture, as they'd traveled in Denmark, on the long exposure technique. He leaned against the windowsill and stared at the frozen river below him. *One photograph, a submarine heading out to sea, and the job is complete.* He shut off the light, locked up, and headed down the stairs. At the bottom of the stairwell there was a middle-aged woman emptying some trash. Her hair was tied with a scarf, and she was humming a Christmas song. She was wearing a housedress that wasn't particularly flattering, but she wasn't that unattractive either. She looked up as he stepped closer. He could see her eyes begin to narrow as she tried to focus on his face. She continued to stare, and it began to unnerve him. Perhaps it was because he was wearing a suit and a topcoat: not something she'd normally see around here. He put on a showbiz happy-face smile, touched two fingers to his eyebrow, and with a wink and a nod, offered, *"Guten Abend."* He heard a gasp as he passed under the overhead light. He turned to face her and saw that she had her hand covering her mouth. She lowered her hand and blurted out, *"Sie sind aus Amerika, ja?"* He nodded as he backed out the front door.

The woman bit her knuckle and started to giggle, then shrieked and ran down the hall.

TWENTY-THREE

Captain Schroeder had instructed Greg to meet him at the east end of his facility, where the building paralleled the Elbe River along the north side of the St. Pauli landing. As they crossed the narrow bridge connecting the two sides of the river, Eddie could see a series of single-story buildings, completely enclosed in corrugated metal, that extended west, paralleling the river for what looked to be more than five hundred meters. He also noticed what he thought was a series of outfitting piers extending out into the river and connecting with a narrow strip of land paralleling the north shore, the St. Pauli Landing. Two ships, Cruiser class, that weren't visible from the south shore, were in port, with construction crews working on deck.

After they'd cleared security, both Eddie and Greg commented on the vast network of rail and roadways needed to supply the large quantities of material required for shipbuilding. Several rail-mounted cranes were offloading railcar after railcar of heavy steel, while trucks were moving some of the steel inside one of the nearby buildings, but it was too far away for either of them to see what was being assembled. A guard ushered them into the nearest building, and after signing in and receiving identification cards, they were seated on wooden chairs facing a large, open office area.

Eddie leaned close to Greg. "Judging from the number of people scurrying about in here, it looks to me like most of Hamburg is employed at these shipyards."

"And," Greg added, "If I'm not mistaken, we're just in the engineering department."

"Greg, there are men and equipment literally moving material everywhere."

Captain Schroeder stepped out of one of the adjacent offices and strode over to greet them. He was dressed in his winter uniform. With neatly combed, graying hair, razor-straight posture, and a confident stride, there was little doubt that this man was in command. Eddie took note of the captain's very pleasant smile. The man seemed very relaxed in these surroundings. He'd ordered coffee in his office.

The captain reminisced on what a wonderful time everyone had had at his wife's party. "And for Eddie to bring his banjo and entertain us with Christmas songs—well, everyone, especially my wife, was properly impressed."

Greg straightened, bowed, and answered, "Herr Peabody, Herr Pitts, and I—we were honored to have participated in your festivities and to have tasted your gracious hospitality."

The captain's phone rang and interrupted them. After listening with furrowed eyebrows, Schroeder barked sharply into his instrument and then quickly returned it to its carriage. Without saying another word, he took a large gulp of coffee, turned to his guests, and handed them each a security badge. He stood, quite abruptly, from behind his desk. Schroeder was now hurriedly ushering them out of his office.

Before directing them down a flight of stairs, the captain briefed them on some safety issues and reminded them to stay close as they toured the facility. "Security is very tight down these stairs, gentlemen. It's very important that you stay close at hand. Unfortunately, throughout this facility, there are some trigger-happy Gestapo who are not under my command. If either of you wanders off, you could be shot."

They both tensed up at the captain's words but nodded their understanding. Greg tried to engage the captain by complimenting him on the cleanliness of such a large facility. There was no response. After traversing four flights of stairs, Greg turned toward Eddie. "It seems as though we're descending into the bowels of the earth."

"Right you are, skipper. It seems to me that we've descended below the level of the river. And have you noticed how much larger the facility is down here compared to the stretch of tin buildings on the surface? It looks like this underground area extends way beyond the road we came in on." Eddie looked up in the direction he thought was north, to get his bearings. He gasped, not believing what he was looking at. A ship hull stretched in front of him that was, in his opinion, as long as an aircraft carrier. He could barely see to the end of the scaffolding; it was larger than anything he'd seen in Norfolk. *What in hell are they building, a German supercarrier? And how are they going to float that thing up a river?*

Greg was also awed by the sight and asked the captain what type of ship was being constructed. It seemed bigger than anything he too had ever seen.

The captain was proud to announce, "Gentlemen, what you are looking at will soon be the largest battleship ever constructed, by any nation." He turned and barked some orders to some civilian contractors and then continued to walk north along this great hull, with sparks often flying near from welding that was taking place above their heads.

Eddie thought he could see the glow of arc welders west of where they were standing and at what seemed to be the level below them. He nudged Greg and pointed to the area he was looking at. "What do you think is going on at that lower level? We must be at least two stories below the level of the river by now."

The captain noticed them pointing out the activity below the current level. "Those are submarine construction bays, gentlemen.

Sorry, but we need to move along. I'm afraid my meeting schedule won't allow me the luxury of a leisure tour."

Eddie was completely dumbfounded. *How the hell do they get a submarine launched and floated when the level of the river is above construction?* He craned his neck upward to where he thought the level of the river was. "I'm sorry, pal, but I can't figure out how they get the damn things out of here."

The captain overheard the question and smiled broadly. "Submarine construction bins are separate concrete enclosures, gentlemen. Each construction bay is separated from the river by two hydraulic locks that can be pressurized and flooded. When construction is complete, the boat's ballasts are flooded, along with the entire concrete bin. The outer doors to the river are then opened, and the submarine is motored out on batteries. Once in the deep channel of the Elbe, the ballasts are blown, and the diesel motors are started. The boat is then motored to a point along the north coast. The completed units are moved only at night, but it is rather spectacular when one is launched at night."

The captain motioned for them to continue. They both noticed that the man was now walking with a swagger to his step. Greg again tried to engage Schroeder in conversation. But before he could ask about production numbers, Schroeder interrupted him. The captain looked straight ahead and continued to speak as though he were talking with an old friend. "You know, we are hoping to have a submarine launch in the next five days. The brass will be here, as always, whenever this happens. But unfortunately I will be stuck down here all night, so I won't get to see much of the launch." He leaned closer to Greg and whispered, "Someone has to make sure everything goes perfectly."

"And with you in charge, sir, I have no doubt that everything will proceed like clockwork."

The captain slowed his pace, tucking his hands behind his back. It always pleased him to inundate people with numbers and statistics. And the two men were suitably awestruck by the incredible production tonnage that Schroeder was responsible for.

"Captain, I want to thank you for taking so much of your

valuable time to provide Eddie and me such a personal and informative tour. I do apologize, but the dean informed me, only last evening, that I am scheduled to give a lecture at American University within the hour. I did mention to him our appointment with you, but I'm afraid that the more I protested, the more he insisted."

Schroeder's empathetic smile was reassuring. "I understand, my friend. Politics seem to permeate all our lives these days. There are some stairs to our right that will take us to the surface."

"Thank you, sir. And if you have no objection, Captain, it would be most helpful if I could telephone you tomorrow and review some mental notes I've filed away for the industrialization research paper I'm preparing. I believe I touched on the subject with you at your party."

"Yes, I recall, Greg. And yes, I would be pleased to answer any questions you may have. But please telephone me at home, sometime after 8:00 PM, if you would. You do have my home number?"

"Yes, sir, I do. And again, thank you so much."

Eddie extended his hand to the Captain and added, "I too want to thank you for your gracious hospitality, sir, and for your patience in helping me to understand a few things I knew nothing about. I'm truly impressed with this incredibly large complex you are responsible for."

Schroeder clicked the heels of his boots, came to attention, crisply bowed his head to his guests, and then gestured with his arm in the direction to the stairwell.

When they were outside, on the way to the car, Eddie stopped and scanned the area, trying to absorb the enormity of the facility he'd just seen. An armed guard suddenly appeared and escorted them, quick time, to their car. He wasn't about to tolerate any dilly-dallying. They quickly drove off the facility and through the security roadblock.

After several minutes of contemplative silence, Eddie couldn't sit still. "There's just no way an outsider could know about the size or complexity of that facility—or appreciate what was going on underground unless you saw it with your own eyes. I still can't believe it. Damn, but I wished to hell I could have gotten a picture of that enormous hull of a battleship." There was a silent pause. He turned sidesaddle and looked at Greg. "When are you going to get the hell out of here and go back to the States? These guys are building warships that even the Brits won't be able to contain."

Greg reached over and took hold of his arm. "Calm down, please. When you get back to the hotel, write down exactly what you saw today."

"I will, pal. But what are you gonna do? I'd say you should be making plans to return to the States, and fast."

"I'm going to stay in touch with the Captain and try to pin down when the next submarine launch will be. I believe he said that in four or five days the brass were returning. If you could get a picture of one of the U-boats, that would be all the proof you'd need. One good picture should convince your superiors that the Germans are continuing to ignore the Treaty of Versailles—and, if it matters, the bilateral agreement with Britain."

"I wish to hell I could somehow just telephone FDR and simply tell him everything I've just seen. The old man would believe me." *And then he could telephone that slug of a prime minister and let him know exactly what the Hun is up to.*

Greg called early the following morning. "I talked with Schroeder this morning. I again thanked him for his hospitality, and he let slip that the brass were due back this coming weekend to witness a midnight sub-launching. He mumbled something about a charging unit, which to me means he's having trouble with the launch schedule. I sensed that the man was stressed, and probably with good reason. Admirals are characteristically unsympathetic to delays. So I'm sure he'll do whatever is necessary to have the boat ready when advertised."

"Or he can kiss any hopes of a future promotion goodbye."

"Well, it looks like this weekend you may want to check into our apartment. I'll stay in touch to determine if there are going to be any delays, okay?"

"Right, skipper. I'll have a look this weekend and let you know if we get lucky. And thanks for the update. Stay in touch, Greg." He rang off and went over to his instrument case, where he'd hidden the camera, and rechecked the number of film packets. *All I need is one picture, and the mission will be complete.*

Johnny was already seated for breakfast when Eddie sauntered in. "Good morning to you, my fine, feathered friend."

"Bloody 'ell, one good night's sleep, and the bloke thinks we're all flamin' birds. I take it you rested well? Speaking of birds, any extracurricular activities?" He poured some coffee for his friend as he raised an eyebrow.

"No, my nosy English friend. But you never know—I might just get lucky this weekend. So if we're on our toes, I just may be able to wrap things up."

"I say, we are articulate this morning, aren't we? And me holding a pocketful of money for you as well. I just don't know." He grinned as he handed him an envelope across the table.

Eddie slid the envelope into his coat pocket. "One good snapshot this weekend, pal, and we've done our job."

That afternoon, Eddie went the theater early to look for Dixie. He caught her eye as she was putting on her makeup in her dressing room. She slipped on a robe, buckled her shoes, and dodged several girls in the cramped space as she made her way to the doorway. One of the showgirls gave her the raspberry as she threaded herself out the door. "Why don't you mind your own business, Sally?"

They embraced in the dimly lit hallway. "So, what's up?"

Eddie just stood staring at her, speechless. He tried to refocus his thoughts. Unfortunately, but much to his delight, her robe parted slightly, and even in the dim light he could see that she was wearing a low-cut corset with fishnet stockings. *Dear God, but this woman is a vision, and she never ceases to surprise me.* He cleared his throat. "Have you got a date Saturday, after the show?"

"No, why?"

"I need a cover escort. I've rented an apartment near the river."

Dixie was puzzled. Suddenly the hallway felt crowded. Stagehands and dancers were scurrying about, bumping into props and into one another. Dixie didn't see anyone nearby, but she still felt uncomfortable. With one hand on her hip, and for anyone who might be listening in, she blurted out, "Sure, honey, but why don't we just go to your hotel room?"

Eddie blushed at her response; he too felt uncomfortable. He wasn't about to explain anything to her in the now-crowded hallway. He pulled her to him and whispered in her ear, "I'll meet you out front, right after the evening performance. I'll explain everything then." He kissed her forehead and stood back and smiled at her. "Bring a warm coat, Dix, and we'll catch a quick bite at the hotel before we head out—that is, if that's okay with you?"

She leaned forward and kissed him lightly on the lips. "I'll be there." She turned on her heels and sashayed back to the dressing room.

He stayed for more than a second and watched her walk away. *Careful, sailor . . . God, what a woman!*

Saturday morning before breakfast, the sky was clear and blue. Eddie warmed his hands and gave a lively two-fingered salute to the doorman as he entered the lobby. He was feeling rested and confident this morning, and it resonated in his gait. He greeted Johnny with a singsong "Good morning, Irene" as he strode toward the dining room.

"And top of the morning to you too, mate. My, my, but aren't we bloody chipper this morning?"

"Clear skies and some moonlight tonight—I can feel some fine snapshots are in the cards for us tonight, my fine, feathered friend."

"That reminds me, have you heard from Greg lately?"

"No, why?"

"Oh, it's probably nothing, but I was expecting a call last night. I'm supposed to deliver a package for him when we return to London. He also wanted to touch base with me sometime before we headed to Berlin. Did he say anything to you?"

"Not really. But if I remember correctly, I think I heard him say that he wants us to leave the car for him to pick up at the train station in Berlin. He won't be traveling with us. He'll be coming in on the train."

After the second show, Eddie met Dixie in the front lobby of the Plaza. They took the first cab, but they said little to each other. The hotel dining room was busy, but the maitre d' found them a quiet table. Eddie excused himself and went up to his room to retrieve the camera. He stuffed several film packets into his coat pockets and wrapped the camera in a white scarf.

When he returned, he noticed Dixie's furrowed brows. He took a quick review of the room: no uniforms. He was about to launch into a brief explanation regarding his need for an escort when a middle-aged woman at an adjacent table recognized him. She waved a folded program and almost shouted to get his attention. He knew she would persist until he went over to their table. He turned toward Dix; she was sitting with her hands folded under her chin, wearing a Cheshire cat smile. "You didn't expect this to be a private rendezvous, did you?"

After autographing the woman's program, he sat back at their table with an audible sigh. "All we need tonight, Dix, is one snapshot." He then leaned forward and began to fill in the blanks for her—the apartment, the camera, and hopefully the midnight submarine launch.

It was about 11:15 when they entered the apartment. Eddie turned on a light in the main room and headed for the second bedroom's window. The night sky was perfect. There was a half-moon, and it lit up the river nicely under a cloudless sky. *I hope Greg was right about the aperture setting. We might just get the whole story on film.*

Dixie tried to get comfortable, slouched in the well-worn chair that the landlord had set near the heating duct. "Nice place you've got here, sailor. Are you going to offer a lady a drink?"

He pulled over a straight-backed chair from the dining table. He sat backward, folding his arms on the chair back. "I'm sorry, babe, but the only thing to drink around here tonight, I'm afraid, is rusty water." He then detailed for her everything he and Greg had seen and done the past week: the anti-aircraft installations, the shipyard with the massive ship under construction, and the very reason why they were sitting in this particular apartment.

"Are you sure you should be telling me all this, Commander?" Her hand went to cover her mouth. She'd mentioned his rank. "Oh damn! I'm sorry. It slipped."

He patted her hand in a reassuring manner. "Forget it. I don't think anyone is listening in just yet." He was pondering her last comment. "Dix, I've had this on my mind for a while now, and this is as good a time as any. Whether or not we get any film of a submarine launch, one of us has got to get back and tell the boss what you and I—and Greg and Johnny, for that matter—what all of us have seen firsthand. This damn country is preparing for another war. And if we are lucky and do get a picture of a U-boat launch, nobody in their right mind will be able to turn a blind eye."

"I do understand. And I do know how important this mission is, for both of us."

He stood and started to pace around the tiny room. "The Navy Department, the State Department—they already know that the Germans couldn't care less about any agreements, with the Brits or the French. Maybe, though, just maybe a snapshot of the real thing, along with our firsthand knowledge—maybe this will be the icing on the cake for Roosevelt? I don't know."

"What time did you say a launch was scheduled for?"

"Greg said we should see something around midnight. The brass were coming in for the launch, but our friend Schroeder told him he was having some equipment problems. So it could be delayed." He glanced at his watch, returned to the small chair, and then resumed where he'd left off. "FDR and the boys in the Navy Department can sense it. I've known that since my commissioning. But the old man's hands are tied. If there is another war over here, he believes that most of Congress will vote to stay out of it. Right now, he can't even help the Brits, even if the chancellor—His Nibs, Hitler—decides to march on London. And after what Greg and I have seen, I wouldn't it put past him. If these bastards bring back the wolf pack, no Atlantic shipping will be safe, including ours!"

Dixie put her hand on his arm. It had the calming effect she'd hoped for. "We'll get the information back, trust me. And it's my job to get you out of here. Right now we're in the lion's den, and we have to be very careful. And if my prior briefings are correct, we must assume that Berlin and the Gestapo are keeping a close watch on what is going on up here. Based on the tour you and Greg were privy to, my guess is that security in the Kriegsmarine may be a little lax."

"What makes you say that?"

"A portion of my training in Virginia included briefings by two British undercover agents. They were convinced that Hitler and his inner circle are suffering from terminal paranoia. They told us that the Waffen-SS, the Gestapo, was created to keep an eye on any political opposition, especially from the old-guard military officers. Many of Hitler's senior officers are from wealthy aristocratic families, and in the past, many of these officers had close contact with some of their British counterparts. But now it's understood that the SS will pull in any officer for interrogation, even if they only suspect he speaks English. I would bet your Captain Schroeder is on a watch list."

Eddie was tired, but her words resonated with truth. He replayed recent scenes, over and over: at the shipyard, the underground secret construction, the Gestapo. *Damn! I've been one lucky sailor. Our boys, the boss, they have to know—and I have to get the hell outta here.*

Dixie again patted his arm. "Hey, are you still with us?"

"Sorry. I was drifting off—your voice one minute, a nightmare the next."

"I've been meaning to tell you this, but this really has been my first opportunity." She moved to the edge of the chair, resting her hand on his arm. "You know that young stagehand who tries to play touchy-feely with all the girls, the guy that fancies himself such a man of the world? Well, he's been pushing me to go out with him nearly every night, so I finally accepted. What I found out, after I learned that he couldn't hold his schnapps, was that he was a big deal in the local Hitler Youth group."

He tried to imagine this scrawny kid trying to hustle a formidable woman like Dix, who likely could sidestep his every move before it even began.

"At a party I attended with some of his brown-shirted friends, he tried to impress me and everyone within earshot. He boasted to one of his friends that in addition to working at the theater, he was also running errands for some Gestapo agent from Berlin. Everyone seemed to put it down to nothing more than hot air, but he kept boasting about his Gestapo connections. So I asked him, was it his job to keep an eye on the people who worked at the Palace? With his chest protruding proudly, he told me that it was his duty—and every loyal German's duty, for that matter—to report anything suspicious he encountered. He kept referred to us as mongrel Americans. I reminded him that I too was an American." She ran her fingers through her hair. "I'm afraid the boy is smitten. And I do intend to keep him on a tight string, perhaps, but interested. If there is any sudden Gestapo interest, I'm certain the boy will let it slip."

"Stay on your toes with this guy, Dix." He returned to the second bedroom's window. "Okay, where the hell is that submarine launch?" *Dixie, girl, you're flirting with danger there.*

The sky was still clear. There were a few more streetlights, but there was no visible activity on the river. It was almost 4:00 AM, and the room was getting colder by the minute. He tried to wriggle the numbness out of his toes. "Well, I think our good captain has postponed the launching, but we'll wait another thirty minutes, just to be sure. That okay with you?"

"Nobody's waiting up for me, but can we get a cab at this hour?"

"I sure as hell hope so." Eddie put his hands in his coat pockets and began quietly to move his feet. "I'm going back to the main room. It's a little warmer in there." Fortunately the heating duct was pumping out some warm air.

Dixie curled up in her coat on the threadbare chair. "Well, I'm completely knackered, so wake me if anything happens."

Eddie pulled the collar up on her coat and then gently rubbed her shoulders. She was out in a minute. He'd never met a woman quite like her. *Another time, another place . . .* He moved a straight-backed chair closer to the warm-air vent. And within a blink, he too dozed off.

Light started to creep into the darkened room. A sunbeam pierced the dirty window and touched his face. He jerked, suddenly awake. "Jumpin' Jesus, it's daybreak." That woke Dixie.

Her voice was groggy. "What happened? What time is it?"

"It's nearly 7:00 AM. We need to get back to the hotel." Eddie turned off the small desk lamp and went to have a last look at the river. *If they launched anything last night, she must have sailed upriver completely submerged. Now, do I believe that?*

Dixie was standing by the entry, still groggy. "Did you say something to me?"

"No, I was just trying to convince myself . . . Let's get outta here."

She walked past him as he held the door, and then she stopped abruptly at the stairway.

As he caught up with her, he noticed someone in the shadows on the first-floor landing.

"It's a woman, with a mop and bucket, I think," she whispered.

They walked slowly down the creaky stairs. The woman at the foot of the stairs was looking out a windowpane at the early morning light. She turned and looked up when she heard footsteps.

He whispered out the side of his mouth. "I think I recognize her. She's the manager's wife." She was dressed in a dark house-dress, and she wore rubber boots. Her hair was wrapped in a scarf that nearly covered her eyebrows.

The woman greeted them with a crooked smile and a *guten Morgen.*

Eddie gave her a stage smile and nodded.

Dixie answered her in German. "It looks like it's going to be a beautiful day." Recognition suddenly crossed the woman's face as she looked at Eddie. She dropped her bucket and mop. "I think she recognizes you. Perhaps she's seen your picture in the newspaper." The woman was now visibly nervous and somewhat shaken.

She spoke to Dixie in a shaky voice. "I had no idea he was actually here, in our building."

When they'd reached the bottom landing, Dixie put her arm around her. "Would you like an autograph from this famous American bandleader?"

"Oh my, could I?" Dix translated for Eddie.

In his topcoat pocket, Eddie found a folded program from a previous performance. "Ask her her name, would you?"

The woman almost screeched, *"Frieda!"*

He autographed the program, buttoned his topcoat, and held the door as they walked out into the cold morning air.

They later learned from Greg that Frieda's husband, Karl, the acting apartment manager, had a day job as a civilian security guard at Schroeder's shipbuilding facility. He'd been asked earlier in the week to work two shifts on Saturday. And Captain Schroeder had canceled all overtime that Friday afternoon. Everyone at the plant suspected the reason for the altered schedule had to have been for a midnight launch for the brass. Karl and Frieda had met at the Hamburger Dom (a fair) and had been married for more than a decade. Times were tough for everyone after the Kaiser's War. Karl was too young to enlist and had escaped military service. Finding a job before the National Socialists took over was nearly impossible, but the Nazis had made good on their promises and had reopened and begun expanding the Hamburg shipyards. Karl's employment had been stable since he'd joined the party, but his lack of military service and love of the local beer had stunted his ability to progress from his civilian security position at the plant.

Karl was disappointed to lose out on the additional pay he'd anticipated for the weekend overtime, but he knew that there would soon be another opportunity. With his cup of coffee, he sat quietly at their small dining table. His thoughts drifted to the good time he'd be having at the beer garden at the end of his shift. The acrid scent of stale tobacco and spilled beer seemed to fill his nostrils. He smiled to himself as he luxuriated in the moment.

Frieda suddenly burst into the room in an excited state. She kept waving a piece of paper at him and nearly screamed for him to look and see the name of the famous American who'd just autographed it for her. She could tell by the look on his face that he wasn't impressed, or even interested—annoyed, yes. And right now she could see that he was trying hard to control his temper. She quietly laid the program on the table and returned to her mop and bucket.

Karl rubbed his head in angry frustration and poured himself more coffee. He tried to regain that pleasant feeling he'd escaped to before his wife had so rudely interrupted. *What is it with women? Who cares about some famous American bandleader? What was his name, Peabody?* Now he was curious. *And just what was he doing in that apartment with that woman?* He remembered an SS officer that had recently visited the plant and cautioned everyone to be on the alert; several British agents had been apprehended snooping around the plant. *I wonder if I should report this American bandleader to my superiors.* After a minute, he shook his head at the thought. *What will I report? My wife saw a suspicious rendezvous and got the man's autograph as a memento.*

Eddie was lost in thought as he stopped at a street corner to let a vehicle pass. He jumped back when he felt something caress the back of his neck.

"Sorry, didn't mean to startle you." Dixie curled her arm around his and stuck her hand in his coat pocket. "I don't know about you, but I'm dead. I sure hope you don't want another rendezvous again tonight."

"No, I'm dead too. But we sure as hell don't have much time left. All we can do is wait for Greg to tell us what, if anything, is happening."

★　★　★

Eddie was running some hot water for a bath when the phone rang. It was Greg. "Good morning. Hope I'm not disturbing you, but I've got some interesting news."

"No, no. Go ahead, skipper."

"Just called Schroeder to invite him and his wife to dinner, but he declined!" Greg's pause was dramatic. He continued, "Schroeder apologized and asked if he could take a rain check, and then went on about the scheduled launch. He mentioned a failure of some sort, and replacement parts being delayed in shipment. I don't know, my friend, but I'd say their aborted launch will be rescheduled for this coming weekend. What do you think?"

"Well, if things continue to fall apart for the captain, I'm pretty sure his superiors will see that his court-martial won't be delayed. But anyway, here's hoping for a successful new launch date, and one successful photo."

"Eddie, listen. There's another reason I called. One of my contacts in Berlin just warned me to be extra careful. It seems that the Gestapo recently questioned two male shipyard workers that have since disappeared. Now, here's the kicker—they were British agents posing as a couple of gay blades but were, in fact, skilled steelworkers. These guys also spoke perfect German."

"Damn! I wonder what happened."

"No one seems to know at my end. They may have crossed swords with one or more of the other workers. Oh, I also found out that the apartment manager is a loyal party member at the shipyard. You've got to be extra careful from here on in, my friend, especially going to and from that building."

"You know we close the show here on Saturday, and it would be near-impossible for me not to attend the closing party."

"I understand. All we can do now is stand by, wait, and hope for the best."

"I've got plenty of practice in that arena. Do keep me posted if anything changes, skipper."

"Right. You know that as soon as I hear anything, I'll get word to you. In the meantime, let's cross our fingers, and please be very careful."

"Right you are, and thanks for the update." Eddie rang off, feeling a chill run up his spine. *Damn! I'm not sure I can stand another night of hurry-up-and-wait.*

Late the following Friday afternoon, Eddie received a call at the theater from Greg. He was brief. "We may have a shot at a photo this evening!"

"Any possible delays?"

"What can I say?"

"Right."

"Best of luck, my friend."

Dixie was at her dressing table and saw him in her mirror as he approached. She caught his eye and continued with her makeup. "Well, to what do I owe this pleasure?"

"Got time for another rendezvous?"

"Tonight? What about the party?"

He shrugged his shoulders. "We play it by ear."

She started to put on her lipstick as she looked up at him in the mirror. "I'll be out front after the last show."

They made their appearance at the party, drank some celebratory champagne, and then ducked out quietly to catch a cab. The place was as dark and cold as they remembered. A quick glance out the window revealed that the quay was well lit from spotlights on the outsides of the buildings. Most of the construction material that had cluttered the dock the previous week had been removed. Armed guards were visible at the corners of the adjoining buildings; Eddie counted four that he could see.

Dixie was shivering. She rubbed her arms for warmth. "Damn

it! We need some heat in here. I'm going to look up that manager or his wife."

"Careful, Dix. I'd hate for you to get stuck. If the guy is there and starts asking questions about what we're up to, just head on back."

"I don't care what he asks. I'm freezing, and he's going to get some heat up here, or I may start my own fire." She hurried down the stairs, and as soon as she located the manager's apartment, she commenced banging on the door. *Maybe he's got guard duty tonight and Frieda won't have a clue about the heat.* After three or four loud knocks, the door creaked open. The light in the hallway was dim, but she could clearly see an overweight man standing in the entryway in a dirty T-shirt, with two days' worth of beard on a dirty face. *Damn!* The smell of stale beer was nauseating when he opened the door.

"Well, well. Look who we have here. And what does this little dumpling want?"

She knew her matter-of-fact, in-charge attitude might put him on the defensive, so she took a deep breath before speaking. "Sorry to bother you, sir, but right now our room feels colder than river water."

He turned his head with a harrumph and a loud burp. He was obviously short of patience. She was glad that Eddie had remained upstairs.

"The damn thing has been working for about half an hour. Hot water should be up and heating your apartment soon now." He paused and grinned at her with a mouthful of decaying, tobacco-stained teeth. "In the meantime, I suggest that you two lovebirds put on an extra coat, share a blanket, or do whatever else you planned for the evening. But whatever you do, don't bother me again with this!" He slammed the door in her face.

He continued to talk to himself behind the closed door. She stayed for a few seconds and listened through the door. "I've been working on that damn old furnace and boiler for the last two days now. And tonight was to be a night for some overtime. Nothing goes right for me. You'd think the owner of this dump would install some new equipment. But no! Arrogant little buggers—to hell with them all."

Dixie turned and scurried back up the stairway.

Frieda had seen her husband in this worked-up state before. And it always was her fault; he said it was her stupidity. *Dear God, but I couldn't stand another beating!* She sat at the kitchen table and watched him as he paced the small room. He turned toward her and began to quiz her about what she knew about this American entertainer and his harlot girlfriend.

Frieda began to cry. "I'd seen the man's picture in the newspaper, and they both seemed nice enough." She said nothing about the autographed program from the Palace.

Karl went to a kitchen cabinet and poured another glass of schnapps. *Something is wrong. I can feel it. What is this American celebrity doing here in a drafty, middle-class apartment when he likely has a luxury hotel room? He can romp with his harlot whenever he wants. I'd better discuss this with my superior tomorrow, after staff meeting. That is, if I still have a job.*

Eddie opened a bottle of wine and filled two glasses. He entered the darkened second bedroom and glanced across the river. He noticed more lights on around the shipyard, but all seemed quiet.

Dixie relayed her encounter with Karl, the apartment manager, and then curled up once again on the chair, now with a glass of wine. "Anything happening out there?"

"No, all seems quiet enough. There are more lights on around the yard. With Karl at home tonight, I hope we're not looking at another delay." He pulled out the straight-backed chair and sat backward, facing Dixie. "So how'd you wind up here, working for the government, Dix?"

She took a long slug of wine and looked at him with a curious smile. "Well, I think you know I left Germany with my mother about three years ago. My father knew Professor Ziemer at the American University. Anyway, Greg made some arrangements with the American consulate in Berlin, and they helped my mother and me with exit visas. We then settled in the Boston area."

He lifted his glass in a silent toast. "And?"

"Eddie, I'm Jewish. I should clarify that by saying that my mother is Jewish. But that, of course, in line with Jewish law and current Nazi doctrine, makes me Jewish." She watched his reaction as he digested what she'd just revealed. "I have a degree in music from the Sorbonne in Paris. I also studied at the conservatory in Berlin. But what I really wanted was to study at the Peabody Institute in Baltimore or, if gender was an issue, Juilliard in New York. I sent applications to both at about the time my father fell ill. Are you familiar with the Peabody Institute?"

"Not really, Dix. I think a distant relative got the school going with a large endowment sometime back in the middle of the last century. But I've never actually visited the school."

"It's beautiful, really. I was at Johns Hopkins University, looking to talk to some professors there, when a man approached me. He said he was from the State Department, and he wanted me to travel to Washington and talk with people in his office. He wouldn't say what they wanted, so I turned him down. By the time I got home, this same man, along with an aide to President Roosevelt—they were sitting in our apartment and talking with my mother. She, of course, was very grateful to be out of Germany and insisted that I be gracious to our hosts, at least talk with them. Well, when the State Department sent a car all the way from Washington just for me, what could I say?"

"You must have felt severely strong-armed."

"I did. The trip to Washington wasn't that long, but as soon as I arrived at the State Department, I was ushered into a meeting room by a Mr. Swanson, where he commenced bombarding me with questions. Some were in German, so I answered him back in German. He told me that citizenship for my mother and me would be guaranteed, even expedited, if I would consent to work four years for the Navy Department. They put me up at a beautiful hotel while I thought the matter over, bought me clothes, and then proceeded to charm me into becoming a spy."

"Did you meet the president?"

"No, but it seemed like I met everyone but him. I was very conflicted by what I was being asked to do. I knew that the Nazis were bad news, but I did struggle with becoming a spy. I love America, Eddie. But I love Germany too—it is my home. The good people of this country far outnumber these barbaric Nazi thugs. But it is difficult for me, at times, to separate the good people from the political and nationalistic nonsense that seems to have taken hold here."

He touched her shoulder. "I'm sorry for what they put you through, but I'm damn glad you're here, Dix."

"It's hard for me to believe I'm saying this, but I'm actually glad I took this assignment."

Suddenly there was a loud groan coming from somewhere along the river, not unlike the sound of large metal doors opening. They both moved toward the window and kneeled, silently glancing up and down the river and watching the yard.

In a short while, Eddie began to feel a dull ache in his knees and feet. "I'm feeling cold, Dix. I need to warm up a bit."

Dixie grabbed his arm before he could turn away. There were massive bubbles in the center of the river about fifty yards out from the docks. A massive structure began emerging from the river. She gently nudged him, with a whisper. "Get the camera."

He dashed quietly to the adjoining room and grabbed the camera, checked settings, removed the lens cap, and hustled back to the window.

"You didn't miss much. It's still surfacing."

He fumbled in the cold and the dim light to get the camera open and adjusted properly. When he looked up, a conning tower had emerged from the murky, semi-frozen river; it was a U-77. The boat began a slow turn, trying to position itself in the center of the river.

He steadied the camera on the narrow windowsill and clicked off as many pictures as his cold fingers could manage. The exhaust from the diesel motors was now visible in the chilly, moist air. In a matter of minutes the boat began to disappear into the night, downriver toward the sea.

Under the window, with his back against the wall, he removed the exposed film. Dixie could see the smile on his face. She wanted to stand and yell out but maintained her composure. *Now all I have to do is get him safely out.*

It was nearly 3:00 AM. They stood up together. "Dix, let's gather up our stuff and get back to the hotel." When she turned toward the main room, he grabbed her in a tight hug. "We've done it, babe." He pulled back but held her shoulders. He kissed her lightly on the lips.

"I'm happy to be of service, Commander, but I think we both know we're not out of the woods just yet."

"Right, so let's get the hell outta here."

TWENTY-FOUR

It was nearly midnight before they reached Lauenburg and the main highway to Berlin. It was still another two hundred kilometers to the capital. Traffic was unusually heavy, and it took nearly four hours to reach their hotel near Bayreuth, about two kilometers from the Scala theater.

Greg arrived by train and immediately caught a cab to the Berlin Ambassador hotel. When the others finally met up with him in the lobby, he knew he needed to caution them quickly and quietly. After handshakes and hugs, he motioned for them to stand a little closer to him. "Welcome to Berlin, folks. Now please listen to me carefully. When we're speaking to one another, particularly in this hotel but in other parts of the city as well, we must be especially careful. Every foreign national that I have had any contact with has been booked into this hotel. And I have heard stories where diplomats have complained that that their German counterparts had advanced information on whatever they were negotiating. This can only have happened through listening in on their private conversations. So a word to the wise—any conversations, other than about the weather? Go for a walk."

"That bad, eh?"

"I'm afraid so. Tomorrow I'll help you get your city bearings. Then you can scope out the Scala prior to rehearsal."

"I do thank you, sir. Now, what about the telephone?"

"Don't use it . . . unless you're ordering room service. We'll meet on the street if there is anything I think you need to know about. And remember, other than your engagement at the Scala, you're simply a tourist."

"We've seen what looks like a large number of street police since we entered the city. Am I imagining things or what?"

"No, I think you're assessing it correctly, Eddie. I too am concerned by what I've seen lately, both in and out of uniform. Ever since the German army marched into the Sudetenland in October, I've had the unsettling feeling that any dissenting voice is promptly arrested. Most of the German officers that I'm acquainted with voice no opinion on any subject that could remotely be interpreted as criticism of the Reich."

Greg turned to face Eddie. "I plan to be here another week, and I would like to take you on a short excursion around Berlin before I head back to Hamburg. There are some installations that you should see before you leave the country. So let's stay in touch as much as we can. Oh, I nearly forgot. Schroeder called to again thank me for arranging your appearance at his wife's Christmas party. He mentioned that rumors were circulating in the German high command that everyone, including the führer himself, was looking forward to seeing this American spectacle, especially the Man with the Banjo."

Before the three left, one of Greg's former students, John Hagenfeld, now a colonel in the regular army, came over to say hello. After a cordial greeting, Greg introduced the colonel to Dix and Johnny. "Colonel, I'd like you to meet a friend of mine from the United States, who also happens to be the star of the new American musical opening at the Scala—Eddie Peabody."

"Herr Ziemer, it is always a pleasure to run into my favorite professor, but now you introduce me to the star of the show everyone in Berlin is talking about. I'm speechless." He turned to face Eddie, clicked his heels together, bowed, and then extended his hand. "Herr Peabody, this is indeed a pleasure."

"Colonel, it's a pleasure to meet you. I do hope that if you or any of your family are attending any of the performances, you won't hesitate to let me know." Just then the front desk motioned for Eddie to approach. "You'll excuse me a moment, sir."

Hagenfeld leaned in to Greg and asked if he would sit with him for a quick cup of coffee. Greg quickly agreed; he enjoyed chatting with his former students.

"So, what have you been up to since I last saw you, Colonel? What has it been, five years now? I believe you were just a captain when you first entered American University."

"Yes, yes. And I have been very lucky in my assignments since those days. Recently, I've been put on temporary assignment to the chancellery."

When the coffee arrived, Greg noticed that the man's cheeks were flushed and he was nervously shuffling his feet. "Is everything all right, Colonel?"

"Professor . . . er, excuse me—Greg. Many of my fellow officers and all the secretaries are frantically looking for tickets to see this famed banjoist. Of course all my superiors want to see are the beautiful dancing girls. Is there any way you could help me with some tickets?"

"Well, we mustn't disappoint a former student and an officer of the chancellery. I'll have four tickets for you at the entrance, good for any performance this week."

Hagenfeld's eyes lit up. "You can do this? That would be simply wonderful, Herr Professor."

Eddie walked over to where the two men were sitting. "I'm beat, mate. I think I'll skip dinner and head upstairs."

The colonel stood as Eddie was speaking. "Gentlemen, I have failed to recognize that you are tired from your journey. Please accept my apology for intruding."

"No intrusion at all, Colonel. Please, stay seated and talk some more with Professor Greg here. I apologize, but I've got a long day tomorrow. Good evening to you, gentlemen."

The colonel leaned over close to Greg. "I am now serving as chancellery aide to General Erich von Manstein, and anything you or Herr Peabody need, anything at all, please do not hesitate to call on me." The colonel then stood, straightened his jacket, and bowed to his former professor. "I do hope you enjoy your stay, Herr Professor. And again, thank you for helping me with the tickets." With that, he clicked his heels and headed toward the street entrance.

The Scala theater was awesome. With its large front columns, it looked more like a Greek temple than a stage theater for the arts. The entrance had a semicircular drive, and there were more than a dozen steps leading up to eight large wooden doors. Men in crisp theater uniforms and white gloves politely greeted patrons at the entrance. Inside the main entry were signs of recent refurbishing: newly added gold and marble fixtures and floor-to-ceiling velvet drapes. The main auditorium was cold, with an uncomfortable feel to it, but it was huge and ostentatious in decoration.

Eddie went up the theater's side stage steps and headed for the rear, where habit directed him to confirm that his instruments had all arrived in good order. He also had a quick look at his dressing room. The show's producer had the dancers and the orchestra rehearsing several numbers as a translator barked out orders in English.

Six separate rooms lined the back wall of the theater, with the room closest to the stage being the largest. More than likely this was where the dancers would manage their changes. A quick look at his room confirmed that all was well; his instruments had all arrived safely. Within roughly twenty feet from his door, with no indication or overhead light, another, heavier metal door opened onto an alleyway. With the rehearsal drill thoroughly occupying nearly everyone, he quietly opened the alleyway door. There were two steps leading down to a small platform. He let the door close gently behind him. The outside air was cool and crisp, and the smells of a nearby bakery sweetened the area. The alleyway itself was wide enough to accommodate two cars easily. *For damn sure, this exit should provide us a quiet getaway—no reporters, and hopefully no too-curious fans.* A sudden chilly breeze caused an involuntary shake of his shoulders. He took a final scan of the area and walked back into his dressing room, where it was slightly warmer. He strolled over to the stage curtain and peered into the orchestra pit. Johnny was also backstage, and he startled his friend with a tap on the shoulder.

"Oh, hi, pal."

"Sorry to startle you, old boy. I was just about to inquire about your instruments."

"All is well there, and my room is over there at the end of the line. That big metal door on the opposite wall opens out into an alleyway."

"You don't say."

"Those band boys in Hamburg were sure a congenial bunch, weren't they? I sure hope these guys are as good to work with. We sure as hell don't need a bunch of stiff-collared Nazis, that's for sure."

Johnny put his arm around Eddie. "Watch your tongue, mate. We'll get through this just fine, so don't you worry about the band." Just then one of the band members stood up.

Eddie grabbed the curtain to steady himself and to look more closely. The man was wearing dark trousers and a white shirt like the rest of the group, but that bulging, overweight physique and curly, unkempt hair atop a ruddy complexion could only belong to one man. "Judas priest! It can't be."

"What is it, mate? Who or what are you looking at?"

"The rhythm banjo man, second row—he just stood up. I think we've seen him before. I know the jerk from New York, a German restaurant."

"Do you think he's the same guy we saw in London? Could this be a problem?"

"I don't know. Maybe it's nothing, nothing at all. But the last time I saw this guy in New York, he was drunk as a skunk and he didn't appreciate being upstaged."

"Look, we can likely have any one of these chaps replaced in a New York minute."

"No, no. Let's just see what happens. Maybe the guy will be okay."

The show's producer walked over to where they were standing and abruptly interrupted their discussion. If they were quite ready, would they please review the music sequencing for the show? Johnny hustled the man away and commenced cussing and discussing the changes from the Hamburg routine.

Eddie retrieved his banjo and started to tune up, while Johnny verbally reviewed individual sheet music and sequencing with the orchestra. The drummer chuckled when Eddie emphasized that his left foot would set all timing and rhythms. The double bass player suddenly commenced stomping his left foot, while two other band members began calling out a rhythm cadence. Laughter soon consumed the rehearsal and took some of the edge off of the uncertainty that comes as baggage with every new performer, especially jazz musicians from America.

Eddie tried to remember the German banjo player's name: *Emhart—Gerhard—Bernhardt—Horst—Earnst—Ernie? That's it, Ernie!*

"Shall we go through 'Lambeth Walk' a couple of times? You know, familiarize the orchestra with the stop-time rhythm?"

"Sure, pal. Maybe some of the boys have heard the song on the radio."

Herr Earnst (Ernie) suddenly stood up, holding his banjo at the neck, and in a loud, thickly accented voice shouted in English, "I have heard this song, Herr Peabody! But most of my colleagues are formally educated fine musicians! I doubt if anyone here would be interested in listening to American Negro jazz!"

The room fell silent. He tried not to stare at the contemptible man. Ernie was standing back by the drummer with a smug look on his face. He then waved his hand in what appeared to be a friendly gesture. No one was sure what to do; should they continue or just leave? Everyone could feel the quiet tension.

With a mutual nod, Eddie and Johnny decided to continue. Johnny started to play the refrain on the piano, and by the time he'd gone through four choruses, most of the remaining orchestra had joined in. Everyone seemed to be enjoying the stop-time rhythm; a few even hammed it up when it came to shouting, "Hey!" Ernie strummed along through most of the song but stopped playing altogether when Eddie took the solo.

During a coffee break, Ernie walked over to where Eddie was sitting. "Herr Peabody, I would like a word please."

"Certainly. What can I do for you, Ernie?"

"I would very much enjoy doing a duet with you at some point during the show. Some in my family think that with the amount of time I have spent here with this orchestra, and with my position in the party, I should insist. But I said I know this Eddie Peabody, and he is a reasonable man. He will see that a duet would be good publicity for both of us."

"Ernie, I'm sorry, but I have no influence on who does what, or when, in this show. If you want to make a suggestion regarding what you think the local audience would like to see, you'll have to take it up with the show's producer." Eddie smiled, adjusted the strings on his banjo, and said nothing more.

Ernie stood and balled his fists. "Well, I see that you are not enthused with my request. Be assured, however, I will have a talk with the producer of this American folly." The bandsman turned angrily on his heels and headed toward the band pit.

Johnny could see Eddie finishing up a conversation with the outspoken rhythm banjoist, and he could now see that his boss was very agitated. "Wasn't that the banjo man? What's happening with him, anyway?"

"That guy scares the hell out of me. I was going to warm up to the guy when I saw him walk over. Then, off the wall, he insists that he and I do a duet as part of the show!"

"Really? And, what did you say?"

"Not a damn thing, pal. I said that he should talk to the producer if he thinks his suggestion has merit." He let out an audible sigh as he set his instrument on a nearby table. "Johnny, that guy couldn't play "Come to Jesus" on a tin flute, but I think you already knew that."

Walking back to his dressing room, he noticed a familiar face. She was dressed in tights and dance slippers, shuffling along, and looking very tired. "Dix?"

She turned toward him with a confused look. When it finally registered, she ran up and threw her arms around him.

Her reaction surprised him. "Well, I'm glad to see you too!" He stood back and looked at her; he could tell she was upset. "What is it? You look like you've seen a ghost."

She forced a smile, took a deep breath, and spoke matter-of-factly. "I overheard the stage manager talking with the choreographer. It seems the entire Third Reich will be looking for a date with an American beauty from the Scala."

"Oh, that's probably just talk. I wouldn't give it another thought. Nobody seemed to bother you gals much up in Hamburg."

"Yeah, but remember Paris? Look, I hope it's just a lot of talk too. But if it's all the same to you, I'll stay a lot closer to you while we're in Berlin. I've had an uneasy feeling about this engagement since the day we arrived."

He touched her shoulder and could feel her trembling. She started to cry. After some deep breaths, she regained her composure.

"Everything's going to be fine, Dix."

"I'm sorry, but ever since we arrived, I've been frightened that someone is going to recognize me." Her eyes were puffy.

"Dix, if we stick together, we'll get through this."

"I know, I know. It's been more than three years, I've changed how I look, my hair, how I dress—I've even changed my name, but I'll be damned if I can rid myself of this knot in my stomach or these terrifying thoughts."

He kissed her forehead. "I know this is tough on you. And as far as your girlfriends are concerned, or anyone else, you're with me, okay?"

Two more dancers approached, and they shuffled sideways to let them pass. No one spoke, but they both noticed the "Well, lookie here" smiles as her friends quietly passed.

"Dix, we're in this together, and by damn, we're going to get the hell outta here together. If ever you feel the need, don't think twice, just come to my hotel.

"Thanks. I needed that." She took his arm as they strolled slowly toward his dressing room. "I am feeling better. By the way, I saw you talking with someone at the break. Who was that man you were with?"

Eddie glanced around to see who might be listening. "That was the rhythm banjo man. I'm not sure, but I think he's got something like a permanent job here with the pit band."

"What was he chatting you up about? Did he want you to give him some lessons?"

"No, no. If only it were that simple. The son of a bitch wants me to put him in the show!"

"What? You have no control over that."

"He wants to do a duet. Can you believe it?"

"What prompted this? Do you know the guy?"

"Unfortunately, I met him in New York maybe a year or so ago, at some German restaurant where he was performing . . . if you'd call it that."

"He looked like his knickers were in a twist. What exactly was his problem? Did you tell him that you had no control over who performs in the show?"

"As a matter of fact, I did." Eddie pointed to a wooden bench against the wall. There was a lull in the post-rehearsal foot traffic, so they sat quietly together.

"As I recall, I was in a two-week engagement at a local theater in New York. Maude and I were having dinner at a German restaurant, the same restaurant where Ernie, the man you saw me talking with, was in costume, playing rhythm for a small band. After dinner some of the band boys wanted me to sit in. Well, it turned out that this Ernie character was a drunken sod. As we were leaving the restaurant, he came stumbling out of the bathroom and made quite a scene."

The show's producer suddenly appeared, with his neighbor in tow. He rudely interrupted, said his neighbor was a supreme fan, and demanded an autograph.

Eddie obliged with a plastic smile, and after the two were on their way, he continued to fill in the blanks for Dix. "Now, where was I? So here in Berlin, I run into the bastard again."

"Do you think he'll be a problem?"

"I don't know. The guy is probably still steamed that I upstaged him back in New York. And who knows how far he'll take this duet nonsense? I can't imagine anyone connected with this show wanting anything to do with him. But I have no idea what kind of union arrangements were in place prior to our show." He turned up the palms of his hands in a gesture of exasperation.

"I'll keep my ears tuned and see what I can find out about him." She touched his shoulder. "Thanks for the kind words and helping me avoid the unwanted advances of who knows what."

"Be careful, Dix, please."

She smiled at him affectionately as she touched his cheek, then hurried back to her dressing room.

Greg called and wanted to take Eddie on a short excursion through the outskirts of the city before dinner. He drove the big Mercedes, and they leisurely toured the city center, Greg actively pointing out all the magnificent new buildings constructed within the last five years. He then turned east, toward the Polish border. When the traffic had diminished some, he cleared his throat and commenced speaking as though he were reciting one of his class lectures. "Germany today is a police state. Since the Nazis took the reins of power, state sponsorship of religion has all but ceased. That goes for the Protestants in the north as well as the Catholics in the south. Grand new government buildings have been built, as you could clearly see, though little information on military spending has been made public. We did, however, see some of their increased military spending in Hamburg. To me, the recent switch in priorities from butter to guns has been staggering." Greg was gathering steam, and his tone became more intense. His foot became heavier on the accelerator as well. "From what I read in the foreign press, I gather that most world leaders suspect this regime is belligerent. My friend, let me be very clear on this—no one really knows how belligerent this Hitler is, or how much of a powder keg Germany is!" He slowed for a stop sign and reached under the seat to retrieve a manila envelope. "I would like you to deliver this packet to the State Department as soon as you can upon your return, if you would, please."

Eddie cautiously accepted the envelope. It was tightly sealed with tape. "Sure thing, pal. What's in here, or shouldn't I ask?"

"No, you shouldn't. So hide it in one of your instrument cases if you can."

Quite suddenly large trucks started to crowd them and congest the roadway. Greg pulled the Mercedes off to the side and stopped.

Eddie turned to Greg and summed up what appeared obvious. "I could be wrong, but I think I'm looking at convoy after convoy of troops. For the last five miles, we've been surrounded by a continuous military presence. Do you think all this is part of an exercise? Where the hell are all these guys going?"

Greg warmed his hands in the air that flowed from under the dashboard. "Two senior diplomats from Czechoslovakia contacted me at American University, Eddie. They were concerned that Hitler's going to invade their country, and they believe he's going to do it before the end of the year. So here we are, witnessing an incredible number of troops being sent to the Polish border. So what's going on? I simply don't know, and none of the newspapers are revealing much, either."

Eddie was visibly shocked at Greg's comment. "My God! War could break out at any moment."

"What can I say? The Czech diplomats wanted me to get their evacuation plan to Britain and the United States as soon as possible. I told them that I'm not in direct contact with either government and suggested that they approach both governments on an official level."

"Right you are, skipper."

"The diplomats said they were desperate, Eddie, and believed that their positions were in imminent jeopardy. They think that their current government has been corrupted by German sympathizers who now occupy key positions." Greg could feel his passenger's anxiety.

"Well, I was sent over here to gather up as much information as I could. So . . . " A German military police officer tapping on the window interrupted him. *Damn, it sure looks like I'm up to my elbows in it now!* The officer ordered them to move the vehicle and make way for another convoy that was approaching.

"As you can see, I've got my hands full just trying to stay on the good side of these bandits. God willing, my friend, I'll continue to get as many people out of this country as I can—and pray that I don't wind up in a concentration camp myself."

Trying to absorb the scene, Eddie quipped, "Well, skipper, it doesn't look like the führer is simply planning a parade."

"And the sad—no, frustrating thing is that many of the people I'm trying to convince to get out of the country have convinced themselves that this too shall pass."

"You can only do what you can do, Greg. Nobody wants to believe that war is inevitable."

"I hope the Brits are strong enough to put a stop to this guy if he decides to move."

"We're in agreement there, my friend. But I don't know. I just don't know."

A Luftwaffe squadron flew overhead as they slowly made their way back to Berlin.

TWENTY-FIVE

The Scala was packed, and the show's producer pointed out to Eddie and Johnny the box locations of some the high-ranking Reichstag members—Rudolf Hess in one box, Hermann Göring and his entourage in another, and Heinrich Himmler and Reinhard Heydrich in a third box. He added that the führer himself would be attending.

"I sure hope those guys like the show."

On the way back to his dressing room, someone grabbed Eddie's arm, her voice low. "The banjo player's name is Heinz."

"Dix?"

"And word is he's a boozer. See you after the show. Bye."

"Wait." But she dashed off to her dressing room.

After the show, reporters from several local newspapers were backstage taking pictures and soliciting interviews with the performers. Two reporters cornered Eddie in his dressing room.

Johnny added to the bedlam with a local radio station promoter in tow. "I've agreed to a fifteen-minute spot on the radio tomorrow, following the afternoon performance. Is that okay with you, chief?"

Eddie nodded in agreement.

After all the reporters and promoters had departed, Johnny lingered in Eddie's dressing room, starry-eyed and silent.

"What's the matter, pal? Everything came together quite nicely tonight. What's bothering you?"

Johnny was surprised that his stormy mood was so obvious. "I can't put my bloody finger on it, mate. All evening I've felt apprehensive and tense, and I don't know why."

"You've got to relax, that's all. You know what they say—a girlfriend is often the best cure. Look, if we can stick it out, stay together for the next two weeks, then we can all blow this powder keg of a country."

The days rolled on, and the shows continued, but each evening before curtain, Ernie Heinz would try to corner and pester Eddie. Eddie remained polite, but one evening the smell of liquor on Ernie's breath was overwhelming, and he snapped. "Look, there's no point in continuing to ask me to do a duet with you! You know that management has made it very clear—they are happy with the current selection of performers and musical arrangements . . . and that, my friend, is that. The folks in Berlin came to see an American jazz performance, not a variety show!"

Rejection had always disappointed Ernie, but Eddie's outburst made him furious. He couldn't just walk away. The inebriated pit musician grabbed the man's arm and swung him around. "You listen to me . . . you . . . you big-mouth hotshot. You think you are not afraid? I know! *Ja*, I can see it in your eyes. You Americans, you love your Jews and your niggers, and you think you are better than me! Mister Man with the Banjo?" He spit on the floor next to Eddie's shoes.

Eddie saw the disgusting look on the man's face but suppressed the impulse to punch his bulbous nose. He wasn't sure what would happen next.

Ernie, angry beyond words, turned and walked away, audibly mumbling to himself.

Johnny noticed that Ernie had once again cornered Eddie. He quickly moved in their direction and listened in, trying to piece together the gist of Ernie's demands. He quickly stepped in front of the retreating man, and he could tell he was inebriated. "Look at me. You're drunk. You dare to harass the star performer? Any more words from you, and I shall be forced to complain to the show's producer. Now return to the pit, Herr Heinz, immediately!"

Ernie spit on the floor, barely missing Johnny's shoe. "Swine!"

Eddie and Johnny were both dumbfounded. Eddie was grinding his teeth when he finally spoke. "Damn it! I told you that guy scares me."

"Not to worry yourself, chief. We'll be watching that fellow's every move from now on. The producer doesn't think he adds one bloody thing to this theater. And if he pesters you any more, we'll have the bastard tossed. I believe everyone will be glad to be rid of him."

Ernie was feeling humiliated and angry. *I would do anything to get back at these pompous Americans. But what can I do? The party meeting is tomorrow night at the Nazi youth hall. I'll talk with my group leader. He's been training with the Waffen-SS. He'll know what to do. He'll expose these inferior men for what they truly are—swine and spies. That's right, nothing but American swine and spies!*

Security around the Scala became noticeably tighter. The show's producer was summoned by the SS to personally verify the identity of each performer. Everyone was ordered to stand in line outside the rear of the theater in the cold, damp air.

Eddie was stamping his feet and blowing warm air onto his hands. He spoke up to no one in particular. "Looks like they're checking everybody's papers tonight. I wonder what's up?"

One of the stagehands answered in a cockney accent, "They sure as bloody 'ell are. Maybe our friend the führer himself will be in attendance. And I'll bet ten quid that we won't be able to get out of this place on time, even if it burns to the ground."

He was right. Everyone was instructed that there would be no exiting the theater until the dignitaries and their guests had safely left the facility. One of the showgirls complained to the producer that cabs were scarce and said that she needed to phone her parents from the hotel. An SS officer stepped forward. In a loud, commanding voice he announced, "Anyone leaving the building in violation of this order will be shot." The silence that followed became deafening.

Eddie broke the silence. "Anyone needing a smoke can use my dressing room."

There was some nervous laughter, but most shuffled off to their work areas in silence. The feeling of captivity soon dissipated with the rigorous preparations. The excitement of the show itself was infectious, but with the high-profile presence of dignitaries, everyone seemed more on edge.

Eddie sat in his dressing room, trying to relax by tuning his instruments.

Dixie knocked softly and then entered without waiting for an invitation. She'd changed quickly, and she looked beautiful all made up. She lit up a cigarette and sat on the threadbare couch. "Dear God, I can't wait to get out of here tonight."

"This too shall pass, Dix." His routine dictated that he press his coat and pants before hanging them back up. His white dress shirt he folded neatly and placed in a pillowcase from the hotel that he was using as a laundry bag. He left his shoes and socks on.

Dixie watched him with curiosity as he stood next to an ironing board, dressed only in boxer shorts and a T-shirt. She started to laugh. "What a great picture this would make."

"What the hell are you talking about?"

"Do you have any idea how ridiculous you look standing there in your shorts with your shoes on?"

He looked down at his shoes. He was interrupted by a loud bang at the door as Johnny stumbled in, terribly excited and breathing heavily.

"Hey, this isn't a bus stop. Can't a guy get dressed in peace around here?"

"Well, you bloody well better get dressed, my friend. You have visitors."

"Damn it! Will you tell whoever it is I'll be happy to see them and sign autographs in . . . can you give fifteen minutes?"

"I'd love to, old chap, but I was just informed that the führer himself was sending over someone to see you personally, and what he wants, I have no idea."

Eddie gave a tired sigh of acquiescence and then slipped on a clean undershirt and some trousers. "Okay, bring 'em on. Let's find out what His Nibs wants."

"My guess is that they want you to perform at some private party."

Dixie was now uncomfortable and visibly nervous. "I think I should leave."

Eddie touched her arm as she rose from the couch. "Please, Dix. Stick around?"

Johnny heard the footsteps and looked over. Eddie nodded just as the door opened. Two German officers entered and stood side by side. Both were in dress uniform, with boots polished to a mirror shine. The air thickened with anticipation.

The senior officer stepped forward, smiled, and spoke in perfect English. "Good evening, Herr Peabody." He turned toward Dixie and bowed. "Mademoiselle. I am Major Schultz, personal appointment secretary to the führer, and this is Colonel Berger of security services."

Eddie walked over and shook hands with the two men. The cordial greetings seemed to relieve some tension.

"The führer, Herr Peabody, is hosting a private party at a residence in Munich this coming weekend. And he would be delighted if you, and perhaps one of the show's female singers or dancers"—he was now glaring at Dixie—"could provide the evening's entertainment. There will be a number of dignitaries and other guests, of course. The affair will take place this Saturday evening in Munich."

There was an awkward pause as Dixie cleared her throat.

Looking directly at Eddie, the major continued, "If you agree, sir, I will arrange for a car to be at your service. You and two additional performers of your choosing"—he again turned toward Dixie—"will be transported, along with whatever equipment you require, to the airport Saturday morning."

There was another awkward pause. Eddie looked to Johnny for reassurance, but all he saw in the man's pale face was fear. Eddie feared the man would bolt, given the chance.

"We are prepared to offer you, Herr Peabody, one thousand marks for your services."

Eddie took a step backward and leaned against the counter. He quickly looked over at his two companions before responding, while he mustered his best plastic stage smile for the major. "Thank you, sir. Please excuse my lack of manners, but I've neglected to introduce you to Mr. Pitts and Miss Parsons."

Johnny nearly fell over as he leaned forward to shake hands. Dixie, however, remained where she stood, posture stiff and arms folded.

"Johnny Pitts is my accompanist and musical arranger, and Miss Parsons is a dancer in the show who also, I might add, sings like a nightingale. And having been with us since Paris, she is well acquainted with all my music." He glanced at her, looking for a sign of approval. What he saw was her eyes rolling upward. "That's a very gracious and generous offer, sir. And I would be pleased to accept, on the condition that you allow me to bring along these two talented folks. They most assuredly will enhance my performance, and I'm quite sure they'll delight your guests as well." He pushed a few items aside on his dressing table and sat with enough weight to cause the flimsy table to utter a loud creak. He quickly stood up. After examining the table, he turned back to face the major. "I hope I didn't break the damn thing."

Dixie started to chuckle.

The major looked at her, and he too started to smile. The tension seemed to ease.

Eddie clasped his hands behind his back and looked directly at the major. "Sir, there is just one more thing." He stretched out his left arm to direct attention to Johnny and Dix. "I believe it is reasonable that these folks should be paid a minimum of five hundred marks each."

Johnny started to cough. He cleared his throat and gave Eddie a sign that he was all right.

"I do hope that you find that reasonable and satisfactory."

Wearing a condescending smile, the major stood at parade rest. He turned his focus toward Dixie, with eyes that scanned her like she was a rare piece of art.

She forced herself to remain calm, wearing a much-practiced happy-face stage smile.

But the major could see that her eyes conveyed an inner strength that radiated caution. It was clear that this woman would not be intimidated. "Your terms, Herr Peabody, are acceptable. I trust a formal written contract will not be necessary?"

"No, sir, your word and a handshake are all I require."

"This is good. The führer will be pleased." They shook hands, and the deal was sealed.

Johnny stepped around to shake the major's hand but received only a head nod.

"You will find that we Germans are also men of our word, Herr Peabody. My card, sir. I will be in contact with you tomorrow. You are staying at the Ambassador?"

"Yes, sir, we are."

Both German officers turned toward the group and bowed. They walked slowly toward the door. *"Guten Abend, meine Freunde* [good evening, my friends], Herr Peabody, Herr Pitts."

Not mentioning Dixie did not go unnoticed. After their departure, the room fell silent.

"Blimey, what have we gotten into now?"

Dixie moved toward the door. "I don't think the major approves of me. I need a drink, guys."

"That sounds good, Dix, but I'm afraid we'll have to wait till after the show. Now, guys, if you'll excuse me, I need to take a minute and finish with my clothes. I'll meet you two out front after the show. First one out front flags a taxi."

★ ★ ★

Sitting close in the taxi provided some warmth from the bitter cold.

Eddie put his arm around Dix and asked, "Why don't you pack a few things and stay with us tonight, Dix?"

"Right. I think I'll call one of the girls from your hotel and let her know where I'll be. I'll ask her if she's overheard anything that may be of interest."

Johnny added, "Several of the girls have been complaining that some young boys in uniform have been following them back to their hotel. Let me know, Dix, if anyone else needs refuge. I'm not sure anyone at the Scala can be of help, but this nonsense has got to stop."

The warmth emanating from the small cozy hotel bar took the chill off. They sat in a secluded corner to keep their conversation private. And the noise level was sufficient that anyone trying to listen in would find it difficult.

Eddie lifted his glass. "Well, guys, an invitation by the head of the German state. How could we refuse?"

No one replied. But it did strike both of them as funny, the way he said it so matter-of-factly.

"And we are getting paid quite handsomely, I might add."

Dix couldn't help herself, and she started to giggle. It was infectious, and soon all three were laughing uncontrollably, as though they'd been watching a Laurel and Hardy clip.

After a minute, things calmed down. "Actually, guys, this should be a cakewalk."

The other two, however, were still digesting all that had happened.

"Well, anyway, I can't think of anyone I'd rather have with me in the lion's den than you guys."

That brought on more giggles from Dix.

Johnny took a large swallow of gin. "Well, I could bloody well think of a few I'd rather have in my place, mate."

Dix leaned forward and spoke in an anxious tone. "You're

right. This could be a real opportunity. For what, I'm not sure. But I'd be a liar if didn't say, and without hesitation, I've never been this scared in all my life! All I'm praying for is that no one recognizes me, that's all."

"Look, I think it's safe to say we're all scared out of our breeches. And given the option, we'd all opt for home. But we've done pretty well so far, by sticking to our plan. Working together, we should be fine. This gig with the German brass should be no different." He sat back with a sigh. "I do think we should let Greg know what we're doing and where we're headed."

"I agree, mate."

"I'll give him a call tomorrow from outside the hotel, as soon as we know the details."

"Well, I'm not sure he could do much if things start to go south, but I'm sure we'd all feel better just the same."

Dixie nodded her approval. "And if it's all the same to you both, I'll continue to play my part. I have to tell you, though, that major gave me the creeps tonight."

Eddie patted her hand. "We're with you, and we wouldn't have it any other way."

"I have a feeling that when the booze starts to flow, at least one of those Nazi goons will get aggressive."

Johnny cleared his throat. "Maybe I shouldn't be asking this, Dixie, but is there anything special I should know about you?"

Eddie looked around casually and then lowered his voice. "Dixie changed her name when she reached the continent. She and her mother escaped from Germany a couple of years earlier. Her name was Marian Graham." He paused and then leaned over to whisper, "Her mother was Jewish."

"My father was a wealthy industrialist. I spent most of my time in Paris, at the Sorbonne, but I did attend some classes here in Berlin. There is a chance, albeit small, that someone from my past might recognize me."

Johnny sat quietly with his hands folded.

"Look, gang, if the three of us stick close, we'll knock their socks off. Then we'll get the hell outta there before anyone gets rowdy. Since you both understand and speak German, I think we'll be fine. We'll just have to be alert, that's all."

"Bloody 'ell. You can say that again."

Ernie Heinz went out of his way to be cordial and friendly throughout the week, since the show's producer had threatened to fire him for being a pest. Heinz, however, still felt that showcasing his talent was his just due. More than anything in the world, he wanted to show up this American hotshot.

Weekly Nazi Party meetings had been frustrating to Heinz. He'd been unable to stir up any strong feelings against the popular American show at the Scala. After the formal meeting, he would press his party captain hard. "I tell you, Captain, this American clown Eddie Peabody is arrogant, insolent, and incompetent. He's a nigger and Jew lover. I tell you, he has to be a spy."

"So what would you have me do? Perhaps you'd like me to haul him into the alley and have him shot. We are not at war with the Americans! And I don't think any of my superiors wants to answer for an international incident based on what you think. So drop it, Heinz! That's an order!"

"But sir, I beg you to please authorize a message, sent to our party headquarters in New York. Ask them for any information on this Eddie Peabody. I have friends there, and I'm sure they'll find something on this imposter."

The captain was unimpressed with Heinz's request. After looking at his file, he noted that the man did participate in party demonstrations, but he also noted that he was drunk most of the time. However, whenever someone used the word "spy," a proper form for party headquarters was required, along with a cursory background check. Most reports of this type were on suspected Jews who had slipped past Gestapo reviews of area synagogues.

The following day, after thinking the matter over, the captain telephoned his superior at party headquarters. He asked for advice on the matter and was told that a message to New York requesting a background check on Eddie Peabody would be authorized. The Gestapo usually handled high-profile inquiries, but he would include this request in their normal radio traffic to New York. The captain's superior cautioned that if there were any repercussions, this would be indicated on his record.

Major Schultz telephoned Eddie at the Scala just prior to the Friday evening show. "Good evening, Herr Peabody. I called to inform you that I have reserved a car to transport you and your two assistants. I have instructed a driver to arrive at the Ambassador Hotel at approximately 10:00 PM Saturday evening. Please inform Herr Pitts and the young lady, Fräulein Dixie, that a change of clothes and any toiletries for an overnight stay would be in order. You will be transported to an airfield, where I have arranged for a private plane to fly you to Munich. I will personally meet you at the Munich airfield and will escort you to the private party. First-class accommodations have been arranged for each of you upon the conclusion of your performance. On Sunday morning you will all be transported back to the Munich airfield for your return to Berlin. Now, Herr Peabody, I must emphasize that no one is to discuss any of these details or arrangements prior to Saturday. Have I made myself clear on this?"

Eddie stood motionless by the phone. "Yes, sir, perfectly clear."

"Thank you. Until tomorrow, then. *Guten Abend, mein Herr.*"

"Showtime, folks!" the stage manager announced and clapped his hands as he hurried past the dressing rooms.

Eddie somehow had to get word to Greg. He hurried to his dressing room and was oiling up the neck of his banjo when he suddenly felt a presence. A tap on his shoulder startled him, and he dropped the small can of 3-in-One Oil. He turned quickly as the can clattered around on the wooden floor. He gasped. "Greg, you just scared the hell out of me, pal! What are you doing here this late?"

"Sorry, my friend. But I've recently heard through the grapevine that you've been summoned to a private party in Munich. Am I correct?"

"Yes. And I was going to get in touch to give you the details."

"Well, that's why I'm here. Something has come up, and I need your help. Several of the prominent Jewish people I've been helping to exit the country are convinced that Hitler and Göring are systematically stealing valuable artifacts from estates that they've closed up and hurriedly left in the hands of an agent. What are being stolen are paintings—valuable old masters. And where they're storing them, no one seems to know. Recently, it appears they've become more brazen. This week a Jewish art dealer in Amsterdam was robbed and beaten in broad daylight. He swears the thugs were wearing German uniforms. But the local commandant dismisses the complaint and charged the dealer with insurance fraud. What the thugs took were two seventeenth-century Dutch paintings—a jester portrait by Frans Hals and a wheat field landscape by Jacob van Ruisdael." He handed Eddie a folder. "Sketches were drawn to illustrate the two missing paintings. Göring and Hitler both use the chateau where you'll be performing to entertain high-ranking officials— even Mussolini has stayed there. It is thought that because this place is so heavily guarded, perhaps it is used to store and even display some of the stolen art. To be sure, we'd need a photograph." He handed Eddie the camera used to photograph the submarine launch.

Eddie quickly set the camera and the folder with sketches in his banjo case and closed the lid. "Jesus H., Greg! I thought my assignment over here was finished."

"I've talked with a counterpart at the embassy here, my friend, and he gave me the State Department's blessing to approach you on this. Please review these sketches and commit them to memory. Then burn them in a stove or fireplace." Greg looked at his watch. "Well, I've got to be going, and you've got a show to do. Good luck, my friend, and be careful. Godspeed." He gave Eddie a two-fingered salute and was out the door.

Eddie's mind was racing as he made his way to the side curtain. The house was packed, and the crowd was noisy. He could feel the anticipation; no substance or tonic could accelerate the pulse faster. The dancers began to line up for the entrance. He looked for Dixie. There she was, her tiny, clinging costume revealing every inch of her lovely figure. He maneuvered around the curtains and the other dancers until he stood beside her. Barely touching her shoulder, he leaned over and whispered, "My place, tonight."

She turned ever so slightly and nodded. The music started, and she and the other dancers pranced onstage.

He turned and headed backstage. "Johnny, you, me, and Dix. Tonight."

His friend nodded.

After the show, the three met again in a dark corner of the hotel bar. Dixie had packed her small travel case with an over-night change. She also carried a hang-up bag with two dresses and a fancy pair of shoes.

After spelling out what the major had barked at him over the phone, including the do-not-discuss warning, Eddie exhaled with a sigh of frustration. "Guys, Greg stopped by tonight before the show. He knows about our summons to Munich, and he presented me with a new assignment." He looked around for any suspicious ears that might want to overhear. "And I haven't a clue as to how to accomplish what he's asked me to do. I need your help." He proceeded to explain about the stolen art and Greg's belief that this chateau might be one of Hitler and Göring's storage depots. "I've got sketches of two paintings that were recently stolen from a dealer in Amsterdam. Greg was hoping that if we saw anything suspicious on display, we could get a photo to offer proof positive as to what these two guys are up to."

The other two were now on edge and had facial expressions that left no doubt that they would rather be somewhere else.

"Listen, mate, your embassy hired me to help get you bookings in Hamburg and Berlin. That's all. I don't know a damn thing about art, stolen or otherwise. However, though it's a bit short on notice, I'll take my chances with you guys and do whatever I can to help."

"Thanks, and look, I'm on pins and needles as well. How 'bout you, Dix?"

"I would like to review those sketches, if it's okay. I too have heard rumors about stolen art treasures. I've taken some art history classes and might be able to recognize something. If what Greg has said is true, we've got to give it a shot. I know some of the families that have had their estates ransacked. So I, for one, have to, at the very least, try. If we're careful, we might just get lucky. Anything we do has to be casual and ordinary, as though we were just tourists."

"Good. Spot on, as His Nibs here would say."

"By the way, what tunes will we be doing for this private show?"

"Nothing fancy, guys, but we should lay out the music."

As they walked to the front of the hotel, everyone was feeling the grip of fatigue, especially Eddie. "I'm going for a short walk, guys. I need to clear my head."

Dixie slid her arm through his and looked up with a coquettish smile. "Care for some company?" The weather was cold this time of year, and Dixie, without her gloves, warmed one hand in Eddie's topcoat pocket while clutching her coat with her other hand. They didn't talk much. They were both feeling numb; the fear and excitement only compounded the cold of the air. They passed a corner coffeehouse with bakery goods displayed in the window. They decided to go in and warm up. They ordered two large cups of very strong coffee and shared an apple pastry.

Looking at the coffee and pastry, Eddie quipped, "Well, this ought to keep us up for the rest of the night."

Dix replied, "Right now I feel so prickly that I couldn't sleep if this coffee were drugged. I hope one of you guys has a good book I can curl up with. I feel like I could walk the streets till morning."

He reached over and patted her hand reassuringly. "We'll get through this."

A well-dressed patron with a young lady on his arm approached and politely asked in German if he was the American performing at the Scala. Dixie translated and then answered. "Yes, this is the Man with the Banjo, Eddie Peabody."

"My girlfriend and I saw your performance last evening. We enjoyed it very much. Please excuse me, but my girlfriend would be very pleased if she could have Mr. Banjo's autograph."

Dixie looked at Eddie, who was smiling up at the couple, not having a clue as to what they were saying. "Well, what?"

"The young man wants an autograph for his girlfriend."

"Oh, okay." He looked around for a napkin. The girlfriend produced a folded program from the bottom of her purse.

"Ask the young lady her name, would you?"

Dixie complied. "It's Della."

Eddie scribbled on the program: *To Della, Wishing you all the Best, Eddie Peabody.*

The young man thanked them and tipped his hat as they shuffled backward toward the entrance. The two lovers giggled at each other as they pawed the program and ogled the autograph.

Eddie paid the bill as Dix bundled up in her overcoat. "Congratulations," she cooed.

"What for?"

She smiled at his furrowed brows. "It's nothing. But you just may have helped that good-looking young man get lucky tonight, that's all."

He shrugged his shoulders. "You're a little devil. Now let's get out of here."

She reached for his hand. "Thanks."

"Now what?"

"For just being you. And for being here, with me."

The cold air was bone-chilling. He stopped walking suddenly and blew warm air onto his hands. He stomped his feet.

"Are you okay?"

"I'm fine—just sensitive to the cold, that's all."

"Maybe we should head back to the hotel?"

"You're probably right." As they turned back, the street was nearly deserted. "Dix, we're going to perform for His Nibs, Hitler, arrogant bastard that he is. He is the head of state! And I think you know I am more than a little nervous about what might happen, given that now we're on a mission to be on the lookout for stolen art."

Dixie put a finger to her lips. She motioned with her hand that his voice was a little too loud.

"Too loud? I think we're alone."

"I know what you're saying, and I agree. I don't think we should be talking about this, though, especially on the street. Let's get back and lay out the music. And I think I'd like to look at those sketches some more, okay?"

She could tell that he still had something he wanted to say.

With his head tilted down, he spoke in a mumbled monotone. "I am confident."

"Eddie, you're mumbling, and I can't understand a word you're saying."

He suddenly stopped and turned to face her. "Dix, we're going to entertain the socks off that Bavarian paperhanger, and whoever else he invites to this shindig." Just as suddenly, he turned and picked up the pace. "And who knows, maybe by the end of the evening, everyone will be doing 'The Lambeth Walk.'"

Dixie had to run to catch up. His sudden surge of bravado made her smile.

TWENTY-SIX

Two uniformed SS men wearing pistols were waiting in the wing as the evening show ended. Johnny asked one of the men if Major Schultz had sent them. He clicked his heels and answered with a polite "Yes, sir. The major was concerned that there might be some delays with taxis or traffic. He wanted to be sure that your trip was not delayed."

When Eddie opened the door to his dressing room after the show, two SS men were standing at attention against the far wall. They gestured to let him know that they would carry the instruments to the awaiting car. Normally he would decline the offer, but under the circumstances, he acquiesced.

When the three of them were settled in the backseat, a junior officer in the passenger seat turned and spoke to them in perfect English. "Gentlemen, mademoiselle. I do hope you are all comfortable. We have the privilege this evening of riding in Reichsführer-SS Heinrich Himmler's personal vehicle. The Reichsführer is already in Munich, attending a conference. My orders are to transport you from the theater to your hotel for your overnight bags and then on to the airport. I trust that is satisfactory with everyone?"

Johnny assumed the role of spokesperson. "Yes, quite. Thank you, quite."

The ride to the airport was uneventful. A Luftwaffe tri-motored Junkers Ju 52/3m was waiting near a hangar. Two more uniformed men were waiting alongside the aircraft to help unload the vehicle as the three exited the limousine. The aircraft was very luxuriously appointed and comfortable.

No time was wasted. Within minutes they were airborne. Their flying time to Munich was just under two hours. The crew captain announced that they would be flying between Leipzig and Dresden, over Nuremberg and into Munich. The aircraft was a bit noisy, but the view at night was spectacular.

Dixie found herself absorbed looking out the window. There was a light dusting of snow, and the seasonal lights seemed to sparkle in the cold, clear air. For a moment she was transported back to the carefree days of childhood, traveling with her parents to visit relatives. She tried to recognize familiar streets. When she turned toward Eddie to tell him about the wonderful time she'd had in Munich as a child, she was instantly reminded of where she was and why.

"What is it, Dix? What were you smiling about?"

"Oh, it's nothing. I was just reminiscing, that's all." She returned to the window, but somehow everything now looked different to her. The mood had vanished.

A limousine was waiting for them as they disembarked in Munich. Very little was spoken as they unloaded the aircraft. The drive to the nineteenth-century chateau took no more than fifteen minutes. There were lighted fountains, a lighted circular drive, and what looked to be a small army guarding the grounds. It was nearly midnight.

Major Schultz was in a walkway adjacent to the driveway, and he greeted them as the vehicle came to a stop. "Good evening, gentlemen, mademoiselle. I trust your journey was pleasant?"

With a nervous smile, Johnny again assumed the role of spokes-man. "Yes, quite pleasant, thank you. Pardon me, sir . . . er, Major. We were wondering if there might be a spare room, perhaps with a bath. We would like to freshen up and change into more formal attire. Before we begin, that is."

"Yes, of course, Herr Pitts. Please follow me. We will use the staff entrance just to the right of this hedge. Please stay close. We don't want to alarm any of the guards."

"No, no. Please lead the way, sir."

The major led them into a small foyer just off the kitchen and then to an adjoining room with a large bath attached. Waiters and waitresses were scurrying about. Two uniformed men with SS insignia followed with the instruments and luggage.

The major stood in the doorway as the uniformed men saluted and returned to their posts. "Gentlemen, mademoiselle . . . I'll return in thirty minutes, after you change. The music room is just through this hallway." He bowed and gently closed the door.

"Thirty minutes! It'll take me that long to put on my makeup."

"Not to worry, Dix. The bathroom is all yours. Eddie and I will use the mirror here on the dressing table."

Dixie took a deep breath and pulled out the dress she'd chosen for the evening's performance. It was a short, low-cut, lacy black cocktail dress with a removable satin drop that attached to the lower back of the dress. She'd only worn the dress for one performance at the Moulin Rouge in Paris.

Eddie had his evening tuxedo with a short satin jacket, while Johnny wore tails.

Johnny whistled softly as she exited the bathroom. "Righto! You look simply smashing, girl."

She did a pirouette and bowed. "Why, thank you, kind sir."

Eddie tuned up his instruments. "You know, pal, I took it for granted that there would be a piano at this party. What do you think?"

"Right, well up to now, it seems that our uniformed friends have anticipated every detail. Let's hope that the music room in this palace will not disappoint us. I daresay that without a piano, I'll be relegated to serving canapés and champagne."

Dixie put her arm on Eddie's shoulder, leaned over, and whispered, "Let me have the camera. It'll fit in my clutch purse. I want to soft-soap the major into letting me take some photos of this place for my scrapbook."

He gave her a wink as he handed her the camera. With his banjo in arm, he walked over and opened the door. The major was talking with one of his lieutenants, and he looked up.

"I'm afraid that we've neglected to ask that a piano be provided. I do hope—"

Major Schultz stopped him mid-sentence with a raise of his hand. "You will find the music room contains a concert grand piano. I have personally seen that it has been tuned for this special occasion. I trust you will find it satisfactory."

They were led through a maze of short hallways that reminded Eddie of his visits to the White House. They emerged in a larger hallway that led to a great room where most of the guests were chatting idly with cocktails in hand. Off to one side were double doors. The major opened the doors for the three, and then he shut them directly after they'd entered.

The room was a miniature theater with a small stage at the front. For a brief moment, they stood in awe.

Dixie quickly turned and opened one of the double doors. "Excuse me, Major." She was running on the toes of her shoes to avoid the loud noise her heels made on the marble flooring. He'd stopped when he heard his title. She caught his arm as she slid past him, almost falling over backward in the process. He caught her and was smiling affectionately as he held her tightly around the waist.

"Oh, excuse me, sir."

"It's quite all right, mademoiselle. Are you feeling all right?"

She was standing upright now, but she did not slide away from his grip around her waist. "Yes, sir. What I wanted to ask you is, would it be all right if I took some photos of this beautiful house and the auditorium for my scrapbook?"

He released his grip around her waist and placed his fist against his mouth to muffle a cough. "I'm sorry, but security measures prevent anyone from taking any unsanctioned photos of the führer or his staff. And I believe that extends to his residences as well."

"Please, I won't take any photos of him or his staff. I would just like my mother to see that magnificent room that we'll be performing in. There wouldn't be any harm in that, would there?' She looked up at him with fluttering eyelashes.

He smiled at her persistence, and it didn't hurt that she was drop-dead gorgeous. He carefully placed his hands on her shoulders, and with a much softer, understanding smile, relented. "Well, if it's just the auditorium, I think we could sanction that."

"Oh, thank you!" She stood on her toes and kissed him on the cheek. She then scurried back to the auditorium and disappeared behind the double doors. She winked and nodded as she rushed in. "Well, looks like we're in business, guys."

The three then walked slowly over to a grand piano, taking in the beautiful brocade wall covering and the crystal chandeliers that lit the ornate room. Comfortable cushioned chairs were set in two rows of six along a center aisle.

"It's a Steinway, for God's sake! I wonder what the poor people are doing?" Johnny sat and adjusted the bench and then ran his fingers over the keys and chorded a few modulations. "First class, my friends. I'm afraid this beautiful instrument will be wasted on my meager talent, but we'll certainly look the part."

Eddie had brought along his small stool with rubber coverings on the feet. He closed the piano lid and then placed the stool on top. He jumped up to check out the seating.

The major had quietly reentered the auditorium, just to check on Dixie. He started to approach the three as Eddie sat on the piano.

They could see the anxiety on the man's face. Eddie tried to short-circuit the anticipated admonishment and spoke up. "I'm too short for the people in back to see me, Major. This stool has rubber feet, sir, and won't hurt the piano or the finish. The lid is quite solid, and we should be just fine with me up here. I've done this many times."

"Yes, I see. Well, any damage will be deducted from your collective salary." The major looked at his watch. "You three seem to be ready. I shall announce that the concert will commence in, say, ten minutes? My lieutenants will usher in the guests."

"We're ready when you are, sir."

Dixie whispered, "If I've added up the number of seats correctly, it looks like the führer is throwing a party for about a hundred of his closest friends. It might have been cheaper if he'd rented the Scala."

Without fanfare the doors opened, and guests started to promenade into the room. The major walked to the front and stood at parade rest to one side of the piano. Junior officers stood adjacent to each aisle and directed the guests to seating until each row was filled. It took several minutes for everyone to get settled. Six ornate satin chairs were then carried in and placed to one side, facing the piano. Four white-jacketed officers in formal attire appeared and stood at attention on either side of the six chairs. A hush came over the crowd. Suddenly everyone stood. Adolph Hitler entered casually with a young woman on his arm. Eddie thought he looked very much like a military chief of staff in his stiff brown dress uniform, bloused trousers, and highly polished knee-high boots. The man looked nervous and impatient, as though wanting to be anywhere but at this event. But it was soon obvious that through sheer force of will, the man had embraced a personable and enthusiastic outward appearance. He smiled and nodded cordially to several guests as he paraded past. All eyes were glued on their führer. After the performance, they learned that the young woman accompanying him was Eva Braun.

Hitler continued to smile and wave at the guests as he stood next to his segregated chair of honor. There was continuous applause until the man was finally seated. Reichsmarschall and Mrs. Hermann Göring followed directly and sat behind Hitler and Miss Braun. Reichsführer and Mrs. Heinrich Himmler then entered and sat behind the Görings. Both Reichsmarschalls were in dress uniform. Himmler, however, wore the traditional dress black of the Waffen-SS. All the ladies were, of course, dressed in beautifully tailored evening gowns.

The major came to attention and began his announcement. "Chancellor Hitler, Reichsmarschall Göring, Reichsmarschall Himmler, ladies and gentlemen. For your entertainment this evening, we are pleased to bring to you, direct from the famous Scala theater in Berlin, three performers from the hit musical *American Jazz*. Featured this evening is the world-famous American jazz banjoist, often referred to in the American press as the King of the Banjo, Herr Eddie Peabody. His musical arranger, Herr Jonathon Pitts, will accompany him. A featured singer and dancer with the troupe, Fräulein Parsons, will also be performing for us this evening. Please give our American friends a warm German welcome." The major turned toward Eddie with his left arm extended. The audience began to applaud.

Before the introduction applause ceased, Eddie and Johnny started to play "Sweet Sue, Just You." Midway through the song, there was a break where Dixie slid in from behind a curtain and began to fill in the rhythm with some fast toe-tapping. The audience whistled, laughed, and started to clap to the rhythm of the song. The song was fast-paced, and Eddie's lightning fingers along the neck of the banjo had many gasping. The three then proceeded through their prearranged routine medleys. Midway through the performance, Eddie switched to the Banjoline and played a medley of soft, romantic American jazz classics. Dixie sang one chorus of "Am I Blue," vamping with the audience while Eddie carried the melody. Eddie put the violin mute on his banjo and asked that the room lighting be dimmed as he commenced playing Liebestraum. This was a familiar tune to many of the assembled guests. They were fascinated by the softened sound of the banjo as a result of the violin mute. At the finish, Hitler himself stood and applauded.

Eddie removed the mute and introduced them to the illusion of two banjos playing at once. The music produced by Eddie's lightning pick hand had the audience gasping in awe. The show concluded with a medley of American Southern tunes that culminated with two choruses of "Saint Louis Blues." At the conclusion, the entire room provided the group with a standing ovation. One of the more enthusiastic guests yelled out in English, "More!" The two men quickly went into "Tiger Rag." At the end of the performance, Eddie jumped off the piano and locked arms with Dix and Johnny, and the three bowed to thunderous applause.

Uniformed men suddenly appeared and quietly formed a human pathway that prevented the main body from leaving the room before the dignitaries and their guests had departed. As the orderly departure commenced, the major walked over and personally thanked the three for their stunning performance. "Thank you, Herr Peabody. I am certain that everyone, especially our führer, was very pleased with your performance this evening." He glanced at his watch. "Cocktails are now being served in the great room, and our führer has asked if you would be kind enough to join him in an informal receiving line."

Though exhausted, they were not about to deny the head of the German state. "We'd be pleased to, sir. We just need five minutes go freshen up, if we may."

"Of course, of course. It will take another fifteen or twenty minutes before everyone settles down and the reception is in place. May I order anything special for you from the bar?"

"Thank you, no. But if three tall glasses of ice water were to appear, we'd label you a saint."

He smiled at the suggestion of "saint." "They'll be waiting for you in your dressing room." He again checked his watch. "I'll meet you on the hour and will escort you to the reception. This will please the führer very much."

At the appointed hour, the three were escorted into the great room. Dixie was feeling underdressed and not the least excited to be stared at in a reception line. When she stepped into the room itself, though, she was awestruck. "My God! This is more opulent than anything I've ever seen, including Versailles." She scanned the room, and her eyes settled on a fireplace at the far end of the room. She touched Eddie's arm, but her gaze was fixed on the painting that hung just above the mantel.

He glanced at her.

"Look at the artwork, in particular the painting above the fireplace at the far end. I need to get a closer look, but from here it might be that landscape from Amsterdam."

"Your eyes are sharper than mine, Dix. This whole room looks like a masterpiece to me."

They both felt a presence approaching and turned in unison to see the major approaching. He was relaxed and beaming as he greeted them. "Hello again." He bowed to Dix. "You look marvelous, mademoiselle. I trust you got your photo for your scrapbook and found the ice water refreshing?"

She beamed a smile back at him and moved ever so slightly to give him an unobstructed view of the front of her dress. "Why, yes, and thank you, kind sir. But this is the most magnificent room I've ever seen. I wonder if it would be possible—"

He quickly interrupted her. "I told you that it is forbidden to photograph the führer or his staff, and that goes for his surroundings as well. I could likely be shot for what I've already allowed. Please remain here, and do enjoy the reception. I will escort you to the receiving line when they are ready." He came to attention, straightened his jacket, and strode off.

Eddie audibly exhaled when the man was out of earshot. "What the hell was that all about?"

"I asked him if I could take some shots of this room for my scrapbook. He said the auditorium was okay, but not this room or anyone in it. He could be shot for even knowing I had a camera."

"He likes you, Dix. He broke the rules for you. You'd better be damned careful. He'll be watching you like a cat."

Hitler was standing with Miss Braun in the far corner. They were surrounded by a group of young SS boys in uniform. Göring and his wife, along with Himmler, were standing to Hitler's left and shaking hands with some of the guests. The major returned and escorted Dixie and the two men toward the group of dignitaries. When the führer saw them approach, he stepped away from the boys, leaving Miss Braun to carry on.

The major commenced introductions and indicated that he would translate everything, first in German, and then in English. When introduced to Eddie, Hitler smiled and shook his hand vigorously. "I enjoyed your performance very much, Herr Peabody. I believe that if my history is correct, your Negro slaves introduced the banjo and jazz music into your country. Well, Herr Peabody, your virtuosity with that instrument truly establishes your wizardry."

"Thank you, sir, for your kind words."

Hitler's eyes immediately went to Dixie. "And this young, talented lady was a marvel as well." The major immediately stepped forward and formally introduced her as Miss Dixie Parsons. Hitler bowed slightly and kissed her hand. "Dixie, what an interesting name. You are a very beautiful and talented young lady. I'm sure you will soon become the belle of American jazz theater."

Dixie gave a slight curtsy. She could sense that the man felt self-conscious. He was delighted with her presence but uncomfortable, like an adolescent on his first date. "It is an honor for the three of us to be here this evening."

Göring and Himmler noticed the führer chatting with the three performers. Wanting to be included, they casually wandered closer. Hitler felt their presence, and when introduced to Johnny, he merely smiled and shook his hand but said nothing. He then stepped to the side and began introducing his Reichsführers to the group.

Dixie could feel Himmler's eyes staring at her. She smiled but avoided eye contact. He then stepped forward, bowed, and spoke to her in broken English. "Excuse me, but you look very familiar. Is this your first visit to Germany? What other countries have you visited with this group?"

She was very uncomfortable and had difficulty looking at the man as he spoke. His eyes were penetrating, and the way they continuously scanned her made her feel like she was naked; this man was dangerous. She bit her lip and lowered her eyes as she replied, "Yes, sir, this is my first visit to Germany. The show has played in England, Holland, Belgium, and France. I was recruited for the show in Boston."

"Ah, yes, yes. Perhaps it was in Amsterdam. I feel certain that I've seen you before somewhere."

Miss Braun quietly appeared and whispered into Hitler's ear. He mumbled something and then begged forgiveness from the guests. He quickly turned and strode off toward the entrance. Himmler and Göring also turned on their heels and followed.

There was a brief period of relative silence. Dixie felt so relieved that she audibly sighed. *Thank God for Miss Braun, and divine intervention—and for leading that awful man away!* She felt sure that the Reichsführer wanted to question her some more—he must have sensed something, perhaps her accent when she spoke.

Johnny caught Eddie's eye and pointed to his watch. "Er, excuse me, Major. I'm truly sorry, but we're all exhausted, and tomorrow is going to arrive very early. Would it be an imposition if we retired to our hotel?"

"Of course, Herr Pitts. I'll have transport out front in two minutes." The major summoned a junior officer standing near the kitchen entrance, and the two of them walked briskly toward an exit.

After the main attraction had left the premises, everyone seemed to coagulate into small, low-key conversation groups. The three entertainers suddenly found themselves standing alongside one another, alone. Dixie nudged Eddie. "I'm going to get a closer look at that painting. Come with me, will you?"

Not hearing Dixie's request, Johnny asked casually, "Well, guys, what are your thoughts?"

"We're heading over toward the fireplace to look at a painting. Come with us."

They walked slowly, like tourists admiring the ornate and lavish fixtures. Dixie lowered her voice to a whisper. "Well, what did you think when you first saw him?"

"His Nibs? He sure as hell's no Roosevelt. Just another tinhorn, in my book. And here he is at a social function, in uniform. He's up to something, I can tell you that."

"Let's keep our voices down. I feel like we're the center of attention here. And with all these gentlemen in uniform . . . "

"Right you are, pal."

Dix added, "If I never see that creep Himmler again . . . My God, would you look at that!"

They both stopped and turned to look at what had caught her eye. On an outside wall between two French doors, with only ambient light for illumination, hung Frans Hals's portrait *Jester with a Lute*. They were standing about ten feet from the fireplace. The landscape that hung over the mantel looked very much like the stolen Jacob van Ruisdael painting. "I must get a photo. You guys shield me as best you can."

They casually looked about. There were only two couples standing about fifty feet away, and they seemed engrossed in their conversation. The two men stepped slightly behind Dix and stood close, pretending to be in conversation while blocking any view as she fished the camera out of her purse. She held the camera waist high, tilted the lens up, and, moving from side to side, clicked away.

Suddenly, from the corner of his eye, Eddie noticed someone approaching. A young lieutenant strode toward them with an authoritative gait. His voice was abrupt and commanding. In broken English he asked, "Did I hear a camera? No cameras are allowed."

Eddie smiled and moved directly in front of the lieutenant to block his view. "Good evening, Lieutenant. Did you enjoy the show?"

"Is there something I can help you with? Why are you looking at this painting? Are you interested in art?"

"No, no, but thank you. We were just admiring this magnificent room and all the beautiful paintings." He tried to distract him by looking at the ceiling. "And all these incredibly ornate fixtures . . . "

In that short space of time, Dixie managed to shove the camera back into her purse. The major suddenly appeared. "What's the problem here?"

The lieutenant came to attention. "I heard the click of a camera, sir. I was about to question them—"

The major held up his hand. "These people are in my custody and my responsibility, lieutenant."

The lieutenant clicked his heels, saluted, and did an about-face.

The major had a grim, admonishing look as he turned toward the three. "Your transport is waiting."

"Okay, guys, looks like our ride is here."

262

The three quickly hustled off toward the exit; the major slowly followed. Before she could exit the room, Dix felt a hand on her shoulder. She stopped and turned to see who it was; it was the major. He said nothing, but she nearly melted under his glare. His mood had darkened, and he looked like he would burst. She stared up at him and thought she was going to cry. Abruptly he removed his hand from her shoulder and waved to her in a gesture that clearly meant get out of here, now! She didn't hesitate.

The two men watched anxiously and then exited the room together. Before entering the car, they were each handed a room key and an envelope.

The major suddenly appeared as they were seated. He bid them good night. "Your driver will pick you up at 0900 tomorrow morning. *Guten Nacht!*"

The hotel was less than a thirty-minute ride from the chateau. No one spoke. As they approached, they noticed dim lighting casting shadows across a quaint half-timbered chalet. The small establishment seemed well kept, with adequate appointments, especially beds. They were exhausted, but they wondered if another shoe was about to drop.

At breakfast they were served cold cuts, cheese, and hard rolls, and thankfully some strong coffee. Everyone looked like they'd been up all night, which they had. They were elated to have the party and its aftermath behind them. Dix wanted to review the evening, while it was still fresh in her mind.

Eddie put a finger to his lips. "Let's wait till we're back in Berlin. What do you say?"

She nodded.

Johnny grumbled as he refilled his plate. "It's no wonder these chaps get their knickers in a twist, eating all this ruddy cheese. And have a look at these bloody rocks they call bread. If they would just try a full English breakfast, everyone would bloody well have a better day."

Their car to the airport was punctual. Discussing German cuisine could wait. A Junker, waiting to take them on their return trip, was warming up engines as they entered the airfield.

★ ★ ★

Gestapo Headquarters, Berlin

A message from New York had been decoded and placed on the desk of SS Colonel Ault. One of his primary duties was to coordinate local area Nazi Party activities. A precinct captain had requested, via radio transmission to New York, all information on an American entertainer currently working in Germany, Eddie Peabody.

The SS radio technician assembled the decoded message and placed it in a folder labeled TOP SECRET. He hurried up the stairs to the office of the duty officer, SS Colonel Ault. The door was open, but the technician stood at attention and gently knocked on the wooden doorframe.

Without looking up from the documents he was reading, the colonel acknowledged the gentle knock. "Yes, what is it?"

"Excuse me, sir. I've just decoded a message from New York. A background check was requested last week on an American entertainer, and you asked to be notified as soon as there was a reply."

"Yes, yes. I recall. Come in, and encapsulate the response for me."

The technician entered and stood at attention until the colonel ordered him to stand at ease. "Well, get on with it, man."

"Yes, sir. The background check was requested on Eddie Peabody. He's currently appearing at the Scala."

"Yes, yes. And what did our agents in New York find out?"

"Well, sir, they were able to chronicle the man's life and career, from his naval discharge in San Pedro, California, to his rise in popularity as a musician, to his current world tour. The message also included a newspaper excerpt from a recent performance of his at the White House. The agents concluded their message with a curious discovery. They recommended Berlin authorize additional follow-up for clarification."

"And what was this curious discovery?"

"Well, sir, one of the agents had found, in an obscure entertainment trade magazine, a photograph of Eddie Peabody in a US naval uniform. His wife had been interviewed for the article and had referred to her husband as Lieutenant."

"Really? That is interesting. Leave the folder here. I'll contact you personally if we require further communication with our New York agents. In the meantime, you are not to disclose any of this to anyone. Is that understood?"

"Yes, sir." The technician came to attention and saluted his superior.

"Thank you. That will be all."

The normal recourse for the colonel would be to follow up with the party section captain that had requested the transmission. He would also brief his superior at their regular staff meeting. But it would be another day before that staff meeting.

Colonel Ault was always prompt, usually arriving at Gestapo headquarters one half hour early. After his regular cup of strong coffee, he would chat with his favorite secretary, Renate, usually about her weekend. This morning was no different, except that as he chatted with Renate, she casually adjusted her stockings and mentioned that she'd seen a message on his desk from New York stamped TOP SECRET. "The message was received and dated yesterday, sir. I was just curious. Are you working on something important regarding some American entertainer?"

The colonel was puzzled and somewhat disturbed by her question. "No, no. It's just routine, Renate." He then went immediately to retrieve the message. He tried to relax and convince himself that no additional follow-up was needed. *This is routine— likely another dead end, of no consequence. After all, many Germans, as well as Americans, served in uniform during the previous war, and many continued their careers in the reserves. I'll telephone the party captain later this afternoon, let him follow up with an interview.* He felt sure his boss would agree. The staff meeting was fast approaching, and he pondered whether or not to even mention the message.

After a few minutes, he returned for another cup of coffee and stopped by Renate's desk. He instructed her to contact the local party captain in the afternoon. "Ask him to make an appointment with us for tomorrow morning. I want the local party chief to interview the entertainer and follow up with a written report, to me. Let me see . . . I believe the entertainer's name is Peabody. Yes, it's Eddie Peabody. He's performing at the Scala."

The secretary's eyes widened. "I've heard of this American. They refer to him as the Man with the Banjo. I intended to get tickets. Have you and your wife seen the show?"

The colonel frowned at her mentioning his wife. "We only attend classical performances, *Fräulein!*" He marched back to his office and reviewed the message one more time. He decided to take the message with him to the staff meeting. He would summarize the findings and report his recommendation for the boss's approval.

The meeting was held in the conference room, and it was chaired by SS-Oberstgruppenführer Richard Heydrich. This was not unusual. Himmler's chief lieutenant, Heydrich, often would chair these meetings when it was felt that emphasis was needed— more often than not to enforce tighter regimentation on Nazi policies. This meeting focused on students and professors at the university at Heidelberg. A small group had been challenging the mandatory military service policies for students.

Heydrich was quiet-spoken but emphatic. He ordered his staff to organize the discreet roundup of all dissidents. "Let them demonstrate in the local stockade for a few days. They will welcome military service to the Fatherland."

During the general discussion portion of the meeting, only a few of the colonel's peers had anything to report. He again pondered whether or not to mention his recent message from New York. As the staff reports were about to end, he raised his hand.

After summarizing the contents of the message, he concluded with his recommendation to let the local party captain interrogate the entertainer and follow up with a written report. He then looked up at Heydrich for approval.

The furious look in the man's eyes nearly made his heart stop. Heydrich's reaction stunned everyone in the room. "For your information, Colonel Ault, this American entertainer has just returned from Munich, where he performed for, and was very close to, the führer himself!" His voice was screeching. Everyone wanted to crawl under the table, but no one dared move a muscle. Heydrich reached for the telephone. He commenced to yell at whomever was on the other end. "Find the Reichsführer, now!" He slammed down the phone. He was now standing, with his fists pressing on the table. "Colonel Ault, I want you to assemble a detachment of men, immediately! I want this Herr Peabody, and whoever else was with him in Munich, arrested immediately! I will attend to his interrogation personally!" Heydrich then dismissed everyone in the conference room except Colonel Ault.

The colonel telephoned his secretary from the conference room and ordered her to connect him with the duty lieutenant. "Lieutenant! Assemble a squad of men and proceed to the Scala theater immediately. All personnel are to be detained for questioning by order of Reichsführer Heydrich. Herr Peabody and all those that have recently returned from Munich are to be separated and arrested! Reichsführer Heydrich and I will proceed at once to the theater. Is that understood?"

Heydrich nodded his approval and then looked directly into the colonel's eyes. "It may interest you that Herr Peabody has recently been performing in Hamburg. It may also interest you that he has been given a personal tour of the shipbuilding facility that is constructing the Bismarck." Heydrich sat motionless for about one minute. He picked up the telephone and called SS headquarters in Hamburg. He instructed the duty officer to locate and detain a Captain Schroeder. "It is extremely urgent that we speak with the captain. Do this quickly, but do not sound the alarm. Is that understood?"

Heydrich and the colonel canceled all their appointments and hurried off to Heydrich's staff car. "Herr Peabody and the other detainees must be escorted back to headquarters. Our in-house interrogations seem to be much more persuasive. And I must have a copy of that photograph—Herr Peabody in uniform! Do I make myself clear?"

"Yes, sir!"

What neither man was unaware of—what all of Gestapo head-quarters was unaware of—was that the colonel's favorite secretary, Renate Oberhoff, was a close childhood friend and relative of Greg Ziemer; she was Ziemer's first cousin, the second daughter of his mother's brother. The two had grown up on adjacent farms on the outskirts of Lübeck, a small town on the Trave River in northern Germany, a town of commerce with medieval roots. Greg and Renate had also spent several memorable summers in their youth exploring the beaches of the East Frisian Islands on family vacations.

Renate found the lieutenant and forwarded Colonel Ault's message. She then went outside the building for her morning break, ostensibly to buy cigarettes. She telephoned Greg. "I can tell you little, Cousin, other than I haven't felt this much anxiety or seen that much activity in the office since Chamberlain's last visit. I'm sure, though, that Heydrich is going to arrest your friend Eddie Peabody."

"Thank you, Ren, for risking this call. Please be extra careful when you return to the office. Everyone is suspicious of everyone these days."

"I want you to be careful too, my favorite cousin. Heydrich is a vicious and vengeful man."

"No more conversation now, Ren. Thank you again for all you have done. There are many who would say they owed you their lives. I must bid you goodbye, for now. I'll contact you as soon as I'm able."

His tone of voice concerned her. She stared at the dead phone.

Greg immediately telephoned the hotel but could find neither Eddie nor Johnny. He telephoned the theater and was able to finally connect with Dixie. He felt relief when she answered. "Dixie. It's time to get Eddie out of Germany, now, as fast as you can! The Gestapo are on their way to the theater as we speak. They want to interrogate him, and likely you and Johnny as well. Good luck, Dix."

Dixie stood motionless momentarily. A cold chill made her shiver. She hoped the theater's phone wasn't monitored. She hurried back to her dressing room to gather her thoughts. *Eddie must be on his way to the theater by now.* She had to hatch a plan, and fast. Three of the chorus girls were in the dressing room, laughing and getting loud. It started to irritate her. She needed to remain calm. She ran out to the front entrance, hoping that she'd see him arriving in a cab. She didn't. She ran to the rear entrance: no Commander Eddie. What she did see in the alleyway, however, was a German soldier, urinating in a walkway next to his Volkswagen jeep. She felt a plan starting to emerge.

She exited the stage entrance and approached the soldier. She was only wearing her robe, and all she had on underneath was her underwear and a corset. She smiled at the young man as he buttoned his trousers and puffed on the cigarette hanging out of his mouth. *This guy can't be more than eighteen or nineteen years old.* She moved closer and stood next to him, and casually she asked him if he had another cigarette. While he fished in his pocket for his cigarettes, she let her robe slide open to expose her bare leg. He couldn't miss the provocative view; he began to blush.

Scanning the immediate area, she saw a narrow walkway between two buildings adjacent to the soldier's Volkswagen. When she glanced down at the jeep, she saw a tire iron on the passenger seat. "So, what's a handsome young man in uniform doing hanging around the Scala at this time of day?"

The young man began to stutter. "I, I'm a d-d-driver for an army group commander. And th-th-the unit's been moved to an a-abandoned base . . . t-two kilometers east of Berlin. I, I just d-d-drove two officers to the train station. So I, I decided to take the rest of the afternoon off." When he'd finished, he stood with his hands in his pockets, staring at her with a broad grin. She noticed that he was missing several teeth.

The sun was starting to set behind some taller buildings, and dark shadows began to engulf the alleyway. Dixie turned up the charm and maneuvered the young man next to the wall adjacent to the passenger side of his vehicle. She gave him a light kiss on the cheek.

"Wh-wh-what was that for?"

"Just a thank-you, for the cigarette." She held it out, indicating that she needed a light. As he searched for a match, she could tell he was getting aroused. He lit her cigarette with a nervous shake of his hand.

She turned suddenly, deftly opened the passenger door, and motioned for him to have a seat. The soldier threw his cigarette into the alley and, with a huge grin, began to unfasten his trousers. She gently pushed the soldier backward and down into the passenger seat, with his pants down around his knees and his feet hanging out the door.

As he sat and tried to lean back, he suddenly grimaced in pain. He reached under his shorts and pulled the tire iron out from under himself. When he saw the cause of his discomfort, he looked up and started to laugh. Dixie took the iron from him and laid it to her side. She then gently began to massage his leg. The soldier closed his eyes and began a low moan as he continued to remove his trousers.

Dixie unobtrusively took the tire iron in her right hand as she continued to massage the young man with her left hand. With his eyes closed, he began to clench his teeth. He then leaned forward to remove his trousers. With suddenness and speed that surprised them both, she whirled the tire iron down on the young man's head with bone-crushing force. The soldier's eyes and mouth opened, and blood began to spurt from the wound. She took a deep breath and then came down at him with another forceful blow. This one produced an audible crack when the iron hit his skull. Blood soon covered his face.

Dix was breathing heavily now as she held her hand to her mouth to stifle a sob. She knew she needed to move him out of the vehicle and into the dark walkway. She dropped the tire iron onto the floor of the jeep and pulled hard on his shirt to get him out of the vehicle. She turned him toward the walkway, but he was too heavy; he fell backwards. But from the alleyway, his feet would still be visible, so she hurried around his body and dragged him by the shirt further into the walkway.

He was a bloody mess, but she had one more difficult job to

do: remove his shirt and shoes. When she'd completed that task, she hurried back to Eddie's dressing room, where he had a sink and she could rinse out some of the blood from the soldier's shirt. When she was satisfied with the quick rinse, she pinned up her hair and dressed in the young soldier's pants and shirt. *I need a hat. Where the hell was his hat?* She felt sick, but she swallowed hard and returned to the jeep to look for the young man's cap.

She found it in the backseat. *He must have tossed it when got out to urinate.* She pulled the cap low on her head and adjusted it to cover her hair. She moved forward and sat in the driver's seat. *Now what do I do?* She tried not to think about it. *I've just killed a man! It will likely be tomorrow morning before he is missed.*

Bright headlights suddenly appeared in the alleyway, illuminating her and the jeep completely. She held her breath.

The oncoming car, an older limousine or Mercedes, pulled up close to the back door of the theater. The driver got out and started up the steps to the theater.

Greg! "Greg! Is that you?"

He stopped and turned toward the high-pitched voice. All he could see was a young German soldier sitting in a jeep. "Did someone just call out?" Dixie exited the jeep and walked over to him. Recognition quickly set in. "My God, Dixie, you sure startled me. What in the world are you—"

"You startled me too, Greg, when I saw those bright lights coming at me."

"But what are you doing in that uniform?"

"Improvising. I wasn't sure how to get Eddie out of here. Truthfully, I'm still not sure."

"Right. I've brought the Mercedes over here for you. Please use it. With you in that uniform, pretending to be his driver, you might just bluff your way out. In short order the Gestapo will close off every route out of Berlin—through Denmark and Holland as well. Your best chance to cross the border will likely be through France. So I suggest you both get moving. Time is of the essence, Dix."

"What about Johnny, and the rest of the troupe?"

"I'm sorry, but there's no time for a coordinated effort. I'm afraid they're on their own. Johnny's German is good, and he knows people in Holland. With a little luck, the SS will be concentrating on stopping Eddie. My source indicated that Heydrich is only interested in you three."

"Swell. Something or somebody must have tipped him off in Munich."

"Anyway, the rest of the troupe should be deported back to England, once they've been questioned."

"What about you?"

"I think my cover is kaput, so I'm leaving as well. I've got exit papers, though. Those should allow me to travel through Denmark—that is, if I hurry. And from there I should be able to catch a fishing boat to Sweden."

"What about Eddie and me? Could we get exit visas?"

"There isn't enough time. I'm sorry, Dix. Damn it! I'm sure, though, if you can make your way into France, you should have clear sailing from there." Greg smiled and tossed her keys to the Mercedes. He then reached into his topcoat pocket and retrieved a German 7.65mm pistol. After he'd handed it to her, he mimicked one of Eddie's two fingered salutes. "Good luck to you both, Dix. And I will see you both in London, soon."

She was staring at the pistol when Eddie emerged with his instruments in tow. "I can't find Johnny, Dix. He was going to stop at the American embassy before coming to the theater. I hope someone got word to him." He stopped just short of running into Greg. "Oh, hi there, pal. What the hell are you still doin' here?"

"The clock's ticking, my friend. The Gestapo will be here soon, so you'd both better head out, and now."

"Right you are, skipper." He sat down and laid his instruments on the floor, then exhaled with a whistle.

Dix turned back to face him. "Try to relax, Commander. I'm going to get us the hell out of here, fast." She started the motor and checked the gas gauge. "I've been crossing these borders since I was a kid. Now, let's you and me see if we can get our butts into France!" She looked up at his face in the mirror as she accelerated. He looked like a lost puppy.

She was out of the alley quickly and onto the main street. She was all business now as she steered the large, cumbersome vehicle toward Potsdam and the main highway to Hanover. She wanted to get to Frankfurt and then on to Mannheim; from there it was a quick dash west into France. From her college days, she remembered that it would take a good day's driving time to get where she wanted to be. She remembered a lot from those days. Things were so different now.

TWENTY-SEVEN

Johnny arrived at the theater about thirty minutes from curtain and rushed back to his room. What he found when he entered brought him up short. A Gestapo major and two armed soldiers came to attention. He tried to act casual. "Good afternoon, gentlemen. How may I help you?"

"You are . . . Herr Pitts?"

"Yes."

Before he could ask what they were doing there, the major stepped closer and nearly shouted. "Where are Herr Peabody and Fräulein Parsons?"

In a voice so calm that it surprised even him, he said, "Unless they are in their dressing rooms, I haven't the foggiest, Major."

The man was turning red, clearly frustrated and becoming quite agitated. "Herr Pitts! You are under arrest!"

"But sir—"

"Take him to headquarters for questioning. Now!" The soldiers quickly hustled Johnny out of the room and toward the alley exit.

The theater manager heard the commotion and came storming into the room. "See here. I'm the manager of this theater, and I demand to know what is going on."

The major looked at him with contempt. "So, you are the manager. Well, theater manager, effective immediately, this show and this theater are closed!"

"On whose—"

"By order of the Gestapo! And if you should receive any communication from Herr Peabody or Fräulein Parsons, Herr Manager, you are to contact me immediately. Is that understood?"

The man was petrified. All he could manage was a nod.

"My people will return here to retrieve all of Herr Peabody's possessions, and those of Herr Pitts and Fräulein Parsons, of course. Am I clear on this, Herr Manager?"

The theater manager was in a state of shock. After he'd informed his boss, he walked onto the stage and addressed the incoming audience. "Ladies and gentlemen, due to unforeseen circumstances, our current show, *American Jazz*, will be closed indefinitely. Please see the ticket agents out front for all refunds."

★ ★ ★

As she headed west, Dix was surprised at how mild the traffic was. She looked into the rearview mirror and saw that Eddie's eyes were closed. *I may be able to convince whomever that I'm transporting this famous American entertainer to perform for . . . maybe some senior Wehrmacht officers?* She shook her head. *No, no. I need to stay focused. I'll do whatever works.*

Eddie sat up and leaned forward. "Do we know if Johnny got the word?"

"I'm afraid that things happened too fast. But I wouldn't worry too much. His German is as good as it gets, and he's been playing theaters in Germany for more than a decade—long before you guys met up in London. They'll probably just deport him."

Eddie sat back. He didn't answer. *Everything was going so smoothly up until now. What happened?*

"Say, I'm getting hungry. How about you?" She pulled into a petrol station near Hildesheim. "Did you bring any cash with you?"

Without answering, he reached in his pocket and handed her five hundred marks.

She gasped at the wad of money. "We've got it made, Commander. With this stash, we might be able to buy our way out." She winked at him.

For the first time since they'd begun their wild ride, her wink brought a grin to his face.

A young service station attendant approached. "Excuse me, sir. Is there an inn nearby where we could get some supper?"

The attendant never looked up. "There are two inns not more than a few miles toward the village." He scratched his head as he returned to filling the Mercedes with petrol. *I could have sworn she was a man.*

A short distance from the service station, they noticed a small chalet that looked cozy and warm. Once inside, the smells from the kitchen enticed them to stay. They were famished.

Dixie loved cozy little places; the interlude had a calming effect on them both. "We'll be heading south now, toward Frankfurt. Why don't you sit up front and keep me company? After that delicious dinner, I may need a shove to keep me awake."

"Sure, I'd even spell you if I knew where the hell I was going. Though I must say that I can't think of anyone I'd rather be on the run with."

It was dark, and the traffic was again light. Soon they'd driven by Frankfurt and were at the outskirts of Mannheim. At an intersection Dixie pulled off the road to review her route. "I thought about going on to Strasbourg, but I've changed my mind. There's a small drawbridge across the Rhine just south of here, near Speyer. Most times, especially late at night, no one mans the gate. My friends and I used to travel this route when we'd forgotten our visas or they had expired. There shouldn't be any river traffic at this hour, and no one should take notice of us. Anyway, I think it's our best chance."

Eddie put his arm around her shoulder. "You're hoping that things haven't changed. Me too."

She leaned into him. "Yes."

"You're in charge, Lieutenant."

"You'd better get in the back, in case we meet up with a curious policeman or security guard." It was difficult for her to remember the exact route to the crossing, especially at night. She turned here, went up a narrow one-lane street there, and finally passed a sign: WISSEMBOURG—11 KILOMETERS.

Eddie didn't have a clue where they were, but he felt sustained by Dixie's confidence.

Around a bend in the road, they came upon a lighted area. A single bar stretched across the road with a large octagonal sign in the middle: HALT. The lights of a village, about a kilometer beyond the gate, twinkled in the dark sky. They approached slowly. No guard was in sight. Dixie stopped in front of the barrier and could see that it was manually operated. She got out but left the car running and walked over to the end of the barrier, where weights were attached. She could lift the bar easily.

Standing out of view, in the dark shadows of a tree, was an elderly man in uniform. He had noticed the uniformed soldier trying to lift the barrier and thought he'd better return to his post. As he walked slowly toward the Mercedes, he thought it odd that the military was using this crossing, and at this time of night.

He brushed off some cigarette ash from his civil service uniform. When he'd reached the lighted open area, he realized that the driver of the beautiful old Mercedes was a beautiful young woman, and in regular army uniform. *This is most unusual. Something is not right about this, and I'm going to find out what is going on.* "Good evening, Corporal. Your papers and your destination, please." After addressing Dix without even a casual glance, he continued on toward the small guard shack.

Unsure what exactly to do or to say, she followed him to the shack. She fumbled in her pockets along the way and found the murdered soldier's papers in the breast pocket. She handed him the stolen papers as she stood in the doorway.

He abruptly snatched them from her hand and commenced to look them over closely. "Where are you headed, Corporal?"

She tried to charm the old gentleman with an engaging smile.

He looked up but continued to glare at her without reaction. "Well?"

She forced herself to hold a beguiling smile. *Damn. This geezer is only interested in asserting his meager authority.*

Now the man was getting impatient. "Corporal, I'm going to telephone—

She quickly interrupted him. "Wait, please." She cleared her throat. "I have a famous American entertainer in the back of that car. I am delivering him to a concert . . . in Nancy . . . for some Wehrmacht officers." She tried to make her voice sound authoritative, hoping to scare the man into letting them pass.

The guard started to walk outside to look into the backseat of the vehicle.

She thought her ruse was working.

He then stopped suddenly and turned around. "Corporal, you do not have an exit visa, and it is my duty to telephone my duty officer in Karlsruhe. I'm sorry, but you and your passenger must remain in the car and wait here until I have proper authority for you to proceed." He reached past her to a small table and picked up a crank telephone. He placed Dixie's stolen papers in front of him. He cranked the telephone, trying to reach a local operator.

Dixie felt her heart start to pound. She had to do something, and fast. By now, it was likely that the Gestapo in Berlin had alerted the border at Strasbourg, and maybe this guy's duty officer as well. She slowly tucked her hand into the pocket containing the pistol that Greg had given her. *Damn it, by now everyone will be on the lookout for us.* She was no longer thinking. She reacted—withdrew the pistol and pulled the trigger. She fired two shots in rapid succession into the man's chest.

The old guard, with a shocked look on his face, dropped the phone and fell back against the wall. His hands went to his chest. She looked at his face as he grimaced and slowly slid to the floor.

With the pistol still in her hand, she ran back to the car.

Eddie was just getting out of the vehicle. "Dixie! What the hell . . . " He stopped mid-sentence as she put up her pistol hand.

"Get in the car—drive it across when I raise the barrier!"

"You got it." As the barrier rose, Eddie hit the accelerator and spun the tires.

★ ★ ★

Gestapo Headquarters, Berlin

Returning from the Scala, Reichsführer Heydrich personally telephoned all checkpoints north through Denmark and west into Holland. He placed all under his command on high alert. Patrols were dispatched from Hamburg, Hanover, and Essen to search every alternate route out of Berlin. All would be on the lookout for a large Mercedes sedan carrying two American agents. Colonel Ault and two junior officers entered and stood to one side of the Reichsführer's desk.

Heydrich suddenly slammed his phone onto the cradle. "Where are they? How could they have slipped by my patrols? They must have exchanged vehicles. All checkpoints have reported—nothing! If they are still traveling by car, they must pass through a checkpoint sooner or later."

He turned to address Colonel Ault. "It's been more than three hours since we arrested that troupe at the Scala. Herr Pitts says he knows nothing of their escape, or of them being foreign agents, for that matter. Colonel, send one of these men to check on the progress of Pitts's interrogation."

The colonel tapped the captain standing at his side. With a sharp click of heels and an about-face, the captain hustled off to the interrogation room.

The colonel cleared his throat. "Reichsführer? May I speak freely, sir?"

"Yes, yes. What is it?"

"Sir, I believe that Fräulein Dixie, mentioned in your brief—well, sir, we now know she too is an American agent. Her real name is Marian Graham."

"Yes, yes. And we now know that the American embassy is saying that they know nothing about the whereabouts of Herr

Peabody or Fräulein Graham. They were offended that it was suggested that perhaps these two could be agents of the American government. This is an embarrassment, Colonel, that I do not care to revisit. Now, what is your point?"

"Sir, you indicated that our intelligence discovered that Fräulein Graham, Dixie, had attended school in France as well as Berlin."

"Yes, yes. Go on."

"Perhaps, sir, instead of trying to escape to the north, they drove south, toward France."

"Yes, that's a definite possibility. However, when I issued the security alert, Colonel, the general description of Herr Peabody and Fräulein Graham was sent to all border stations. None, including those along the French border, have reported anything suspicious."

Heydrich stood up and walked toward the office window. There was a long silence before he spoke. "But Colonel, since you are convinced that they have taken this longer and more exposed route, I want you to personally telephone all checkpoints that border with France and Belgium. Have all sightings and actions reported immediately to this office!"

The colonel saluted and retreated to the conference room. En route he passed in the hallway his aide, whom he'd sent to check on the interrogation of Herr Pitts. "Captain, any new information?"

"Yes, sir. He revealed that their contact in Germany was a Herr Greg Ziemer, a professor at the American University."

"Where is Pitts now?"

"His holding cell, sir." The captain turned pale and started to gasp for breath. He didn't tell his boss that he'd sought to speak with Pitts personally. And what he'd found had made him wince: a broken man lying prone on a cot, motionless. When he'd approached, the unconscious man's face was blood-red and severely swollen. His left eye was swollen shut, and the bone surrounding it looked smashed. He'd exited the cell quickly and nearly vomited in the corridor.

"What is it, man?"

"Nothing, sir." The captain came to attention and abruptly left the area. His superior, bewildered, watched the man disappear, then he too left abruptly.

The Reichsführer looked up from his desk. "Yes, yes. Come in. What is it, Colonel?"

"It seems there has been a disturbance at a remote border crossing near Karlsruhe, sir. A guard station south of Bad Bergzabern failed to acknowledge receipt of the security alert. And when the security officer in Karlsruhe dispatched a rider to hand-deliver the message, the guard was found dead at his desk. He'd been shot. Additionally, Interrogation has determined that a Herr Greg Ziemer was the American's local contact."

Heydrich stood and, with hands clasped behind his back, started to pace. "Yes, we've been suspicious of Herr Ziemer for some time now. I issued a detain-and-arrest order for the man two hours ago. But it appears that our American University professor had a pass and has already crossed into Denmark. So I'm afraid he will be of no use to us now."

He stopped pacing and turned to face the colonel. "Well, it appears that you were correct, Colonel. That little minx Dixie has traveled our back roads and used her charm to escape into France. But this game is far from over. We still have some cards to play, like our well-placed agents in France. I believe these criminals did cross south of Bad Bergzabern, and now they will likely head for either Strasbourg, Nancy, or Metz."

"What makes you so certain of their route, sir?"

"Trains, Colonel! The availability of regular train service to either coast—to Switzerland, Italy, or Spain."

Heydrich began to thumb through a file on his desk. He wrote four names on a separate sheet of paper. "Come, Colonel. We must get a message to these agents immediately!"

On the outskirts of a small village, Dixie noticed light emanating from either a large home or what she hoped was a bed-

and-breakfast. Though it was a dark night, she turned off the car's headlamps and drove slowly past. "Oh, thank you, God."

"What are you thanking him for?"

"I think I've found us a place for what remains of the night." She turned down a narrow side street and pulled the car close to the edge of the road, under a large tree, out of direct sight. "Okay, I'm going to check this place out, so please remain in the car until I return."

She walked around the front of the B&B and entered. Two cleaning people were speaking French in the entryway. They stopped talking when she cleared her throat. They both stared at her uniform. In fluent French she asked, "When will someone be at the desk? I would very much like to rent one of your rooms."

They seemed pleased that she spoke French. One woman stepped forward and smiled. "The manager will be over shortly. He's just finishing his breakfast, mademoiselle, and getting his children off to school."

"Thank you. May I wait over here by the front desk?"

"Oh, *oui*, mademoiselle."

Across the small street, a well-dressed man scampered down the steps of a two-story white house. Two children rushed by him and ran off toward the town. He entered the B&B and caught the eye of one of the cleaning ladies. He immediately turned to Dixie. She could see him tense up the minute he saw her uniform.

She'd waited patiently, but he seemed frozen in place. Maybe she could calm the man by simply speaking to him in French. "Good morning, sir. I was hoping you had a room available for me and my American friend."

Eddie had been sitting in the car no more than fifteen minutes when Dixie returned. "Well?"

"We're in luck."

"Wonderful. And I didn't hear any shots."

Dixie's stomach tightened. "Did you have to say that?"

"Sorry. I guess I'm a little overtired."

"Okay, okay. Let's go. I've got us a room."

They walked together to the front of the house. "The manager mentioned to me that there were a few shops in the village. I'll need to do some shopping, but my body is telling my head to hit the pillow, at least for a little while."

"Do you need some more cash?"

"No, you've given me plenty. I've got to find some wearable clothes and get rid of this damn uniform. Then we can try our luck at trying to catch a train."

Their room was small but comfortable, with brightly colored wallpaper and two windows. One window overlooked the narrow street out front; the other provided a view to a wooded area just beyond where she'd parked the car. To Dix, the bed looked divine. But she was afraid that if she even sat down, she might not get up. She needed to stay alert and review what she needed to do—get some traveling clothes, find a train schedule—Phalsbourg was likely the nearest connection. The bathroom was at the end of the hall, right next to their room. "Why don't you take a bath, and while you're at it, wash out your underwear and socks. I'll go for a short walkabout and try to find some travel clothes, and maybe some shaving gear for you while I'm in town."

A knock on the door startled both of them. Dixie motioned for Eddie to stand behind the door and remain quiet. She coughed and resurrected her perfect Parisian accent. "Yes, what is it?"

"Your coffee and biscuits, mademoiselle."

They sat at a small table and devoured their meager breakfast. The snack and the freshly brewed coffee revived them both. As they sat back and reflected on their harrowing flight out of Germany, Eddie asked casually, "How long before you think they'll find him?"

"I don't know." The words echoed in her head, and a flood of emotion enveloped her as she recounted the incident. She removed the pistol from her pants pocket and began to sob uncontrollably.

Eddie touched her arm. "I'm sorry, Dix, but you did what you had to. Let me carry the pistol from here on. Okay?" He set down his cup and retrieved the weapon. "We're here, and we're safe, thanks to your quick thinking. If it weren't for you, who knows?

We could be in a Gestapo jail somewhere, waiting for our finger-nails to be trimmed."

She looked up at him, tears leaking out the sides of her eyes. The humor helped. After a minute, she leaned back and gave him a smile. "Thanks. I needed that." She pushed away from the table and dried her eyes. "If I'm not back in two hours, make your way to the train station at Phalsbourg. If no trains stop there, head for Nancy, and book passage to Paris. From there take the first train to Spain, and on to Gibraltar. Do you understand?"

Eddie stood up. "Yes, I got it, babe.

"You know the Brits will find a way to get you back to England." She turned to leave him.

"Be careful out there, Dix, and come back to me."

"Just leave some hot water for me." She started to giggle as she went out the door.

Eddie finished his coffee and was soon staring out the window as he tried to remember what she'd said about which trains to take, and from where. *What did she say, Fazeburg? Nancy, Paris, Spain, then Gibraltar—I think that's the order she gave me. If that gal doesn't return, I'll be one lost pup if I can't find someone that speaks English.*

About three blocks toward the village center, a sympathetic shopkeeper in a small boutique helped her find two casual outfits that fit. The successful shopping revived her spirits. She also found a men's straight razor, some soap, and a couple of toothbrushes. She was also able to exchange her remaining marks for French francs. Passing a small *boulangerie*, she picked up some *croute au fromage*, ham and cheese sandwiches, and a bottle of wine.

The creaking of the door opening awakened Eddie. She had returned. "Well, aren't you a sight for sore eyes?"

"Sorry to wake you, but it looks like we've got to move on to Nancy—another 125 kilometers." She placed her purchases on the bed and then opened the wine bottle. "I was able to look at a schedule, and there are three trains we could catch. Unfortunately, two of them originate in Germany. I think it would be best if we took the one that leaves at seven-thirty tomorrow evening. It travels only within France. It stops at several small villages, but it's not likely the Gestapo will target it. We should arrive in Paris close to midnight." After tasting the wine, she handed him a glass. "And now, good sir, I believe I will retire to the bath."

At six o'clock the next morning, they heard a car door slam. Instantly they both sat upright. Eddie toddled over to a window and looked out: it was a delivery truck.

After settling their bill, they drove along the outskirts of the village to avoid any curious eyes. Within ten kilometers they connected with the main highway to Nancy. As they approached the town, they again used secondary roads that paralleled the train track. Once they sighted the station, they parked the Mercedes on a side street and walked the two remaining blocks to the central station.

The building was nearly empty and eerily quiet when they arrived. They spotted a ticket agent and purchased two first-class tickets to Paris. Eddie looked at his watch. It was 2:00 PM. They had another five hours to wait. Dixie produced a sandwich she'd saved from her previous village outing, and they sat together in silence on the nearest wooden bench, both trying to relax.

Later that afternoon, a bus pulled up to the entrance, and suddenly the station was filled with businessmen and families. The noise level had elevated considerably.

The incoming train commenced expelling steam as it trudged to a halt. By 7:20 they were settled in their compartment. Dixie stowed a package that contained extra clothes she'd brought with her. "I'm going to check out the rest of the train. I think it would be wise if you stayed here. I won't be long."

The train pulled out of Nancy Station promptly at 7:30. The conductor came by their compartment and startled Eddie when he entered. "Tickets and passports, *s'il vous plaît*."

Eddie handed him the tickets and his passport. The man looked closely at his passport and face. Immediately Eddie started to tense up, but the conductor just smiled and punched his ticket. The conductor held up the other ticket and asked for the corresponding passport; he started to say something just as Dixie returned to the compartment. After punching her ticket, he bid the couple a *bon voyage* and continued on his rounds.

"There's a dining car only one car up. Are you up for some dinner?"

"Babe, I'm hungry enough to eat a hobby horse." He opened the door and grabbed her arm in one motion.

"As I walked about, I didn't see anyone that looked suspicious—no gentlemen traveling alone, or in pairs."

"Do you think there might be some Gestapo goons trying to chase us down?"

"Well, I'm not going to take any chances."

"Good God Almighty! I can't wait to get off this damnable continent!"

They did enjoy their lamb dinners with *pommes de terre* and vegetables. They ordered a bottle of wine, but Dix abstained, knowing she had to remain alert. "I wonder if the porter can find us a schedule of trains out of Bordeaux."

Eddie let out an audible sigh. "Damn, and I was just starting to relax. Why don't you ask him when he brings us our bill?"

Back in their cabin, the wine and the rocking of the train soon had Eddie lulled into a twilight sleep. The porter had found a train schedule for Dix, and she studied it for routes into Spain. As she leaned back in her seat, sleep soon overtook her as well. The train rolled to several stops, but neither was awakened until they pulled into Reims. There was an engine change at this stop, and it rocked and jarred their car during the transfer.

Dix awoke startled with the first bump as the new engine was brought into place. She leaned over Eddie and looked out the window at the boarding passengers. She noticed several men in topcoats but saw that they were all carrying briefcases. *Probably just businessmen traveling to Paris.*

They arrived at the North Central Station in Paris about fifteen minutes late. According to her recently acquired schedule, the next train leaving for Bordeaux wasn't departing for another three hours. They exited the train and purchased tickets to Bordeaux.

It was now 1:00 AM. Two or three couples milled about, but all of them looked like they had arrived from other destinations. A vendor wandered by, and they each ordered strong coffee to fend off the damp cold that permeated the sparse waiting area.

At 3:00 AM their train was moved into place, and passengers started to board. They were tired, and they walked slowly down the ramp toward the first-class car. As they passed two men boarding standard class, Dix suddenly felt the hair on the back of her neck rise. She felt sure that she had seen these men, but where? Was it in Reims? She said nothing to Eddie, but she could feel herself start to tense up. As they approached their compartment, she stopped. "Do you still have the pistol?"

"Sure. What's up? Did you see something?" He pulled out the small automatic from his coat pocket. "You look like the coffee was too strong or you've seen something suspicious." He opened the door to their compartment.

"It's probably just my imagination, but I could swear that I've seen the two guys that were boarding two cars down from us. They looked like the same guys I saw standing on the platform in Reims, but I'm not sure. It's probably nothing. Just the same, I think I'll lock the door."

Hotel Gutenberg, Strasbourg

SS Captain Karl Meyer sat in his office-room at the Gutenberg, rereading the urgent message from Colonel Ault, cosigned by Heydrich himself. The Hotel Gutenberg was an old mansion, built in the nineteenth century and recently purchased by a German company set up through the office of Reichsführer Himmler. The basement had been remodeled to accommodate an SS communications center for the Alsace-Lorraine area. A runner had been sent to Captain Meyer's room as soon as the top-secret message had been decoded. Meyer, a favorite of Heydrich's, had been recruited from the Wehrmacht. He was tenacious and thorough. Heydrich believed that he was the brightest agent he had in all of France. The man was also fluent in French and had studied some English at the American University in Berlin.

The message was clear:

> URGENT—Arrest and detain suspected American agents Eddie Peabody and Marian Graham (goes by "Dixie")— Agents are suspects in the murders of Army Corporal Lintz in Berlin—and civilian security guard Oster in Bad Bergzabern—Suspects are believed to be traveling by train within France—Check all American rail passengers traveling to Paris and the French coastal areas—Report to Office of SS-Oberstgruppenführer Richard Heydrich.

Physical descriptions of Eddie and Dixie followed. Meyer was certain that if these American agents entered France from the remote outpost at Bad Bergzabern, any French train connections they made had to be booked from Nancy. He called his friend and fellow SS captain Herman Beck. "Herm, we've got an assignment. Pack light, and meet me with a staff car at the Hotel Gutenberg in ten minutes."

The two men drove to the train station in Nancy. After questioning all of the station ticket agents, they learned that an American couple fitting the descriptions had boarded the evening train for Paris. Meyer knew that with luck, they could beat the Paris-bound train and board it when it stopped in Reims.

When the Paris-Bordeaux conductor arrived, Dixie gave him their tickets and passports. She smiled. "I'm going to lock the door. We need to get some rest."

"No one should be disturbing you, mademoiselle. Oh, the dining car will be open in approximately one hour. If you like, I will knock to alert you about thirty minutes before arrival in Bordeaux." He tipped his hat as he backed out the doorway.

"Thank you, but that won't be necessary." Dixie locked the door and wedged a package she'd been carrying against the opening, for what she thought would be some extra security. She pulled out the bench seats into a makeshift bed and laid the pistol on the floor.

They were exhausted. Eddie touched her shoulder reassuringly. "Come on, babe. No one's gonna break in here. You've thought of everything, I'm sure."

"Almost home, Commander." She took one last look around the compartment before she fell back on the pullout bed. "If some Gestapo goons are on board, I'm going to make it very difficult for them to get either one of us back to Germany."

Dixie stared at the ceiling and then moved the pistol closer. She closed her eyes, her body a bundle of nerves, but sleep finally enveloped her. Suddenly she sat upright, drenched in sweat. Her watch indicated that she'd been asleep for three hours.

The little noise she made woke Eddie. "What's the matter? Did you hear something?"

"No, no. It was just a bad dream. May as well get up. Care for some breakfast?" She rummaged around in the small package on the floor and took out a new set of underwear. With her back to Eddie, she removed her slip and used it to give herself a dry bath.

Eddie's eyes were bleary, but he would forever remember her image. The light formed shadows on her body, like living art. She was, without a doubt in his mind, a very beautiful woman. Feeling self-conscious now, he turned his head away. "Tell me about your dream."

She put on a skirt and a blouse and rummaged in her purse for a comb. "Not much to tell, really. It was like when, you know, you're being chased by an animal and can't seem to get away."

"Did this animal have only two legs?"

She put her hand on his cheek. "You need a shave, Commander. I'll meet you in the dining car. Your shaving kit is in that bag on the seat." She reached down and put the pistol in her purse before she unlocked the door. "I'll order you some eggs and sausage, and some hot coffee. Okay?"

"You're too good to me. I'll be right behind you."

In the dining car Dix took the table nearest to the door. As the porter was pouring some coffee, she looked around at the people having breakfast. One couple had two small children with them. She didn't remember any children at the station in Paris. *Maybe the train stopped in Orleans or Tours. I must have been out of it.*

Eddie came bouncing in by the time the porter had finished taking her order.

"Well, don't you look refreshed?"

"That shave was what the doctor ordered. I should have taken your lead and bought some clothes in Nancy. This suit could likely stand up on its own."

"You look fine. When we get to Spain, I'm sure you'll be able to pick up whatever you need."

The dining car door suddenly opened with a loud whoosh. A man walked in wearing a black wool overcoat and a felt hat. His hands were tucked in his overcoat pockets. They looked up as he passed. He stopped, smiled, and tipped his hat but then moved on through the car and exited. Dix started to get up. "Please watch my purse while I go to the lavatory, would you?"

He nodded as she slid out. The stranger in the dark topcoat passing them: was he one she'd seen before? After he heard the whoosh of the car door opening, he reached over, picked up her purse, and removed the pistol. He felt a sudden cold chill, and he returned the purse to her side of the table. There was another swoosh as the door opened; it was Dix.

As she returned to her seat, he leaned over the table and spoke softly. "Do you think that guy was a goon?"

"Until I hear him speak, I can't be sure. I thought maybe you'd seen him before, but we can keep an eye on him."

"If he is, I'm sure he has a partner. I think it's best if we keep to our cabin. If they continue to follow us when we leave Bordeaux, we can be reasonably sure they're not tourists or businessmen."

Back at their compartment, Eddie looked toward the door connecting their car to the next car downstream. He thought he saw a shadowy figure moving at that juncture. A surge of anger suddenly enveloped him. The thought of sitting around and waiting for some Gestapo goon to get the drop on them was not appealing. He stood in the open entry as Dixie straightened the seats.

She opened the curtains covering the window. "We'll be in Bordeaux soon."

Eddie slammed the compartment door shut. "Dix, if these guys are German Gestapo, wouldn't they have tried to arrest us by now?"

"I don't know. If those two are who we think they are, we'll know soon. My guess is that right now, there are too many people around. When we get close to Bordeaux, they may make their move, using the local authorities to back them up."

"Well, right now I'm half inclined to step outside and pop one of those bastards. My nerves are ready to pop."

She looked up as he spoke and quickly moved close to him. She wrapped her hands around his wrists and pleaded. "Don't think like that, please. Let me handle these guys. I've been trained and won't let anything happen that I don't want to happen. Understand?"

He reached up and put a finger to her lips. "And I'm not the kind of guy that just lets things happen, to you or to me. Tell you what—let's agree that we're partners. You look over my shoulder, and I'll look over yours. Deal?"

She grinned at his bravado. "Okay, okay. But now tell me what brought this on."

He motioned for her to follow. They went outside into the area where he thought he'd seen a shadowy figure lurking. Only now, there was no one there.

They returned to their compartment. Dix retrieved a train schedule from her purse and began to study it. "Wait a minute. I'd been planning to travel to Bayonne, and then on to Bilbao, Spain. But now . . . maybe we should try to lose these characters in Bordeaux. If we catch a train to Toulouse, we could then head south to Barcelona. What do you think?"

"Hey, you know your way around here, and I don't. I'm just along for the ride, remember?" He was starting to feel frustrated and trapped, and he wanted to pace. "I can't believe these guys would follow us to the ends of the earth. What about trying to catch a plane in Bordeaux? Surely there are flights from Bordeaux to England."

"There are, but my orders are clear. There aren't that many commercial flights to and from England, and if we took a commercial flight, they'd nail us—either at the airport or, God forbid, in the air. I'm to get you to British soil as quickly and safely as possible. Our best chance is Gibraltar." She took a deep breath. "I just didn't figure on having to shake off a couple of these swine bastards en route, that's all."

"It's hard to believe they've got agents on this damned train. They must want us real bad." He sat down and looked out the window at the passing scenery. *If anyone in Washington believes that Germany is not preparing for war, they're daydreaming.* He watched her as she sat next to him and lowered her head into her hands. "We'll make it—I can feel it. I'm just glad you're on my side."

The train started to slow. They gathered up their meager possessions, disembarked, and headed for the nearest station exit. Once out the station entrance, they hailed a cab. Dixie gave the cabbie directions to the little village of Mérignac, just west of Bordeaux.

As they drove to the outskirts of Bordeaux, she looked back periodically to see if they were being followed. Once outside the congestion, the road narrowed and followed the contour of the land. The countryside was winter-bleak.

She nudged Eddie. "There's a country inn in Mérignac where I used to vacation with my family. I'm hoping it still exists. I remember a nearby pub or wine bar where we'd go sometimes for lunch. I think we should stop there first. We'll have a good view of the village streets, in case anyone followed us. When it's dark, if the coast is clear, we can walk to the inn."

"Sounds good to me. I could use a drink right about now."

At the edge of the village, the cabbie dropped them at the St-Albert, a small, turn-of-the-century country house that had been converted to a restaurant and bar. They sat near a large front window and ordered some bread, cheese, pickled onions, and wine. They were pleased to see no vehicular traffic on the main street. After their meal, Dixie telephoned the chateau near the Gironde inlet, Chateau Cordeillan-Bages.

They started their walk to the chateau north out of Mérignac. The road was one lane, and they could see no vehicles in front or behind. The village was surrounded by beautiful vineyards, but it was too dark for them to see much.

The matron of the chateau was waiting for them with a welcoming smile. The building was very old but well maintained. It radiated charm. Hot spiced wine and cheese were waiting for them in the sitting room. They sat by the fireplace, drank the delicious brew, and snacked before calling it a night. Their upstairs room was large and beautifully furnished with period pieces. The matron had placed on the bed two deliciously soft robes. After placing their freshly washed garments on the large steam heater, they collapsed.

The Bordeaux Train Terminal

Meyer had questioned the ticket agents, and Beck quizzed the cabbies at the main entrance. "It looks like we've lost them, Herman. None of the agents recall ticketing two Americans, either to Spain, back to Paris, or anywhere. Any luck with the cabbies?"

"No. And there aren't any rental agencies within walking distance either. If they took a cab, the driver must have returned to his home or taken a fare in town. What do you suggest we do now?"

"If they were going to take a commercial flight, they would have stayed in Paris, near the airport. No, I'm convinced they're headed for Spain. We may as well get something to eat and try to pick up their trail early tomorrow. So, tomorrow you take the earliest train to Perpignan. I'll wait here for them and question any cabbies that you may have missed. At 9:00 AM, you call me at this number. It's the outbound ticket counter."

Sunshine was spilling into their room when they awoke. Some machinery was starting up in a barn that backed up to the east end of the chateau. Dix leaned over and kissed him full on the lips. "The bathroom is mine."

Her robe parted, and Eddie found himself staring at her beautiful olive skin and shapely legs. She noticed and smiled as she tied her robe. "Too much wine last night. I'm in need of the loo."

Returning to Bordeaux Central Station, they booked the first train to Toulouse. There were two trains leaving Toulouse for Barcelona, and Dix booked that route as well. She remained vigilant in checking out the passengers as they came and went, but no one looked like the two she'd seen following them from Paris. *Maybe, just maybe, we've lost them.*

The Toulouse train was on time, and the train to Barcelona was already on the adjacent track as they pulled in. Dixie tucked her arm in Eddie's as they walked slowly to the Barcelona first-class car. She mused at some of the Spanish and French names for the passenger cars, beautifully painted on small plaques at each car's entrance. She loved Europe. She blurted out her feelings as they approached their car. "Why the hell do they always have to be fighting one another?"

Eddie glanced sideways at her. *Now what?*

10:00 AM
Bordeaux Central Station

Captain Beck was late calling in from Perpignan. Captain Meyer was worried and impatient. When the agent handed him the phone, he nearly dropped it. He acknowledged Captain Beck and glanced up at the main entrance. Eddie and Dixie had just entered and were searching for a ticket agent. Meyer interrupted Beck mid-sentence. "They're here, Herm. I don't think they've seen me. Stand by. I'll call back as soon as I know where they're traveling to." Captain Meyer quickly handed the phone back to the agent and walked slowly to the restroom.

★ ★ ★

Dixie was going to explain her outburst, but before she stepped up to enter their first-class car, she turned and casually scanned the passengers boarding standard class. Her hand moved to quickly cover her mouth; it was her natural reaction. *Oh my God! The same two men that boarded the train in Reims—same topcoat, same hat.* Tension gripped her like an iron fist.

Eddie could feel it in her arm, rigid.

He started to speak, but she interrupted him and pushed him on board. "Find our compartment, and fast."

Their compartment was right next to where their car joined standard class. She sat on the padded cushion with a thump. The sudden grip of fear had her gulping for air. "I can't believe it!"

"What?"

"Those guys that boarded in Reims . . . "

"Yeah?"

"I just saw them boarding our train!"

"You're kidding! How in the hell . . . ?"

"I haven't a clue. But if they are the same two, they must be part bloodhound."

"Maybe they've been riding trains all night, looking for us. Do you think they saw us?"

"I don't know. But I'll bet a year's pay they check out every compartment before we reach Barcelona."

"Son of a . . . "

"Let's just sit tight for now. I want to give this some thought."

The train was ten minutes late getting out of the station. The conductor said that the delay was due to an unscheduled engine change. "When crossings the Pyrenees, it's a government rule to change engines." After he'd stamped their passports, Dix asked him when the dining car would be open.

The conductor looked at his watch. "Another two hours, mademoiselle—about nightfall, when we begin our climb through the mountains."

They decided they would wait in their compartment until dark and then move to the dining car. Dining cars were usually well lit, and hopefully it would be filled with people later on.

Dix tried locking their door, only to discover that the lock was broken. She didn't panic, but the broken lock made her uneasy. She picked up her purse and started to rummage in it. "Uh, do you still have the pistol?"

He reached in his pocket. "Yes. Here, do you want it?"

She took the pistol from him and checked the clip: five more shots. She placed the gun back in her purse and sat down. They looked at each other in silence; both could feel the tension.

"I'm glad we rested well last night. I only hope those two guys are so flipping tired that they drop off the first time the light dims."

Eddie nodded. He started to shuffle his feet nervously. "I'm going to the bar and get us a drink."

Dixie scrunched her lips together in a painful smile. "I'd love one, but I think we'd be better off without just now. Okay?"

"You're probably right. I just feel the need to do something."

"Please stay here with me, and let's try to help each other relax, at least till the dining car opens. Okay?"

Eddie sat back down and turned to look out the window. "They were right on the money, sending you along to keep an eye on me. You know, in the last war with these bastards, you shot first, then you asked questions. And right now I'm keyed up enough to—"

She started to laugh. "Funny, you don't look like a cowboy."

Her laughter was infectious, and the tension subsided.

The train was navigating some gentle curves, and through the window Eddie could see an approaching tunnel. The country-side was beautiful and peaceful-looking. Rolling hills gave way to sheer rock cliffs and scrub mountain foliage. He closed his eyes and started to daydream.

There was a knock on their compartment door.

Dix grabbed for her purse. "Who is it?

"The dining car and bar will be open in ten minutes."

They both stood and rearranged themselves. Dix took out a pocket mirror and then quickly replaced it with a sigh. He recognized the reaction.

"You're beautiful, babe." He straightened his coat.

"I look like a rag bag, but thanks." She slid open the door.

She checked her purse and counted out the French notes she still had. "Do you have any more German marks?"

"I think so. Let me check."

"I have plenty for dinner, and we'll have time to stop at a local bank in Barcelona."

When dinner was served, Dix ordered a half-bottle of Bordeaux wine.

"Dix, I thought—"

She interrupted him. "Yes, yes. I know what I said. Well, I thought about it, and maybe it's just what we need." She wouldn't look at him as she spoke.

The dining car wasn't a fashionable Paris restaurant, but they were enjoying the moment. Many of the tables were filling up now, and the elevated noise began to distract them. Dixie's eyes scanned the dining car as several couples passed by.

Suddenly a porter turned, and like a flashback she felt a presence. The man in the charcoal overcoat was standing next to their table. He removed his hat and tucked his hand in his coat pocket. He bowed and with a thick German accent addressed them in English. "Goot evening, Fräulein Graham, Herr Peabody." A plastic smile now shaped SS Captain Meyer's face. He had found them! "I do hope you are enjoying your journey. Do be careful, though. I've heard this route into Spain can be very treacherous."

They both stared up at the dark figure, speechless. Eddie dropped his spoon into his coffee cup.

The SS man broke the silence with a click of his heels and a slight bow. "Now I bid you goot evening—Fräulein Graham, Herr Peabody." The plastic smile never left his face.

Before the man could exit the car, Dixie's anger boiled over. She stood. In clearly enunciated German, she spat, "Leave us alone, you Gestapo pig, or it may be you who finds the trip treacherous!"

Captain Meyer maintained his composure and didn't reply. Several nearby diners were staring in silence at the confrontation. He walked backward out of the dining car, never taking his eyes off them.

The porter appeared at their table without being summoned. "Is everything all right? May I offer you coffee or desert?"

With a smile and nod she answered, "Yes, everything is fine, thank you. We'd both like coffee and dessert. He takes cream with his coffee." When the afters arrived, she was somewhere else, lost in thought. She stared at her coffee cup and then leaned over and spoke softly. "I need to wash my hands and freshen up. I'll be right back." Without waiting for him to reply, she quietly slid out of the booth.

He noticed that she'd left her purse. He hesitated and then quickly removed the pistol. He saw her talking with the bartender and slid out to catch her. "Dix?"

She turned in his direction.

"Your purse. I thought you might need it." He handed her the much lighter purse and quickly returned to their table.

He too began to stare at the coffee and dessert. He looked over at the bar, but Dix was gone. He couldn't just sit there, so he got up from the table, planning to return to their compartment. Just as he was leaving the dining car, the train entered a tunnel, and momentarily everything went dark. It startled him, and he immediately reached for the pistol. Within a few seconds, overhead lights brightened, and he could again see. The sound was deafening, though, and he felt his ears pop.

As he approached their compartment, he looked through the

window in the door at the passageway where their car adjoined another car. He saw nothing, but he was curious. He opened the connecting door and immediately felt the vacuum of air pressing in on his eardrums. It was pitch-black, but as the train began pulling out of the tunnel, he could see a man standing with his back to the other doorway. He could also see the glow of the man's cigarette.

"Vell, goot evening again, Herr Peabody."

He felt a cold chill as the man spoke. He remembered his training and spread his feet to brace himself. He thought he was about to go toe-to-toe with this guy.

The man started to snuff out his cigarette just as the train entered another tunnel. The vacuum sucked Eddie backward slightly, but instinctively he went for the pistol. He couldn't see the man, but he felt movement just in front of himself. Without hesitation he fired two rounds in rapid succession. The deafening sounds of the tunnel passage muffled the crack of the pistol. He could see the man's arm fall and the shadowy figure slump backward toward the door. The body fell forward against Eddie's legs, causing him to stumble back a step. The train was now beginning to exit the tunnel, and he could clearly see the body. *One goon down, one to go.*

He looked around, searching for the handle that opened the door to the outside. He moved the body toward the door; suddenly the train entered another tunnel, and again everything went black. He fumbled for the door handle, but the back pressure made it nearly impossible to open. Using every ounce of strength he could muster, he lifted the body and pushed the door with his foot. When he got it slightly ajar, he gave a grunt and pushed the body out the opening. He heard a thump before the back pressure slammed the outer door shut. He staggered back to catch his breath and felt his arms shaking. He nearly stumbled again trying to enter their compartment; his legs had turned to rubber.

Dix found him staring out the dark window when she entered. "Where have you—Dear God! What happened?"

Eddie's face and neck was drenched in sweat, his tie was askew and untied, and his hair was stuck to his forehead. He looked at her with a tired smile. He reached into his pocket and handed her the pistol. "One shadow down, one to go, babe."

She knelt down. "Speak to me. Tell me what happened."

Though he had not completely regained his composure, he replayed what had just transpired.

"Thank God you're all right. That was a very brave and foolish thing you just did."

"Well, I couldn't just sit there and have coffee and dessert while that arrogant goon sauntered off, taunting us. Besides, I looked up, and you were gone."

"I had asked the bartender where I could find the conductor. It only took a minute, and then I told him about the two men that had been harassing us. He seemed to know these guys. He said he'd warned them once about entering the first-class car and that if he caught them again, he would ask them to leave the train. He gave me this little rubber doorstop to wedge under our door. If someone wants in, it won't stop them, but it should slow them down. Anyway, are you sure you're okay?"

"I think I need a drink . . . maybe two. Wanna come to the bar with me?"

This was a good sign. She smiled as she stood up and took his hand. One other couple and a lone businessman were at the bar when they arrived. They sat a table and tried to soothe their nerves with a glass of wine. They'd finished their second glass when the train started slowing for its arrival at Barcelona Central.

They were gratefull the station was well lit. As they walked toward the central ticketing and waiting area, they saw a man in a dark overcoat and hat running through the dining car, looking out the windows on both sides of the train. The conductor was standing outside the dining car, waving his arms and shouting at the man running inside. No one seemed to pay any attention.

Eddie quipped, "Seems that someone has lost his partner."

Dixie rechecked her wallet inside the station and realized they had plenty of money left to get them to Gibraltar. The crowd had thinned, but no one looking suspicious was hanging about. "Well,

Commander, would you like to spend a night here, or push on to Madrid? I know of a lovely little hotel . . . "

He grabbed her by the arm and escorted her toward the cabstand. "I've had enough of these damn trains for one night. I don't care if I stay the night in a fleabag, as long as the room is stationary. There's only one thing still bothering me, though. Do you think that guy's partner saw us as he was running through the dining car?"

"I doubt it. I got a good look at his face. And all I saw was a frightened little man who couldn't find his buddy. These guys were likely looking for a promotion of some kind, but only if they could bring you in. It is scary, though. Why the hell would anyone hound us like those two have?"

The taxi area was crowded, but again, no one was looking suspicious or looking at them suspiciously. The cab ride, about eighty kilometers out of Barcelona, took about an hour. The cabbie turned off the main highway to a secluded village, Girona, near the ocean. They drove through some iron gates that led to a beautifully restored estate house surrounded by what looked like a well-manicured park. As they drove up the circular drive, they could see a gleaming reflection of the Mediterranean, which the cabbie referred to as Playa Santa Cristina. The air was alive with the delicious scent of the nearby ocean mixed with pine and forest humus.

She closed her eyes. "I think I want to stay here forever."

The house was nearly empty of guests, and the lady desk manager spoke the King's English. So they opted for a large room with an adjoining bath.

Dix turned and smiled at Eddie. "A bit extravagant, but we deserve it, don't we?"

In addition to an adjoining bath, there was a small balcony that overlooked the sea. When the door to their room closed, Dix ran to Eddie and threw her arms around his neck. She squealed with delight. "I get the bathroom first!"

Eddie gave her a light kiss and patted her on the butt as he steered her to the bath. "Just save some hot water for me, or I might just come in there and join you."

"Don't you dare, or you'll sleep on the beach tonight." She laughed and latched the door.

Eddie took off his suit and tried to brush off some of the accumulated dust and dirt. It was hopeless. *No amount of cleaning is gonna restore this battle-worn rag.* He collapsed on the super-soft bed. *This is wonderful.* He started to drift off.

Dixie emerged from her bath wrapped in a towel and waltzed over to the bed.

Eddie felt her presence and opened one eye. She was mesmerizing. Only now, her eyes had a determined and desirous look.

Without saying a word and with fluid movement she leaned over and kissed him, full on the lips.

He pulled her down toward him.

The only sounds were of the gentle lapping of the ocean, muffled through the beveled panes in the balcony's French doors.

TWENTY-EIGHT

Dixie awoke leisurely to the sights and sounds of their incredible surroundings. She didn't want to move, but soon the reality of where she was and the flood of recent events brought her to full alert.

Eddie emerged from the bathroom, towel-drying his hair. "Mornin', babe."

"And a beautiful morning it is, sir. But . . . "

"But? Something tells me there's more to come."

"Yeah. Much as I would love to stay here another night, I think it would be prudent for us to move on."

"You're right. Who knows when or if that Gestapo bunch will regroup? They might have found the body of their fallen comrade by now."

"Right, and now we'd have the Spanish authorities on the lookout for us." Dix could see the disappointment and resignation on his face after she spoke. She too wanted to forget everything that had happened and absorb some more of these magnificent surroundings, but it was not to be.

It was mid-morning by the time they emerged. The matron of the house had arranged for a light breakfast. While they were enjoying the delicious pastries and coffee, the matron recounted a telephone call she'd received from her nephew, the cabbie that had delivered them the previous evening. "He said that a German security agent had been conferring with the authorities at Barcelona Central late last evening. All the cabbies were being questioned about two Americans that were wanted in Germany for murder. Naturally, my nephew said nothing. I don't know what is going on, but I can't imagine you two being involved in any murder. Personally, I don't have much use for Hitler—or Franco either, for that matter. But for the record, does either of you know what's going on?"

Both were stunned speechless. Dix took a chance on the matron's sympathetic posture and kind smile. "Thank you for your kind hospitality, and for sharing with us your nephew's conversation. Yes, we've indeed been running away from the German SS. We are American entertainers, and we were performing in Berlin. Then, quite suddenly, the show was canceled, and soon truckloads of Gestapo were rounding up all the performers. No one would tell us anything. We weren't allowed to contact anyone, including our embassy. Everyone was under arrest. That's when we decided to make a run for it. It's been frightful!"

"You poor dears. What's gotten into those Germans? Do they want to start another war? Well, finish your breakfast, and don't worry. If you'd like, I'll have my man drive you to the airport, or back to the train station if you'd prefer. If anyone should show up here asking about you, I'll tell them that you've already left the area by motorcar." The matron smiled at Dix and patted her hand.

They hurriedly gathered up what little they'd brought with them and took the matron up on her offer. Once on the main highway, Dix asked the driver to take them to Barcelona Central Station. She turned to Eddie and whispered. "I still believe the train is our best bet, but I also want to see if there is any increase in security."

"We could find a car in Barcelona and drive to Gibraltar."

"That'll be Plan B if security is tight at the train station."

Central Station, Madrid

SS Captain Herman Beck, phoning from a Spanish transit security office, was pleading with his superior in Berlin to allow him to continue tracking the Americans. Before the man mysteriously disappeared, his last conversation with his fellow agent and friend Captain Meyer had been clear. *We've got them, Herm. We'll arrest them at Barcelona Central and use Franco's men to help transport them back to Germany. You take a rest while I have a smoke.*

"Yes, sir. But Captain Meyer was convinced that if the Americans entered Spain, they would head straight for Lisbon. They would have no problem getting to the Azores, which is the continental port destination for the Pan American airline. And the quickest route to Lisbon is by train, through Madrid. Please, sir, allow me one more day. I know I am close. I will not let these American spies escape me!"

At Barcelona's Central Station, passenger travel seemed crowded but normal. They spotted no additional Spanish police, or men in dark coats looking over incoming passenger traffic. The driver dropped them on a street across from the station, at a busy intersection. They quickly blended into the crowd. At the ticket counter, a Spanish transit security officer was standing next to the agent but took no notice of Dix as she paid for first-class passage all the way to Gibraltar. Eddie busied himself by looking at the newspapers in a nearby kiosk. She bumped him in passing, and they quietly hustled off to their connecting train to Madrid.

Once settled in their compartment, Eddie sighed in exasperation. "If I never see the inside of another one of these damned trains, it'll be too soon."

"Try to relax if you can. We should be in Gibraltar before dark.

I could use a cup of coffee. I hope this train has a decent dining car." She turned to open the compartment door. Standing in the doorway was a tall man wearing dark clothing. She gasped and stumbled backward. As the man stepped in, out of the shadows, she realized that it was only the conductor, who needed to check tickets and passports. After he'd punched their tickets and left, tears started to stream down her face. "I'm sorry, Commander. I guess I'm still a little on edge."

Fortunately, the remainder of the trip was uneventful.

They had to disembark in Madrid to change trains. This was a major terminal, very busy and very confusing.

In a glass booth above the concourse, Captain Beck was in the process of having his German National Transit Security identity and boarding pass validated by the local authority. He glanced casually out the window at the incoming passengers. "My God! It's them!" He grabbed his security pass from the agent and ran from the tiny room.

Eddie and Dix were running down the concrete walkway paralleling the train to Gibraltar. The noise was deafening, and clouds of smoke and steam from the engine enveloped them. They jumped aboard the last car just as the train started to pull out. They had to walk up through three more cars before they reached first class. Everyone seemed to stare at them as they tried to maneuver through. Dix was frazzled from her run to catch the train. All she could think about was getting reassurance that they were in fact on the train to Gibraltar. When they reached the first-class car, she almost ran over the conductor. Communication was difficult, but she was finally reassured that they were in fact on the correct train.

All of the first-class compartments had been taken, but the man indicated that there was plenty of open seating in the next car up. Disappointed, they continued to trudge on up to the next car. They settled in next to a family traveling with two small children: a little boy and girl. Eddie sat close to the aisle and laid his banjo on the facing seat. The little boy seemed fascinated.

Dix sighed with relief. "This is okay, don't you think? I like it up here with all the windows."

He patted her hand. "Just fine, babe. Just fine." He laid his head back against a small pillow and closed his eyes. He felt someone bump against him and was instantly alert. The little boy was standing right next to him, with his right hand caressing the banjo case. The boy's large dark eyes, charged with curiosity, were staring up at Eddie. The boy's mother rushed over to retrieve him. She spoke harshly to the boy, grabbed his arm, and apologized. He was smiling at the little guy's curiosity; then he sat up and opened the banjo case.

The boy couldn't help but look over, and when he saw the gold and rhinestone-studded instrument, his eyes widened in astonishment. The boy whispered to his mother, but she held onto her son's hand firmly.

Eddie took out the instrument and began to tune it. He placed a violin mute on the banjo's bridge and smiled at the boy as he started to play "Blue Spanish Eyes." The boy's sister had now left her seat and was standing next to him, intently watching his fingers slide over the instrument. When he finished the song, the whole car seemed to burst out in applause. He removed the mute and started to play a familiar tune, "Old MacDonald Had a Farm." The boy had disengaged from his mom and was standing next to his sister. When he sang the verse, the children chimed in and helped with the E-I-E-I-O's.

Dix sat sidesaddle in her seat as she watched the mini-performance in delight. When he'd finished the song, the little boy and girl began jabbering excitedly. Their mother quickly appeared and escorted them to their seats.

As if the children had put her up to it, Dix asked, "Is that all? Aren't you going to play another?"

Eddie grinned. "Always leave them wanting more, Dix. Then you'll always have a job."

No sooner had they sat back to relax when a man, topcoat on his arm, strolled through their car. He passed them by, then stopped and turned around. "Herr Peabody, Fräulein Graham, how nice to see you again."

They both sat up abruptly as Captain Beck smiled, nodded, and continued on to the back of the car.

Dixie was stunned and speechless.

Eddie could feel his blood pressure rise. "Jesus H. . . . Where the hell did he come from?"

They arrived in Gibraltar on time, right at dusk. Everyone appeared to stand and disembark at once. In the melee of shuffling to the exit, they nervously looked over the crowd, but the Gestapo agent was nowhere in sight.

"Stay close to me, Commander. Once outside the train, I'm going to run as fast as I can to the cabstand."

"Right. I'll be no more than ten steps behind you."

At the cabstand she looked back and saw that Eddie was close behind. She also saw the SS agent on a dead run, heading right toward them. She yelled at the oncoming cabbie to hurry, and when the car arrived, they quickly loaded themselves and their baggage. She yelled at the cabbie, "The British compound! And please, as fast as you can—we're being chased!"

The cabbie tipped his hat and took off with tires screeching. There were other cars on the road, but the cabbie took her plea seriously. He hit the accelerator and weaved in and out of traffic at racecourse speed. The white-knuckle ride took only twenty minutes, and with the gate in sight, the driver put the cab into a four-wheel slide as he stood on the brakes.

They jumped out, and Eddie threw a fistful of money at the driver. There was a young soldier standing guard at the gate.

"Sergeant, I'm Lieutenant Commander Eddie Peabody of the United States Navy, and this young lady is Lieutenant Graham, also a US naval officer." He handed the young man their passports. "I wonder if you'd be good enough to let us pass and contact your base commander."

As they stood outside the gate, speaking to the security guard, the sound of screeching tires caused the sergeant to look up. The man in the dark topcoat jumped from the still-moving cab and started to yell. "Halt! Halt! By order of German Reichsführer Heydrich, these people are under arrest!"

Eddie turned and saw Dixie motioning for him to push through the gate. She suddenly stumbled and fell to her knees. He turned back and rushed over to help her up. He grabbed his banjo with one hand and her elbow with the other. Captain Beck was now closing in fast and reaching for Eddie.

By this time, the young British sentry had leveled his weapon at the approaching German. He gestured for Eddie and Dixie to quickly step inside the gate. Captain Beck grabbed Dixie's arm, trying to prevent them from crossing over.

Dix had sidestepped around Captain Beck and was pushing Eddie ahead of her through the gate.

The sentry stepped forward, directly in front of Captain Beck, blocking his entry. They were now on British soil.

The SS captain was furious. "This is outrageous! These people are fugitives of the German Reich! You must release them to me at once!" But as he was yelling out his demands, two more British guards suddenly appeared on each side of the sentry, with their weapons at the ready.

Captain Beck stomped his feet in frustration. "I demand to speak with your superior!"

The sentry turned to Eddie and spoke calmly. "Right, sir. Is Major Bartlett expecting you?"

"I'm not sure, son, but we would appreciate it if you would contact him."

Captain Beck stood within inches of the sentry's weapon as he held up his identification. "I am Captain Beck of German Special Security. These people, Herr Peabody and Fräulein Graham, are wanted for questioning in the investigation of two murders on German soil. I must take them into custody at once!"

The British guard continued to level his weapon at the German agent. "I'm sorry, sir, but this is British soil. They are in our custody now. You'll have to take up your request with the British consulate." The sergeant ordered one of the standby guards to call the duty officer.

Everyone stood motionless for the two minutes it took for the soldier to return. When the soldier returned, a British marine accompanied him, carrying a barricade. The barricade was immediately placed at the gate entrance, blocking Captain Beck and some local citizens that had gathered to view the commotion.

The sentry directed Eddie and Dixie to a plain-looking building to the right of a flagpole about one hundred yards from the main gate.

An armed guard standing just outside the door came to attention as they approached. When they entered the building, a British major came out of a nearby office. "Commander Peabody and Lieutenant Graham. Jolly good to see you chaps."

After being seated in the major's office, Eddie started to reconstruct why they were in Gibraltar.

The major raised his hand to interrupt. "I know why you're here, Commander. London has been waiting for communication from me concerning you two for the past week. We knew from your people that you were on the run and would likely surface here. My standing orders are, if and when you did make it to Gibraltar, to get you aboard a submarine and on to London ASAP. Since receiving the call from the gate, I've alerted London that you did indeed make it. They send their congratulations and a hearty 'well done'! I've sent a signal to one of our submarines in the straits. They should be in port in roughly forty-five minutes and will hold for emergency passenger transfer." The major picked up his phone, and instantly two orderlies arrived, one male and one female.

Things were happening fast. When the door opened, Eddie and Dix exchanged a puzzled glance at each other. "Right, then. Off you go, Commander. The orderly will fit you with some submarine travel clothes. And we should have you on your way in about an hour."

At the doorway Eddie stopped and turned toward the major. "Excuse me, sir. But what about Lieutenant Graham?"

The major looked up from his desk and said casually, "The lieutenant will be flown to Lisbon, where she is booked on a commercial flight to London. She'll then board a Pan Am flight for New York." The major cleared his throat. "Ah, Commander? You weren't thinking that she should travel aboard a submarine with a boatload of sailors, were you?"

Eddie gave him a halfhearted smile.

"Right, then. Off you go."

Eddie turned to her and touched her arm. Their eyes met, but they said nothing to each other. She blinked her eyes, and a tear rolled down her cheek.

The major broke the silence. "Right, well, carry on. Your rides back to civilization await."

Eddie emerged from an adjacent building about twenty minutes later wearing standard-issue British sailor pants and a blue shirt, both of which were too big. A jeep pulled alongside to transport him to the dock. About one hundred feet away, a woman in dark slacks and a light-colored blouse stood at attention, faced him, and saluted. Eddie recognized her immediately. He returned her salute.

The driver's voice interrupted the silence. "Commander, the *HMS Medway* has docked and is ready for you to board, sir."

TWENTY-NINE

The submarine ride to the English coast was swift, as they ran on the surface for most of the night. Eddie was returned to Washington via a US Navy flying boat, after a short stopover in Brighton, where he met briefly with US embassy personnel. Once he arrived in Washington, the Navy Department sequestered him at a remote location in Virginia. He turned over all of the exposed film he'd been carrying. The images were developed at labs within the Navy Department. They were far from perfect, but they were clear enough to recognize the size and class of submarine launched that moonlit evening in Hamburg. Then he recounted his meetings with Greg Ziemer; Captain Schroeder, who was responsible for the shipyard in Hamburg; and Hitler and his hierarchy, at the party where he'd performed in Munich. The information Eddie brought back confirmed what other agents had been reporting, though no other agent could report being that close to Hitler and his immediate staff.

President Roosevelt was very pleased to see Eddie when he returned. He invited him to accompany him, as his only guest, on the presidential yacht as it cruised up to Boston Harbor. During the voyage, the president spent hours having him recount every detail of what the president referred to as his exciting journey. Upon their return to Washington, the president informed Eddie that German agents, likely in hiding somewhere in the United States, might want to exact revenge for his escape from their invincible SS; therefore, the president extended Eddie's active-duty status and assigned him to assist in reopening the Great Lakes Naval Training Center near Chicago.

As history reveals, by the time Eddie had returned to the United States and delivered his report, the Germans were indeed violating the Anglo-German naval treaty of 1935. And the British, ever so slowly recognizing that Hitler was less than trustworthy, finally realized that the German head of state would not be appeased, even by the cession of the Sudetenland. After German soldiers marched into Czechoslovakian territory, with the blessings of both Britain and France, Hitler turned to Poland and demanded the return of the free city of Danzig. After the Polish government refused, the British government finally abandoned its policy of appeasement. The dawn of World War II was ushered in by September 1939, with the German invasion of Poland.

Lieutenant Marian Graham (Dixie Parsons) returned to her home in the Boston area. She resigned her commission soon after her debriefing. The Navy Department, however, had made good on its promises to her. She and her mother were now naturalized citizens. And due to the men-only admissions policy at the Peabody Institute of Music, she enrolled at the Juilliard School of Music in New York.

Eddie tried for months to persuade the Navy Department to provide him with Marian's address, but each time, he was refused. In the fall he was booked into a theater in the Baltimore area. He tried to locate her through a private investigation agency, but it seems that no one could confirm the whereabouts of a Miss Marian Graham.

On a Friday evening, after his last performance, Eddie was walking back to his hotel, reviewing in his mind the changes he would make for the upcoming theater engagement in New York. Suddenly, a dark figure appeared from an alleyway ahead of him.

The figure turned and stood facing him. The person's face was hidden and shadowy. He could see a trench coat with its collar turned up, but the figure wasn't wearing a hat.

He didn't panic, but he did look around for an escape route. He was about to walk across the street when two couples exited the hotel and turned toward him. The shadowy figure backed up against the wall to let them pass. There was a lighted hotel sign above. The shadowy figure's facial features became clear. *My God, it's Dixie!* He ran to her when recognition finally set in.

No words were spoken as they embraced for more than a minute.

"Aren't you going to offer a girl a drink, sailor?"

"Dear God, but it's good to see you, Dix." He bent down his head to kiss her gently on the lips. They walked, arm in arm, to the lounge but said little.

Marian told Eddie about becoming a citizen and filing an application to enroll at Juilliard.

Eddie recounted how he and Maude had split the sheets, and how he'd tried to contact her through the navy, but to no avail. He reached over to touch her hand as he spoke.

She sighed. "Eddie, I want you to know how much you mean to me. But you have your career in the navy now, as well as show business. I think you know this is hard for me, but I want—no, I need a career of my own. The navy just wasn't for me, but you knew that." She gave another deep sigh. "Oh, I do hope you understand." She needed to change the subject. "So, now, tell me. Whatever happened to Johnny and Greg?"

Eddie took a large swallow of his drink. "Greg Ziemer, after learning of the pending Gestapo arrest, retrieved travel documents he'd prepared in advance of what he knew would surely one day be his fate. He traveled west into Holland before the Gestapo had a chance to alert the border stations. From there, he traveled by boat to London. He remained in Britain, assisting intelligence personnel with his intimate knowledge of the German physical and political landscape. I also heard that he was writing a book about his experiences. Johnny Pitts was the only member of our show that was arrested and detained by the Gestapo. The rest of the troupe was deported back to Britain. Johnny, bless his soul, was interrogated day and night for more than a week in hopes of gaining information regarding our escape. When they discovered he also played the piano, the bastards broke all the fingers on his left hand. He, of course, knew nothing. By the time the Gestapo found their dead agent in the mountains, we were in Gibraltar. Frustrated, the bastards blamed poor Johnny and labeled him a political subversive. They transferred him to a concentration camp called Buchenwald. I also learned that the Gestapo had arrested Captain Schroeder. Remember me telling you about the German Kriegsmarine captain in Hamburg? Well, they questioned him regarding his association with Greg Ziemer and me. The man was immediately retired from the German navy."

Eddie paused while Marian absorbed what he'd just recounted. "Dix, I don't want it to end here."

"I'll bet President Roosevelt was glad to see you in one piece."

"Yes, he was. He told me personally, on his yacht, that what we all did over there was nothing short of heroic. He also said that should the Germans decide to attack Britain, that little tinhorn bastard with a mustache will be stopped dead in his tracks."

Dixie was looking intently into his eyes as he spoke. She suddenly reached over and took his hand in hers. She leaned over and kissed him on the cheek. A tear slid down her cheek. "Gotta go, Commander. Classes start early tomorrow." She slid back her chair and stood. "Thank you for everything, but most of all, thanks for just being you. I shall always remember you, fondly." She turned and buttoned up her trench coat. Within a blink of his eyes, she was gone.

THE END

Selected Biographical Briefs

George Dern

Fifty-Second United States secretary of war under President Franklin D. Roosevelt, in office from March 1933 to the time of his death, aged sixty-three, August 27, 1936. He was a lawyer who entered state politics in 1914 in Utah. He served two terms as governor of Utah from 1924 to 1932. During his tenure at the War Department he oversaw the administration of the Civilian Conservation Corps (CCC), which employed more than three hundred thousand out-of-work men who joined the ranks of the CCC to work in the preservation and conservation of America's public lands.[1]

Rudolf Hess

German deputy führer to Adolf Hitler, in office from April 1933 to May 1941. He served in the German army during World War I and received the Iron Cross, Second Class, for his gallantry in the Seventh Bavarian Field Artillery

---

1 Encyclopaedia Britannica, Volume 19, 1957; Wikipedia.org.

Regiment. As deputy führer he wielded a great deal of power within Hitler's Third Reich, but he was privately distressed by the war with the United Kingdom. His hope was that the UK, through contact with the Duke of Hamilton, would seek peace and accept Germany as an ally. On May 10, 1941, he secretly flew to Scotland to contact the Duke of Hamilton but was arrested and sent to the Tower of London by Winston Churchill, the UK prime minister. He was held prisoner in various locations throughout England until his trial in 1946, when he was convicted of crimes against peace (planning and preparation of aggressive war) and conspiracy with other German leaders to commit crimes. Rudolf Hess died in Spandau Prison, Berlin, Germany, on August 17, 1987 (aged ninety-three).[2]

Heinrich Himmler

Reichsführer-SS to Adolf Hitler, in office from January 1929 to April 1945; **director of the Reich Main Security Office,** June 1942 to January 1943; **Reich minister of the interior,** August 1943 to April 1945. He had authority over all German uniformed law enforcement agencies. The main office of law enforcement was also the headquarters of the German secret service (SS). He personally oversaw the construction and operation of the concentration camp system in Germany and in all occupied territories. In April 1945, recognizing that Germany's war efforts were hopeless, he tried to negotiate surrender to the Western Allies. He was unsuccessful in his surrender attempt to British and American forces, and General Dwight Eisenhower labeled him a major war criminal. He was captured, dressed in disguise, by Allied forces in May 1945 near the Danish border. He was sent to Lüneburg, Germany, to await trial as a war criminal. On May 23, 1945, he committed suicide.[3]

---

2 Encyclopaedia Britannica, Volumes 10, 11, 1957; Wikipedia.org.
3 Encyclopaedia Britannica, Volumes 10, 11, 1957; Wikipedia.org.

Edwin Ellsworth (Eddie) Peabody

A vaudevillian entertainer, musician, and showman from 1921 to 1970. He joined the US Navy in 1916. A gifted self-taught musician, he joined a dance band in 1921 in San Pedro, California, after being discharged from the navy. He played rhythm banjo in the band, but his unmistakable talent and dexterity with the instrument landed him a solo performance on a local Los Angeles radio station. This performance caught the attention of several vaudevillian theater producers, and his career began to skyrocket. Large metropolitan newspapers now labeled him "The King of the Banjo." In addition to performing for major theater companies across the country, he made many appearances on nationwide celebrity radio programs. He also made numerous popular musical recordings for Victor and Columbia and several film shorts for Vitaphone and UM&M. His musical talent, personality, and previous naval experience caught the attention of President Franklin D. Roosevelt, who secretly commissioned him as a lieutenant in the US Naval Reserve. During his 1938–39 European musical tour combined with some intelligence gathering in Germany for the president, German spies in the United States discovered a photo of him in his naval uniform. After Eddie's narrow escape out of Germany, the president, upon Eddie's return to the United States, ordered him to remain on active duty. The onset of World War II in 1941 resulted in the transfer of Commander Eddie Peabody to the South Pacific under Admiral Charles Lockwood, US Commander of Submarine Warfare in the Pacific Theater. In 1946 he reignited his show business career, performing in nightclubs and what remained of theaters in major metropolitan centers. He maintained his reserve officer status in the navy and retired at the rank of captain. In the 1950s and 1960s he recorded thirteen albums for the Dot label and appeared on several nationwide celebrity television programs. He was honored for service to his country by President Dwight Eisenhower, receiving the People to People award. In November 1970 he died of natural causes in Covington, Kentucky.[4]

Maude (Kelly) Peabody

Maude Kelly was born, raised, and educated in Texas around the turn of the twentieth century. She traveled to Southern California around 1920 seeking adventure, excitement, and fortune. She met and fell in love with Eddie Peabody, and in March 1924 they were married in Cleveland, Ohio. Throughout his early musical career she personally managed his theater, radio broadcast, and recording bookings, and she acted as his publicity agent when required. She was socially very conservative and actively supported the Women's Christian Temperance Union. They divorced in 1939. She died in 1947 of natural causes.[5]

Erich Johann Albert Raeder

Erich Raeder attained the highest possible German naval rank, Grossadmiral (Grand Admiral), in 1939. He had been awarded the Knight's Cross of the Iron Cross and was leader of the German Kriegsmarine (German navy) from 1939 to 1943, when he resigned at the age of sixty-seven. He was convicted of waging a war of aggression at the Nuremberg Trials and sentenced to life imprisonment but was released in September 1955. He wrote an autobiography, *Mein Leben*, in 1957 and died at the age of eighty-four in November 1960.[6]

Claude A. Swanson

Forty-fifth United States secretary of the navy under President Franklin D. Roosevelt, in office from March 1933 to the time of his death (aged seventy-seven), July

---

4 Lowell H. Schreyer, *The Eddie Peabody Story;* Wikipedia.org.
5 Lowell H. Schreyer, *The Eddie Peabody Story.*
6 Encyclopaedia Britannica, Volumes 10, 11, 1957; Wikipedia.org.

7, 1939; **US senator from Virginia**, in office from August 1910 to March 1933; **US representative of Virginia's Fifth Congressional District**, in office from March 1893 to January 1906. The Swanson Middle School in Arlington, Virginia, is named for him.[7]

Hubert Prior (Rudy) Vallee

A singer, actor, bandleader, and entertainer from 1922 to 1986. He became most prominent as a singer in the mid-1920s, capitalizing on his suave manner and boyish good looks. He was, arguably, the first of a new style of popular singer at the time: the crooner. He quickly landed recording contracts with Columbia, Harmony, Velvet Tone, Diva, and Victor. His first feature film was *The Vagabond Lover,* made in 1929 for RKO Radio. That same year he began hosting the very popular *Fleischmann Hour* radio show out of New York. With the onset of World War II he enlisted in the Coast Guard and directed the Eleventh District Coast Guard band. In 1944 he was placed on the inactive list, at the rank of lieutenant, and returned to radio. Some of the films in which he appeared are: *The Palm Beach Story, I Remember Mama, Unfaithfully Yours, The Bachelor and the Bobby-Soxer,* and *Gentlemen Marry Brunettes.* He performed in approximately twenty other films and also on Broadway in the show *How to Succeed in Business Without Really Trying.* He appeared in three episodes of the 1960s *Batman* television series as "Lord Marmaduke Fogg" and in eight or nine other shows in the 1960s and '70s. His marriage to Leonie Cauchois early in his career ended in annulment. He was briefly married to Fay Webb and then to Jane Greer, which marriage ended in divorce in 1944. In 1946 he married Eleanor Norris, who remained with him until his death (aged eighty-four) in July 1986.[8]

---

7   Encyclopaedia Britannica, Volumes 10, 11, 1957; Wikipedia.org.
8   Rudy Vallee, The Official Website; Wikipedia.org.

Gregor (Greg) Ziemer

He was an American educator who lived in Germany from 1928 to 1939. While in Germany he served as headmaster of the American School in Berlin. He fled Germany in 1939 and returned to the United States but was called back to Europe in late 1944 as a war correspondent embedded with General George Patton's Third Army. He later provided information to the Nuremberg Trial prosecutors about Nazi society. He wrote two notable books on Nazi society: *Education for Death* and *The Making of a Nazi*, which was the inspiration for Walt Disney's animated film short of the same name and, more directly, Edward Dmytryk's film classic, *Hitler's Children*. Ziemer also wrote, with his daughter Patricia, *Two Thousand and Ten Days of Hitler*. In the 1950s he wrote many short stories, articles, and some screenplays, often contributing articles and commentary to the popular magazine *The Saturday Evening Post*. He also served as a director for the American Foundation for the Blind and was a director of the Institute of Lifetime Learning. He died in August 1982 (aged eighty-three).[9]

---

9 Lowell H. Schreyer, *The Eddie Peabody Story*; Wikipedia.org.

CPSIA information can be obtained at www.ICGtesting.com
Printed in the USA
LVOW072142171111

255526LV00003B/12/P